TEAL INK
PRESS

THE VEIL
BOOK 1

REALM OF THE FAE

S.J. KADILE

THE VEIL:
REALM OF THE FAE

S.J. KADILE

ISBN: 979-8-9939125-1-6

Library of Congress Control Number: 2025925531

Cover Design: Nada Orlic
Editorial Design: Luca Funari

First Edition

Printed in the United States of America

Published by Teal Ink Press

TEAL INK
PRESS

 www.tealinkpress.com

 @sjkadileauthor

 @sjkadileauthor

For my dad,
who fought for every dream I dared,
and my mom,
whose love of magic made it all possible.

REALM OF THE FAE

CHAPTER 1

The sticky cocktail of crushed medication dripped down Clara Valenwood's scrubs. She backed out of the room, the resident's shrieks still echoing behind the closed door. Her fists clenched from the effort it took not to scream back. In six months at Brookhaven Manor Nursing Home, she'd been yelled at, kicked, cried on, and splashed with every bodily fluid imaginable. Somehow, she still couldn't make it through a shift without wearing someone's puked up or thrown out meds.

She sagged against the hallway wall and took a deep breath. The sweet medicinal smell made her stomach turn. The fluorescent lights hummed overhead, casting a bluish-white glow on the scuffed linoleum. Some days it felt like the call-ins never stopped, like she was always the one being shuffled between halls. She should just quit and—

Her smartwatch vibrated against her wrist.

Hope you got the package! Tracking says delivered!

Clara stared at the tiny screen, breaking out of her spiral. Package? Typical Dad and his surprises. Probably another *pasalubong*—he'd been obsessed with this Filipino tradition ever since learning about it from Mom. Buying little gifts from their trips and sending them to her. They'd been traveling nonstop since she moved out, finally living their best life. She wished she could join them. Her thumb hovered over the watch face.

At work now. I'll check when I get home. Rough day.

A reply appeared immediately.

Have a better day, sweetheart. Remember, you're a Valenwood.

Yeah, right. Being a Valenwood didn't help when she was covered in meds. Dad had been saying that her whole life, as if the name carried some hidden meaning. Maybe it was just a dad thing.

"*¡Ay, bonita!*"

Clara's hand flew to her chest as she stifled a gasp. An elderly man in a wheelchair had suddenly appeared beside her, his face creased with concern. He gestured at her stained scrubs, murmuring in Spanish. She caught bits and pieces: *pobrecita* and *qué terrible*, mixed with the word he kept repeating: *bonita*. People always assumed she was Latina. Thanks to the Philippines' colonial history, they weren't exactly wrong.

"Tell me, *bonito*," she said, even though she guessed that he probably couldn't understand her, "why did I even become a nurse?"

The old man's expression softened. He reached out and patted her hand gently, his skin paper-thin but warm. Then, he placed that hand over his own heart and pointed to her, his eyes crinkling with kindness. The gesture was unmistakable: from my heart to yours. He produced a tissue from his pocket and pressed it into her palm, then began humming as he wheeled himself away. Was that the wedding march?

"*Bonita, bonita,*" drifted back down the hallway.

Clara stood frozen, her throat tight. These moments were her "why." Not the salary that barely covered her loans, but the small connections that reminded her why she became a nurse.

She pushed off the wall and dabbed at her soaked scrubs with the tissue. Maybe tomorrow would be better. Maybe not. But for now, she had rounds to finish. Clara headed down the hallway, shoulders straining as she shoved her medication cart forward. Being short and skinny didn't help, and her scoliosis had her back aching halfway through every twelve-hour shift. *Ugh*. Her thoughts tangled. She'd thought nursing was her life's purpose, but she wasn't so sure anymore.

She stopped in front of the next room on her list. Mrs. Alcott. Clara knocked gently before pushing the door open. Morning light filtered through the half-drawn blinds, casting long shadows across the room. The older woman sat propped up by pillows, her silver hair braided neatly. Clara gave her a soft smile. "Good morning, Mrs. Alcott."

Mrs. Alcott's gaze lifted. "Ah, my favorite nurse has come to visit. Or should I say, the Guardian of the Valenwood legacy?"

Clara laughed softly. She probably shouldn't have told Mrs. Alcott her full name when she'd been admitted a few weeks ago, but the woman had been so insistent, and she was too sweet to say no to. "You've been reading too many fantasy novels again."

"Perhaps," Mrs. Alcott said, her voice lilting playfully. She reached out a shaky hand, and Clara took it gently. Her skin was cool, the veins visible beneath.

Something sharp glinted in Mrs. Alcott's eyes. "Names are never just names, dear. You're special, you know. A Valenwood."

"You and my dad would get along great with all the family sayings." Her dad's phrases sounded like they could be plastered on motivational posters, except they were always tied to some family history her father had yet to share. She reached for the blood pressure cuff, trying to steer things back to normal. "Let me just check your vitals."

As Clara wrapped the cuff around Mrs. Alcott's thin arm, the woman suddenly clutched her wrist with surprising strength.

"The veil is thinner than you think."

Clara stilled, the half-secured cuff dangling awkwardly. She knew dementia could make people say random stuff, but it didn't make moments like this any easier. Clara cared so much about her patients, especially Mrs. Alcott. Despite her episodes, she had made Clara feel like a granddaughter—and she didn't have a living grandma. It pained her to see Mrs. Alcott slipping away.

She kept her voice calm and steady as she gently extracted her hand and finished securing the cuff. "You should try to rest, Mrs. Alcott. Let's check your blood pressure and then I'll be here to check on you later." The machine hummed to life, numbers climbing on the display.

Mrs. Alcott's eyes drifted to the window while the cuff tightened on her arm. The sunlight seemed less bright than before. "There isn't much time. You'll understand soon enough."

Clara stayed quiet, finishing up the vitals checks. It had to suck living with a mind that just came and went like that. The thought made her genuinely sad. Maybe she should mention it to the psychiatrist, see about adjusting her meds.

"Let's get you comfortable," Clara whispered. She adjusted the blankets carefully and handed the older woman her morning pills. After Mrs. Alcott obediently took them—sparing Clara's scrubs from further mess— her eyes fluttered closed and her breathing grew soft and even.

Clara lingered for a moment, watching the rise and fall of her chest. She shook herself out of it, straightened up, and brushed a loose strand of dark hair behind her ear. She jotted down Mrs. Alcott's vitals on her clipboard. As she turned to leave, she glanced back one more time. The door clicked shut behind her, and Clara checked who was next on her rounds. But the woman's words stuck with her all the way down the hall. Why was she so fixated on Clara's name? Dementia or not, it was honestly kind of creepy.

Twelve and a half hours later, Clara was fumbling with her keys outside her studio apartment, mail tucked under one arm.

The hallway reeked of Chinese takeout. Someone's TV was blasting through the paper-thin walls. Home sweet home. She kicked the door shut behind her and dumped everything on the entryway bench. Her feet were killing her as she toed off her sneakers. The apartment was tiny—just four hundred square feet of so-called "affordable" New York living—but it was hers. Mom's knitted throw was draped over the couch. Dad's old paperbacks were stacked on the coffee table. Little pieces of Ohio scattered throughout her Queens life.

Clara flipped through the mail until rough brown paper caught her attention. Her father's handwriting stared back at her: *Clara Valenwood.*

The excitement she'd been pushing down all day bubbled up. She tore into the padded envelope at the kitchen counter, tissue paper crinkling everywhere. Inside, a pendant on a golden chain caught the light. She gasped softly. It was gorgeous. Dad had seriously outdone himself this time. She couldn't help but smile.

Clara lifted it for a closer look. A teardrop-shaped crystal about an inch long, capped with delicate golden scrollwork, hung from the chain. Strange symbols spiraled across its surface, flowing together like a language she couldn't read. Each line was etched so finely it seemed to shimmer.

As she held the necklace, the crystal warmed in her hand as if it had been sitting in the sun. She frowned. Then, just as quickly, it cooled against her skin. For a moment, it almost felt like the pendant was greeting her. Clara turned it under the light, wondering if she was imagining things. Maybe it was just exhaustion or the weirdness of the day messing with her. She shook her head. Ridiculous.

Under the tissue paper, she found a note in her father's neat handwriting:

You're twenty-one now, Clara. This pendant has been in our family for generations. Now, it belongs to you. Keep it close. It's more important than you know. Love, Dad.

Generations? Since when did her family own anything like this? Her grandparents had been totally working class, and this thing looked expensive. Really expensive. She hadn't expected such an extravagant gift. She reached for her phone to call her dad, then stopped—it was past seven, they'd be eating dinner. Her stomach growled. She shot off a quick thank-you text instead, still staring at the pendant. Dad was getting eccentric with each passing year.

Clara smiled at the thoughtful gift and let the note fall back into the box.

She fastened the chain around her neck. The crystal settled just below her collarbone—it felt different having something there. She touched it once, half-expecting that warmth again. Nothing. Obviously. What was she even thinking?

Clara tucked it under her shirt, then flicked off the kitchen light and headed for the shower. Still, an unsettling feeling curled in her chest that she couldn't explain. The pendant just sat there quietly against her skin, a reminder that some things weren't that easy to brush off.

Later, after scarfing down some leftover pasta, she was lying in bed with the city humming softly in the background. Headlights flickered across the ceiling. Outside, New York kept moving. But here, everything felt still. Like that moment right before something big happens.

She shifted, and the chain brushed her neck.

It was dumb, but the pendant made her feel closer to home. Ohio was so much quieter than New York, more chill. Moving here was supposed to be this big adventure. And it was. But lately, it just felt like constant noise. Endless shifts. Conversations that didn't go deeper than the type of "How are you?" that didn't want an answer. That was New York for you. She loved parts of it—all the energy, everything there was to do— but it wasn't home.

And the noise was starting to feel heavy.

Her mind drifted back to her father's note and Mrs. Alcott's bizarre comments. She breathed out slowly, trying to clear her head. Clara had never been great with too many unknowns; she felt everything too deeply. But she was handling it. She'd be fine. She liked working at the nursing home overall. She'd stick with it and try to focus on her patients. Yeah, that's what she'd do. Her eyes started getting heavy. She just needed to sleep.

Then . . . the world around her changed.

Clara blinked and found herself standing in a forest bathed in silver light. The air was crisp and smelled like pavement after summer rain. Towering trees rose toward the sky, pale blue veins shimmering across their trunks and branches. Leaves of gold and emerald floated down around her, gliding weightlessly before vanishing into mist.

Clara took a step forward, the ground springy under her feet. The forest was quiet, but not empty. Somewhere ahead, a distant, melodic whisper drifted through the air.

"Clara . . ."

She spun around, looking for whoever was calling her, heart racing. The trees seemed to lean in closer, their glowing branches forming a tunnel that stretched deeper into the forest. Light pooled at the end, warm and inviting.

"Come . . . find me . . ."

The whisper grew clearer, like it was tugging at her chest. She felt this strange pull, like the air itself wanted her to move forward. Her feet moved on their own, carrying her down the glowing path as her mind wavered between curiosity and fear.

She reached the end of the tunnel where the light became blinding. The pendant around her neck was burning now, the warmth sharpening into searing heat.

"Clara . . ."

The voice called one more time, urgent and pleading. Clara stepped into the light.

Clara jolted awake, gasping for air.

The room was dark again, the familiar shadows of her apartment settling around her. Her chest heaved as she tried to catch her breath, her heart pounding.

She sat up, fumbling for her bedside lamp. The light chased away the darkness, but it couldn't get rid of what was left of the dream. The forest, the voice, that blinding light. Her skin prickled with leftover cold, as if she'd actually walked through that otherworldly place.

Clara's hand drifted to the pendant at her throat. It was warm again. Much warmer than her body heat. She lifted the crystal to look at it. The pendant glowed faintly before fading back to its normal crystal surface.

A chill ran up her spine. She looked out the window at the city beyond, its lights steady and indifferent to whatever strange thing was happening in her tiny apartment. She swallowed hard and pressed the pendant to her chest, the metal cool again beneath her palm. The pendant felt heavier, like it was carrying something more than just some old family tradition.

She shivered and lay back down, pulling the covers up to her chin. Why did the forest, that voice, all of it feel like more than just a dream?

"For you," she whispered, pressing the box into Clara's hand. "Keep it safe."

What the hell was Mrs. Alcott talking about? What could she possibly be giving her?

Clara held it carefully. The box was warmer than it should've been, almost as if it had been dipped in hot water. Patterns etched along the top glowed for a moment, then faded. First the pendant. Now this. She couldn't possibly accept it.

"I can't . . . Mrs. Alcott?" Clara's voice faltered. "Alira?"

Mrs. Alcott's fingers went limp. *No, no.* Clara squeezed her hand, hoping for any sign, but nothing. Her eyes closed. Her chest lifted once more, then stilled. It always struck like this, no matter how much she told herself it was inevitable. This was the part of the job she could never get used to.

Another nurse entered quietly, drawn by the call light. She glanced at Mrs. Alcott, then at Clara. "I'm sorry. I know you were fond of her. I'll take care of it. You should step outside."

Clara hesitated, her professional instincts clashing with the heaviness in her chest. She finally nodded, her mind still hazy. The thought of never seeing Mrs. Alcott's smile again left her hollow. At the very end, Mrs. Alcott had treated her as someone special, even entrusting her with an antique box.

Clara didn't understand why, but she knew the least she could do was honor that trust. She would keep the box, and whatever was inside, safe. Whispering a soft goodbye, she stepped into the hall with the box pressed tight against her chest.

The night air was colder than usual, slicing through Clara's scrubs, even beneath her coat. She shoved her hands inside her pockets. Her tote bag pressed against her side, the small box, nestled deep inside. City lights flickered, casting long, jagged shadows onto the cracked sidewalks.

She had just gotten off the train a few blocks back. Her phone vibrated against her thigh, but she ignored it. Something didn't feel right. The city felt quieter tonight, like the volume had been turned down. Each squeak of her sneakers sounded too loud. Clara pulled her coat tighter around her, but the chill still prickled her skin. Above her, the half-moon hung in the sky, its light barely cutting through the low-hanging clouds. The trees lining the sidewalk rustled, their skeletal branches swaying. Clara quickened her pace.

You lost a patient today, she told herself. *You're just tired and imagining things.*

But a jolt of unease ran through her stomach, one that had nothing to do with fatigue. She heard a shift in the air, the whoosh of something brushing against a surface. It both pulled at her and made her want to run. She glanced back over her shoulder, growing panicky.

Nothing.

Just empty sidewalks, parked cars, and pools of shadow. Clara swallowed and turned for home but hit something solid. She screamed as she sprang back.

The person she'd bumped into swore and placed a hand over his heart.

Clara's eyebrows shot up as she fought to calm her racing heart. "Mal?"

"Jeez, Clara! You nearly gave me a heart attack."

"I'm so sorry." Clara readjusted her tote bag and fought the urge to peer back into the shadows. Maybe she hadn't heard anything strange. It was just Malrik.

A streetlamp cast its warm glow across her friend's face. Malrik's dark hair was tousled and his black-rimmed glasses sat slightly crooked on his nose.

"What are you doing here?" she asked.

Malrik pushed his glasses up the bridge of his nose, then thrust his hands into his pockets. "I texted you a million times! When you didn't show up, I got worried. I was coming to check on you."

Clara's heart sank. With the arrival of the strange pendant and losing Mrs. Alcott, she'd completely forgotten about meeting Mal. "I'm so sorry. Today has been . . . weird."

Malrik threw a friendly arm around her shoulders. "Well, you can tell me about it over dessert."

Clara thought about asking to reschedule. Her eyes felt like sandpaper and her legs were aching. But the idea of sitting with Mal in a brightly lit restaurant, far away from the dark alleyways, was too tempting to pass up. "Okay."

They walked toward their favorite spot. Mal filled the silence, and Clara let him, too distracted to join in.

The bell above the door chimed softly as they stepped into Penny's Brew. The warmth of the café was a welcome contrast to the chilly night air. Inside, golden string lights crisscrossed the ceiling, casting light over the mismatched wooden tables and fogged-up windows. The smell of baked bread and cocoa lingered in the air.

Clara slid into their usual booth as Malrik went to place their order. A few moments later, he joined her. He sprawled across the bench seat, his long legs stretching out under the table. He was always so relaxed. The corner of his mouth tugged into a lopsided grin, his gray eyes crinkling. "So. Weird day?"

"You're lucky I came," Clara said, dropping her tote bag with a soft thud. "My legs gave me at least three different warnings on the way here."

A waitress slid a warm ceramic mug toward her, steam rose gently from the top. Despite her exhaustion, Clara smiled.

"Hot chocolate," Mal said. "And yes, I got the one with the marshmallows. Because I care."

"You're too good to me," she said, wrapping her fingers around the mug, inhaling the scent of chocolate. She blew on the steaming drink and took a tentative sip. It warmed her from the inside out. "I lost a patient today."

Mal pressed his lips into a thin line as his brows drew together. "I'm sorry."

"Thanks." She took another sip of her drink. She didn't know how to tell him about the pendant from her father or the strange box Mrs. Alcott had given her. Not yet.

They chatted a bit until Malrik leaned down and pulled a small white box from under the table. "Happy belated birthday," he said, placing it in front of her.

Clara blinked. "You didn't have to—"

"I did," he said simply. "You're twenty-one. I'm not letting that go uncelebrated."

Inside the box was an ube cupcake—her favorite. He lit the single candle with a match, and the flame danced between them.

"Make a wish," he said.

Clara stared at the candle for a second. Her thoughts scrambled to settle on a wish. Rest, a vacation, maybe something bigger. Something more. She wasn't sure what that meant yet. She blew out the candle.

Malrik gave a satisfied nod. "There. Now it's official."

She laughed softly. "Thanks, Mal. Really."

"Anytime." For a while, the two of them sat there, talking between bites of cupcake and sips of hot chocolate, their little corner of the café lit with soft light and familiar comfort. After an hour, they pushed themselves out of the booth. Despite her protests, Malrik insisted on walking her home. "It's on the way."

As they stepped farther into the darkness of side streets, Clara was glad to have him with her. She couldn't shake the sense of eyes on her, no matter how many times she glanced over her shoulder.

Every shadow, every shift in the light felt wrong. If Malrik noticed, he didn't say anything.

Clara's pulse kicked hard in her throat. The box in her bag bumped against her with every step. As they turned onto a quieter street, their breath clouded in the cold air. Streetlights flickered, a few dying out completely. Shadows stretched over the pavement, keeping her on edge. She scanned the empty street, parked cars and doorways looming like threats.

A dark figure shifted near an alley entrance, just out of reach of the streetlight. Clara froze. The figure began to slink closer, slithering unnaturally from the shadows. She took a step back, shoulders tensing as she clutched the strap of her bag.

Every instinct screamed at her to run.

Malrik stopped beside her, his eyes snapped to the figure in the alley. His expression hardened. He took a step forward, his shoulders squared, his presence a shield.

"Hey!" he called, his voice sharp. "Who's there?"

The figure melted back into the shadows. The alley was empty again, silent.

Malrik didn't move until the tension ebbed away. Then he turned back to Clara, his eyes narrowing. "Clara, what was that?" His voice was low, concerned. "And don't tell me it's nothing."

"I don't know," she whispered, the hairs on her arms standing up. "But something's happening, Malrik. And I don't know what to do."

He sighed and stepped closer, his hand resting lightly on her shoulder. "Let's get you inside."

She nodded. The warmth of his hand eased her nerves. But the chill in her bones wouldn't fade completely.

Somewhere out there, in the dark, something was watching.

CHAPTER 3

Clara closed the apartment door behind her, locking the deadbolt. She let the warmth of the familiar space wash over her, a relief compared to the chilly, odd night. She slipped off her coat and hung it by the door but kept a firm hold on her tote bag. She didn't want to let go of what was inside. She kicked off her shoes and moved further into the apartment.

Malrik followed, his glasses fogging up briefly before he pushed them up the bridge of his nose.

"Make yourself at home," Clara murmured. Malrik dropped onto the couch, stretching out his legs. "Already ahead of you."

She smiled and lowered herself onto the couch beside him. Between the pendant, the box, and the strange shadow, she didn't know where to begin.

Malrik broke the silence for her. "So . . . are we talking about that shadow or pretending it didn't happen?"

Clara shifted her weight, unsure of what to think or feel. "I don't know what it was. I just know it didn't feel right." It was a feeling she sometimes got. Certain places or smells made her feel as if there was something she'd forgotten. Since moving to New York, a moment of *deja vu* would hit her so hard she swore she'd been to places that were entirely new to her. But those flashes were just strange. This had felt sinister.

Malrik's jaw clenched slightly, his eyes narrowing. "Whatever it was, I didn't like it. And I don't like to see you so freaked out."

He nodded toward her bag. "What's in that, anyway? You've been guarding it like it holds the meaning of life."

Clara drew the box out slowly and rested it in front of her. "Mrs. Alcott, my patient, gave it to me before she died . . ." Her voice trailed off. "I haven't opened it yet."

Malrik's expression softened. "You want to check it out together?"

She nodded. They sat side by side on the couch, the box between them. She hadn't taken a long look at it yet. Now, she could finally study the delicate carvings pressed into pale wood that carried a strangely familiar scent. As she leaned closer, the pendant began to glow, filling the room with warm light. Clara reached out with careful hands and lifted the lid. The light flared, and she gasped.

Inside the box was a tightly folded piece of fabric. She frowned and pulled it out, expecting paper, but the material was different. It was soft, thin, and supple, like silk, yet it had the resilience of something much stronger. She carefully unfolded the square.

Lines and symbols spread out before her, glimmering dimly in the pendant's golden glow. The markings pulsed softly, like they were alive.

"What is this?" she whispered.

Malrik leaned closer. "Is that . . . a map?"

"It does look like it," she muttered. "Or something else."

"Whatever it is, it's definitely not normal," Malrik said, his voice dropping to a murmur. His eyes reflected the same blend of curiosity and apprehension that she felt. "And neither is that necklace."

Clara's gaze fell to the teardrop-shaped crystal resting on her collarbones. The glow wasn't subtle this time. It pulsed steadily, casting light that seemed to dance across the map's surface.

"I thought it was just my imagination," she admitted. "Before, I thought the glow was a reflection or a trick of the light. But now . . ."

Malrik nodded, his brows drawn together. "I don't know what's going on. Are you sure nothing is making it light up? It doesn't make any sense."

"No. I swear it. It just lit up like that when I touched it."

"Well, I don't know, then," Malrik continued. "It's like the map and the pendant are connected somehow. And they're both trying to tell you something. Except, that doesn't make sense. There must be a rational explanation."

She slowly nodded, then shook her head. Malrik was right. There couldn't be a connection like that.

The glow wasn't frightening. At least not in the way she expected. Instead, it brought a strange comfort. She felt that the pendant was a tiny beacon of safety against encroaching darkness. With a jolt, Clara realized her dad hadn't responded to her text yesterday. That wasn't like him. He usually sent twenty follow-up messages whenever he mailed her something. "I should call my dad," she murmured, reaching for her phone. Her fingers were cold against the screen as she tapped the familiar number.

The call rang, each tone growing louder in the silence of the room. Her heartbeat quickened. She clutched the phone tighter, as if sheer will-power could make him answer. Finally, his voicemail clicked on.

Hey there, this is Richard. Leave a message, and I'll get back to you when I can!

Why wasn't he answering? Something strange was happening. Was Dad okay?

She lowered the phone as a hollow ache settled in her chest. Then she remembered. Just a few days ago, her dad had mentioned a hiking getaway with her mom. No phones, no signal. She'd been so buried under work and exhausted from her string of long shifts that she'd completely forgotten.

"They're off the grid." She muttered the words under her breath. "Great timing."

Malrik leaned toward her. "You okay?"

She forced a smile that didn't quite reach her eyes. "Yeah. They're on a trip. I forgot." She wrapped her arms around herself.

Malrik studied her face. "You want me to stay over? I can take the couch."

He lingered a moment longer, looking at her with concern and a hint of something else that made Clara's stomach flutter.

She shook her head. "I'll be fine. Thanks, though."

He nodded. "All right. But you text me if anything happens, got it?"

She straightened slightly. "Got it."

Malrik squeezed her shoulder gently before he stood. "Tomorrow's your day off, right?"

"Yeah," she replied. "It's a good thing, too. I don't think I can handle another shift right now."

"Perfect," he said, his smile reassuring. "I'll pick you up in the morning. We'll check the bookstore. I've got some things there that might help."

"Thanks, Malrik." Her voice was barely above a whisper. Then, she smiled a little. He was so proud of running his own shop.

He grinned, his usual warmth returning. "Anytime, Valenwood."

Valenwood.

She'd never given her last name a second thought. Who does? But Mrs. Alcott knew more, and Clara hadn't been able to ask. The regret sat heavy now. Her dad better have some good explanation when he got back.

The door clicked shut behind Malrik, and the stillness pressed in. Clara stared at the map and the stubborn glow of the pendant. Fine. If no one else would give her answers, she'd hunt them down herself tomorrow.

The small bell above the door jingled as Clara followed Malrik into Tomes and Tales. The shop smelled of old paper and polished wood, the kind of scent that settled instantly into her bones. Morning light filtered through the dusty front windows, casting long, golden shadows across rows of overflowing bookshelves. Malrik locked the door behind them, adjusting his glasses as he smiled. "We'll figure this out."

Clara's gaze drifted to the brass nameplate mounted just inside the door: *Malrik Hawthorne, Proprietor.* "You finally put that sign up, huh?" She knew he'd been putting it off.

He crossed his arms, eyes going distant for a second. "It was time."

Malrik had inherited the bookstore from his grandfather two years ago. Clara had only been in the city a few weeks when Malrik texted to say he was moving there too to take over running Tomes and Tales. He'd shared such fond memories of spending time here with his grandfather.

He'd always come back to their small hometown raving about how much he loved the city and the bookstore. Clara knew it was important to him that he carry on his grandfather's legacy.

The bookstore's warmth contrasted sharply with the chill outside, and for a moment, Clara let herself breathe. The cluttered coziness of Tomes and Tales felt like a different world. Her fingers brushed the chain at her neck. It was a new habit she was developing.

Malrik led her past shelves of novels and into the back section where the older, more obscure texts were stored. He cleared a space on a wide wooden table, scattering a few stray papers and closing a book that looked like it hadn't been opened in years. He gestured for Clara to sit.

"Okay," he said, leaning over with his hands on the table. "Let's see what we're dealing with."

Clara placed the box on the table, lifting the lid to reveal the folded fabric inside. She felt her pendant grow warm against her skin, tucked safely under her sweater, as she carefully unfolded the fabric, revealing the map. The unusual material spread out smoothly, its surface shimmering dimly in the bookstore's soft light.

Malrik nodded, his fingers hovering over the shifting lines and symbols. "And these markings. They don't look like any language I've seen before."

As Clara set the pendant down beside the map, a sheen rippled across the fabric, the lines subtly rearranging themselves. Her head jerked toward Malrik. "Did you see that?"

Malrik leaned in closer, his eyes narrowing behind his glasses. "Yeah," he murmured, his voice tight with disbelief. "It reacts to the pendant."

Clara's fingers hovered just above the map. The air between them thickened as they exchanged a glance. The map seemed to pulse with a quiet, enigmatic life of its own.

Malrik straightened abruptly, rubbing his palms against his jeans. "Wait here. I think I have a few books on ancient artifacts and symbols."

He returned with two thick tomes, their leather covers cracked with age. He flipped through the pages of the first book, muttering under his breath as he skimmed the texts. Clara watched him, contemplating whether she should touch the map again or not. The soft patter of rain on the roof and the sound of turning pages were the only sounds in the stillness of the store.

After several minutes, Malrik's finger landed on a passage. "Here. This mentions something called the *Vaelithar*. It's an ancient artifact described as a stone that carries sacred light. It also says something about a 'Bearer of Light.'" He glanced at Clara. "It sounds awfully similar to what we're looking at."

Clara's gaze drifted back to the pendant. The words *Bearer of Light* seemed to resonate with something buried deep within her, though she couldn't explain why.

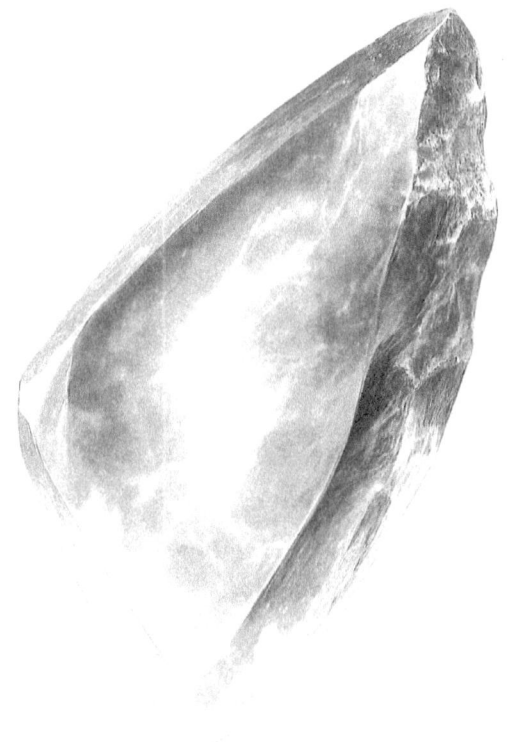

Malrik leaned back, rubbing his eyes. "There's something big here, Clara. Bigger than either of us." He looked at her, concern darkening his eyes. "Are you sure you're okay?"

She took a deep breath, the pendant's muted beat stirred against her skin. She remembered Mrs. Alcott's words: Guardian of the Valenwood legacy. "I don't know. But I feel like whatever this is, it's not going to go away by ignoring it."

Malrik closed the book with a soft thud and exhaled slowly. "I won't lie, Clara. This map, this pendant, they feel off. Like they're not meant for us to understand." He pushed his glasses up, his fingers lingering at the bridge of his nose. "It's like they belong to a different world entirely."

"I know." Malrik was scaring her. He was always the logical one. She reached for her necklace and withdrew the pendant, wrapping her fingers around it. "But somehow, it feels like I'm supposed to have this. Like it's protecting me." The pendant surged with warmth.

Malrik's gaze softened. "Then keep it close. Whatever it is, if it makes you feel safer, hold onto it." He hesitated, his gray eyes clouded with uncertainty. The rain outside grew heavier, a steady rhythm that filled the silence. The shadows beyond the window seemed thicker now, stretching along the pavement. Clara glanced over her shoulder again, her nerves prickling. The memory of the figure in the alley, the footsteps too close behind her, played like a phantom reel in her mind.

She forced her fear down. "I'll keep the pendant on me. At all times."

Malrik gave her a firm nod. "Good." His hand brushed her shoulder, a brief, steadying touch. "Let's lock up. Want to stop by Penny's Brew?"

The thought of a steaming cup of hot chocolate lifted her spirits. "Sounds good."

They moved to the door, the old bell above it jingling softly as Malrik turned the lock. The rain was a thin curtain outside. The mist clung to Clara's eyelashes as they walked toward their favorite cafe.

Later that night, Clara drifted in a hazy space between sleep and wakefulness, the comforting warmth of her blanket a distant anchor. Her breaths grew slower, deeper, as the edges of reality blurred, giving way to something ethereal.

The darkness behind her eyelids softened, replaced by a silvery glow. A forest gradually took shape. The air thrummed with a soft, otherworldly light, illuminating trees with bark like polished ivory. Their leaves had a soft, pearly tint that stood out against the dark. The ground was blanketed in moss that glowed under the full moon hanging above, too large and too bright to belong to her world.

The whole thing was strange and frightening. The clarity of the landscape, the way she felt every detail around her, made it seem real.

A rustle came from the trees. Probably the wind. Or animals. She refused to guess what else. It felt like the forest knew she was there.

Clara moved forward, her footsteps silent. A mist coiled around her ankles, cool and light, dissipating with every step. The pendant rested against her throat, unusually cold. A stark contrast to the vibrant warmth it had held earlier.

A voice whispered her name.

"Clara . . ."

She turned but saw nothing. Just endless trees, their luminescent leaves rustling in a breeze she couldn't feel.

"Protect the key . . . Mend what is broken . . ."

Clara spun, trying to find where it came from. The voice filled the air, close and distant at once, its presence larger than anything human. Goosebumps prickled her arms.

A sudden flash seared her vision. Fragmented images raced through her mind. Jagged shards of a radiant artifact scattered in a void. A tree split the sky with its branches while its roots sank into shadow. The chaos blurred together, burning into her memory. She fought to make sense of it.

The voice returned, clearer now, edged with desperation.

"You must mend it before the veil shatters . . ."

Clara fell to her knees. She reached for the pendant, hoping its warmth would steady her. Her vision blurred. She blinked, trying to clear the haze, but she felt something scraping against what she saw. Shadowy figures, twisting and writhing, their eyes glowing with malevolent light. She knew these shadows meant her harm. They weren't supposed to be here. Her limbs grew heavy, and she tried to focus her vision, even as her head swam.

Ahead, shifting subtly between two trees, a figure watched her. The shadows fled from this presence. Ocean-blue eyes glinted from the dark. Something about them was so familiar. They beckoned to her, like she was meant to meet their owner. She wanted to move toward them.

Before she could call out, the forest wavered beneath her. The trees shivered and blurred like a broken projection. The shadows stretched unnaturally long as the air grew colder, sharp with the scent of rain-soaked earth.

The shadows moved, crawling closer, reaching for her.

"No!" she gasped, her voice breaking through the quiet.

The world cracked like glass, and she fell—

Clara's eyes flew open. The room was dark, lit only by the soft glow of the pendant against her skin. Its golden chain lay cool across her neck. The crystal pulsed once before growing completely dark.

Her hand, slick with cold sweat, pressed against the stone, the same way it had in her dream. The images from that place still clung to her mind. She told herself it was only a dream, but her body refused to believe it.

She glanced toward the window. The city outside was cloaked in darkness, but the distant hum of traffic was a reminder that the world was still turning, still going on as it always had. The dream's words reverberated in her mind.

Protect the key . . . Mend what is broken . . .

She tightened her grip on the pendant. Fully awake now, Clara turned on her bedside lamp. She took a deep breath, exhaling slowly as she tried to shake the tension from her limbs. The familiar warmth of her apartment felt fragile now, like a thin barrier against something vast and unknown.

Her eyes drifted to the map, still lying on her desk where she'd left it. The silken material seemed to shimmer in the dim light. She hesitated before rising to her feet.

Carefully, she unfolded the map, spreading it out over the desk. The intricate lines and symbols glowed, the patterns shifting and pulsing in time with her still-pounding heart. The markings looked different than before, as if the map itself were trying to communicate something new.

"What are you trying to show me?" she whispered.

She leaned closer, squinting as the lines twisted and merged. The pendant swung free, slipping through the neck of her baggy t-shirt. For a moment, the lines seemed to form an image, a fragmented outline of something she didn't recognize. The partial shape blurred at the edges, refusing to settle into clarity.

The pendant winked with a feeble light. Not the soothing glow she'd seen before but something more urgent. Almost *pleading.*

Then she heard whispers. They were thin, brushing against the edge of her consciousness like a breeze through brittle leaves.

Safeguard the key . . . Repair the fractures.

Clara inhaled sharply. The words from her dream looped through her mind like a haunting refrain. She pressed a hand to her forehead, willing the whispers to fade. But they grew louder, swelling until they filled her mind completely.

Protect what matters . . . Mend what's broken.

The map's glow flared as lines of light raced across the fabric like veins of molten gold. The partial image wavered, almost solidifying. Then, just as quickly, the light dimmed and the markings faded. Clara staggered back, her fingers gripping the edge of the desk. She stared at the map, now inert, the fabric as smooth and unreadable as before. A wave of exhaustion tore through her, making her knees wobble. The pendant, too, had cooled, its glow reduced to a weak beam.

The room felt colder, the shadows deeper. She swallowed, her mouth dry. Clara pressed her fingers against her temples. This wasn't normal. People didn't hear whispers or have strange dreams like this. Her mind drifted to an array of diagnoses, flipping through a mental catalogue of possible explanations that stemmed from illness. She squeezed her eyes shut and took a deep breath.

When she opened them, the map and pendant lay before her. The necklace still glowed with a soft yellow light that shone from within. Whatever was happening, it was beyond coincidence. The pendant, the map, the whispers. Clara knew, deep within her, that they were pieces of something bigger, something she was now tangled in whether she liked it or not.

Her gaze remained fixed on the map as her mind raced. What was this key she was supposed to protect? What was broken, and how was she supposed to mend it? And why had her dad sent her this pendant in the first place?

Clara felt a strange resolve settle within her. Her eyes remained on the map, the dim glow casting shadows across her face. She clenched her jaw. She'd figure this out. Whatever it took.

A creak echoed beyond the window. The shadows outside shifted, then melted back into the darkness.

CHAPTER 4

few days later, Clara sat at a table in Tomes and Tales, barely visible beneath a mountain of yellowed pages and stacked books. Morning light filtered through the dusty windows of the bookshop, casting golden beams over piles of books and half-toppled shelves. Outside, New York City hummed with life, but within the shop, an almost oppressive silence wrapped around her.

Shadows ringed her eyes, a testament to too many nights spent wrestling with relentless dreams. She couldn't escape them. Sleep, when it came, was a fragile thing, shattered by whispers, visions, and the suffocating dread that something terrible was edging closer. Her fingers toyed with the corner of a page, her movements restless.

Clara felt like her world was coming apart. With her parents still away, she could not be more grateful for her friend's presence. The threads of reality were fraying at the edges, and no matter how hard she tried, she couldn't shake the feeling that the pendant nestled against her throat was the key to it all. The map, the dreams, and the ever-present shadows were all threads in a tangle she was desperate to unravel.

"Nothing," she muttered, slamming a book closed. The sound fractured the silence. She pressed her fingers to her temple, wincing.

Across the table, Malrik looked up from the tome he was examining, his black-rimmed glasses slipping slightly down his nose. His brow furrowed, his mouth pulling into a tight line. He didn't flinch at Clara's frustration. He never did. Where she was flighty at times, he was solid. When she'd confessed how convoluted the dreams had become, Malrik had redoubled his efforts to dig through the most obscure books on myths and legends his grandfather had collected. Clara was grateful for his steady presence.

"We'll find something," he said, his voice calm and sure. That steady, logical tone had been her anchor more times than she could count. "We have to be missing something."

He pushed the glasses back up with a knuckle and glanced down at the book in front of him. The pages were brittle with age. Malrik had always been methodical and patient. It was part of who he was; the boy who lived next door in Ohio, the boy who always had a book in his hand and a plan in his mind. He was one year older, but their friendship had been forged in scraped knees, summer nights, and whispered secrets between backyards. Now, in the heart of New York City, that bond felt more vital than ever.

Malrik's eyes narrowed, and he carefully shut the book in front of him. "Another bad dream?" he asked softly.

She let out a slow, shaky breath and ran a hand through her dark waves. "Yeah," she whispered. "I see . . . fragments. Shattered things. Symbols. And there's always this voice whispering to me, '*Come find me.*' Or sometimes, '*Mend what is broken.*' It feels like if I don't figure this out, something terrible will happen. I can't shake it."

Malrik leaned back in his chair, his face serious. He rubbed the back of his neck, absorbing her words. "These can't just be dreams. Not with everything else happening."

It's what she'd been trying to say. She didn't have to explain. Malrik understood her. Her gaze dropped to the pendant hidden beneath her sweater. It hummed against her skin, a reminder that her world was no longer the safe, predictable place it had once been.

Malrik's fingers tapped the table, a steady rhythm that mirrored his thoughts. "Based on what we've found so far, I think we need better resources." He spun the book he'd been reading to face her, flipping back open to a particular page. He pointed at a collection of strange symbols that curled and twisted. "See this? Every time the Vaelithar is mentioned, which has only been three times in all these books, these symbols appear."

Clara leaned forward and squinted hard at the curling shapes, trying to see them more clearly. They didn't look like anything from her pendant or map.

Malrik was undeterred by her silence. "I've seen these symbols before."

Her eyebrows shot up in surprise. "Where?"

"In the restricted section at the New York City Public Library."

"And how, exactly, did you come across them? I didn't even know the library *had* a restricted section."

"Research." Malrik shrugged. "Some of the books my grandfather left me cross reference with some of the ones they have. He used to take me there. Told me it was important that I know that collection existed. Maybe this is why."

A fragile bubble of hope swelled in Clara's chest. "And how, exactly, are we going to get into a restricted collection of books?"

Malrik smiled. "I know someone who can get us in."

The thought of finding answers, of finally understanding the tangled mess her life had become, was both terrifying and exhilarating all at once. Clara's hands clenched into fists, nails biting into her palms.

"Let's go," she said, the words brittle but determined.

Malrik offered a small, reassuring smile and stood, his chair scraping against the worn wooden floor. "No time like the present." They gathered the scattered books, the map, the questions that refused to be silenced. As they stepped outside, the roar of New York City crashed over them, the screech of taxis and the hum of life weaving together into a symphony. The cold air whipped across Clara's cheeks, anchoring her to reality.

Clara and Malrik resurfaced onto the street after a short subway ride. The air was crisp and laced with the bite of autumn. The scents of damp pavement, exhaust fumes, and the occasional drift of roasted peanuts from a street vendor's cart mingled. Pedestrians surged through crosswalks. Cars weaved and jostled, drivers exchanging curses and glares. The city was a relentless tide, moving forward no matter who got caught in the current.

The crosswalk changed, and the wave of people swept forward, carrying her and Malrik with them. Clara pulled her jacket tighter, her eyes lifting to take in the building before them.

The New York Public Library rose like a marble fortress, its grand steps spreading wide like a barrier daring them to cross. The two stone lions, Patience and Fortitude, flanked the entrance, their gazes stoic and unyielding. The facade's carvings depicting leaves and mythological figures stood out against the morning light. Corinthian columns framed massive arched windows. Clara's feet felt rooted to the pavement. The library was solid and had stood unyielding through decades of change. Her own world was crumbling, yet this place remained untouched. Stable. Ordinary.

For a moment, doubt gnawed at her. What if this was pointless? What if the answers weren't here, and she was chasing shadows through myths and legends? What if she was losing her mind, piece by piece?

A cold gust of wind cut through Clara's thoughts. She shivered, but the sensation snapped her out of her spiral. The pendant beneath her sweater felt warm now, a subtle weight against her skin. It was a reminder of why she was here. The dreams, the map, the sense that something was coming. It all pressed beneath the surface of her thoughts. Urgent. Undeniable. She glanced at Malrik, who stood beside her, his expression a mixture of determination and concern. His gray eyes were steady behind his glasses as he gripped the straps of his backpack.

"You okay?" he asked quietly.

She nodded. "Yeah. I just hope there's something here that can help me figure this out."

He smiled, a brief curve of his lips that held more reassurance than words ever could. "I have a good feeling about it. Shall we?" Malrik's tone was his usual measured, positive one. She'd never known him to be a skeptic. It was both a good and bad quality—sometimes you needed to be on guard, like Clara was. But she smiled and relaxed a little. Maybe everything would be okay.

They climbed the steps, footfalls slapping against the marble. The shadows behind the lions' unseeing eyes watched, unblinking, as if judging their resolve. Clara felt the air grow taut as she passed between them, as if she was walking through a wall of static electricity. Her cheeks grew warm despite the cold. The feeling continued as they climbed the steps. She fought the urge to place a hand over her pendant, unsure if it was the source of the strange feeling or if there was something more to the library than first met the eye.

As they reached the top, Malrik pushed open one of the heavy wooden doors. The hinges groaned softly. Clara took a deep breath and stepped inside. The door shut quietly behind them. The roar of the city faded. Malrik led the way, taking her through rows of deep oak tables that stretched across rooms, each crowned with brass lamps casting pools of golden light. Shelves lined the walls, their spines a mosaic of stories and knowledge, each book filled with often forgotten truths. Clara's heart thudded, doubt lingering in the back of her mind. But beneath it, her determination took root.

She could feel it. This was a crossroads. A place where myth and reality might blur. The answers might be buried here, hidden in the shadows of ink and parchment. Or they might be nowhere at all.

But she had to try.

The quiet of the library pressed around them, each whisper and rustle of pages like a secret being shared.

Clara trailed slightly behind as an oppressive sense of urgency gnawed at her. At last, they stopped in front of a heavy door labeled "Restricted Access. Authorized Personnel Only." The brass plaque gleamed dully in the subdued light. Clara's heart fluttered. The door seemed to loom larger than it should, as if it knew the importance of the secrets it kept locked away.

Malrik knocked twice. A woman with sharp hazel eyes stood on the threshold.

"Malrik," she said, a teasing edge in her voice. "I was starting to think you'd gotten lost among the fiction shelves."

Malrik smirked. "Hello, Lydia. You know me. Always chasing stories."

Lydia's gaze flicked to Clara, her eyes softening slightly. "And you must be Clara." A knowing smile tugged at her lips. "The nurse he can't stop talking about."

Clara's cheeks flushed, and she shot Malrik a quick, questioning look. He coughed and avoided her gaze, suddenly engrossed in adjusting his glasses. Clara felt a flicker of warmth beneath her anxiety, a brief respite from the unknowns closing in on her.

Lydia chuckled. "Relax. It's good to finally meet you." Her expression turned serious, her eyes flicking to the door behind her. "I'm bending a lot of rules here, Malrik. Some of these texts are older than anything in your shop. Handle them with care."

"We will," he promised. His voice was tinged with relief. She was letting them inside.

Lydia reached into her pocket and pulled out two pairs of thin white gloves, handing one pair to Clara and the other to Malrik.

"These texts are irreplaceable," Lydia announced tersely. "No smudges. No torn pages. And you've got two hours. Don't push it."

Clara nodded, slipping the gloves on. The weight of the task settled around her shoulders. "Thank you, Lydia."

Malrik took his gloves, slipping them on with the same careful precision he applied to everything. "We owe you."

Lydia's gaze lingered on them for a moment longer. "Good luck," she said softly, then stepped aside, the door opening wider.

Malrik walked through first, his posture tense but resolute. Clara followed, her steps careful, her heart pounding. The door shut behind them with a soft, final click.

They were in a narrow room flanked by towering shelves that loomed like ancient sentinels. The air was colder here, tinged with the damp scent of stone. Light filtered down in weak beams from high, narrow windows, barely cutting through the dense shadows. The shelves stretched upward, their dark wood polished smooth by time.

The quiet here felt different, heavier, as though the room itself was listening. "So, how do you know her, again?" she asked, trying to break the tension.

"She's a friend of my grandfather. He took me here a few years back. Right after he got his diagnosis. She helped him with some manuscripts." Grief tinged Malrik's voice, and her heart squeezed. She knew just how devastating cancer could be.

Malrik turned to her, his gray eyes reflecting the dim light. "It feels different here today. Almost as if this place was waiting for us. Can you feel it?"

She sighed. Malrik was being a bit dramatic, but underneath her own doubts she understood what he meant. She nodded, her fingers instinctively brushing the outline of the pendant beneath her sweater. The metal felt cool and smooth, its presence grounding her.

"Let's get to work," Clara whispered.

They stepped deeper into the room. As they moved through the stacks, looking for anything that might be of use, the shadows shifted, as if reluctant to reveal the secrets hidden among the shelves. The narrow room was silent, except for the soft shuffle of their shoes on worn carpet and the slight creak of leather bindings being opened.

An hour later, Clara ran gloved fingers along the spines of ancient tomes. What hope she had of finding answers here had almost completely extinguished. The lack of sleep wasn't helping, either. Her eyes had trouble focusing on the books. Everything blurred together. Dammit.

Just as she was about to suggest to Malrik that they leave, maybe return another day, Clara paused. Something caught her eye. The spine of one of the books looked different from the rest. The cover was embossed with faded symbols that seemed to shake under her gaze. Beside her, Malrik was already engrossed in another volume, his eyes narrowed in concentration. He turned pages carefully. Clara took the book to a nearby table. She opened it, and the scent of old ink and parchment wafted into her nose. The first pages were filled with symbols of twisting lines and delicate curves that seemed both familiar and foreign.

As she flipped through the pages, she read stories of realms entwined, of ancient light and encroaching darkness. The words blurred and faded, as though time itself was trying to erase the truth.

Then, a passage caught her eye. Clara read aloud, *"When the realms were entwined, there existed a bearer of light, destined to guard the key that held their unity."*

The words seemed to flicker, their meaning hovering just out of reach. Something about the phrase felt important, like she needed to hold onto it.

Malrik's head snapped up, his eyes sharp. "Wait. That sounds familiar."

"It should. We found those exact words, *bearer of light*, in that fragment at the bookstore." Her voice trembled as the pieces of the puzzle shifted closer together. "We thought it was just another myth."

Malrik pushed his book aside, his gloved fingers clenching around the edge of the table. "But it's here too." His gaze flicked to the passage, then back to Clara. "That can't be a coincidence."

Clara felt something pressing against her ribs. The pendant beneath her sweater hummed, a subtle vibration that thrummed through her bones. It was as if the metal itself was responding to the words, resonating with something ancient and half-remembered.

She swallowed hard. "The pendant. It's reacting again," she whispered. "I can feel it."

Malrik's eyes darkened with worry. "What does it mean? Is it agreeing with us, or is it . . . something else?"

She shook her head, confusion and fear threading through her thoughts. "I don't know. But every time we get closer, it reacts." She took a slow breath, steadying herself. She thought of her dad, and how this pendant had come from him. "Like it's guiding us. Or warning us."

She turned another page, her fingers faltering slightly. More words swam before her eyes, half-obscured by age and decay. A new passage glimmered in the dim light.

"Protect the key. Mend what is broken."

The whisper from her dreams echoed in her mind. The sense of urgency, the feeling of something shattered, the voice telling her to protect . . . everything aligned with these legends.

Her gloved hand clenched into a fist. "I've heard these words before. In my dreams." Her voice was brittle. "It's like they've been trying to tell me something all along."

Malrik exhaled slowly. His logical side grappled with the surreal nature of it all, but Clara could tell he still trusted her. "If your dreams are connected to this and if the pendant keeps reacting, then maybe these myths are more than just stories." He leaned back, rubbing the back of his neck. "But how do we know what's real and what's just legend?"

A sudden chill seeped through the room, colder than before. The pendant's vibration shifted, the hum growing sharper, almost electric. The metal felt cool one moment, then surged with a charge of hot energy the next. Clara's pulse quickened.

They sat in silence for a moment. The whispers of ancient myths, the threads of dreams, and the pull of the pendant converged into a single, undeniable path. Clara exhaled; she needed to understand. A sudden thud shattered the stillness.

Clara jumped, her heart leaping into her throat. The sound of a heavy book hitting the floor echoed through the room, bouncing off the cold stone walls. Her eyes darted toward the aisle where the noise had come from. Shadows pooled like ink between the shelves.

Malrik was on his feet, his body tense. "It's just a book," he finally said. Clara swallowed, her throat dry. "Yeah. Just a book." His logical side comforted her.

They exchanged a glance, the unease simmering beneath the surface. Was Malrik right? God, she hoped so. They settled back into their seats. Clara turned her attention back to the book in front of her, but another sickening thump ricocheted from between the shelves.

One noise like that could be easily explained away. Two was more than a coincidence. Clara and Malrik locked eyes across the table.

The pendant beneath Clara's sweater stirred against her skin, a low vibration thrumming in her chest. The sensation was no longer comforting. It felt like a warning. She opened her mouth to share its warning with Malrik, but a soft whisper drifted through the air.

"The key belongs to our queen . . ."

Clara froze. The whisper was distant, but it coiled inside her mind, cold and sinister.

She swallowed hard. "Did you hear that?"

Malrik's face was pale. "Yeah. I heard it."

Another whisper slithered through the air, closer this time. *"Give it to us . . ."*

Another sharp thud sounded behind them. Clara leapt from her chair and spun around, her heart pounding. A book lay splayed on the floor, its pages fluttering as though gasping for breath. The shadows between the shelves twisted and writhed, stretching toward them.

The temperature plummeted. Frost crackled along the edges of the bookshelves, delicate patterns blooming across the spines of ancient tomes. Their breath clouded in front of them. It was so damn cold her fingers were cracking.

Malrik stepped closer to Clara, scooping up his backpack in one fluid motion. "We need to get out of here."

The pendant's vibration surged, the hum intensifying to a sharp, electric buzz. At the same moment, the map in Clara's bag grew hot against her side, the heat spreading like wildfire. A pulse of light seeped through the fabric, bright enough to pierce the gloom.

Clara yanked the map from her bag. The parchment glowed with swirling symbols. The markings twisted, aligning with invisible patterns etched into the marble floor beneath them. The glow pulsed.

"Malrik!" she gasped. "Something's happening!"

The shadows surged forward again, a wave of darkness that swallowed the weak light from above. The voices overlapped in a sinister chant.

"The key belongs to our queen . . ."

"Give it to us. Give it to us!"

The pendant flared, and a brilliant burst of light erupted from beneath Clara's sweater. Her heart pounded. What the hell was happening? The glow poured out in waves, meeting the map's light and fusing into a swirling vortex of golden energy. The air around them warped, the walls and shelves stretching and blurring as if reality itself were being unraveled. Clara's hair whipped around her face as the energy churned around them.

The shadows recoiled, hissing as the light seared their edges, but they regrouped, pressing in from all sides.

"Clara, we need to move!" Malrik's hand found hers, his grip firm despite the tremor in his voice.

"Don't you think I know that?" she gasped.

The symbols on the floor blazed brighter, lines of molten gold carving intricate patterns into the marble. The vortex spun faster, pulling at their clothes and their hair.

The shadows recoiled and then . . . they lunged.

Darkness swiped toward Clara's back. Malrik yanked her forward just in time, the icy chill of the shadow grazing her spine. She screamed, but no one could hear her.

"Hold on!" Malrik shouted, his fingers digging into her gloved hand.

Books flew from shelves, pages scattering like startled birds. The shadows shrieked. The cyclone expanded, becoming a tidal wave of light that swept them off their feet. Clara clung to Malrik's hand, the world fragmenting around them into shards of light and darkness.

"Clara!" Malrik's voice barely broke through the surge.

She opened her mouth to respond, but the light engulfed them, pulling them into its blinding heart. The library shattered, reality fracturing.

They fell through a void of swirling gold and shadow. Clara tried to scream, but the sound dissipated as the wind tore through them, and they fell.

CHAPTER 5

The world settled and everything was still. The roar of the vortex faded, leaving only the sound of Clara's ragged breathing and the pounding of her heart. She forced her eyes open, fighting against her lingering fear. Pressing the pads of her fingers to her temples, she tried to calm herself before hazarding a glance around them. It would be okay. Eventually. She needed Malrik to talk her down. His earth to her fire could only help them.

Her knees dug into impossibly soft moss. She looked down at it. Where was she?

Its surface glowed with a pale, bioluminescent light. It pulsed like a living thing, sighing beneath her weight. She lifted her hands, the green and gold particles of moss dust clinging to her gloved fingertips.

The air was dense and carried a scent that was both sweet and sharp. Every breath tingled in her lungs, flooding her with energy. An unfamiliar undercurrent threaded through her body. Next to her lay the map, now quiet and still. Her favorite tote bag had also made it to this strange place. She picked up the map and stowed it safely in her bag. Then Clara removed her gloves and slowly pushed herself up, her gaze lifting to take in the world around her.

The forest was painted in twilight hues of violet, indigo, and deep teal. Trees with trunks like pearly marble stretched toward a sky she couldn't see. Their branches hung with leaves that cast dapples of light on the ground. Flowers of impossible blues, silvers, and luminescent pinks bloomed in clusters, their petals shimmering. Tiny motes of light drifted lazily through the air. Clara's breath hitched. The beauty of the place was jarring, an almost unbelievable contrast to the cold darkness they'd just escaped. Her mind struggled to process it, but the forest floor beneath her feet was solid.

And Clara knew that some part of her recognized this strange place she found herself in.

Her hand went to the pendant beneath her sweater, its metal now cool and smooth. Her dreams echoed in her mind. The silver light, the glowing trees, the feeling of being drawn somewhere she couldn't name. It was the same place as in her dreams.

She had known it deep down—they hadn't been dreams at all. They were meant to lead her here.

A low groan broke her reverie.

Malrik was sprawled beside where she stood. He stirred, his eyes fluttering open. Confusion darted across his face, giving way to awe as he took in the forest around them. His gray eyes widened behind his glasses, reflecting the soft light of the leaves.

"Where . . ." he whispered, his voice trailing off as if words couldn't form around the wonder in his throat. "Where the hell *are* we?"

Clara swallowed, her voice quivering. "We're not in New York any-more." She had to laugh at the absurdity of the situation.

He pushed himself up on his elbows, his gaze darting between the glowing trees and the ethereal flowers. Malrik turned to her, his brows pinched together.

"That's for sure," he said, his voice low. "This place feels almost sen-tient . . . Like it's *observing* us."

A shiver slid down Clara's spine. The feeling was subtle but insistent, as if something hidden in the shadows was quietly taking stock of them. Despite the forest's beauty, the possibility of danger lingered at the edges. Her fingers curled around the pendant. She drew a steadying breath. Malrik rose to his feet, offering her a hand. She took it, letting the warmth of his grip steady her. A hushed rustle stirred the air.

Clara's head snapped around, her eyes narrowing into the shadows between the trees. The motes of light flickered. The leaves shifted slightly, though no breeze touched her skin.

"Did you hear that?" she whispered.

Malrik's shoulders went rigid, his gaze scanning the darkness. "Yeah."

The forest held its silence, but the feeling of being watched intensified. "There's something out there," Clara murmured, her voice barely audible.

Malrik's hand tightened around hers. "We need to move. Standing here doesn't feel safe." Clara hated that Malrik sounded afraid; it made the dangers of their situation feel more real.

She nodded, her heart thundering in her chest. Her free hand brushed against her bag, feeling the map shift inside, its surface warm and strangely reactive. It was as if it knew more than they did, guiding them deeper into the unknown.

They took a step forward, the moss muffling their footsteps. The glow of the trees lit their path, leading them further into the heart of the peculiar forest. As they walked, the air grew colder. The shadows thickened. Each breath felt like a leap away from the world they knew, into a place woven with secrets and danger.

Yet, Clara couldn't shake the feeling that something—or *someone*—was waiting for them just beyond the light. She glanced around constantly, her eyes searching for movement, but all she found was the eerie stillness of the forest.

Malrik's grip on his backpack strap was tight, his knuckles white. His shoulders were rigid with tension, his steps quick. He was trying to stay strong for Clara; that much she could tell. But his gray eyes betrayed him as he scanned for signs of danger. He was scared too, and this made Clara anxious. They stopped to rest for a moment. Clara's chest heaved with effort. She would not weaken. They had to keep going; her resolve strengthened. She continued to scan the shadows but could not help but marvel at the soft lights that winked among the trees and undergrowth.

"How are we here, in my dream?" Her voice was hushed. "It doesn't make sense. It shouldn't be possible."

Malrik's jaw clenched. He exhaled sharply, a cloud of mist forming in the cold air. "There's some strange energy in this place." He gestured vaguely to the iridescent landscape.

Clara's fingers brushed against the pendant beneath her sweater; its firm outline steadied her. "It has to be a portal of some kind. There's no other explanation." Her voice wavered. "Right?"

Malrik swallowed hard and frowned. "I don't know. And right now, I'm not sure I want to think about it." His gaze swept the darkened forest. "Not until we're somewhere safe."

They shared a glance, and the hair on the back of Clara's neck rose. Malrik was right. The need for survival was more important than her need for answers. At least for now. The quiet of the forest pressed down on them.

"Then, let's try to find someplace safe."

They walked on, and the glow from the moss weakened, as if the forest itself were reluctant to help them.

The cold seeped deeper, numbing her fingers and toes. How could it be this green but this cold? Clara's breath misted in front of her. The thought of her parents, blissfully unaware of her absence, gnawed at her mind. Soon, they'd return from their vacation to find her unreachable. Panic twisted in her stomach. What would they think? How long before they realized she was truly gone?

And what about her patients at the nursing home? She had promised to be there for them, to help them heal or find comfort in their final days. The idea of abandoning them, even unintentionally, felt like a betrayal.

"Everyone will think I just disappeared."

Malrik's expression tightened. "And the bookstore. I can't stop thinking about it. It's the last piece of Grandpa I have left. If I'm not there . . ." His words trailed off, the fear he didn't want to voice hanging between them. "I have to get back, Clara. No offense—this has been a fun adventure—but we've gotta get out of here."

Clara reached out and squeezed his arm gently. "We'll find a way back," she said, trying to sound certain.

He nodded, but his eyes reflected the same uncertainty she felt.

The chill in the air deepened, carrying a sense of dread that crept into their bones. The shadows pressed closer, more solid than they should have been.

Her voice cracked. "We can't keep wandering around out here. We need to find shelter. It's getting cold."

Malrik's eyes narrowed, scanning the path ahead. After a moment, he pointed. "Look. There's something up there."

Clara followed his gaze. A towering tree loomed in the distance, larger than any of the others around it. Its long roots stretched wide, winding through the soil. Nestled between them, a dark opening offered a sliver of hope, a place where they might finally escape the dangers of remaining out in the open.

They exchanged a glance, understanding passing silently between them. Without speaking, they moved quickly toward the massive tree. At the base, they found roots twisted into a natural arch that led into a hollow beneath the trunk. Its surface was mostly smooth, traced with dim veins of light that seemed to come from within the wood.

Clara stepped forward. Her fingers brushed one of the roots, its cool, solid surface steadying her as they ducked beneath the arch and entered the hollow.

Inside, the air felt calm and still. The hollow widened into a cave-like space, its walls lined with clusters of luminescent fungi. Their soft glow filled the space with pale blue and silver, casting gentle shadows around them. Moss grew here too, forming a thick carpet underfoot. Clara stepped forward carefully, her foot sinking slightly into the springy ground. Then she heard a low trickle breaking the silence. On the far side of the hollow, a thin silver line caught the dim glow of the fungi.

"Is that . . .?" she murmured. She rushed forward, falling to her knees beside a narrow stream that wound its way along the hollow's edge. The water was clear as crystal, catching the pale light. Clara scooped a handful of the icy water, it's cold shocking her palms. She brought it to her lips, too thirsty to care if it was a good idea or not. The taste was clean and crisp.

"It's water," she whispered, a shaky smile breaking across her face. "Clean water."

Malrik knelt beside her, his own face lighting with relief. He splashed a handful on his face, gasping at the cold. "Shit, that's cold. But finally, we found something good." He let out a half-laugh. He wiped his face, then set down his backpack and started rummaging through it. After a moment, he pulled out a crumpled bag of chips and a few slightly squished granola bars.

Clara's eyes widened. "You brought snacks?"

"Never underestimate the power of emergency rations." Malrik managed a grin, though his eyes were tired. "It's not much, but it's better than nothing."

"*Way* better than nothing." She took a granola bar, tore it open, and took a bite, savoring the familiar taste of peanuts and chocolate chips.

They ate quietly, accompanied only by the trickling stream and their muted chewing. The relief of finding water and food settled some of the tension in Clara's chest. It wasn't comfort exactly, but it was enough to keep the fear at bay.

Malrik leaned back against the moss-covered wall, stretching out his legs. He exhaled slowly, eyes flicking toward her. "Okay. Now what?"

Clara's fingers traced her pendant through her sweater. "The pendant and the map brought us here, right? They might be able to get us home. But . . ." Her voice trailed off. "If we go back right now, those shadow creatures could still be waiting for us. It's not safe."

Malrik nodded, his expression hardening. "Now that I'm not starving, I have this strange feeling. Like we're supposed to be here."

"Let's go through everything we know," Clara said, her voice thoughtful. "Something might make more sense now."

Malrik shifted, latching onto a task that felt productive. "We read about the Vaelithar and the bearer of light. The book said, 'When the realms were entwined, there existed a bearer of light, destined to guard the key that held their unity.'"

Clara's eyes narrowed in thought. "The Vaelithar . . . Maybe it's connected to the pendant. Like a link between this world and ours."

"Or a lock." Malrik's voice was cautious. "A lock that someone wants to break. I just wonder what it's keeping in. Or out."

Clara shivered. The shadowy figure's whisper echoed in her mind: *The key belongs to our queen.* "Whoever or whatever that shadowy figure was, it wants the pendant. And it knew I had it."

Her thoughts tangled further. Her father's words returned to her: *Keep it close. It's more important than you know.* And Mrs. Alcott's warning about the veil being thinner. Clara chewed her lip, the implications heavy.

"What if the Valenwood name is part of this?" Malrik asked tentatively. She could tell he was trying not to offend her, but the words lay unspoken between them—maybe her family had caused this to happen. "Your dad always said Valenwoods are special. Maybe it's not just a saying. Maybe your family's connected to all of this."

Clara's fingers tightened around the pendant's smooth surface, its weight suddenly more significant. "If that's true, then everything, my father sending me the necklace, Mrs. Alcott's messages, and my dreams, are all part of something bigger." She met Malrik's gaze. "But why now? Why us?"

Malrik stared at the domed ceiling above them. "I wish I knew." He glanced around the hollow. "But whatever the reason, we're in it now." The pieces of the puzzle were there, but the full picture remained maddeningly out of reach. Whatever was about to happen, they were in it together.

Clara's eyelids grew heavy, exhaustion creeping in. Malrik noticed and began shrugging off his jacket. "Here. You need rest."

Clara shook her head. She couldn't take his jacket; he would freeze. She brought her knees to her chest and leaned back against the wall. "It's fine. I can take the first watch."

Malrik's lips pressed into a slight frown and stilled. "I don't think I'll be able to sleep."

"Me either."

They sat for a moment, shoulder to shoulder, in silence. Malrik's shoulders fell slightly. "Stubborn as always, Valenwood. I'll take second watch."

Clara's lips quirked up as Malrik slid down the wall and rolled onto his side, tucking in his arms.

She was tired. Her body ached, and her eyes felt incredibly heavy. Her fingers toyed with her pendant. The events of the last few hours played in her mind. She still struggled to fully grasp what had happened. The soft glow of fungi dimmed as the minutes ticked by. The gentle trickle of the stream soothed her, relaxing her muscles.

At some point her eyes closed. She felt warm fabric around her shoulders, and the familiar scent of old books and cinnamon wrapped around her.

"You can go to sleep, Clara." Malrik whispered.

It took no time at all for sleep to claim her. Silver light filled her dreams, soft and ethereal. A voice whispered through the glow.

"You have come."

The words echoed through her mind, resonating with inevitability. She couldn't escape it, couldn't shake it off. Something was about to happen. Something dangerous.

Then, there was only silence.

A hand on her shoulder shook Clara from her sleep. She sat up, startled, heart pounding. Malrik pressed his fingers to his lips, eyes wide with fear. It had to be bad for Malrik to look so afraid. Clara's eyes darted around the hollow, taking in the dim silver glow and the three silhouettes that stood at the entrance of their sanctuary.

The figures were tall and elegant. They remained still, and the three travelers' attention was fixed on them.

Malrik's body tensed as one of the figures, a female with long silver hair, stepped forward and ducked into the hollow. The light from the entrance played across her pale skin, casting pearlescent hues that shifted with her movements. Her gaze swept over Clara and Malrik. The other two figures followed.

The three beings were clad in garments of light gold, cream, and earthen brown. Their coats, high-necked and refined, bore the unmistakable patterns of chainmail, though they floated as if they weighed no more than regular cloth would. The intricate links trailed down the sleeves like fine embroidery. Cream colored tunics peeked from beneath their outerwear, and all three wore knee-high boots.

"Children of dust," the female said, her voice clear, with a tone that felt unfamiliar but not unkind. "Your presence ripples through the land of Avenora."

The name felt important, though Clara didn't know why. *Avenora.* She repeated it in her head, trying to stay calm. She didn't miss the thin dagger belted to her hip. Though their clothes were sophisticated, they were clearly meant for battle.

Clara rose beside Malrik. Her words faltered in a whisper, "Who are you?"

The silver-haired female tilted her head slightly, her features calm and observant. "We are the Aelvor. Where you come from, we are known as fae."

Malrik spoke, his voice rough with disbelief. "Fae? You mean . . . fairies?" He shifted to place himself between Clara and the strangers.

The Aelvor on the left, a male with copper-toned hair and eyes like embers, let out a sound that might have been a laugh. It rumbled, low and distant. "The stories your kind tell are only shadows of the truth."

Clara's fingers curled around her sweater, gripping the spot where the pendant rested beneath. Fear tangled with disbelief. They looked human, but it was layered with beauty and danger in a way that felt unnatural.

"How do we know you're telling the truth?" Clara asked, her voice steadier than she felt. Malrik nudged her with his elbow, but she didn't care. Sometimes, you had to be direct if you wanted to get somewhere. And Clara needed to know where they were, how they'd gotten here, and why they were here.

The third figure stepped forward. His skin was the color of rich earth, his hair dark and glossy. He lifted one hand, and behind him, a soft rustle sounded as a vine from outside the tree snaked into the hollow, as if responding to his will. "If we meant you harm," he said, "you wouldn't have woken up."

Clara stared, her mouth slightly open. Her mind scrambled for logic, searching for anything that might explain what she was seeing. Maybe it was a dream. Or some kind of hallucination. But it didn't feel like either. Everything around her was too vivid. Deep down, something in her gut told her this was real, no matter how impossible it seemed.

Malrik's jaw clenched as he stepped forward, shoulders squared. "Then, why are you here?"

The silver-haired Aelvor regarded him with eyes that shifted from violet to blue. "It is not a question of why *we* are here. It is why *you* are here. The threads of fate have tangled, and your presence is a knot that must be unraveled."

"Great," Clara said with a light smirk.

Her gaze drifted toward the forest beyond, where the shadows seemed to deepen. "This land is no longer safe for wanderers. Darkness prowls beyond sight."

The Aelvor with brown skin spoke with authority. "We will take you to Ceyndor. He holds the wisdom of ages and will know what path you must walk."

The name rang with power. Clara's pulse quickened. Her thoughts flashed to her parents, to the life she had been pulled out of. Everything familiar felt impossibly distant, like a dream she could barely remember. They were stuck in a land wholly unknown. It was impossible to know who was friend or foe.

Malrik gave voice to her thoughts. "How do we know we can trust you?"

Clara struggled to trust people in general, and she *really* didn't trust a group of fairies.

The copper-haired Aelvor's lips lifted in a wry smile. "Trust is not demanded—it is earned. But linger here and the choice to trust may be stolen from you."

The forest beyond the hollow darkened further, the air carrying an edge of warning. Fear tugged at Clara, but she knew staying here, vulnerable and exposed, wasn't an option.

The silver-haired Aelvor extended a slender hand. "The choice is yours. We offer guidance, not chains."

Clara's hand betrayed her nerves as she reached for Malrik's. His fingers closed around hers, steady and warm despite the cold seeping into their bones. He squeezed once, trying to convey everything they could not say aloud in the presence of these strange people.

Her voice was barely a whisper. "Let's go."

Dawn's pale light spilled into the hollow as the Aelvor stepped aside. The path ahead was uncertain, but with them leading the way, they moved deeper into the unfamiliar lands of Avenora.

The Aelvor moved with a grace that seemed effortless, gliding over mossy ground and weaving through trees without hesitation. Clara and Malrik followed behind them, their footsteps heavy and awkward in comparison. The air was cool and crisp, carrying a clean, fresh scent. The soft light filtering through glassy leaves bathed everything in a muted green glow.

Malrik studied the Aelvor's fluid movements, his brow furrowed in thought. He leaned toward Clara and whispered, "Do you notice how they never seem to stumble? Or even get tired?"

"Crazy," she said. "But it makes sense since we're in their world."

The copper-haired fae with ember eyes glanced back, his voice low and calm. "Our forms are shaped by magic and time, molded by Avenora itself. Where you see obstacles, we see pathways. The land bends for us."

Magic. The word stayed with her. She knew it would take time to accept this new reality.

Malrik's brow rose. "Magic? Like spells and stuff?" He glanced at the forest, clearly reevaluating everything, then looked at Clara.

She shrugged but smiled at his having been caught whispering about their guides. Clearly, they had exceptional hearing too.

"Must be nice," he muttered as he narrowly avoided tripping on a tree root.

The silver-haired female slowed her pace slightly. "Your steps are laden with the gravity of humanity. That is not a flaw. It is the measure of your strength."

Her words, though cryptic, held a warmth that soothed Clara's fraying nerves. She took a deep breath, the cool air clearing some of the tightness in her chest. "You're saying we're strong because we're slow?"

The Aelvor with deep black hair sounded slightly amused as he responded. "Because you endure. Time flows differently for humans, yet you persist. That is a strength we do not possess."

Malrik rubbed the back of his neck. "I never would have thought of it that way."

They walked on, the forest glowing softly with bioluminescent moss and flowers in vibrant colors. Warmth slowly wrapped around Clara and Malrik, easing the chill from her fingers. The silence between them began to lift, replaced by a tentative calm. Eventually the copper-haired Aelvor turned his gaze toward Malrik and Clara. "You carry names, do you not? We are called Selandor," he gestured to himself, "Lythara," he indicated the silver-haired female, "and Vaelin." The dark-haired Aelvor inclined his head.

Clara's mouth curved gently. "I'm Clara. And this is Malrik."

Malrik gave a hesitant nod. "Nice to, uh, meet you."

Lythara turned to face them, something thoughtful in her expression. "Your names are brief, yet they hold echoes of your world. The simplicity of them offers a steady strength."

Clara stepped over a gnarled root, glad that the Aelvor had slowed their strides. "I guess we don't really think about names that much. They're just . . . what we're called."

Vaelin tilted his head slightly, studying her. "A name is never just a sound. It is a thread woven into your essence, binding you to your past and your path."

A shiver crept down Clara's spine as she wondered what path her name bound her to. She shook the thought away, trying to focus on the present. "How much further until we reach . . . Ceyndor?"

Lythara offered a serene smile. "Not far. At your pace, an hour. At ours, mere minutes. But we will continue to walk as you walk."

Malrik exhaled sharply, relief flashing in his eyes. "An hour I can handle." His stomach grumbled loudly, echoing in the stillness of the forest.

Selandor's gaze softened. "You have traveled far already, through realms you do not yet understand. Your weariness is earned."

Clara's shoulders relaxed a fraction. The Aelvor patience was like a balm to her. She felt a cautious thread of trust forming between them.

As they continued, Malrik's curiosity got the better of him. "So . . . the fae, sorry, Aelvor, can all move super fast then?"

Vaelin glanced at Malrik, his tone carrying the hint of a dry laugh. "Compared to humans, yes. Our bond with Avenora grants us strength, endurance, and sight beyond what you know."

Lythara added gently, "We are not bound by the same limits as humans, but we are bound by other constraints. You may not see them, but they are there."

Clara tilted her head, absorbing their words. "So, you're faster, stronger, and . . . what else?"

Selandor lifted an eyebrow. "Wiser, we hope. Though wisdom is a river that flows differently for each soul."

Malrik snorted softly. "That sounds like something a wise person would say."

A soft ripple of laughter passed between the trio of Aelvor. The sound was oddly reassuring, a reminder that these beings, for all their pretty words and power, were not unfeeling.

For the first time since they arrived in this strange realm, Clara allowed herself to hope. Surely, the Aelvor would help them find their way home. The fear hadn't vanished, nor had the uncertainty. But here, surrounded by beings who spoke of guidance and patience, the weight felt just a little easier to bear. She exchanged a glance with Malrik, whose shoulders seemed more relaxed. He felt it too.

They pressed forward. Clara's legs burned and her back ached, but she knew they must be getting close to their destination. Lythara had said they were only an hour away.

Malrik leaned in toward her, not bothering to whisper this time, but he did not speak too loudly either. "I can't believe I'm saying this but having them almost makes this place less terrifying."

Clara nodded, brushing her fingers against the chain around her neck. The pendant was still safely hidden beneath her sweater. She wasn't quite convinced. "Almost."

An eerie quiet settled in the woods. The stillness grew too pronounced, the air thickened like a storm cloud about to break. The moss beneath their feet stiffened, no longer soft but brittle and cold. The leaves in the trees grew muted.

Clara's heart pounded. She shot a glance at Malrik, whose eyes mirrored her unease. Selandor's copper hair caught a glint of dying light as he suddenly froze. Vaelin and Lythara halted too, their movements sharp and alert.

A whisper, low and distorted, scraped across her mind. The shadow creatures had found them.

Lythara's eyes widened in alarm. Her voice sliced through the stillness, sharp and urgent. *"Dravok!"*

The shadows between the trees writhed and stretched. Figures peeled away from the darkness, their movements jerky and unnatural. Clara's mouth fell open as she beheld them, rendered more corporeal than ever before. The shadow creatures bore features that seemed to have once been fair but were now veiled in a terrifying shroud. Their eyes swirled with pure black and blazing red, reflecting the malice burning within. Long, obsidian tendrils extended from their fingertips. Clara watched in horror as the soft wisps of smoke turned razor-sharp and deadly.

Malrik's hand clenched around Clara's. "Run!"

But there was nowhere to go.

They stumbled back as a flash of glowing silver cut the space between them and the creatures. Selandor leapt forward, and a sweep of light carved through the advancing darkness. What had first looked like a dagger extended as he moved, morphing into a glowing blade. Vaelin and Lythara moved beside him, their own swords igniting with blinding radiance and extending to reach for their attackers. The creatures, what Lythara had called Dravok, hissed, their whispers rising.

One lunged at Malrik and Clara. Selandor spun, intercepting it, but its claws raked across his side. A cry of pain escaped him, and he staggered, blood spattering onto the moss.

"Selandor!" Lythara barked as she leapt to shield him, her blade a whirl of silver light.

Another Dravok slipped past their defenders, its predatory gaze locking onto Clara.

Fight. Flight. Freeze. Each reaction battled for supremacy in her.

The creature lunged, its obsidian tendrils reaching for her.

She couldn't move. Fear rooted her to the spot.

A flash of movement descended from above. A figure landed between Clara and the Dravok, a blade of pure light cleaved the creature in two. It screeched as it dissolved into shadow.

Clara barely had time to process what she was seeing. The newcomer stood tall and poised, his presence commanding. Pale hair swept across his forehead, catching the dim light. His beauty was fierce, impossible to look away from, like a force of nature brought to life.

He turned his head slightly, his voice low and firm. "Stay down."

Clara obeyed, dropping to the ground and pulling Malrik with her. She kept her eyes fixed on the Aelvor who had just saved her. He moved with deadly grace, his blade a streak of light, cutting through the encroaching darkness.

He blocked another attack, but a Dravok slipped past him. They were so *fast*. Its burning eyes fixed on Clara.

Clara's heart stopped. The Dravok lunged, its claws stretching toward her. She tried to scramble to her feet, to run, but there was nothing she could do. The creature would be on her in half a second. She was going to die.

A burst of blinding white light erupted from her pendant, searing through the darkness like a star exploding. The Dravok shrieked as it was obliterated, the light consuming it completely. The force of the blast knocked Clara backward.

The world tilted out from under her feet. Her vision blurred, the edges fading to black. As she crumpled to the ground, she saw the Aelvor who had leapt from the trees turn toward her, his eyes wide with shock. He reached out, his silhouette blazing against the darkness.

Then everything went dark.

CHAPTER 6

Clara's world teetered on the edge of consciousness. Fragments of sensations swirled around her. Cool air rushing past her cheeks, the rustle of leaves, the rhythmic thud of footsteps far too swift to be human—it all felt like disaster descending upon them.

She drifted as the darkness pulled her down. But there was something else beside her there in the dark. A warmth, a presence she couldn't name, steady and strong. It wrapped around her like a cocoon. Behind her closed eyes, she caught whispers and fleeting bursts of light before everything fell into stillness. The air shifted, filling her lungs with new scents. Aged wood and a trace of sweetness, like wildflowers blooming at night, trailed through the air. She was dimly aware of being lowered gently onto a soft surface. Her hands clutched at a woven blanket beneath her, its rough texture oddly reassuring.

Once her head stopped swimming, Clara's eyelids fluttered open. The blur of shapes sharpened into distinct forms: a ceiling of smooth, living wood, its grain spiraling in patterns that pulsed softly with light. The air was cool but no longer hostile; it carried a serenity that felt almost sacred.

A presence shifted beside her. With great effort, Clara turned her head and met a gaze that unraveled her thoughts.

He was there. The one who had jumped down from the trees, appearing out of nowhere.

His pale hair shimmered like a warm sunbeam, cascading around a face that was both fierce and beautiful. His eyes were an impossible shade of blue, locked onto hers, holding an unspoken intensity that made her heart skip a beat. His lips were thin, and his eyes creased at the corners, as if trying to solve a riddle hidden in the very core of her being. Those eyes . . . something about them was so familiar. Clara swore she'd seen them somewhere before, but she couldn't place it. Her head hurt too much to think.

Clara fought to open her mouth, to ask what had happened, where she was.

The Aelvor's voice was low and rich, like a strand of silk warmed by fire. "You're safe."

The sound wrapped around her, resonating through her bones. His voice spoke to something deep within her. The magnetism of his presence was inescapable.

A low groan broke her trance. Clara turned her head toward the doorway just in time to see Malrik stumble into the room, his fingers pressed against his temples. His eyes, clouded with fatigue, widened when they met hers, relief melting the strain on his face.

"You're awake," he rasped, his voice rough. He leaned against the frame for a moment before pushing himself into the room, his movements stiff. "I thought . . ." He swallowed, shaking his head. "I'm glad you're okay."

Every small movement took monumental effort, but she managed to speak. "What happened?" Her voice was barely audible.

Malrik's gaze flicked toward the Aelvor kneeling beside her. "They saved us."

Her fingers gripped the blanket as she tried not to think about what would have happened if the Aelvor weren't there. As her head cleared and her eyes regained their focus, she realized there were more people there.

Across the room, Selandor sat propped against the far wall. A pearlescent bandage wrapped tightly around his side where the Dravok's claws had struck. Vaelin stood near the entrance to the clearing beyond, his dark eyes vigilant, scanning the world outside with unwavering focus. Lythara whispered to an older Aelvor.

The older Aelvor stepped forward, his presence filling the space with an unspoken authority. Fine lines were carved into his face, betraying just how old he must be.

"Welcome," he said, his voice a calm river flowing through the room. "I am Ceyndor, leader of this camp. You are among allies."

Relief washed through Clara, loosening the tight knot in her chest. "Thank you," she whispered, the words feeling too small.

Ceyndor inclined his head with grace. "Rest. There will be time for answers soon." He turned slightly, his gaze meeting the blue eyes of the Aelvor beside her. "Ashael, watch over them."

Ashael. The name resonated through her mind, fitting perfectly, as if it had always belonged there. It was so familiar. Ashael nodded respectfully. "I will."

As Ceyndor moved away, Clara's eyelids grew heavy, exhaustion tugging her back toward the darkness. The warmth of the refuge seeped into her. The last thing she saw was Ashael's captivating blue eyes before the world faded to black.

Clara pushed herself up and tried to blink away the dregs of exhaustion that clung to her. She'd been disoriented and overwhelmed the last time she woke. But now, in a moment of stillness, Clara took in the room around her.

They were inside the heart of a tree. The living wood curved like a protective cocoon, creating domed ceilings and arched windows. Veins pulsed through the wood, emitting a bluish-white glow. Clara stifled a groan and swung her feet over the edge of the bed. A curtain of leafy vines that hung from an arched doorway shifted aside on a gentle breeze, revealing the world beyond.

Clara peered around the leaves. She gasped as she swept the curtain fully aside and stepped onto a balcony. She stood at the base of a colossal tree, as tall as any high rise in New York City. Its roots spread wide, clutching the earth. Above her, the tree stretched skyward. Branches and vines wove together, forming living quarters that grew from the heart of the tree itself.

And there were more trees like this one that stretched into the distance. Each one held dwellings. Some glowed with a soft internal light, nestled within the branches like radiant fruits. Others were tucked beneath tree roots, their entrances framed by curved wood and sparkling crystal. Delicate stairways and winding pathways spiraled up the trunk, connecting each home in a seamless, organic flow.

Aelvor moved effortlessly through the network of paths, their grace a striking contrast to the rugged beauty of their surroundings. The air hummed with life, a gentle symphony of rustling leaves and distant, melodic voices.

Malrik brushed away the curtain of leaves and stepped onto the balcony to join her. He let out a low whistle, his eyes wide. "This isn't just a camp. It's . . . it's a whole world."

Clara's heart fluttered with awe and relief. Malrik was unharmed. Tired but unscathed. They had made it. They were alive. Clara turned her attention back to the wondrous sight before them. "It's like the homes are alive."

A soft, musical laugh broke through their wonder. Lythara approached, coming up the path. "That's because they are," she said, her voice gentle. "Our homes are not built. They are grown. The trees of Avenora shape themselves to our needs, offering shelter and light. In return, we care for them as family."

She gestured to the crystalline orbs and vine-wrapped hollows. "What you see is harmony, life supporting life."

Clara ran her hand along the smooth wooden railing. It hummed pleasantly beneath her fingers. From the outside, the homes appeared small. But the room behind her had felt expansive, like stepping into a space that defied logic.

"How is it so much bigger inside than it looks from the outside?" she asked. Lythara smiled, the corners of her eyes crinkling with amusement. "The trees are connected to the magic of Avenora. Space bends for us, folding in ways your kind would not expect. What appears small to the eye holds vastness within."

Malrik shook his head in wonder. "You know, in the human world, we have stories about fairies living in trees. I always thought they were just myths or children's tales." He gestured to the labyrinth of homes around them. "But this feels like those stories come to life." Clara surmised he was thinking of the bookstore. She gently squeezed his elbow.

"Your stories are echoes of truths long forgotten," Lythara reminded them. "The veil between our worlds may hide much, but it does not erase everything."

Malrik rubbed the back of his neck, still trying to wrap his head around everything. He glanced around at the Aelvor, his brow furrowing. "If you're fairies, why don't you have wings? Aren't fairies supposed to have wings?"

Lythara's laugh was a soft melody, gentle and kind. "We are fae, as you know them, but not all fae are the same. The ones with wings are called Nyths. They are smaller than your kind, no taller than your hand. We are of a different kind."

Clara leaned her forearms against the wooden banister, intrigued. "So, there are different kinds of fae?"

Lythara nodded. "As many kinds as there are leaves on the trees. Each with their own gifts, their own purpose." Her gaze softened. "You will come to know more in time."

Clara took a deep breath, the scent of moss, wood, and distant flowers filling her lungs. Despite the strangeness of it all, the fear that had clung to her since they arrived was loosening its grip. The wonder of this place was starting to seep into the cracks of her disbelief.

Perhaps here, amidst the magic and life of the Aelvor, they could finally find the answers they needed. A question tugged at the back of her mind. Where was Ashael? Ceyndor had specifically told him to watch over them, yet he was nowhere to be seen.

Lythara seemed to sense her unspoken question. "Ashael had to attend to the camp's defenses. The Dravok have been relentless in their pursuit. He made sure you were safe before he left."

Clara nodded, a strange mix of relief and disappointment settling in her chest. The memory of Ashael's piercing blue eyes lingered, and she couldn't shake the feeling that his absence left the air around her a little colder.

Lythara followed Clara and Malrik back into their sanctuary beneath the roots. The air inside was cool and fragrant with a hint of moss and wildflowers. The sense of safety within these living walls was a fragile comfort after everything they had been through.

Malrik stretched, rolling his shoulders with a groan. "I don't know how long we slept, but it wasn't enough." Indeed, dark circles still bloomed beneath his eyes.

Clara was sure she bore similar signs of her exhaustion, but she managed a tired smile. "At least it was something." Her eyes drifted toward the two archways framed by twisting vines that led to their separate bedrooms. The woven moss beds had been surprisingly comfortable.

Lythara, standing by the entrance, tilted her head with an amused glint in her violet-blue eyes. "Rest is precious, but I sense you have other needs now."

Clara's stomach growled in agreement. She winced. "Yeah, I guess food and water are next on the list."

Malrik rubbed his face. "And maybe a way to clean up. I feel like I'm wearing half of the forest."

Lythara waved a graceful hand through the air. "The tree provides for all of this. Come, let me show you."

She gestured toward a low table in the center of the room, where an assortment of vibrant fruits, dark seeded bread, and slender cups were laid out. The woven tray they rested on was crafted from intertwining vines.

"These were brought while you were sleeping," Lythara explained. "I thought you might wake with an appetite. The water is provided by the tree," she continued as thin tendrils unfurled from the table's edges, forming a pitcher that filled with a shimmering liquid.

"Please, eat," Lythara encouraged. "This is *ilvara* fruit, sweet and rejuvenating. The bread is *thornel*, made from seeds and herbs. And the drink is *alunel*, water blessed by the essence of the stars. It will replenish you."

Clara hesitated for only a moment before picking up one of the glowing fruits. The skin was smooth and cool, and when she bit into it, a burst of honeyed citrus filled her mouth. She closed her eyes, savoring the refreshing taste.

Malrik grabbed a chunk of the bread and took a bite. "This is incredible." He poured himself a cup of the *alunel*, sipping cautiously. His eyes widened. "It's like drinking pure energy."

Clara took a sip as well, the cool liquid spreading a soothing warmth through her body. For the first time in hours, maybe days, she felt a brief sense of normalcy.

When they finished eating, Clara glanced at Lythara. "Thank you. That was exactly what we needed."

Lythara inclined her head. "There is more to show you."

She led them to a small alcove off to the side. Short vines hung down from the ceiling in a delicate curtain, their tips glistening with droplets of glowing water. The floor beneath was a shallow basin lined with soft moss.

"This is where you may cleanse yourselves," Lythara explained. "The water flows from the heart of the tree."

Malrik eyed the setup with a look of curiosity and relief. "So, it's like a shower?"

"In essence, yes," Lythara said with a smile. "The moss will wick away the water, and the tree will absorb it harmlessly."

Clara nodded, her shoulders relaxing. "That sounds perfect."

Lythara gestured to another section of the alcove, where a hollow in the wall held a series of smooth, glistening leaves and a vessel filled with more fragrant water. "You can cleanse your teeth here. These leaves serve as brushes, and the water contains natural mint essence. It will leave your mouth refreshed."

Malrik picked up one of the leaves, his eyebrows raising in surprise. "Toothbrush leaves? Okay, that's pretty cool."

Lythara chuckled softly. "They are gentle yet effective. And for other needs," she continued, pointing to a narrow passage screened by thick vines, "there is a private space beyond. The roots form a natural basin that carries waste away and nourishes the earth. Everything here exists in balance."

Clara's cheeks flushed slightly, but relief washed over her. "That's . . . good to know. I was wondering about that."

Malrik exhaled, running a hand through his hair. "So, we've got showers, toothbrushes, and even bathrooms."

Lythara smiled warmly. "The trees provide for all needs, as long as we respect them."

Malrik glanced down at his dirt-streaked clothes. "And, uh, what about these?" He plucked at his shirt, grimacing. "I don't suppose there's a laundry service?"

Lythara chuckled. "Your clothes can be cleaned, but I would suggest wearing something more fitting for Avenora."

She gestured to a nearby shelf where folded garments lay, woven from delicate fabric. "These are Aelvor clothes. They will be more comfortable and suited to your needs here."

Clara stepped to the shelf and ran her fingers over the fabric. It was soft, almost like silk, but with a strength that hinted at magic woven into its threads. The garments, tunics, pants, and long overcoats were in a variety of pale greens, deep blues, and silvers that seemed to shift under the light.

Malrik picked up an intricately embroidered tunic, holding it up to his chest. "Well, it beats wearing the same sweaty clothes."

Lythara smiled warmly. "Take your time. Once you are ready, I will be waiting outside."

She left them with a graceful nod, the curtain of vines swishing gently behind her. Clara exchanged a glance with Malrik, a hint of humor in her eyes.

"This place really does think of everything," he said.

Clara chuckled. "Yeah. It's like living in a magical bed-and-breakfast."

Malrik grinned. "With a side of impending doom."

She laughed softly, the sound easing some of the tension that still coiled in her chest. For now, at least, they could take a moment to breathe, to eat, to wash away the grime and fear. Clara wanted to hold onto this moment of peace for as long as she could before she had to face the reality that she was in a strange land, far from home, being hunted by shadow creatures. So, she moved toward the bathing chamber. "I call the first shower!" She grinned as Malrik huffed his protests.

Clara ran the comb through her dark hair, its sleek teeth gliding easily through the freshly washed strands. She had found it tucked neatly in the corner of her room, a delicate tool crafted from a material that shimmered delicately, almost like pearl. With each stroke, her hair fell in loose waves over her shoulders, free of the tangles and grime that had clung to her since they found themselves hurled through the portal.

Her new outfit hugged her figure perfectly. She'd chosen a long, tunic-style dress that opened at the front to reveal fitted cream-colored leggings underneath, offering both elegance and freedom of movement. The sleeves were long, tapering into graceful curves at her wrists, and the neckline dipped just enough to give it a refined touch. The fabric shimmered in hues of teal, green, and blue. She moved her arm experimentally, marveling at how the material seemed to stretch and adjust effortlessly, always comfortable.

Her shoes, a mix of practicality and beauty, rose just above her ankles, their sleek design sturdy yet delicate. They were lightweight, with a subtle inch of heel and the same shimmering hues as her outfit. Clara flexed her toes, surprised by the comfort they offered despite their refined appearance.

She caught her reflection in the smooth, crystalline surface of the room's walls and paused. For the first time since arriving in Avenora, she felt like herself, only . . . different. Stronger, perhaps. More capable. They'd been through so much already. But she was going to make it. They were going to be okay.

"Ready?" Malrik's voice startled her, and she turned toward the doorway.

Malrik leaned casually against the wooden frame, his usual nonchalance tinged with something else she couldn't place. His outfit suited him better than she would have expected. His shirt, a pearlescent white, peeked out from under a coat of dark forest green, its sharp lines softened by the flowing material that moved with him as he stepped closer. His pants matched the coat, and his knee-high boots bore the same practical elegance as Clara's.

"You look . . ." He faltered for a moment, rubbing the back of his neck. "Different. In a good way. Really good, actually."

Clara felt heat rise to her cheeks. "Thanks. You don't look so bad yourself," she said with a smirk, though her voice wavered slightly.

Malrik chuckled, brushing his coat sleeve. "Guess I clean up well." He hesitated again, his gaze lingering a little too long before he cleared his throat. "We should probably head out. Lythara's waiting for us."

Just as Clara nodded, Lythara appeared in the doorway. "Ah, there you are," she said warmly, her violet eyes scanning the two of them. "You both look splendid. The Aelvor attire suits you well."

Clara smiled, smoothing the fabric of her dress. "It's amazing. I don't think I've ever worn anything like this before."

"The trees of Avenora provide the fabric," Lythara explained as she gestured for them to follow. "It adapts to your needs. It keeps you warm in the cold and cool in the heat. It's alive, in a way, like everything else here."

They stepped out into the bustling pathways of the camp, where the rhythm of Aelvor life unfolded before them. Clara couldn't help but marvel at the seamless harmony of it all. Children darted between the roots of trees, their laughter light and musical. Adults tended to glowing plants, their hands moving with precision and care.

Malrik's curiosity broke through the awed silence. "So, uh, how do you even have children? If you live so long, wouldn't the whole realm be packed by now?"

Lythara laughed, a sound like wind chimes in a gentle breeze. "We do not have children often. Each child is a rare and cherished gift. Our pregnancies lasts only a short while. But the children grow slowly, their connection to Avenora shaping their development."

Clara tilted her head. "Slowly? How slowly are we talking?"

"They reach adulthood in decades," Lythara explained. "But once they do, their aging slows to a crawl. Many years pass before the first signs of age appear. An Aelvor may live hundreds of years before their time comes to an end."

"They die eventually?" Malrik asked, his tone cautious.

"We are not immortal," Lythara admitted. "While our lives are long, we can still die from wounds, illness, or the passage of time. When we are ready, some choose to return to Avenora's essence, completing the cycle. Rarely, they are reborn, their spirit finding new life within the forest."

Malrik let out a low whistle. "That's . . . different."

"It is our way," Lythara said simply.

As they continued, Lythara introduced them to a few Aelvor along the way. A healer tending to a bird with glowing herbs and a warrior who inclined his head with solemn grace. Each interaction added new layers to the world of Avenora, and Clara felt herself drawn deeper into its magic.

When they finally reached the base of another towering tree, Lythara turned to them with a kind smile. "Ceyndor is ready to see you now."

Clara exchanged a glance with Malrik, her stomach knotting with both anticipation and unease. Whatever answers they were about to receive, she knew they would change everything.

They followed Lythara. From the outside, the dwelling seemed no larger than the other trees in Avenora, but as they stepped through the arched doorway formed by twisting vines, the space inside expanded, defying all expectations.

The interior was vast yet welcoming. Roots from the floor wove upward to create natural columns, while glowing veins traced their way through the walls, emitting a warm, steady light. In the center of the room, a broad table rose organically from the floor, its polished surface reflecting the light. The air inside carried a trace of floral fragrance, calming Clara's frayed nerves.

Around the table stood figures whose presence immediately commanded respect.

Ceyndor, the Aelvor with flowing hair and a lightly lined face, stood at the head of the table. To his left was a regal Aelvor woman dressed in teal robes, her demeanor calm and nurturing. Beside her stood a sturdy male with cropped hair, dressed in garments that seemed made from bark and stone. Lythara moved gracefully to her place, her sharp gaze sweeping the room. At the far end, Ashael leaned lightly against a column, his piercing blue eyes taking in Clara and Malrik with an intensity that needed no words.

Ceyndor stepped forward, his expression both welcoming and grave. "Clara and Malrik, you have walked a path fraught with peril and uncertainty. Your presence here is no small matter. Humans seldom find their way here, and rarer still under such dire circumstances. Allow us to officially welcome you among the Aelvor." He gestured to the others around the table. "Before we proceed, let me introduce those who guide this sanctuary."

He motioned toward the woman beside him. "This is Aelina, the eldest of our healers. She leads those who mend both body and spirit."

Aelina inclined her head, her voice warm and steady. "It is a pleasure to meet you both. You carry burdens, but you also carry strength. That will serve you well."

Ceyndor continued, turning toward the sturdy male. "Darion, our master builder. He oversees the creation and maintenance of all that thrives within Avenora."

Darion offered a slight bow. "Every part of this place lives because of the unity we share with nature. It is our purpose to guide, not harm."

Lythara offered a small smile as Ceyndor gestured toward her. "Lythara, leader of our scouts, ensures that the shadows do not overtake us. You have already met Selandor and Vaelin, two of her most trusted."

Finally, Ceyndor turned toward Ashael. "And Ashael, our commander of warriors. His duty is to protect our people from the threats that seek to destroy us."

Ashael stepped forward slightly, his expression carefully neutral. Clara's gaze lingered on him, her chest tightening as his words settled in the air. She couldn't quite place the strange pull she felt, but his presence was undeniable.

Ceyndor gestured for them to sit, and Clara and Malrik took their places on smooth benches placed around the table that were formed from living roots that grew out of the floor.

Once they were seated, Ceyndor's expression softened. "Now," he began, "share your story. Start from the beginning and tell us everything that led you here. Leave nothing out."

Clara and Malrik exchanged a glance. The Aelvor had given them no reason not to trust them. And if they were ever going to get home again, they needed help. Clara cleared her throat and began. "It started when my father sent me this pendant." She placed her fingers on the stone, which pulsed like a cat's purr. She unclasped it from her neck and set it on the table so everyone present could see it clearly. She recounted her strange dreams. She withdrew the map from a pocket of her dress and placed it next to the pendant, sharing how Mrs. Alcott had given it to her. Clara recalled the shadow attack at the library and the portal that pulled them into this world. Malrik chimed in with details here and there, making sure she left nothing out.

Ceyndor listened intently, his expression changing subtly with recognition at certain moments. When Malrik mentioned the shadows whispering about their queen and Clara told them about the phrases that haunted her dreams, Ceyndor leaned forward. "The queen they speak of is Veylora. The whispers and dreams you describe are deeply troubling but not unexpected."

Clara's eyes widened. "So, she's the queen they want to give the key to," she murmured. "But why us? Why now?"

The older Aelvor's gaze bore into Clara. "To answer your question," he began, "you must first learn the history of our realms. To understand why you were brought here, you must know the truth of our past."

He straightened, his silver hair catching the light as he spoke. "Long ago, the fae and human realms were one, living side by side in harmony under the guidance of the Eternals, beings of immense power and wisdom who maintained the balance of existence. The Eternals were protectors, ensuring peace and prosperity across the realms. Under their guidance, the fae and humans flourished together."

Clara leaned forward, captivated. "But then . . . something changed?"

Ceyndor's gaze darkened. "Yes. Among the Eternals was one who believed that humans were inferior, who were unworthy of the equality bestowed upon them. This Eternal, Veylora, became consumed by a belief that humans should be ruled, not guided. Her view was a stark departure from the Eternals' principles, but it went further. She sought to enslave humans, claiming their subservience was necessary to preserve order."

Malrik interjected, his voice tense. "What made her think that way?"

"She was corrupted," Ceyndor replied, his tone grave. "A darkness beyond even the Eternals' light touched her. A force ancient and insidious. It began to twist her, drawing her away from the harmony of the realms. Veylora's actions grew increasingly cruel. She enslaved humans, bent their will, and sought to dominate their existence entirely."

Ceyndor's voice dropped, heavy with reverence. "The other Eternals acted swiftly. To protect both realms, they banished Veylora, imprisoning her in the farthest, darkest corner of Avenora. Yet, knowing her influence could still spread beyond her prison, they took decisive steps to safeguard humanity and ensure balance."

He gestured to the pendant and map. Both lay quiet and still on the table. "The Eternals divided the realms, creating the Veil Gate to separate fae and humans while ensuring a balance was maintained. To hold the Veil Gate intact, they forged the Vaelithar, an object and source of unimaginable power, and entrusted the fae realm to the Aelvor, the guardians of Avenora. A special family among the Aelvor was chosen to lead, their bloodline said to carry unique gifts bestowed by the Eternals themselves."

Clara's brow furrowed. "And the humans?"

"The Eternals made a pact with the ancient humans," Ceyndor continued, "an agreement forged in mutual respect. They entrusted an artifact to a chosen human family, an artifact believed to work in harmony with the Vaelithar to sustain the balance of the realms. It was thought to be a single object, but now . . ." He gestured again to the pendant and map. "It seems the truth may be more complicated than we realized."

Aelina, the healer, spoke then. "For thousands of years, peace reigned in both realms. But then, without warning, the Eternals vanished. Some say they transcended to another plane, leaving behind traces of their essence in the Vaelithar and within the fabric of the realms. Others claim they simply faded, their purpose fulfilled. What remains is uncertainty."

Malrik's voice was low. "And what about Veylora? What happened to her?"

Ceyndor's expression darkened further. "Eons after the Eternals disappeared, Veylora escaped her prison. Though weakened, the darkness she had clung to for centuries had grown stronger, corrupting her completely.

She used this dark magic to amass power, leading a coup against the Aelvor monarchy. In the chaos, the Vaelithar shattered into shards, its protective force broken."

He paused, his voice thick with gravity. "Though her magic gave her great strength, the Vaelithar shards eluded her. Each fragment was protected by ancient magic, hidden in places she cannot penetrate. This has frustrated her plans for total domination, but her ambition remains unchecked. She seeks the shards to corrupt them, destroy the Veil Gate, and finally dominate both realms."

Lythara spoke next, her tone sharp but steady. "When she seized the throne, many fae fell under her sway, either out of fear or a lust for power. But not all succumbed. Those of us who could, fled, gathering in secret to resist her tyranny. That is how this sanctuary came to be."

Darion added, "There are other resistance camps scattered across Avenora, each working to oppose her in their own way. But the Dravok, her corrupted fae soldiers, hunt us relentlessly. Many of our kind have been lost, but we endure."

Ceyndor's gaze softened as he looked at Clara and Malrik. "Now, your arrival changes everything. The activation of these artifacts may signal the prophecy's beginning, the first tremors of the balance being restored."

The room was heavy with silence, the kind that seemed to press down on the soul. Malrik took Clara's hand, pressing it gently in his. The pendant and map on the table glimmered, their light casting shifting patterns across the room.

Malrik broke the quiet, his voice steady but laced with curiosity. "What prophecy?"

Ceyndor clasped his hands together, resting them on the table. "The Vaelithar was created to preserve balance, but when it shattered during Veylora's rise, it released more than just fragments of power. It is said that at the moment of its breaking, a prophecy was cast across the realms."

Clara frowned. "Cast? What does that mean?"

"An event like that, the destruction of something so integral to the fabric of both realms, cannot pass unnoticed," Aelina explained gently. "The Vaelithar's shattering did not just weaken the Veil; it echoed through existence itself. And in that echo, a vision was shared. A prophecy of what might come to pass."

Lythara nodded. "It is said that the prophecy appeared as a fiery projection in the skies of both realms, words burning so brightly they were visible to all who looked up. Many witnessed it, but time has blurred the exact details."

Ceyndor's silver brows pinched in thought. "Ancient records suggest the prophecy spoke of a bearer of light, a force to mend what was broken, and a path to restore balance. The full meaning remains obscured, but the words left an indelible mark on those who saw them."

Clara and Malrik exchanged a glance, recognition sparking in their eyes. Clara's voice was soft but insistent. "The bearer of light . . . We've come across that phrase before. It appeared in books from our world. When we were looking for information about the Vaelithar."

"Yes," Ceyndor said, his tone grave. "The bearer of light is a central figure in the prophecy, though their identity is unknown. Some believe it refers to the one destined to restore the Vaelithar. Others think it represents a force of hope, a guiding light in the darkness."

The tightness in Clara's chest eased. For the first time in days, she was able to take a deep breath. Of course *she* wouldn't be a bearer of light. The unspoken fear, the anxiety that she was responsible for these things happening, vanished at Ceyndor's explanation. It was the pendant that was important. It had certainly brought her hope and comfort and a heap of trouble, but it was only an artifact, just trying to fix what had been broken.

Malrik's brows furrowed. "But what does that have to do with us?"

Ceyndor's gaze rested on the artifacts. "Your arrival here, the activation of these artifacts, is no coincidence. These objects, entrusted to the human realm long ago, have awakened now for a reason. They have already shown their power, creating a portal to bring you here. Together, they may reveal more. We must study them carefully to uncover their secrets."

Malrik leaned forward, his voice laced with urgency. "If the pendant and map created a portal once, does that mean they can do it again? Could we use them to go back?"

Clara's heart sank at the hopeful desperation in his voice. He missed the bookstore.

Ceyndor's expression grew thoughtful, his tone measured. "It is unlikely. The creation of that portal required an extraordinary convergence of events. The artifacts' power was awakened not just to protect you, but because the prophecy is now in motion. Their magic is tied to the Vaelithar and the balance of the realms, not simply to serve as a gateway. For now, the Veil Gate remains the only passage between the realms."

Malrik's jaw tightened, frustration flashing across his face. "So, we're stuck here until we figure this out?"

"For now," Ceyndor said. "But your arrival here was no accident. This realm holds answers. Answers you were meant to find."

Clara exchanged a glance with Malrik, her fingers brushing the edge of the table. She felt like this was her fault that they were trapped here. She had thought that the leader of the Aelvor would have answers for them. A solution to get back home. To her parents. Her life.

Her stomach clenched. It seemed that it wouldn't be that easy.

She couldn't just sit around, hoping that the pendant and map would suddenly decide to let them go back home. She needed to be doing something. Something that would give her and Malrik purpose. "What do you think we should do now?"

"You stay," Aelina said gently. "Learn our ways. Train, so you are prepared for what lies ahead. This is not a journey you can undertake unprepared."

Lythara added, her tone decisive, "And you stay hidden. Veylora's Dravok are relentless, and she will not rest until she finds what she seeks."

Ceyndor stood. "For now, recover your strength. In time, the path will reveal itself."

As the rest of the Aelvor departed, disappointment settled over Clara and Malrik. They had come seeking answers, but the truths they had uncovered only led to more questions. As they sat in the council's presence, the enormity of their situation began to sink in. They had stumbled into something far greater than they could have ever imagined. Something that had been set in motion long before their time.

The room fell into a reflective silence, the light of the pendant casting wavering shadows across the room. Clara stared at it and wondered if her father had entrusted her with a blessing or a curse. She wished she could have asked him before finding herself here.

CHAPTER 7

The pendant and map lay on the council table, their soft glow illuminating the intricate patterns carved into the wood. The chamber seemed to hum with magic, the air thick with an energy that shifted between silver and gold. Above, the intertwined branches forming the ceiling allowed glimpses of Avenora's violet sky, casting shifting patterns of light and shadow.

Clara hesitated before picking up the pendant. The moment her fingers brushed its surface, a gentle warmth spread through her hand and arm. Reluctantly, she looped the chain around her neck, its weight settling against her chest. She couldn't deny that it provided her comfort. It reminded her of her dad. Thinking of him made a soft lump form in her throat. She wondered if they would ever make it home. With equal care, she folded the map and placed it in her pocket.

"We'll stay," Clara said, her voice steadier than she felt. Her gaze met Malrik's, his eyes a mix of fear and resolve mirroring her own, before turning to Ashael. He had remained unnervingly quiet during the meeting. His expression was neutral, though something like approval or concern glinted in his eyes.

Malrik exhaled sharply. "Better than waiting for death to find us," he murmured, tense. "Whatever comes, we face it standing."

Ceyndor inclined his head, his voice weighted with centuries of wisdom. "The path you choose is arduous but wise. The Aelvor will prepare you if you can endure what lies ahead."

His words provided little comfort. But what else were they to do?

Ashael stepped forward from the chamber's archway. A slight twitch in his jaw betrayed the only trace of tension in his otherwise composed demeanor. His gaze lingered on Clara a moment too long, sending an unbidden shiver through her.

"Training begins immediately," he said, his voice carrying the weight of authority. "The Dravok are gathering, building strength in the shadows beyond our reach." His eyes flicked briefly to Lythara, who nodded.

"We start with the basics," Ashael continued, addressing Clara and Malrik. "Combat, movement, and defense. These are not separate disciplines but parts of a whole, flowing together like streams into a river. You will learn them as one."

"And healing," Aelina added, stepping forward in green, opalescent robes. Her voice was warm yet commanding. "Human bodies are fragile, but they can be taught to mend. You must learn to channel Avenora's magic and let it strengthen you."

Darion's deep voice followed, drawing every eye. His robes were entwined with living vines that shifted subtly as he moved, adding to his imposing presence. "Understanding Avenora is vital. Its signs and magic are your lifeline here. Without them, survival is impossible." He fixed his intense stare on Clara and Malrik. "The forest speaks to those who listen. You must become fluent in its language."

Clara's chest churned with each new requirement. The pendant's warmth offered little comfort against the mounting pressure. "We're just human," she whispered, the words catching in her throat. "How can we possibly learn all that?"

"You were brought to Avenora for a reason. One we might not yet understand, but the fact remains that you are here." Ashael's voice cut through her doubt like a blade through silk, quiet but intense.

When Clara looked up, his blue eyes had locked onto hers with almost physical force. The air between them seemed to crackle with unspoken energy, making the pendant warm against her skin.

"Don't worry. I will protect you," he continued. The intensity of his gaze held her captive, making her forget, for a moment, that anyone else was in the room. Clara found herself unable to look away from the fierce promise in his eyes.

"Both of you," he added after a moment, almost as an afterthought, breaking the spell that had briefly wrapped around them.

Malrik shifted his weight, drawing attention back to himself. "Well," he said, attempting a grin that didn't quite reach his eyes, "it beats sitting around waiting for those shadow things to find us again." He straightened his shoulders. "We'll do what we must to return home."

Ceyndor raised his hand, and silence enveloped the chamber. Even the light in the walls seemed to dim, drawing all focus to him. "Your training begins this afternoon. Combat and movement with Ashael and Lythara. After that, healing with Aelina, followed by nature-craft with Darion." His sharp gaze rested on Clara and Malrik. "Every moment matters. Time is not our ally."

Across the room, Ashael's thoughtful gaze lingered on her. When their eyes met again, he didn't look away. Her pulse quickened.

"You'll also need new rooms," Ashael said. "The guest quarters are too exposed. The warriors' quarters near the silver-barked trees will provide better protection."

"The trees there are ancient and wise," Lythara added. "They'll provide what you need. Armor, weapons, shelter. They have taught before and will guide you now."

Ceyndor walked to the exit. "Lythara will lead you to your new quarters." His gaze lingered briefly on the pendant at Clara's throat. "Some choices cannot be undone, but they can be met with honor."

Clara exchanged a glance with Malrik as Lythara gestured for them to follow. As they left the council room, Clara could feel Ashael's stare burning into her with fierce intensity.

The path ahead was uncertain, but it was the only way forward. Lythara led them deeper into Avenora, where ancient silver-barked trees rose so high their trunks could house entire dwellings. As they passed by, Clara noticed how the branches bent subtly, forming archways that hadn't been there moments before.

She and Malrik followed as Lythara guided them along elevated walkways winding through the canopy. Warriors moved with effortless grace on parallel paths, their armor and weapons catching the light. Some nodded in greeting while others watched with open curiosity. Clara felt the weight of their stares, wondering if they saw her and Malrik as outsiders fumbling for a place in this enchanted world.

"The trees know you now," Lythara said, pausing where several paths converged beneath a woven canopy of branches. "They will respond to your presence and intent. This is your first step toward belonging in Avenora."

Malrik hesitated, brushing his fingers against a nearby trunk. He yanked his hand back as the bark quivered under his touch. "They're alive," he said, awe softening his voice. "I mean, they feel sentient, not just tree-alive."

"Everything in Avenora lives with purpose," Lythara replied. "The trees are our oldest allies, our strongest defenders. They remember the First Dawn and will endure long past us."

They stepped into a vast clearing where more silver-barked trees formed a perfect circle, their branches interwoven to create a natural dome. Sunlight filtered through, casting shifting rainbows across the ground. The air here was charged, making Clara's skin tingle and stirring a subtle hum in the pendant at her chest.

Warriors moved with precision across the clearing. Some sparred in rapid duels, while others meditated with glowing weapons before them. At the clearing's center, a group performed synchronized movements that sent ripples of energy through the air, their actions more art than combat.

"This is the Warriors' Grove," Lythara said, leading them along the edge. "Here, physical training and magical attunement merge. Watch."

She gestured to a warrior mid-form. His blade cut glowing symbols into the air, each lingering briefly before dissolving. Clara felt the pendant resonate subtly with the patterns, responding to the energy.

"That will be part of your training," Lythara continued. "The forms aren't just combat. They are a language, a way of connecting with Avenora."

Malrik stared, awe and doubt in his expression. "How long does it take to learn that?"

Clara suppressed a smile. She'd seen Malrik with that stunned determination plenty of times.

"For most Aelvor? Decades," Lythara said plainly. "But you have advantages: the pendant and necessity. Sometimes urgency teaches faster than time."

Their new quarters were nestled within the sprawling roots of one of the largest trees. Warm light framed the entrances, radiating gently from the bark. Though smaller than their guest quarters, the spaces were practical.

"These are for our newest warriors," Lythara said as Clara stepped inside. "The tree will provide for you."

Clara's chamber was simple yet remarkable. A glowing moss bed rippled under her touch. A clear stream fed a crystal basin, its water shimmering lightly. Shelves curved naturally into the walls, and an alcove held training clothes: tunics, pants, and coats in muted greens and browns.

Across from her room, Malrik explored his own quarters, his usual skepticism giving way to genuine wonder. He traced his fingers over the wood, his posture relaxing as though the space itself had eased his tension.

In the central chamber, a table had grown organically from the floor, set with silvery rolls wrapped in leaves and a crystal flask of sparkling water. "Lunch is ready," Lythara said. "The rolls are *telavryn*. A food favored by warriors, as they are light, small, and packed with energy. The flask holds *quenya* water. Drink sparingly. It enhances stamina."

Clara took a bite of the fluffy bread and was caught off guard by the flavor: sweet nectar with earthy undertones, light yet deeply satisfying. It reminded her of *hopia monggo* and *pandesal*, the kind her mom used to set out for breakfast back home. Warmth spread through her with each bite. Malrik grabbed a roll, his expression brightening. "Not bad for tree food."

As they finished, Lythara gestured toward the alcoves. "Change into your training clothes. Clara, it would be wise to secure the pendant," she added. "Its light could draw attention during combat."

A leaf unfurled next to a shelf, bearing silver links of a strange metal and a clasp. Clara recognized it as a chain extender. With this, she could wear the pendant lower beneath her shirt, nestling it closer to her heart.

Clara nodded and took what the tree had provided for her. "Understood."

"We will be waiting for you in the clearing," said Lythara. "Do not linger too long. Time grows short."

Malrik paused at his doorway and threw Clara a small smile. "At least the food's good."

Clara managed a hesitant smile. "Yeah. Malrik, look, I'm sorry—" Her throat closed up as guilt settled in her stomach. It was her fault they were stuck here. Malrik should never have been brought into this. He missed his bookstore. His whole life was in New York.

Malrik shook his head, cutting her off. "You don't have anything to apologize for. I took us to the library where those shadows first came after you. I mean, yeah, we're stuck here for the foreseeable future, but there are worse places to be. We could be running through the woods with those shadow creatures still after us."

"I guess so." She relaxed a little.

"Exactly," he replied, his voice firming. "We can do this. We don't have a choice."

She nodded, the weight of their decision settling into resolve. The distant clash of weapons echoed through the grove, reminding them that they had a training session to get to.

"Let's go get our butts kicked, shall we?"

Once they had changed into their new clothes, Malrik and Clara stepped into the clearing. The training grounds hummed with an energy that seemed to vibrate in Clara's chest as they stepped around the outskirts. Their training attire was a marvel: long coats in green and silver, made from Sylvanite, a rare and extraordinary material of Avenora. Their texture was soft but resilient, capable of withstanding strikes that would fell ordinary armor. Beneath the coats, their form-fitting tunics and pants shifted to blend seamlessly with the forest.

The thought of striking someone made Clara's heartrate spike—she wasn't a fighter. What had they gotten themselves into? She was a nurse who spent her days caring for the elderly. Clara was gentle, kind. But the clothing was beautiful. Clusters of Aelvor warriors moved across the grounds, their forms blurring as they demonstrated the incredible speed Clara and Malrik had only witnessed briefly before. When the warriors slowed, their movements became a mesmerizing dance, delicate and deadly. The ground beneath their feet was packed firm, marked by the rhythmic pounding of countless training sessions. Afternoon sunlight filtered through the high canopy, creating shifting mosaics of light on the earthy floor.

Clara's breath caught as she spotted Selandor and Vaelin sparring nearby. Their motions were impossibly fluid, glowing arcs trailing behind their blades with every strike and parry. The spectacle left no doubt about the centuries of practice behind their mastery. How would Clara and Malrik ever fight like them? Clara wasn't remotely athletic, and her curved back didn't help. She gritted her teeth, thoughts spinning in her head. She didn't think any amount of training would help.

Selandor was the first to notice them, halting his match with a grin. "Malrik! Clara!" His voice carried the warmth of familiarity, though it was tinged with curiosity. "You decided to join us, I see."

Malrik offered a lopsided smile. "We'll try to keep up. No promises." He and Clara exchanged a glance. He sold books for a living, it's not like he was an MMA fighter. Still, he smiled, appearing more confident than Clara felt. Masculinity, she thought. He was acting far more capable than he could possibly be.

Vaelin sheathed his blade with ease, his sharp features calm but focused. "Keeping up is not your task. Learning is." His tone was measured and authoritative. "Only fools run before they walk."

Clara gave a small smile, appreciating the subtle wisdom beneath Vaelin's bluntness. The Aelvor's demeanor, though intimidating, carried a strange reassurance. Something pulled her attention away from the two warriors. A dominating presence prickled at her neck. Clara looked to the edge of the grounds and found the source of the strange feeling. Ashael stood beside Lythara, unmistakable. He gestured for Clara and Malrik to approach. Clara's heart dipped into her stomach at the gesture. They bid Vaelin and Selandor farewell and moved to join Ashael.

"You will begin with the group," Ashael said as they arrived. "Movement and balance come first. Mastering the basics is the foundation of all skills, whether with blades or without." He nodded toward the

Aelvor warriors practicing nearby. "For now, you'll observe and follow. Watch closely and match their pace to the best of your ability."

Malrik squared his shoulders. Fierce determination flashed across his face. Clara resisted the urge to roll her eyes. What did Malrik know about fighting? "We'll do our best."

Lythara added, her voice softer, "Speed will come with time, though not in the way you might think. Tools to aid your progress exist, but they are rare, kept in Darion's domain. First, you must earn the right to use them."

Clara's curiosity piqued, but Ashael's next words pulled her focus back. "The simplest moves are often the hardest to perfect," he said, his piercing gaze meeting hers. "Do not let your mind wander."

Her stomach tightened at the command, but she nodded. "Understood."

Clara and Malrik joined a group of Aelvor warriors practicing foundational forms. The training began with simple stances, shifting into coordinated movements that felt more like an intricate dance than combat. The Aelvor moved with grace, their motions weaving a silent rhythm that Clara struggled to emulate. Her steps were hesitant, her balance unsteady, and more than once, she stumbled, earning a gentle correction from Lythara.

Malrik fared little better, though his determination kept him moving, even when his footing faltered. Clara couldn't help but admire his resolve, though she felt embarrassed every time she fumbled. The gap between human and Aelvor abilities became increasingly evident as the session progressed. While Clara and Malrik moved with all the effort they could muster, the Aelvor's blinding speed and grace made them seem untouchable. The warriors blurred between positions, their forms barely visible at times. Only when they slowed for demonstrations could Clara follow their motions enough to attempt mimicry.

After a particularly complicated set of movements that involved stepping with her right foot and striking with the back of her left hand, they were given a short break. Clara's legs quivered as she drank from a cup of water.

"Patience," Lythara said, her tone firm but encouraging. "You are not expected to match them. Remember, you are here to learn first. The forest does not grow overnight, yet it endures."

The words gave Clara pause, grounding her amidst the growing frustration. She took a deep breath and, once her legs had stopped shaking uncontrollably and her back had eased its familiar twinge, rejoined the warriors. She focused on each movement, no matter how clumsy it felt. With every repetition, the forms became slightly less foreign, and her body began to understand what her mind could not yet grasp.

After another hour, sweat poured from Clara's brow into her eyes. Malrik didn't fare much better. His chest heaved as he fought to regain his breath. Clara fought the urge to plop onto the ground for several minutes or hours. Every muscle ached.

Golden hues of sunset filtered through the canopy as Lythara signaled the end of training. She stepped over to Clara and Malrik and bade them to follow her. Clara's body protested every step as she followed Lythara and Malrik along a winding path that led deeper into the forest. Even the lightweight Sylvanite coat felt like it weighed twenty pounds.

"The healing pools await," Lythara said, her tone calm but carrying a note of sympathy. "Their magic will restore your strength and prepare you for what lies ahead. Then we shall dine."

The trail curved beneath arches formed by intertwining branches. The air grew warmer and more humid, rich with the scent of herbs and the gentle hum of energy that seemed to cradle the path. Clara noted how the luminescent patterns in the trees pulsed slower here, as though echoing the forest's restful state.

They emerged into a secluded grove encircled by ancient silver-barked trees. Their massive roots intertwined to form an organic dome. At the grove's heart lay a cluster of pools, their surfaces reflecting the deepening purples and blues of Avenora's sky. Gentle ripples spread across the water, though there was no breeze to disturb it.

"These are the restorative pools," Lythara explained, gesturing to the steaming waters. "The trees channel their energy here, infusing the waters with their magic. Even the Aelvor rely on them after rigorous training."

Clara approached the nearest pool. She knelt and dipped her fingers into the water, drawing back in surprise. The water wasn't just warm. It enveloped her in comfort, as if the water itself welcomed her presence.

"Don't just stand there!" Malrik called from another pool. He was already submerged to his shoulders, his face transformed by a rare expression of contentment. "It's like . . . I don't know how to describe it. Better than any bath back home."

Lythara chuckled softly. "The pools adapt to your needs, channeling the restorative magic of Avenora. They mend what is strained."

Encouraged, Clara removed her Sylvanite coat and hung it on a waiting, low-hanging branch. Then she stepped into the pool, still wearing the training undergarments provided earlier. The moment the water touched her skin, she gasped. The warmth was immediate and profound, seeping into her aching muscles and unraveling the tension that had gripped her since training began. "Ahh," she said. "This is better than any spa I've been to."

The pendant resting against her skin responded to the water, sending gentle waves of warmth through her chest in sync with the pool's ripples. As Clara sank deeper, she noticed the light from the water form-ing delicate patterns on its surface. Patterns reminiscent of the symbols left behind by the Aelvor's blades during practice.

"It resonates with the ancient magic here," Lythara explained as she eyed the glowing ripples and runes. "The pendant, the water, the very essence of Avenora are all connected. In time, you will learn to draw strength from these connections."

Clara closed her eyes, letting the water carry away her fatigue. The aches in her muscles faded, replaced by a profound sense of renewal.

"I never thought magic could feel like this," Malrik said from his pool, breaking the silence. His voice held an uncharacteristic softness. "It's . . . real. Not just something out of a story."

"Avenora's magic is not separate from life," Lythara said. "It flows through all things: the trees, the waters, even the air you breathe. To embrace it is to embrace the world itself."

Clara listened, leaning back so her hair fanned out in the water. The clarity brought by the pools wasn't just physical. Her thoughts felt sharper, more focused. Yet they kept returning to the pendant's gentle warmth and the fluttering feeling she got whenever she locked eyes with Ashael.

Lythara knelt beside Clara's pool, her voice lowering as she spoke to Clara alone. "The waters often reveal truths we guard too closely. Both in our bodies and our hearts."

Clara's blush deepened. She avoided Lythara's knowing gaze by study-ing the rippling water, though her heart beat faster.

When they finally rose from the pools, Clara was astonished to find herself completely dry, as though the water had left its essence behind. The undergarments she wore for training now bore intricate patterns, glowing softly like dewdrops in the light.

"Your garments reflect your time in the pools," Lythara explained. "The patterns are a sign of attunement, a small step toward becoming part of Avenora."

Clara ran her fingers over the fabric, marveling at its transformation. Beside her, Malrik inspected his own attire with similar care.

Lythara handed them fresh evening robes, elegant and weightless. Clara's were a deep indigo, reminiscent of twilight's tranquil skies, while Malrik's were a soft green, like the first leaves of spring. The robes' subtle shimmer reflected Avenora's magic, their craftsmanship both practical and beautiful.

"The dining pavilion is just ahead," Lythara said as they changed behind the privacy of shifting branches. "Evening meals are shared there by tradition. It fosters unity and provides guidance for those in training. While you may eat in your quarters if you wish, I recommend you join us, at least for tonight. Your presence, or lack thereof, will be noted."

Clara understood that this was more than just about food. She stepped from behind the screen and found Malrik waiting.

It was remarkable just how quickly he had taken to their new environment. The Aelvor clothing suited him. He looked both more confident and more at ease here, surrounded by the forest. The guilt Clara felt about taking him away from the bookstore started to abate. "I think we should go," he said.

Clara brushed the front of her robes, smoothing invisible wrinkles. A queasy tension stirred in her gut at the prospect of being ogled, but there was nothing for it. "Agreed."

Lythara smiled and gestured for them to follow. As they walked along the softly lit path, the tantalizing aroma of roasted meats and herbs filled the air, stirring her hunger. After a few moments, a pavilion came into view, its warm glow inviting and alive with low conversation.

The dining pavilion was seamlessly woven from the heartwood of an ancient silver-barked tree. Subtle patterns of light shifted across its surface, glowing softly as the last hues of sunset faded into twilight. It was an open-aired structure made of sweeping arches and pillars, but there was no roof. The night air glimmered above the tables laden with food and the warriors who sat speaking in hushed tones.

Lythara led them inside, and the pendant at Clara's throat stirred softly as if acknowledging the gathering's importance. She'd adjusted the chain to place it on display once more.

They weaved between long tables, naturally shaped from the tree itself, stretched beneath lanterns that floated above, casting soft light around the pavilion. "Here," Lythara said, guiding them to a central table where Selandor and Vaelin sat, their weapons leaning casually against the table. Selandor's auburn hair gleamed as he offered a welcoming grin, while Vaelin gave a curt nod.

"Just in time," Selandor said, gesturing to a platter of food. "Tharien roast, fresh from today's hunt near Crystal Falls. You won't find anything like it in your world."

Malrik slid into the seat beside Selandor, mirroring the warrior's easy demeanor. "Finally, something hearty," he said, then hesitated, glancing at Lythara. "Safe for humans, I hope?"

Selandor laughed, a warm, easy sound. "The tharien graze in Avenora's enchanted groves. Their meat holds the magic of this realm. It'll help your bodies adjust. The hunters blessed it before bringing it here. Trust me, you'll feel the difference." He served Malrik a generous portion, the rich aroma already promising its power.

Clara settled across from them, flanked by Lythara and Vaelin. The feast was unlike anything Clara had ever seen. Bowls of golden soup steamed invitingly, their surfaces glimmering. Platters of meat lay blanketed beneath tempting swirls of steam. Even the bread, still warm and crusty, carried a subtle glow, suggesting the touch of magic worked into every crumb.

As she ladled a portion of golden soup into her bowl, Vaelin spoke, his voice low and weighted. "The food here does more than sustain. It prepares you for what lies ahead."

Clara glanced at him, catching a trace of sadness before his expression smoothed. "I remember my first meal here, centuries ago," he added. "The taste of magic lingers long after the meal is done."

The first spoonful of soup warmed her from within, its flavor rich yet delicate, suffused with a vitality she couldn't name. The *tharien* meat followed. Clara couldn't help closing her eyes and humming with pleasure.

"The meat is marinated in sap from the boundary trees," Lythara explained, watching Clara's reaction. "It deepens the bond between you and Avenora's energy. Everything you take in here becomes part of you."

Clara nodded, her mouth too full to speak. She chewed and glanced around the pavilion, taking in the other warriors. Not all the gazes directed at their table were friendly. Clara noticed some warriors' eyes linger on Vaelin, their expressions veiled but unmistakably wary. She also caught a few curious glances aimed at her and Malrik. They were newcomers in a world where they clearly did not belong.

"Not everyone is pleased to see me here," Vaelin murmured. "Some grudges are older than memory."

Before Clara could respond, two Aelvor women approached their table. Both were clad in the flowing garments of hunters, their movements assured.

"Selandor. Gathering strays again?" the taller of the two teased, placing a hand on his shoulder.

Selandor laughed, his charm as warm as the lantern light. "Nyshara, you wound me. Malrik and Clara are no strays. They're part of our circle now." He gestured toward them with a flourish. "Nyshara and Elyndra, two of our finest hunters. They'll outpace anyone in the forest and charm you with stories afterward."

Nyshara's dark eyes sparkled as she inclined her head toward Clara and Malrik. "Welcome to Avenora. I hope you know what you've gotten yourselves into."

Elyndra's gaze lingered briefly on Vaelin, her expression neutral. "Avenora has seen many arrivals," she said softly. "Few make it through the trials ahead. But then, few come wearing such marks of destiny." Her eyes flicked briefly to Clara's pendant before returning to Selandor with a slight smile. "May your circle stay unbroken."

With a nod, the two hunters departed, leaving Clara with an uneasy tightening in her chest.

Clara's eyes wandered across the pavilion, taking in the vibrant energy of the gathering. Her gaze inevitably settled on Ashael, seated at a table near the far end of the hall. Even here, surrounded by senior warriors, his presence stood apart. He listened intently to those around him, but Clara sensed his awareness extended to the entire room.

Lythara leaned closer, her voice quiet. "Ashael rarely joins these meals. When he does, it's because something significant is unfolding."

Clara's cheeks flushed as Ashael's piercing gaze met hers briefly from across the room. She quickly looked down at her plate.

"He's been . . . different since you arrived," Lythara continued, studying Clara with a knowing expression. "More present."

Clara busied herself with her soup, avoiding Lythara's gaze. "He's just focused. Like you said, there's a lot at stake."

Lythara's smile deepened, but she didn't press further.

The conversation at the table grew livelier, with Malrik asking Selandor many questions about weapon techniques. Vaelin added dry comments that drew surprising laughs from Malrik, their camaraderie easing the tension that had lingered since the day began.

"Your training tomorrow will test you," Vaelin said during a quieter moment. "The food here prepares you, but you'll need more than magic to prevail. Strength comes from within. It is earned, not given."

Clara felt the pendant pulse subtly at his words. Vaelin's gaze lingered on her a moment longer, his expression unreadable, before Selandor launched into another story, breaking the solemnity.

As the meal wound down, Clara saw Ashael rise from his table. As he passed through the pavilion, his eyes briefly found hers again. This time, she didn't look away, and something unspoken passed between them. A silent acknowledgment or perhaps, a challenge.

Then he was gone, leaving Clara with questions she couldn't yet answer and a growing sense that her place in Avenora was tied to him in ways she had yet to understand.

The days flew by, and soon Clara and Malrik grew used to the rhythms of life in Avenora. Between training, meals, and spending time wandering the many paths around the camp, the hours passed with blinding speed.

Malrik quickly found companionship with some of the warriors, Selandor and Vaelin especially. He laughed with them at his clumsy mistakes during their forms. It had been that way for him ever since they were children. Malrik was always quick to make friends on the playground or at school.

There had been no progress yet on their return home. Ceyndor had counseled patience. But it was hard to be patient given everything she now knew about the Vaelithar.

After a week had passed, their routine was disturbed by Ashael, who cornered Clara and Malrik at the end of their training. As the group drills concluded, he stepped forward, his gaze settling on Malrik. "You will train with me first," he said, his tone leaving no room for argument. "Then you," he said, eyes flicking to Clara. "Come with me."

Malrik swallowed but nodded, following Ashael toward a shaded sparring hollow at the edge of the grounds. Clara watched as Ashael demonstrated defensive stances, his movements sharp and honed from years of training. Despite her nerves, she couldn't help but admire the way Ashael commanded the space, his authority woven seamlessly into every motion.

Selandor and Vaelin joined Malrik after his one-on-one session, offering additional guidance as he worked on his stances. Their camaraderie eased Malrik's tension. Clara watched him spar with Selandor, his strikes growing more confident, his balance steadier. She was glad that he fit in so well with them.

"Clara," Ashael called, his voice cutting through her thoughts. "Your turn."

Clara stepped into the hollow, her heart pounding. Ashael's gaze was as intense as ever, though a subtle softness in his expression hinted at something more than formality. She straightened her posture, determined not to let her nerves show.

"We begin with stances," Ashael said, his voice low but firm. "Show me what you've learned."

Clara moved through the basic forms, her motions still awkward but slightly more fluid than when she had first started. Ashael's sharp eye caught every mistake, his corrections swift and precise. When she stumbled, his hand shot out to steady her, his grip firm.

"Your balance is improving," he said, his tone almost approving. "But your hesitation will cost you in battle. Trust your instincts."

She nodded, her cheeks warming under his scrutiny. Despite his stern demeanor, there was a surprising patience in the way he guided her, his corrections meant to teach rather than criticize. As they worked through the basic forms over and over again, Clara got the distinct impression that behind his tough exterior, there was more to him.

By the end of the session, Clara's muscles ached, but a spark of pride burned in her chest. She had stumbled less, her movements were less awkward, and though she was far from mastering the forms, she felt the first hints of progress.

Ashael stepped back and studied her. "You are beginning to understand," he said, his tone quiet. "But there is still much to learn."

Clara nodded, meeting his eyes briefly before looking away. The warmth of his approval, however small it might be, lingered as she returned to the main grounds, where Malrik was still practicing with Selandor and Vaelin. Clara observed from the edge of the clearing. Malrik laughed easily with the Aelvor, joking with them and teasing. As she watched the warriors spar, a hollow ache, one she had grown used to in New York, settled in her chest, dispelling the glow of Ashael's praise. It seemed she was destined to be on the outskirts. That was how life had always been for Clara.

Malrik would be done soon. Besides, she didn't want to interrupt his training. She walked off to the healing pools alone, ready to soak away the ache in her muscles. Even if she knew the water could not evaporate the ache in her heart.

The path to their quarters was quiet, illuminated by the light filtering through the towering trees. Clara and Malrik walked side by side, their footsteps muffled by the soft forest floor.

They stopped in front of their quarters, the entrances glowing softly, inviting them inside. Clara hesitated at the threshold. There was something she needed to say. "I'm grateful, you know. For the Aelvor. For you. I know it's not ideal being stuck here, but if it was going to be with anyone . . ." Her throat tightened, thinking of her family still living their lives back in the other world. "Well. I'm glad it's with you."

Malrik's expression softened. "Me too. We'll figure everything out, Clara. One step at a time."

She managed a weary smile despite the heaviness in her chest. "Goodnight, Malrik."

"Goodnight," he replied, his voice quieter now.

Clara stepped into her quarters, and the soft glow of the moss walls wrapped around her like a comforting blanket. As she settled onto the moss bed, the past few days replayed themselves in fragments: the council meeting, the training drills, the dinner under the glowing pavilion. The memories intertwined with flashes of the days before their arrival in Avenora. Her nursing job, the ominous shadows that had driven her and Malrik to flee, the chaotic moment they'd crossed into this realm. Every event felt impossibly distant yet vividly immediate, the sensations overwhelming.

She touched the pendant at her throat, its warmth steady against her skin. Her thoughts turned to the Aelvor. Their otherworldly grace and strength had initially felt intimidating, but now she saw them as protectors. They didn't have to help her and Malrik, yet they had, with unrelenting dedication. Gratitude swelled in her chest despite the uncertainty of the future.

Then there was Ashael. His intensity lingered in her thoughts, unbidden but undeniable. The memory of his hands correcting her stance, his sharp gaze watching her every move, made her pulse quicken. *I will protect you.* He had spoken with such firm conviction that it still sent a shiver through her. She wasn't sure if it was admiration, or something else entirely.

And Malrik, steady at her side, helped her navigate every challenge. Between them and the Aelvor, she felt supported in a way she hadn't expected.

Still, doubt lingered.

Sleep claimed Clara quickly, dragging her into a dreamscape unlike any she had ever known. She stood in a vast expanse of light, the ground beneath her shimmering like molten crystal. The air vibrated with a silent melody, ancient and otherworldly, pulling her forward.

Ahead, a pool appeared, its surface rippling with light that shifted in mesmerizing patterns. The pendant on her chest glowed brilliantly, as if in recognition of the place.

A voice, neither male nor female but resonant and commanding, filled the space. *"Hover the key and map above water. The way will reveal itself."*

The map materialized in her hand, its markings glowing, shifting in response to the voice. She stepped closer to the pool, compelled by the force of the command, but something in the dream changed.

A fissure cracked across the lightscape, spreading outward like shattered glass. Clara froze, the hairs on her neck standing on end as the melody faltered, replaced by an ominous silence. Something was watching her. It wasn't one of the shadow creatures, nor anything she could see, but she could *feel* it. The pendant flared suddenly, its light intensifying into a protective barrier around her. The presence recoiled, though it did not retreat entirely. Clara clutched the map tighter as a force pressed at the edges of her consciousness.

"Hover the key and map above water," the voice repeated, sharper now, insistent.

The barrier around her shattered into fragments. Clara gasped as the dream dissolved, leaving her flailing in the dark.

Clara woke with a jolt, her chest heaving. The pendant glowed softly in the dark. She rested her hand on it, breathing slower as its warmth calmed her.

The dream lingered, its details vivid.

The instruction was clear, but the danger hinted at by the dream felt just as real. Whatever had tried to break into her dreamscape wasn't merely a figment of her imagination. She knew now that something, or someone, was watching. Waiting.

For a week she'd had dreamless, peaceful sleep. The Aelvor's sanctuary had felt like a haven, but now it seemed fragile, its safety no longer absolute.

As exhaustion tugged her back toward sleep, Clara resolved to act on the dream's message. Tomorrow, she would hover the map and pendant over water. She prayed that, finally, answers would be revealed.

CHAPTER 8

The early light of Avenora seeped into Clara's quarters, refracting patterns across the walls. She stirred, her muscles aching from the past day's efforts, yet her thoughts felt sharper, more focused than they had in days. The warmth of the moss bed beneath her offered fleeting comfort, but her thoughts quickly turned to the dream.

Hover the key and map above water.

She sat up. The map lay folded on the shelf nearby, its surface catching the light as if waiting for her. Maybe she could finally get some answers, some direction on how to return home.

Moving with focused determination, she grabbed the pendant and map. A basin of water across the room glimmered, reflecting the light of early dawn that seeped through the walls. Taking a deep breath, she stepped closer, her heartbeat loud in her ears.

Clara positioned the pendant and map above the water, the memory of her dream clear in her mind. "Show me," she murmured. Then she held her breath and waited.

Nothing happened.

She furrowed her brow, lowering the artifacts slightly closer to the surface. The pendant remained warm, but no light, no resonance, no sign came from the basin. Frustration bubbled in her chest, and she tried again, this time closing her eyes and concentrating on the intent: *Uncover the path. Show me what to do.* Still, nothing happened.

Clara heaved a sigh as she placed the pendant back against her chest and folded the map. The dream's instructions had felt so vivid, so clear, yet she was no closer to understanding what it all meant.

Her thoughts wandered to Ashael. "Trust your instincts," he had said, his gaze so piercing it still lingered in her mind. If she couldn't figure it out alone, perhaps he could help. For now, though, she would set it aside. Morning lessons with Aelina and Darion awaited, and the last thing she wanted was to show up distracted or frazzled.

Clara slid the map into her pocket and turned to glance out the window. Birdsong floated through the trees, and the gentle hum of the forest filled the air. Despite her failure, a spark of determination stirred in her chest. At least now she had a direction. She would figure it out.

After dressing and rousing Malrik from a deep sleep, the two made for their morning lessons, munching on *ilvara* fruit for breakfast. After a week of training, they were finally ready to start their other lessons, now that they had proven they could handle the warriors training. They couldn't hope to keep pace with the swiftness of the Aelvor, but they threw themselves into the training. Malrik did so because he enjoyed it and thrived on sparring with Selandor and Vaelin. Clara because the physical movement gave her something to channel her energy into. And she hoped to earn Ashael's praise.

The path to the healer Aelina's quarters was serene, lined with golden-leaved vines that emitted a low, melodic hum. As Clara and Malrik stepped closer, the air shifted, enveloping them with a sense of peace like the aura that hung around the healing pools.

Aelina's quarters were enclosed in a lattice of living vines. Inside, shelves lined the walls, brimming with jars of dried herbs, glowing vials, and neatly bound bundles of plants. At the center of the room, a table carved from living wood displayed an array of leaves, roots, and flowers, each labeled in a delicate script.

Aelina greeted them with a serene smile. "Welcome," she said, gesturing to the table. "Healing begins with understanding the tools nature offers us. Before magic, there is knowledge."

Clara's attention lingered on the plants, her curiosity piqued. "What are these for?"

"Each one holds a purpose," Aelina explained, brushing her hand over a bundle of silver-veined leaves. "This is *nythril,* used to treat fever and inflammation. When steeped in water, it cools the body and calms the spirit." She pointed to a thin, pale root with glowing edges. "And this is *silvara* root. It counteracts venom from some of the more dangerous creatures in Avenora. Snakes, stinging insects, and the like."

Clara leaned closer, her interest growing. "This . . . feels familiar. In my world, we study plants too. Well, some people do. I'm a nurse. I worked with medicine, mostly pills, but the principle's the same, I think."

Aelina's eyes lit with understanding. "A nurse? Then you already carry the essence of a healer. The skills you honed in your world are not so different from ours. Avenora offers its gifts through these plants, just as your world offers its remedies in other forms."

Clara smiled, feeling a spark of confidence. She may not have been any good at battle forms, but she knew about medicine. "So, how do we use them?"

Aelina placed a small mortar and pestle on the table and handed Clara a bundle of glowing petals. "Let's begin with a simple salve. These petals come from the *celindar* bloom. When crushed and mixed with sap from the boundary trees, they create a soothing paste for burns and abrasions. It is a skill any healer can learn, even without magic."

Clara set to work, her hands moving carefully as Aelina guided her through each step. The petals released a light sweet scent as they were crushed, and the sap blended smoothly under the pestle's weight.

"Like this?" Clara asked, holding up the paste.

Aelina nodded, clearly pleased. "Exactly. Apply it thinly to the skin, and it will heal surface wounds within hours."

Malrik, who had been content to observe, picked up a small jar of dried leaves. "And what's this one for?"

Aelina smiled knowingly. "*Cindral* leaves. Chewing them numbs pain, though the taste is unpleasant."

Malrik grimaced as he sniffed the jar. "I'll take your word for it."

Aelina chuckled softly before turning back to Clara. "There are methods only the Aelvor can perform. Things tied to our connection with Avenora's magic. But what I'll teach you first are skills you can use as humans. Healing begins with practicality. I will teach you about the plants and remedies available to you, but I will also explain the methods beyond your reach. Knowledge, even of what you cannot do, is still valuable."

The lesson continued, with Aelina explaining the properties of various plants and how to prepare them. Clara listened intently, her earlier doubts about her usefulness fading as she realized how much of her human knowledge could apply here.

By the time the lesson ended, Clara had prepared a small kit of salves and poultices, each labeled with its purpose. She clutched the kit to her chest, feeling a sense of accomplishment she hadn't expected.

As they left, Aelina placed a gentle hand on Clara's shoulder. "Healing is not about grand gestures. It is about the small things. Knowing when to act, what to give. You have the heart of a healer, Clara. Never forget that."

Their next appointment was with Darion, the builder. His domain radiated a calm yet potent energy, unlike any they had felt since their arrival at the camp. Towering silver-barked trees formed a natural cathedral, their branches weaving an intricate canopy that softened the light into a kaleidoscope of hues. It would have rivaled any great building from the human world.

Beneath this intricate architecture of intertwined branches and roots, alcoves housed tools and artifacts. They spied armors etched with runes, shields that shimmered with subtle radiance, and more of the daggers that they had seen the Aelvor use to defend them from the Dravok. Every piece was imbued with Avenora's essence.

At the grove's heart, Darion waited, his robes subtly entwined with vines that seemed to shift in response to his movements. Symbols carved into his staff glimmered subtly, a silent testament to his mastery over Avenora's mysteries. His calm expression settled on Clara and Malrik as he beckoned them forward.

"Welcome, children of dust. Avenora thrives not on domination but on partnership," Darion began, his deep voice resonant and calm. "It is a force that neither bends nor breaks. To survive here, you must learn to listen to what it offers, not demand what you desire."

Clara tilted her head. Lythara had said that the trees provide so that they could exist in harmony. "You mean the forest decides for us?"

"In a way," Darion said with a small nod. "Avenora's energy is deeply intuitive. It senses intent and responds to harmony. For the Aelvor, this bond comes naturally. We are born into it. For humans, it requires patience, trust, and an openness to its rhythm."

Darion knelt, pressing his palm gently to the earth. The soil stirred, shifting as if responding to an unspoken command, and a slender sprout emerged, its leaves glistening as they unfurled. "This is the relationship we share with Avenora. The forest responds to our thoughts as readily as it responds to the wind."

He looked up at Clara and Malrik. "But humans interact with Avenora differently. You cannot draw upon its essence as we do, but you can channel it through tools or deliberate actions, like cultivating herbs or crafting natural remedies. Where Aelvor create by instinct, humans refine through effort."

Clara's brow furrowed. "So, we'll always be at a disadvantage here?"

"Not at all," Darion replied with a small smile. "Your strength lies in adaptability. Aelvor are bound to Avenora's rhythms, but you can innovate in ways we cannot. For example, while an Aelvor might call upon the forest to shield them instantly, a human can craft protective wards and enchantments that last far longer."

Malrik raised a skeptical brow. "Sounds like you're saying we need tools to keep up."

Darion nodded, gesturing toward the alcoves. "Exactly. Tools are extensions of your bond with Avenora. They amplify what you can already do, but they cannot replace effort or understanding."

He retrieved two small seeds from his satchel, their surfaces radiant. "Let's see what the forest offers you today. Plant these and focus not on what you want, but on what the forest might provide."

Clara pressed her seed into the soil, her fingers trembling slightly. She closed her eyes, inhaling deeply as she turned her senses to the quiet hum of the grove. At first, nothing happened. Then, a gentle warmth spread beneath her palm and a soft rustling reached her ears. When she opened her eyes, a tiny shoot with translucent leaves had emerged.

"I did it," she whispered, awe lighting her face.

Beside her, Malrik frowned at the bare patch of soil beneath his hand. "Mine's not doing anything," he muttered, sitting back with a frustrated sigh. "Maybe this whole connection just doesn't work for me."

Darion approached, his expression patient. "Do not worry. The forest isn't rejecting you. It's waiting. Doubt clouds your intent. These lands respond to clarity and trust, not force or frustration." He gestured toward the tools and artifacts resting in the alcoves. "These are examples of what our realm offers. They are gifts of its essence shaped into tools and weapons. For the Aelvor, such things are often extensions of ourselves. For humans, they are pathways to connection."

From a smaller alcove, he retrieved a pair of silver bands, their intricate etchings gleaming. "These anklets were forged during Avenora's earliest days. They are called the Zaralis. Each enhances speed and sharpens instincts, but it does not grant its gifts lightly. Only a few have been chosen to wear them."

Clara's curiosity deepened as she studied the anklet's craftsmanship, but she did not reach for the silver band "It's beautiful," she murmured. "But . . . we're not ready, are we?"

Darion replaced the anklets with care. "No, not yet. Such tools are earned, not given. When Ashael and Lythara deem you ready, it will be yours to wield."

Malrik folded his arms, a trace of skepticism evident in his expression. "So, why show it to us now?"

Darion met his eyes evenly. "Because you must understand that Avenora's gifts are not prizes. They are responsibilities. The anklet, like the forest, requires trust and intention. Its rarity is a testament to its significance."

He turned back to the grove's center, gesturing for them to follow. "Today, you have glimpsed the wisdom of our land. Tomorrow, we will explore the forest's defenses, how it shields its own and how you might harness that protection."

As they left the grove, Clara's fingers brushed the pendant at her throat, its warmth echoing the solemn promise of Darion's teachings. Beside her, Malrik cast one last glance at the unmoving soil, his earlier frustration giving way to a determined glint in his eyes.

After lunch, Clara and Malrik returned to the training grounds. The atmosphere thrummed with energy, sharper and more demanding than their earlier lessons. Clara stepped into the clearing beside Malrik, her nerves tingling with anticipation.

Clusters of Aelvor warriors moved with a grace that was both mesmerizing and intimidating. Clara's eyes instinctively searched for Ashael. Her heart fluttered at the thought of him observing her, though she immediately chastised herself. *He was ordered to protect you*, she reminded herself. *He's a teacher, nothing more.*

"Back at it," Malrik said beside her as he rolled his shoulders. He bounced on his feet, eager to begin.

Lythara approached with her characteristic calm, her silver hair catching the fading light. "Today builds on what you've already learned. Defense transitions into offense. Precision and endurance are your goals."

She gestured for Clara and Malrik to join the group. They fell into formation, following the Aelvor as they began their drills. The movements were like a combination of yoga, martial arts, and boxing. It took all of Clara's strength to keep up, to engage her muscles in just the right way so she didn't fall over.

"Balance and timing," Lythara reminded, placing a firm hand on Clara's shoulder to steady her. "Every move flows from your center."

Clara exhaled and reset her stance, her muscles aching but responding better than before. She pushed herself to stay present, even as her mind wandered to thoughts of Ashael. Where was he? Was he even coming today?

The drills intensified, but Clara finally began to find her rhythm. Then, as she moved through another sequence, a commanding voice broke through the clearing.

"I'll take Clara."

Her heart leapt. Ashael strode toward her, his movements purposeful. His light blond hair, streaked with darker, sandy-brown strands, blew away from his face as a gentle breeze swept across the clearing.

Lythara inclined her head in silent agreement, stepping back to let him take over.

His presence sent a strange thrill through her chest, though she fought to suppress it.

"Let's go," Ashael said, his tone firm but calm.

She followed, her steps growing more confident with each stride, her focus drawn entirely to Ashael. The other warriors continued their drills, oblivious to them. Or at least they pretended to be. Ashael led Clara to a shaded hollow at the edge of the grounds, where the air felt cooler and still. She took her position opposite him, exhaling slowly to calm her beating heart, though the charged space between them made her hands tremble despite her effort.

"Show me what you've learned." He began with slow, deliberate strikes, testing her reactions. Clara deflected the first but stumbled on the second.

"Your stance," Ashael said, stepping forward. He placed his hands on her hips, squaring them. The contact sent a spark as strong as lightning through her. Clara's breath hitched, and she tried to focus.

"Again," he said, stepping back.

Clara braced herself and tried again, deflecting two strikes before faltering. She bit her lip, frustrated.

Her irritation evaporated as she found herself transfixed by the way his muscles shifted beneath his tunic, the controlled power in every motion. Even the way his hair caught the light seemed distracting.

Her lapse cost her. Ashael's next strike slipped through her guard, tapping her lightly on the shoulder.

"You're distracted," he said, his tone carrying both reproach and curiosity, though a slight twitch at the corner of his lips made Clara wonder if he'd noticed more than he let on or if she was just imagining it.

"I'm not," Clara replied too quickly, her cheeks flushing.

His expression stayed calm, though there was a trace of amusement as he chided her. "Focus," he said, his voice steady but quieter this time, the challenge in his tone unmistakable. "Again."

Clara adjusted her stance, forcing herself to concentrate, though her heart still raced. As they continued, Ashael increased the speed of his strikes, pushing her to react faster. Clara stumbled as he sidestepped around her, but she quickly recovered as her movements gradually became more confident.

She deflected a particularly swift strike, her foot slipping as she whirled to meet him. Ashael stepped forward instantly, his arm wrapping securely around her back to steady her before she could fall. For a moment, Clara froze. His arm lingered just long enough to make her chest tighten with uncertainty. The warmth of his hand against her sent her thoughts scattering, but it was the way his eyes seemed to hold hers, glinting with restrained humor, that left her reeling. The faintest hint of a smirk tugged at his lips. Did he *like* her? No, it couldn't be. He probably acted this way with everyone he trained. Still, a spark of hope ignited in her chest.

"Careful," he said, his voice low, almost teasing. "You're trying too hard." Ashael let her go and stepped back smoothly, his hand brushing absently at his sleeve. The motion was so slight it felt almost intentional. Was it his way of regaining composure? "Here. You need water." He extended a flask to her.

Clara hesitated, the feeling of his arm around her still imprinted on her senses. Her fingers brushed his as she took the flask, and her thoughts tumbled into self-consciousness. Did he notice the effect he had on her, or was she reading too much into it? She hoped not. How embarrassing. Quickly, she looked away and drank, her cheeks warming under his steady presence.

Clara cleared her throat, trying to steady her thoughts. "Darion showed us something today," she began. "An anklet. He said it could help us in the future, but only when we're ready."

A shadow of intrigue flitted across his face. "The anklet is no ordinary tool. It enhances speed and instincts, but it's not freely given. Darion must see potential in you to even mention it."

"He said it's a promise, not a prize," Clara added. She tried not to think about how close he stood to her, how intense his gaze was.

Ashael nodded. "It's rare for him to show such faith. Consider it a challenge to prove him right."

Clara nodded.

"Reset," Ashael commanded.

She thrust the flask awkwardly into his hands and placed her feet hips-width apart. This time, Clara moved with renewed determination. She deflected three strikes in a row, her confidence growing with each successful attempt.

They sparred for another half hour until Clara's muscles trembled uncontrollably. "That's enough for today," Ashael said.

A part of Clara hoped for more praise or another correction of her stance. Her heart sank as she realized she was being dismissed. She left, returning to the main clearing, not bothering to say goodbye.

As she returned to the main training area, Clara's body ached, but her mind buzzed with a strange energy. Malrik jogged over to her, his face flushed from exertion.

"How'd it go?" he asked, his tone light but curious.

Clara managed a small smile. "I think I'm getting better."

"Better than me, probably," Malrik quipped, though his grin faded as his focus shifted to something behind her shoulder.

Clara turned and found Ashael, who was speaking with Lythara now, his expression composed, but his attention lingered in her direction for a moment longer than necessary.

Before she could stop herself, Clara called out, "Wait!" She'd completely forgotten about her dream. She'd been far too distracted.

Both Ashael and Lythara turned toward her.

"There's something I need to tell you. It's about a dream I had last night. It felt important."

Lythara tilted her head, curiosity softening her sharp features. "Dreams tied to Avenora often carry significance. What did you see?"

Clara reached for the pendant at her throat. "It was like a vision. A voice told me to hover the key and map over water."

Ashael's attention sharpened, his intense focus making her cheeks warm. "Did you try it?"

Clara nodded. "This morning in the basin in my quarters. But nothing happened."

"Then, perhaps, you weren't using the right water," Lythara suggested.

Clara glanced between them, unsure. "Do you think the restorative pools would work?"

Ashael exchanged a brief look with Lythara before nodding. "It's worth a try. The pools are deeply tied to Avenora's essence. If your vision was guiding you, those pools might be the answer."

"Let's go now," Lythara encouraged.

Clara's heart quickened. "No time like the present, I guess."

As they moved toward the pools, Clara couldn't shake the excitement and apprehension bubbling in her chest. What if this latest attempt didn't work? And, more importantly, what if it did?

The restorative pools were calm and undisturbed, their surfaces as smooth as glass. Clara knelt at the edge of the largest pool, gripping the pendant and map tightly. The stillness around her belied the anticipation thrumming in her chest.

Behind her, Ashael, Lythara, and Malrik stood in a silent semicircle. Clara hesitated, her fingers tightening on the pendant. Her earlier failed attempt, and the presence of the Aelvor and Malrik at her back, made her stomach flutter with nerves. She felt silly. What if nothing happened?

"This has to work," she murmured to herself. Taking a slow breath, she held the pendant and map over the pool, the memory of her dream urging her forward.

"Trust what brought you here," Ashael said quietly.

Clara let his encouragement settle her nerves. Her dreams had led her here. The pendant's soft glow intensified, spreading to the map as both artifacts responded to her intent. The light rippled across the water, creating intricate patterns that danced across the clearing.

"What's happening?" Malrik asked. Clara heard him take a step closer to her, but her attention was focused on the swirling runes and shapes before her.

Lythara's usually calm voice was tinged with excitement. "It's responding. Let's see where this leads."

As the light grew brighter, Clara felt the world around her shift. The air hummed with energy. She blinked, and her surroundings melted away in a surge of radiant light.

Her head swam as she got her bearings. When her vision cleared, she stood on a narrow path carved into the side of a towering cliff. The sharp tang of salt filled her nose, and the wind whipped around her, carrying the distant crash of waves. She reached out instinctively, her fingers brushing the rough, uneven surface of the cliffside.

The path ahead curved toward a cavern obscured by the shimmering veil of a waterfall. A haunting melody drifted from within. It urged her forward, its notes threading through the air with an irresistible allure. Clara's steps felt purposeful, each one anchoring her more deeply in the strange yet vivid reality.

Seawater sprayed her skin, cool and stinging. Waves pounded below. The pendant at her throat resonated, almost as if urging her onward. Her heart raced as she approached the cavern, the melody growing louder, filling her with both wonder and unease.

The cavern's entrance loomed ahead, the cascade of water reflecting light as it fell. Clara stepped closer, her hand reaching out toward the curtain of water. The air vibrated around her with anticipation. But just as her fingers touched the edge, the scene shattered into fractals of golden light.

Clara gasped, her knees buckling as she was pulled back to the present. She swayed precariously on the edge of the pool, and both Ashael and Malrik moved simultaneously. Malrik steadied her by the elbow, while Ashael's firm grip on her shoulder kept her upright.

"I'm fine," Clara said quickly, though her voice was shaky. They both stepped away, but Clara was too focused on the objects in her hands. She furrowed her brow, her gaze fixed on the map. Her eyes widened as a subtle trail of light wove across its surface. Relief swept through her.

"It worked," she said softly, more to herself than anyone else. The realization that her dream had guided her correctly filled her with a tentative sense of purpose. "The map. It showed me something."

"What did you see?" Lythara asked, stepping closer.

"A path along cliffs and waves crashing below. There was a cavern hidden behind a waterfall, and I heard singing. It was haunting and beautiful. It felt . . . important, like it was leading me."

She held out the map, showing them the glowing path. The lines etched on the parchment were like threads of gold, a wordless affirmation of her vision.

Ashael leaned forward, examining the map. "The place you described . . . it feels familiar," he said. "I might know what it is, but I'm not certain. We need to bring this to Ceyndor."

Clara nodded, her grip on the map tightening as her vision replayed in her mind. She could still feel the sting of saltwater on her face.

"Then we'll bring this to him," Lythara said. "His wisdom is great. He may know of what you saw."

Clara straightened, determination and apprehension swelling within her. Why had the map shown her this place? What did it mean? The light from the pendant and map dimmed. "Let's go."

They wasted no time, making up for Ceyndor's domain. Malrik walked next to Clara. He kept glancing at her, his brow furrowed, but there was no time to speak about what had just happened.

Inside Ceyndor's dwelling, the air was heavy with the scent of aged parchment and the aroma of dried herbs. Shelves laden with books, scrolls wrapped in silk ribbons, and artifacts that gleamed softly in the stillness adorned the space.

At the heart of the room stood Ceyndor. He stood over a table, transfixed by charts etched onto translucent crystal and a large, circular mechanism that shifted and rotated with an almost sentient grace.

He straightened at their approach, his silver-blue eyes catching the ambient glow as they settled on the group with sharp intensity. "What is the matter?"

Ashael stepped forward, motioning toward Clara. "We've uncovered something. The pendant and map responded to Clara, revealing a path and a vision. It's . . . significant."

Ceyndor's attention shifted to Clara, who stepped forward with the map clutched tightly in her hands. She recounted the dream, the voice instructing her to hover the pendant and map over water, and the vision it revealed. She described the cliffs, crashing waves, the hidden cavern, and the haunting melody that seemed to call to her.

When she finished, Clara held out the map. "This appeared after the vision," she said quietly.

Ceyndor took the map, his long fingers tracing the glowing path with care. His expression sharpened as he studied it. "These markings align with a formation I've seen before." He turned to his shelves and pulled down a book bound in deep green leather.

He flipped through the fragile pages, their edges crackling lightly, until he stopped at an intricate drawing of cliffs rising above tumultuous waves. "Does this match your vision?"

"Yes. That's exactly it." She leaned closer. "The path, the waterfall, even the cliffs. It's the same place."

Ceyndor nodded gravely. "This is the Syralen's Cove, a perilous place few dare to approach. The Syralen are enigmatic beings, half-human and half-aquatic, known for their haunting songs and their ability to lure others into their domain. Their cove, shrouded in legend, has resisted Veylora's corruption. Perhaps due to protections tied to the Vaelithar."

Lythara folded her arms, her expression thoughtful. "The Vaelithar's remnants must still be active there if even Veylora's reach cannot penetrate it. Could the Syralen be aware of this connection?"

Ceyndor inclined his head. "It's possible. The Syralen are deeply attuned to the balance of Avenora, but they reveal little of what they know. Their cove could be a refuge or merely a byproduct of their ancient magic."

Malrik crossed his arms and cocked an eyebrow. "Syralen, huh? Sounds a lot like the sirens from stories in the human world, luring people in just to destroy them."

Ceyndor's lips twitched at the corner. "The legends of the human world likely stem from glimpses of truth. The Syralen are not to be underestimated. They are powerful, ancient, and their intentions remain as elusive as the tides they command. If Clara's vision led her there, it is not without purpose. But purpose does not guarantee safety. I've never met such an attuned human. There is something different about her." He eyed

Clara with a strange look of distrust and admiration. His face was stoic, but his eyes betrayed him. He didn't trust easily. This much she could tell. Clara and her visions had sent him off balance.

Clara swallowed, the memory of the haunting melody from her vision lingering in her mind. She hesitated before speaking, her voice steady but tinged with unease. "Do you think the Vaelithar is guiding me? Through the dreams?"

Ceyndor's expression remained stoic as he studied her. "It's possible. The pendant, the map, and the Vaelithar shards are undoubtedly connected," he said. "If your dreams are tied to the Vaelithar, then—"

"There's more," Clara interrupted, her voice quieter now. All eyes turned to her and she took a steadying breath. "In the dream I had, it felt off, like an outside force was trying to push through. It wasn't part of the dream. It was invasive."

Ceyndor's expression darkened. "You sensed interference? Something trying to disrupt your connection?"

Clara nodded, her voice steady but tinged with unease. "Yes. It felt hostile, like it was trying to stop me from seeing what I was meant to. It reminded me of those shadow creatures, the Dravok."

Ceyndor's tone turned grave. "That is troubling. If something attempted to disrupt your dream, it could very well be Veylora. Her reach extends far, even into realms of thought. If she suspects your connection to the shards, she may already be trying to intercept it."

"My connection to the shards?"

"Do you doubt your connection, even now? After all that has led you here?" Ceyndor's eyes were searching yet tinged with that same unease.

Clara swallowed, trying to clear the lump in her throat. It was a truth she didn't want to fully acknowledge. Part of her still hoped that this had all been a terrible mistake.

Ashael's jaw tightened, a spark of urgency in his voice. "If Veylora is interfering, we can't afford delays."

"Yes," Ceyndor replied firmly. "But do not act recklessly. The Syralen's Cove is treacherous enough on its own. Rushing in unprepared could lead to failure, or worse."

Lythara crossed her arms, her voice steady but pragmatic. "A few more weeks of preparation will make all the difference. The journey alone will be difficult, and we can't risk facing the Syralen without being ready."

"Ready? For what?"

The group paused and stared at Clara. She fidgeted with the edges of the map. Surely, they did not mean that they should all go to this place? Was that why she was brought here, to follow visions into places she'd never been for reasons she had yet to understand?

"Your vision is guiding you to Syralen's Cove for a reason, Clara," said Lythara softly. "It would be wise to investigate why."

Ceyndor's expression softened as his eyes rested on Clara. "Your vision has shown you the path. Trust in what you've seen but also trust in yourself. I believe that the Vaelithar chose you for this task."

Clara nodded, her mind swirling with the memory of the haunting melody as she clutched the map closer. Her mouth was dry. They had barely made it to this sanctuary. They might not have survived if Lythara, Vaelin, and Selandor hadn't found them, or if Ashael hadn't come to their rescue. Now she was supposed to blindly follow a vision and a map that never showed the whole picture. Her gut pinched with unease. None of this made sense. She wanted to understand, and there didn't seem to be time.

As they left Ceyndor's domain, the group made their way toward the dining pavilion, the light crunch of their steps through the forest filling the spaces between their thoughts. Clara's mind churned with everything that had happened that afternoon.

Malrik broke the silence, muttering, "Syralen. Of all the things we could be walking into, it had to be them. Are we even sure this is worth it?"

Ashael replied, "If the Vaelithar shards are tied to the cove, then we have no choice. This is the first tangible lead we've had to stabilizing the Veil."

Clara stopped on the path and balled her hands into fists. Ashael spoke as if she had decided to go to the Syralen's Cove already. But no one had really asked her what she thought. She clenched her jaw.

Malrik stopped walking too and turned to face her. His skeptical expression softened slightly. "Are you all right?"

Clara took a deep breath. He was always there for her, always had been. "Yeah. It was just . . . a lot."

Lythara nodded. "Replenish your strength. I imagine the visions must be draining."

Clara saw hope in her eyes, determination in Ashael's. She didn't want to take this hope away from them with her own doubts. So, she shoved her hesitations aside. For now. Besides, she did have a headache, right behind her temples. Between training and the vision, she was tired. "Yes. You're right."

They continued to the dining pavilion. Clara caught Malrik studying her out of the corner of her eye, but he didn't press her.

When they reached the open-aired structure, Clara's attention caught on vibrant banners strung between the trees near the entrance. Their bold reds, blues, yellows, and intricate designs stood out sharply against the greenery of the camp, fluttering lightly in the evening breeze. "What are those for?"

Lythara glanced at the banners and offered a small smile. "The Festival of Lumina is approaching."

Clara exchanged a look with Malrik, both equally puzzled. "Festival of Lumina?" Clara echoed.

Ashael nodded but said only, "It's an important tradition."

"When does it happen?" Malrik asked, his tone edged with suspicion. "And why haven't we heard about it before?"

"Soon," said Lythara as they stepped into the pavilion "Preparations are just beginning."

Clara's thoughts lingered on the unfamiliar name as the warm glow of firelight enveloped her. The banners snapped cheerfully in a light breeze, bold and celebratory, at odds with the unease in her heart. She inhaled deeply, trying to be strong, to push away the headache. Clara wanted to go home. And she'd even pulled Makrik into this. But what could she do? Nothing. There was nothing to do but wait and see, even if it was killing her inside.

CHAPTER 9

Three weeks had passed since Clara and Malrik had entered the Aelvor Sanctuary, and in that time, life had taken on a rhythm that was both exhausting and fulfilling. They spent their days learning healing techniques, combat drills, and exploring Avenora's unique connection to its people. Evenings brought calm conversations by the fire or solitary moments of reflection. Though the sanctuary still felt strange in some ways, it had begun to feel less foreign.

Clara hadn't had another dream or another vision. The pendant still glowed faintly, resonating with the land's magic, but her sleep was sound, and the map had remained unchanged. She'd even stopped panicking about being there, realizing that focusing on staying present would help more than anything. No one had brought up Syralen's Cove again. At first, Clara was worried that her lack of enthusiasm had offended the Aelvor. They had seemed eager to rush off into the dangers of the cove, ready to find answers about the Vaelithar. But after a few days passed and neither Lythara nor Ashael mentioned it again, Clara was more than happy to push her unease about it away and focus on her training.

On the morning of their fourth week, Clara and Malrik were surprised to learn that training exercises had been paused to prepare for the

Festival of Lumina, a seven-day celebration of light and renewal. The festival marked a time for unity, remembrance, and hope. It was a chance for the Aelvor and their allies to strengthen their bonds. The first day was dedicated to decorating the festival grounds, transforming the space into a vibrant area filled with banners, garlands, and lanterns.

Clara stood near the central pavilion of their quarters, weaving wildflowers into vibrant garlands alongside other Aelvor. Her fingers moved with care, arranging the blooms, while she observed the bustling scene around her. The atmosphere carried a lightness unusual for the sanctuary, filled with laughter and playful exchanges.

"I can't believe it's already been a month," she said softly, more to herself than anyone else.

"Talking to yourself again?" Malrik's voice cut through her thoughts. He approached with a crooked grin, carrying a bundle of banners draped over one shoulder. "You've picked up that Aelvor habit, you know. Always muttering like the trees are going to answer."

Clara nudged him playfully. "I'm just thinking how much has changed. Remember how lost we felt when we first got here? Now look at us. Almost blending in."

Malrik raised an eyebrow, his grin widening. "Speak for yourself. I still feel like I'm one step away from accidentally offending someone. I'm pretty sure Darion hates me. I still haven't managed to make one single seed grow. And you grew a whole garden the other day."

"He doesn't hate you," Clara said with a shake of her head. "You just don't listen." It had felt good, taking Darion's teachings and being able to let the magic of Avenora flow through her. It felt good to *make* something, rather than just train for battle, to prepare to defend. Or destroy. Like Lythara said. Everything had balance here.

"Or maybe I'm just a slow learner," Malrik replied, dropping the banners onto a nearby table. "But hey, at least I'm good at hauling things around. A useful human, right?"

Before Clara could respond, a group of Aelvor children darted past, their laughter trailing behind them as they chased each other with colorful ribbons. One of the younger ones slowed, clutching a handful of fresh flowers. They hesitated, then stepped closer to Clara and held them out.

"For the garlands," the child said sheepishly.

Clara knelt, accepting the offering with care. "Thank you. They're perfect." She held them gingerly between her hands, careful not to crush their petals. "Are you helping with the lanterns?"

The child nodded enthusiastically. "We're putting them on the big trees in the festival grounds!" they exclaimed before darting back to their friends, ribbons streaming behind them as they wove through the clearing.

"Come on, humans," Elyndra said, drawing Clara back to the task at hand.

Clara got the distinct impression that she still thought of her and Malrik as strays, but after training with Elyndra and Nyshara for the past few days, a tentative acceptance was forming between them, despite their frosty interaction the first night at dinner.

"The festival grounds won't decorate themselves. Let's see if we can make our section stand out." She instructed Malrik to bring the banners and made for the main clearing, not bothering to see if they followed.

Clara rolled her eyes at Malrik, feigning exasperation, but her heart felt light as she followed the determined Aelvor.

Seven days of celebration stretched ahead. Tomorrow would bring the official opening of the Festival of Lumina, filling the sanctuary with music, dance, and countless lights. For now, she embraced the simple pleasure of contributing to something larger than herself.

Activity filled every corner as Clara, Nyshara, and Elyndra arrived at the warrior's pavilion, their arms laden with ribbons and lanterns. Earthy green and brown banners marked their territory, framing an open area where hunters strung colorful ribbons between posts, warriors arranged shields and weapons into striking displays, and scouts added final touches to the entrance decorations. It reminded Clara of a county fair, with booths competing for the attention of patrons.

"Let's hang the lanterns there," Elyndra directed, indicating the pavilion's archway. "Nyshara, those ribbons need picking up before someone trips."

"I was going to." Nyshara turned to Clara with a teasing smile. "And you? Ready to test your balance with these lanterns?"

Clara scrunched her lips. Though her balance had improved with training, it still was nothing compared to the grade of the Aelvor. "I'll try not to disappoint."

As they worked, competitive banter drifted between groups of hunters, warriors, and scouts, each section determined to outdo the others. Clara caught fragments of good-natured challenges, the usual military discipline giving way to playful rivalry.

Lythara had said that she could choose any group to join and help with their preparations for the festival. At first, Clara had thought about joining the healers. But Malrik had quickly declared that he'd help the warriors, and Clara didn't want to be separated from him. Besides, Ashael would be helping the warriors too.

Midway through their task, Clara felt the atmosphere in the clearing shift. As if her thoughts had summoned him, Ashael emerged at the pavilion's edge, his stride purposeful, fresh from his council with the elders. His inspection of the preparations was methodical, acknowledging the warrior's weapon arrangements with brief nods.

Their eyes met briefly across the space, but his expression remained neutral. He continued his assessment before heading toward the central clearing. Clara returned her attention to the task at hand, frowning. Why had he left so quickly? Ashael's actions could be confusing—he was either hot or cold, never in between.

There had been no further individual training sessions with Ashael. Not since the day the map had revealed the path to Syralen's Cove. Clara tried not to dwell on it, but she was sure something had changed between them. The thought of his hands on her hips, correcting her stance, made her cheeks flush. She added more blooms to a garland, turning her back on him.

With the pavilion decorated, Elyndra clapped her hands. "Time to inspect the competition. For quality control, of course."

Nyshara arched an eyebrow. "You mean to confirm we're winning."

"Naturally," Elyndra agreed, grinning.

They moved to the Healers' section first, where green banners announced their domain. The pavilion showcased elegant craftsmanship, its structure adorned with fresh herbs and wildflowers. Inside, carved totems and carefully arranged remedies created an atmosphere of measured tranquility.

Aelina adjusted a wreath near the entrance, acknowledging them with a serene nod before returning to her task.

"They make it look deceptively simple," Clara observed.

"That's their strategy," Nyshara said, feigning conspiracy. "Understated perfection."

They inspected the Builders and Artisans' pavilion next, its brown and gold banners distinct against the forest backdrop. A masterfully crafted arch of vines and roots framed the entrance, appearing as natural as the trees themselves. Lanterns illuminated displays of ornate carvings, marked tools, and detailed tapestries. Darion supervised a group of artisans, offering composed direction.

"Every year," Elyndra sighed dramatically. "They're impossibly good at this."

Clara studied the details. "The integration with the surroundings is remarkable."

"We'll compensate with spirit," Nyshara declared.

The Scholars' pavilion completed their circuit, its white and gold banners pristine and dignified. Carefully arranged scrolls, maps, and books filled the tables. Ceyndor stood at the rear, overseeing the placement of a detailed historical tapestry.

Clara paused to admire the woven scene depicting the sanctuary's untouched splendor. "The atmosphere here feels different," she noted.

"The Scholars prefer subtlety," Nyshara explained. "They let history speak for itself."

Returning to the central clearing, they found preparations underway for the festival's performances. Musicians arranged their instruments while others prepared seating for the elders.

"Everyone contributes something unique," Clara remarked, taking in the diverse displays.

"The Festival of Lumina represents more than celebration," Nyshara replied. "It reminds us of our purpose and our shared destiny."

As the day's light began to fade, the first lanterns were lit across the grounds, transforming the woods into something more enchanted. Clara noticed Ashael speaking with Ceyndor near the Scholars' pavilion, their expressions serious despite the festive atmosphere. Whatever they discussed seemed at odds with the celebration, a reminder that even during festivals, the resistance's work continued.

Conversations quieted as attention turned toward the forest path leading into the sanctuary. Figures emerged from the deepening shadows, illuminated by the lanterns' glow.

"The guests are here," Elyndra said, nudging Nyshara with a grin.

Clara watched the path with growing interest. She'd heard whispers about the Festival of Lumina drawing allies from across Avenora but seeing them in person was another matter entirely. Each arriving fae stood distinct, their bearing revealing their origins and roles.

The first arrivals were Aelvor from distant resistance camps. Their clothing bore subtle variations that reflected their homelands. One group's attire was dark and practical, suited for navigating dense forests, while another's lighter fabrics hinted at open plains. Their faces, though marked by fatigue, brightened as they were greeted by sanctuary dwellers.

"They make the journey every year," Nyshara explained. "It's dangerous, but they know how to move undetected."

Clara watched as a visiting Aelvor handed a message to Ceyndor at the Scholars' pavilion. The elder lifted his head in acknowledgment before leading his group to mingle with the crowd. Despite their varied appearances, there was an ease in their interactions, a shared purpose that transcended their differences.

A sharp cry, like that of an eagle, drew Clara's attention to the sky. Two birds, one sleek and black, the other golden, soared over the clearing before shifting mid-flight into humanoid forms. They landed effortlessly at the edge of the festival grounds, their transformations leaving traces of their bird nature. The first fae's midnight-black hair fell past her shoulders, her skin a deep obsidian that caught the lantern light like polished stone. Her companion stood in striking contrast, with hair the color of sunlit gold and bronze-tinted skin. Both wore fitted attire that mimicked their feathered forms. Dark plumage patterns traced along their sleeves and collars, while delicate feathers adorned their forearms like natural bracers. A third figure with silver-streaked hair stepped out from the shadows of the trees to join them.

"They are Shantera," Elyndra said, her voice tinged with awe. Her eyes brightened as she said, "They rarely travel in groups."

The three Shantera moved with grace, their keen eyes taking in the scene. The golden-haired one exchanged a few words with Ashael before heading toward the Scholars' pavilion. The other two lingered, their attention sweeping the pavilions with an air of calculated observation.

"They're essential for communication between camps," Nyshara added. "They know the terrain better than anyone and can travel swiftly."

Two Dwarven were next to arrive, their sturdy frames standing no taller than four feet. Clara did not need an introduction as to who they were. They closely resembled the dwarves from her world's stories. Yet something about them seemed more refined, more elegant, despite their compact strength. One carried a hammer slung across his back, but unlike the crude weapons of fairy tales, this tool caught Clara's attention with its extraordinary head. The hammer's crystal surface shifted between deep green, sapphire blue, fierce red, and rich amber, its colors dancing and blending in continuous motion.

The other Dwarven bore a satchel that clinked softly with each step. Their attire featured masterful metalwork. What struck Clara most were their eyes. They were dark as night but reflected light like a cat's, adapted for seeing in the deepest mines and darkest caves.

"They always bring something useful," Nyshara said, nodding toward Darion, who approached the Dwarven with his arms outstretched in welcome.

The hammer-wielding Dwarven removed a bundle from his pack, carefully unwrapping a set of tools marked with runes. Darion's expression brightened as he accepted the gift, exchanging a few words with the visitors before inviting them to the Artisan's pavilion.

Laughter rippled through the crowd as a lively tune drifted over the clearing. Another fae strolled in, drawing every eye with his striking presence. From the waist up, he could have passed for a remarkably handsome human with high cheekbones, perfectly tousled dark hair, and an impossibly charming smile that promised both mischief and seduction. But below, powerful goat-like legs carried him with natural grace as he strummed a lute slung across his back. His polished horns caught the lantern light, curving elegantly back from his temples, and his smile held a hint of delicious danger.

"That's Rynn," Elyndra said, rolling her eyes fondly. "He's a Satira and impossible not to like."

The Satira paused to play a quick melody for a group of children, who clapped and spun around him in delight. His movements were theatrical and charming. Clara couldn't help but smile as Rynn bowed with dramatic flair before moving toward the Scholars' pavilion. He greeted Ceyndor with a flourish before leaning casually on a post, his lute still in hand.

"He's more than just a performer," Nyshara said. "Satira are sharp strategists when they need to be. Don't let his charm fool you."

The final arrival was impossible to miss, yet Clara realized with amazement how easily such a being could vanish in the forest. A fae as tall as the surrounding trees stepped into the clearing. Though her features were remarkably human, her skin mimicked bark with such perfection that parts of her seemed to fade into the forest behind her. When she moved, Clara caught glimpses of how the patterns across her skin shifted and adapted, allowing her to blend with any tree at will. Her towering form wore a cloak of moss and flowers, and she carried a staff that seemed born from the forest itself.

Clara watched in admiration as the fae stooped to accept a garland from one of the children, her immense height making the gesture all the more remarkable. She draped it over her staff with a gentle nod, the movement causing her skin's patterns to ripple.

"She's here to represent the highlands," Nyshara explained. "The Granovar don't leave their territories easily. It's a sign of how important this festival is."

As the guests settled into the festival, Clara observed the vibrant mix of faces and cultures around her. Each visitor—Aelvor, Shantera, Dwarven, Satira, and Granovar—added their unique presence to the gathering. The sight was a testament to the resilience of those who refused to yield to Veylora's rule.

"It's something, isn't it?" Clara said quietly, her tone reflective. "All of them, here together."

Nyshara's features softened. "It's more than a festival. It's a promise to each other and to what we're fighting for."

Clara scanned the gathering, taking in the colorful pavilions and the hum of life that surrounded her. The music, laughter, and easy conversations blended into a harmonious rhythm.

"Let's get a good spot." Nyshara extended her hand to Clara. "Ceyndor's about to make his address and open the festival."

Clara took her hand, knowing that the gesture meant more than an offer of guidance. It was one of friendship. Her heart squeezed as she, Nyshara, and Elyndra navigated the busy grove and settled before a circular dais that had been woven from the earth.

The glen hummed with anticipation as Ceyndor ascended the circular platform. His robe, embroidered with the sanctuary's emblem, a tree that shone with light, sparkled beneath the lanterns. Ceyndor carried an air of solemn authority as he raised a hand for silence.

"Tonight marks the official opening of the Festival of Lumina." His voice resonated throughout the clearing. "This festival is not only a celebration but a time to reflect, to honor our history, to remember the trials we have endured, and to strengthen the bonds that unite us. It reminds us of what we fight to protect: our people, our lands, and the balance that once joined all realms."

A ripple of agreement spread through the crowd. On the platform, a troupe of performers took to the stage behind Ceyndor, their costumes adorned with carefully crafted details that reflected their roles in the story to come. Ceyndor gestured toward them with an inviting sweep of his arm. "We begin this celebration with the story of Avenora, brought to life to ensure we never forget the strength we carry within."

The performance began with the low, melodic notes of a Satira's flute, the haunting tune weaving through the festival grounds. The narrator's dramatic voice accompanied it. "In the beginning, the realms of fae and humans were one, their harmony intertwined with the essence of Avenora itself."

Crystals set around the stage and held aloft winked to life and projected vivid imagery, painting scenes of lush forests, cascading rivers, and the vibrant life of Avenora's early days. Around the platform, the environment shifted to match the narrative: trees arched toward the performance, their leaves forming a natural canopy, while vines curled gracefully to frame the stage.

"The lands were ruled by the Eternals, otherworldly beings who existed beyond time. Under their care, the lands flourished. Balance, wisdom, and elemental power thrived in the world." The scene glimmered with hope and promise. It was truly beautiful.

"To preserve this peace forever more, the Eternals forged the Vaelithar." The projections displayed its radiant form, an object of unity and balance. The performers raised their arms in unison, mimicking the forging of the artifact. "Its purpose was to bring fae and humans together in shared existence, bound by mutual respect," continued the narrator.

A sudden cool breeze tore through the glen. The atmosphere darkened as the tale reached Veylora's corruption and betrayal. Shadows crept outward, twisting the trees as their branches gnarled and their leaves fell like ash. The projections mirrored the growing corruption, revealing forests wilting, rivers drying, and the Vaelithar's light dimming. The performers' movements grew jagged and dissonant, portraying discord and despair. Their costumes darkened, reflecting the collapse of harmony.

Figures of Dravok emerged, monstrous and foreboding, their exaggerated forms embodying destruction and chaos. The narration described their rise under Veylora's influence, their shadowy presence spreading fear and devastation.

Clara shivered.

"The artifact, once whole, fractured under the strain of battle, and the balance it upheld was lost." Projections depicted the artifact breaking apart, shards scattering across distant lands as the realms descended into disarray.

Light began to creep into the stage once more. The shadows receded, and the surrounding trees regained their natural splendor. Projections showed fae and humans alike standing side by side, their unity defying the encroaching darkness. They held lanterns aloft, their lights keeping the shadows at bay. The performers' movements became fluid and purposeful, embodying the resolve of those who fought to protect what remained.

As the Vaelithar's light returned in the projections, the performers reached upward, their final act symbolizing resilience and hope for restoration. The environment around the stage responded in kind: trees stood tall, flowers bloomed anew, and the air felt lighter as the triumphant melody swelled.

The audience erupted into applause, their cheers echoing across the festival grounds. The performers bowed deeply, their expressions reflecting both pride and humility.

Clara joined in the applause, her chest tightening with emotion. The performance had struck a chord deep within her. It was a reminder of the stakes, of everything the Aelvor were striving to protect. She glanced at Nyshara, who stood quietly beside her, her expression thoughtful.

"It stays with you, doesn't it?" Nyshara said, her voice low. "A reminder of what's worth fighting for."

Clara nodded, her attention drifting toward the platform as the performers dispersed. Out of the corner of her eye, she noticed Ashael at the edge of the crowd. He stood with a composed stillness, though his focus seemed elsewhere.

To her surprise, Ashael started moving in her direction. Clara straightened instinctively, unsure of what to expect. But as he neared, a group of children dashed through the crowd, their laughter breaking the moment. She looked toward them, and when her attention returned to where Ashael had been, he was already walking away.

"What was that?" Elyndra murmured, leaning closer to Clara with a knowing smirk.

Clara shook her head, unsettled. "I'm not sure," she admitted, though curiosity lingered at the edges of her thoughts.

Moments later, Malrik appeared at her side, his expression warm as he nudged her shoulder. "Quite the performance, huh?"

"It was," Clara said.

"It helped me understand that there's a lot at stake here. This," he gestured to the festival, and to the people gathered, "is what it should be like all of the time. We've only seen this camp. But there's a whole world out there. People are scared. But they're determined to make things as they once were." His eyes darkened in contemplation.

Clara's stomach twisted. He was right. This was much bigger than she had first thought. She thought guiltily of the map, of her vision. Were her own fears, her doubts, keeping them from banishing the darkness in this land? The map had shown her the cove for a reason. Her mouth pulled tight as she wrestled with her thoughts.

As the festival carried on, the music swelled, and the hum of voices blended into the night's rhythm. Clara shoved away her guilt and let herself be present, the joy of the festival settling her thoughts. Yet, despite her best efforts, her mind kept circling back to the map and the feeling that she should be doing more. She should understand what those dreams and that map meant. She couldn't help but feel she held the key.

The Festival of Lumina entered its second day. Nyshara, who had seemingly changed her mind about Clara, dragged her to the warrior's clearing with a bounce in her step. "It's not about being better than anyone else," she said with a grin. "It's about celebrating the strength we still carry and the strength that keeps us standing."

The clearing, which was usually packed with warriors training in forms or weapons, had been transformed into a competitive arena. Fae were grouped in front of different skill challenges that focused on weapons proficiency, speed, balance, and strength.

Malrik was already here. Clara watched as he stepped forward for the spear-throwing competition, his confident swagger impossible to miss. "Watch and learn," he announced to anyone within earshot, spinning the spear in his hands before taking aim. Clara laughed under her breath; his newfound cockiness was almost endearing. Almost.

The weapon soared through the air but landed just shy of the center target. The onlookers broke into cheers, though a few hunters exchanged knowing smirks.

"Not bad," Clara called, meeting him halfway as he returned, his expression somewhere between pride and playful frustration.

"Not bad?" Malrik echoed, his eyebrows raising dramatically. "That was a masterpiece!"

Nyshara snorted. "Sure. If you're aiming for second place."

The banter carried through the grounds, blending seamlessly with the cheers and challenges of the other contestants.

As Clara moved between the events, she caught sight of Lythara and Selandor seated under a tall tree, their postures close but unassuming. Lythara let out a sharp, sparkling laugh and Selandor leaned closer, his expression playful as he whispered something to Lythara. Her demeanor softened, and Clara was struck by the contrast. She'd never seen Lythara's usually sharp countenance melt into such unguarded warmth.

Clara's suspicions were confirmed. The two weren't just comrades; they were a couple. She smiled as they continued to laugh together. Selandor tucked a strand of hair behind Lythara's ear. The gesture was kind and intimate. "They make it look effortless," Nyshara murmured as they passed by, her tone half-amused, half-admiring.

Clara nodded as her cheeks grew hot, her thoughts lingering on the bond between them. Something in her chest twinged. A longing to be close to someone like that. A longing for something she'd never really had.

She turned, ready to ask Malrik about just how many events he had entered, when she spotted Ashael weaving through the crowd toward her. His approach was deliberate, but an uncharacteristic hint of hesitation marked his steps. Her stomach swooped.

"Clara," Ashael said when he finally reached her, "have you had the chance to see the view from the central pavilion?"

Clara shook her head. "Not yet. Is it special?"

"I think you'd find it . . . meaningful."

A loud call interrupted them. "Malrik! You're up for the sparring match!"

Malrik jogged past, tossing a quick grin their way. "Don't go anywhere! I'll be back for my victory dance."

Clara rolled her eyes, laughing softly. But when she turned back, Ashael had already stepped away, his focus now on the sparring grounds.

Her smile faded. What had he wanted to say? Was it just about the pavilion or something more? Her head spun. She was always so confused when he was around.

At the edge of the Artisans' pavilion, Clara noticed Elyndra and Vaelin standing a little apart from the others. Elyndra nudged him lightly, her voice teasing. "You should join one of the games. Show them how it's really done."

Vaelin's expression didn't shift, but his body tensed. "I don't think that would be wise," he said quietly, stepping back.

Elyndra hesitated, her playful smile dimming. Clara couldn't help but notice the way her eyes followed him as he walked away, her usual ease replaced by restrained frustration.

Nyshara leaned toward Clara, lowering her voice. "Vaelin's past still haunts him, you know. Elyndra sees it, but it's not my place to say. Some walls aren't easy to break."

Clara nodded, a pang of sympathy stirring within her. Whatever Vaelin carried, it was heavier than she'd realized.

As the sun dipped lower, the central pavilion brimmed with music. The Satira led the melodies with their vibrant pipes, while drummers set an energetic rhythm. The crowd became a swirl of color and motion as dancers filled the space.

Clara lingered near the edge, content to watch. Elira, Kalen, and Mirin, the children she'd grown fond of over the days, darted around her, waving ribboned sticks with wild enthusiasm.

Ashael appeared at her side, his presence quiet but steady. "You're not dancing?"

Clara shook her head, a shy smile touching her lips. "Not really my thing."

"Nor mine," he admitted, surprising her. "But it doesn't seem to matter here."

Before the moment could linger, Malrik bounded over with good energy. "Clara! Enough standing around. Come on, you've got to dance at least once!"

Caught off guard, Clara hesitated. "I—"

But before she could respond, Kalen and Mirin grabbed her hands, dragging her into their circle. "You have to!" they insisted, their laughter infectious.

She let them drag her toward the center of the clearing. She stole a glance over her shoulder and saw Ashael and Malrik exchange a brief look. Then Malrik shrugged and headed toward the refreshments. Ashael lingered on the fringes of the dancing. Their eyes locked for a moment, and Clara felt her cheeks grow hot. She turned back to the children who grabbed her hands and let them pull her into a spinning circle.

At breakfast the following morning, whispers rippled through the sanctuary. A neighboring Aelvor camp, invited to join the festival, had not yet arrived. Though the absence had been noticed yesterday, the growing tension among the leaders suggested something more troubling.

As Clara ate, she saw Ceyndor and Lythara. They stood to the side, heads bent close in hushed conversation. Around the dining pavilion, the air felt different. The joy of the festival now carried a thread of unease. Elyndra caught Clara's questioning look and gave a small shake of her head, silently urging her not to press the matter.

The games continued with gusto, though the crowd's energy seemed more subdued than before. Ashael was absent from the morning activities, and Malrik's growing confidence in his sparring tactics was tinged with a subtle edge, as though he, too, sensed the shift.

By late afternoon, the festival unveiled a beloved tradition, a partner's game that combined balance, rhythm, and a fair amount of trust. The rules were simple. Two partners had to keep a smooth, luminous orb steady between them as they moved to the music without using their hands. The orb, roughly the size of a melon, demanded just enough proximity to make every movement deliberate. For the Aelvor, it was a playful test of harmony and coordination, met with eager laughter and friendly competition.

"Don't worry, Clara, I already put your name in!" said Nyshara as she gestured to a large wooden bowl. From here, partners would be selected to compete.

"You didn't." The idea of moving in perfect sync with someone, especially with so many eyes watching, made her stomach tighten.

"You've been standing on the sidelines all day. Time to participate," Nyshara laughed.

Clara crossed her arms as pairs quickly formed and names were drawn from the bowl. Clara stood at the edge, watching the unfolding matches with apprehension.

"Clara Valenwood," Lythara called out, pausing theatrically before drawing the next name. "And Ashael."

The name rippled through the crowd, drawing eyes toward the pavilion's edge where Ashael stood. He moved forward calmly, unruffled by the attention on them both.

"Well, this just got interesting," Nyshara whispered, smirking as she gave Clara a nudge.

Clara hesitated, but with every eye on her, she stepped forward, meeting Ashael in the middle of the clearing.

He extended a hand, his tone steady but unreadable. "Shall we?"

Clara hesitated, glancing at the orb in Lythara's hands. "We don't really have a choice, do we?"

"No," he said simply, a subtle, almost teasing smile playing at his lips.

Clara barely registered the murmurs from the crowd as she stood across from Ashael. The orb, radiant in the evening light, rested on a wooden stand between them.

Ashael stepped closer, his composed manner only heightened Clara's nerves. "We'll need to move together," he said.

Clara nodded, brushing her fingers along the fabric of her dress in an attempt to steady herself. "No pressure," she muttered under her breath.

They leaned forward simultaneously, positioning the orb between their chests. The closeness was unavoidable, and Clara's heart raced as the smooth surface pressed lightly against her. A slow, melodic tune began, and they stepped into motion.

To Clara's surprise, their movements synced. Ashael led with an effortless control that she hadn't expected, and she quickly found herself matching his rhythm. Each step required complete focus, the slight pressure of the orb a steady reminder of how closely they had to move together.

"I thought you said you couldn't dance," Clara said softly.

"I said I'm not much of a dancer," Ashael replied, his voice carrying a slight lilt. "This is merely a test of coordination."

Clara let out a giddy little laugh, her awkwardness easing. For a fleeting moment, she forgot about the crowd and the game itself, focusing only on the balance they shared.

"You're surprisingly good at this," she admitted, unable to resist the observation.

"So are you."

Clara glanced up, meeting his eyes, and felt the air between them shift. His eyes held an intensity that sent an unsteady flutter through her chest.

Ashael hesitated, then said quietly, "Clara . . ."

The way he said her name, soft and purposeful, made her stomach flip. She opened her mouth to respond, but the moment was broken as the music suddenly quickened into a lively tempo.

Startled, Clara misstepped. The orb wobbled precariously, and they both instinctively leaned closer to steady it. But their movements were no longer in sync, and the orb slipped free, landing on the ground with a soft thud.

Laughter and cheers erupted from the crowd as Clara stood frozen, her cheeks burning. Ashael exhaled, his composure intact as always, though his lips twitched with what might have been amusement.

Before Clara could say anything, Malrik's voice rang out from the sidelines. "If I were your partner, we'd have nailed it!" he teased.

Clara groaned, shooting him a mock glare. "Thank you for that vote of confidence, Malrik."

"Anytime," he said with a wink, clearly enjoying the moment.

Ashael retrieved the orb. As he handed it back to the attendant, he turned to Clara and said quietly, "Perhaps we'll do better next time."

Clara blinked, but before she could respond, he gave her a small nod and stepped away, disappearing into the crowd.

Nyshara appeared at Clara's side, her grin unmistakable. "Not the best performance, but definitely the most entertaining."

Clara groaned. "You two are diabolical." Though a small smile tugged at her lips. It had been a mess, but somehow, it felt like a moment she wouldn't soon forget.

The evening had settled into a gentle rhythm, the crackle of the central fire blending with the soft murmur of conversation. Music hummed in the background, mingling with the laughter of children darting around the firelight. Clara's eyes rested on the flames, her thoughts wandering back to the dance she'd shared with Ashael.

The stillness shattered with the thud of a body hitting the ground. Gasps echoed through the crowd as heads turned toward the shadows. A figure staggered into view, steps faltering, their labored breaths audible even above the murmurs. A dark stain spread across his chest.

Ceyndor and Lythara moved swiftly, their expressions grim. "Aelina!" Ceyndor's command cut through the rising tension like a blade.

The healer emerged at once, her steps precise as she knelt beside the fallen figure.

Clara's chest tightened as she watched two warriors lift the fae, carrying them toward the Healers' Pavilion. The crowd parted silently as unease crept across every face.

Another fae entered the clearing, clutching their arm. Clara was moving before she even realized she'd gotten to her feet. Her instincts took over, the need to help. To heal.

The Aelvor in the clearing let her pass. When she reached the injured fae, she removed the shawl she'd been wearing and wrapped it around him. He looked young. His clothes were torn, and dirt streaked his face. "It's all right," Clara soothed.

"There are more of us. The Dravok . . ." he said shakily.

Clara steered the fae toward the path that Ceyndor and the others had taken. "We'll take care of them," she said, pushing her own fear aside as she remembered the terror she'd felt as the Dravok had attacked. First, she needed to attend to his wounds and alert Ceyndor that there were others who needed aid. She focused on what needed to be done, her hard-earned skills pushing back the anxiety.

As she led the injured fae through the forest, she did not miss the feeling of a dark foreboding settling across the camp, heavy as fog.

CHAPTER 10

The arrival of the injured Aelvor shattered the festive atmosphere like glass. Clara could still hear the echoes of music that had abruptly stopped as she helped the fae toward the healer's pavilion. Tension blanketed the sanctuary.

The Aelvor stumbled. Clara braced to wrap his arm around her shoulders, but before she could finish the movement, Malrik appeared from the path behind her. He smoothly took the fae's other arm, lessening the load of carrying him. Clara shot him a nod of thanks.

They were silent as they approached the healer's quarters. Ceyndor and Aelina stood just inside the doorway, speaking in hushed voices. A team of Aelvor healers attended to the injuries of the fae who had stumbled into camp shortly before.

Aelina rushed forward as they crossed the threshold. "Another?" Her brows furrowed as two Aelvor stepped in to lead the injured fae to a moss bed that glowed with healing light.

"There are more of us, more who need aid," croaked the fae as he was led away.

Ceyndor was quick to issue orders, instructing that the scouts go to the border and search for more wounded and secure the perimeter of the festival. A flurry of activity followed as fae swooped in and out of the pavilion with swift grace.

Clara hovered on the fringes of activity, wanting to be useful. A touch on her shoulder made her turn to find Malrik at her side.

"Come on. Let's leave them to it."

Clara hesitated. "I want to help," she said softly. The fae had said more were wounded. Surely, they would need more healers. But even as she scanned the healer's quarters, Clara saw that the wounded fae had drifted into a restful sleep and were tended to by two Aelvor for each of them.

"Let's come back in the morning. I'm sure we can be of use then," he said gently.

Something pulled at Clara's chest. The pendant felt uncharacteristically cool against her skin. But perhaps Malrik was right. She dipped her chin and left the Aelvor to do their work.

Clara sat up and rubbed her eyes, catching fragments of conversation outside that floated through her open window. Words like *"defenses,"* *"attack,"* and *"Dravok"* pricked at her ears, though the details eluded her. She dressed quickly.

As Clara stepped outside, a low fog pooled around the roots of the towering trees. The sanctuary was already a flurry of purposeful activity, with Aelvor moving between their posts. Warriors inspected weapons, while others worked in pairs, their movements synchronized as they carried objects she couldn't identify. Clara's eyes followed one group to the edge of the sanctuary, planting glowing orbs into the ground.

She paused, watching as one of the orbs settled into place. Suddenly, it emitted a straight, brilliant beam of white light that shot upward into the sky. The air rippled where the beam connected, revealing an almost imperceptible dome that shimmered briefly before fading back into invisibility.

Clara recognized the protective barrier from her lessons with Darion. She'd learned how it cloaked the sanctuary from view and repelled enemies by responding to their intent but seeing it in action was entirely different. The beams of light wove into the air like tightening threads, forming a dome above them.

The sound of familiar voices drew her attention back to the sanctuary. Nyshara and Elyndra stood near the center of the activity. Not far away, Ceyndor stood with a small group of Aelvor, his commanding presence unmistakable as he gestured toward the perimeter and spoke in low, firm tones. Clara couldn't make out the words, but his authority was palpable.

Clara approached Nyshara and Elyndra first. Both were fully equipped, their weapons polished and ready. Nyshara's expression was sharp, her focus unshaken as she adjusted the fletching on her arrows. Elyndra stood beside her, speaking softly but urgently about patrol routes.

"What's going on?" Clara asked, her voice hesitant but insistent.

Nyshara glanced at her, her usual confidence tinged with weariness. "The eastern sanctuary was attacked." Her voice tightened and her fingers brushed the shaft of an arrow. "Veylora's forces used the festival as a distraction."

"A distraction?" Clara frowned.

Elyndra's expression was grim. "The Dravok descended on the camp with purpose. The eastern sanctuary was protected, like all our camps, but Veylora's forces are moving differently now. The attack wasn't random—it was calculated."

"For centuries, she has ruled over those who surrendered or aligned with her, leaving most sanctuaries untouched," Nyshara added. "Our resistance wasn't worth her effort. But something's changed. She's hunting us now, actively and relentlessly. And it's no coincidence that this began after you and Malrik arrived."

Before she could respond, Ceyndor strode over. "The eastern camp is gone," he confirmed, his voice steady despite the gravity of his words. "Survivors have made it to other sanctuaries, but many were taken. We're fortifying our defenses here. The sanctuary's barrier is being reinforced, but we're also preparing for the possibility of a direct attack."

Clara hesitated before asking, "Why now? Why would Veylora escalate like this?"

Ceyndor folded his hands together. "Because she feels threatened. Your arrival tipped her hand." He paused, then added, "I'm waiting for updates from Selandor and Vaelin. Their scouts are gathering more information about the Dravok's movements."

As if on cue, Selandor and Vaelin approached, their expressions grim. Selandor's sharp features were set with purpose, while Vaelin's gaze carried a shadow. The two exchanged brief nods with Ceyndor before speaking.

"The Dravok have been sighted patrolling closer to our borders," Selandor reported. "Their numbers are larger than before, and their formations are more coordinated. It's as if they're testing us."

"They're not just moving randomly," Vaelin added. "They're tracking survivors and probing for weaknesses. The sanctuary is still hidden, but it's only a matter of time before they find it if we don't act."

Clara listened intently. The sudden attack on the sanctuary was because of her. People had gotten hurt because she'd come through the portal. They truly didn't belong here. She didn't feel like she belonged anywhere. Not New York. And certainly not here. Guilt enveloped her body, and her stomach sank.

Ceyndor's voice brought her back to the present. "We can't waste any more time. We will meet in the council chamber in one hour. We need to discuss our next move."

Clara's heart pounded as she watched the Aelvor move with renewed urgency. The calm of the sanctuary was gone. Now, it felt like a fortress preparing for war. She needed to find Malrik, to tell him about the council meeting. She headed toward his quarters first, only to find the dwelling empty and his bed neatly made. Frowning, she turned back to the warrior's clearing. When she emerged, she spotted Lythara emerging from a group of scouts, coming from near the southern boundary. She spoke in a low, firm tone, and the others listened without question.

Clara approached her hesitantly. "Lythara, have you seen Malrik?"

Lythara paused, her sharp eyes softening slightly as she turned to Clara. "He's in the healers' quarters. Likely helping Aelina with the refugees."

Clara nodded her thanks, feeling foolish that she hadn't thought to go look for him there.

Inside the healers' pavilion, the Aelvor moved with efficiency, tending to the refugees who lay on moss-like beds. More had been brought in since she was last here. As Clara surveyed the room, her nurse's instincts flared to life, assessing and analyzing. She noted the neat rows of supplies, the composed order amid the chaos. A child's muffled whimper drew her attention to a small family in the corner. A mother cradled her young one, her expression weary but relieved. Nearby, an older Aelvor sat upright, his features etched with exhaustion but brimming with gratitude.

She spotted Malrik near one of the beds, talking to a young Aelvor that she recognized as the one they had helped the night before. The refugee was propped up slightly, his features still pale but his voice steady.

Malrik glanced up as she neared, a warm smile tugging at his lips. "Clara, this is Faelor," he said. "He's been filling me in on what happened."

Faelor studied her for a moment before a friendly smile curved his lips. "You must be the other human," he said with a hint of amusement. "Malrik's been talking about you."

Malrik rubbed the back of his neck as a hint of color rose to his cheeks. "I wasn't—"

Faelor waved a hand gently. "No harm done," he said, his tone warm and reassuring.

Clara managed to smile, tucking away the sudden surge of warmth to think about later. "It's good to meet you, Faelor. I'm glad you made it here."

"Barely," Faelor admitted, his voice carrying a trace of humor before it softened with weariness. "Thank you for your help."

The brief exchange tugged at Clara's heart, and she felt a gentle pull at her dress. She looked down to see the child from earlier, peeking up at her with wide, curious eyes and a hesitant smile. Clara knelt slightly, her smile softening as the child took a tentative step closer before darting back to her mother's side. The simple interaction solidified something within Clara. Something that she was hesitant, even scared, to admit. She focused instead on her resolve. Things had gone on long enough.

"Ceyndor wants to meet in an hour," Clara said, turning back to Malrik. "The council is gathering."

Malrik nodded. "Someone already informed Aelina. I was about to head over."

Together, they left the healing quarters, the weight of the morning's events settling over them. As they approached the council chamber, Clara noticed the growing number of Aelvor gathering. Groups exchanged hushed conversations, their expressions tense but determined. Among them, the guests from the festival stood out, their presence a reminder of the alliances they would need to rely on in the days ahead.

Clara and Malrik stepped inside the chamber, the hum of voices growing quieter as they joined the crowd. The room was spacious and charged with anticipation. The space was far larger than Clara remembered from her previous visit. The great tree had expanded seamlessly to accommodate the growing gathering, its interior shifting in response to their needs. The outer circles were lined with seats that curved naturally along the tree's contours, creating ample space for the attendees.

At the center, on a slightly elevated platform formed by the tree itself, stood Ceyndor, Aelina, Darion, Lythara, and Ashael. Senior Aelvor advisors gathered nearby, their faces solemn, while a few refugees sat quietly along the edges, their presence a poignant reminder of the urgency at hand.

Clara's gaze lingered on Ashael. His presence brought a sense of reassurance, though she noted the tight set of his jaw, betraying the weight of his thoughts. Malrik pointed to a pair of empty seats, and she followed behind him.

A moment later, Ceyndor stepped forward. "We face a moment that will define the future of our sanctuary and perhaps all sanctuaries," he began as a hush fell over the assembled council. "The attack on the eastern camp was not an isolated event. It was calculated, deliberate. Veylora's forces are emboldened, and their reach extends further than we had believed."

His words hung heavy in the air, and a wave of unease spread through the gathered Aelvor.

An Aelvor Clara had not met was the first to respond, stepping closer to the platform. "I am Khelvar, leader of one of the northern camps. Three of our sanctuaries have reported signs of Dravok activity just beyond their borders," he said, his voice rough with frustration. "They tested our defenses, prodding for weaknesses. We fought them off, and they didn't breach our barriers, but they're relentless." He hesitated, his expression darkening as his eyes shifted toward the refugees. "And the eastern camp . . ." His voice faltered before he continued softly, "I am deeply sorry for what happened. It is a tragedy."

A murmur of agreement spread through the chamber, but it was soon drowned out by another voice, sharp and tremulous. "And what makes you think we'll fare any better?" The speaker, an elder whose face was lined with age, stepped forward, his ceremonial robes swaying with his movement. "I've seen sanctuaries fall. I've seen the devastation. If we wait for them to come to us, we'll share the same fate. We need to evacuate now while we still can."

"Evacuate to where?" Lythara's voice cut through the sudden din, her sharp tone silencing the elder. She stepped forward, her stance firm. "The other sanctuaries are no safer than we are, Vaeris. Splitting ourselves up will only make us easier targets."

"We can't just wait to be attacked!" a young warrior shouted, his voice cracking with barely controlled panic. He stomped his foot against the ground, the dull thud resonating through the chamber like a physical echo of his unease. "We need to act now. We need to fortify and strengthen the barriers—"

"Barriers won't hold forever!" Khelvar shot back, his frustration boiling over. "We've held them off so far, yes, but for how long? They're growing stronger, and they won't stop until they find a way through."

The tension in the room rose like a storm cloud ready to burst. Clara flinched as another Aelvor slammed their hand against a table, the sharp crack cutting through the air. The display of emotion was unlike everything she had come to understand about the Aelvor. She had come to rely on their calm approach to the unexpected. As voices overlapped, anger and fear mingling into a cacophony, Clara realized just how dire the situation was. She caught snippets of arguments, pleas, and accusations. She shivered, wondering if this was fixable, wishing they could go home.

"I left my daughter behind!" A woman's voice rang out, trembling with emotion. Clara turned to see one of the refugees, a burn-scarred Aelvor, standing with her hands clenched. "We did everything we could. We reinforced our barriers. We fought with everything we had. But there were too many of them." On the verge of tears, she glanced toward Faelor, seated among the other refugees. "We're fooling ourselves if we think they'll stop there."

Faelor nodded, sounding weaker but steady. "She's right. The Dravok knew what they were doing. It wasn't a random raid; it was a message. And if we don't act, we'll all suffer the same fate."

The chamber erupted again, voices clashing in anger and fear. Aelvor pounded fists on the living furniture, the wood shifting subtly under the force of their blows. Some leaned against the walls, their faces tight with worry, while others paced like caged animals. Clara could feel the tension thick in the air, pressing down on her chest. The arguments grew louder, more chaotic, blurring together into an overwhelming roar. It was like the war and instability her own world showed sometimes.

Clara's eyes drifted back to Ashael. He hadn't moved, his calm demeanor unshaken by the chaos around him. But there was a fire in his eyes that made her pulse quicken.

Clara knew what she had to do. "I think I can help," she said, pushing herself to her feet. Malrik rose beside her, offering silent support. Her voice was lost in the tumultuous arguing. A lump formed in her throat, tight and unyielding. She balled her hands into fists but didn't know how to get the attention of everyone in the room.

Ashael stepped forward. His presence commanded attention, the tension in the chamber shifting as every eye turned to him. "We have a direction," he began. He gestured to Clara. "The vision Clara received, and the map's guidance, point us to the Syralen Cove. It's a path forward."

Vaeris scoffed, his tone brimming with skepticism. "A human's vision? You'd have us risk lives on a dream? The Dravoks are testing barriers, and the eastern camp is already lost."

"Vaeris," Ceyndor interjected sharply through the rising unrest. "We cannot dismiss anything that offers us a chance to push back against Veylora. But nor can we act recklessly."

"What map?" barked Khelvar.

Clara could hear her heart pounding in her ears. Malrik's steady presence at her side and Ashael's calm gaze gave her the courage to continue.

She glanced at Ceyndor for confirmation that she could share what she knew with the larger council. The Aelvor here knew how she and Malrik had come to their sanctuary, but was it wise to share everything?

Ceyndor extended his hand, gesturing for her to continue.

"I was given a pendant and a map that led me here from my world. The human world." She summarized her strange dreams, her and Malrik's journey, their encounter with the Dravok, and the visions that had revealed Syralen's Cove to them. When she finished, the room remained quiet, tension thick in the air.

It was Ashael who broke the silence. "I'll lead them to the Cove myself."

"Impossible," an elder protested, half-rising. "You know your position."

Ashael didn't waver. "I trust Lythara to protect the sanctuary in my absence. Waiting will only make us weaker. Veylora is growing bolder, and every delay gives her the advantage."

Lythara stepped forward. "I'll ensure the sanctuary is defended. We need answers, and the vision gives us a way to move ahead."

The chamber erupted into heated debate. Some called for fortifying defenses, others argued the vision was too uncertain, while a few voiced fears of abandoning their stronghold. A young warrior's eyes filled with tears. "How do we defend without you, Ashael? You trained us!"

"That's why I must go," Ashael said. "Defending alone isn't enough. If we wait, we'll lose everything."

Ceyndor hit his staff on the ground. The sound resonated through the chamber. "Enough. Ashael's decision is made, and it is the path we will follow. The sanctuary will stand, and preparations will begin immediately."

As the crowd murmured and the tension gave way to a settled resolve, Clara glanced around the chamber. She would no longer sit idly by, waiting for more of a sign. Her desire to forestall the inevitable was gone.

Now, she felt determined to go to Syralen's Cove and see what the map was leading her to.

Clara noticed the Shantera exchange a subtle glance, their grave expressions hinting at a shared decision. The golden-haired Shantera stepped forward, her metallic hair catching the light and drawing every eye.

"I am Kira," she began. "With me are Calyen." She motioned to the storm-gray Shantera, who met their gaze without flinching. "And Sidia," she added, nodding toward the dark-haired Shantera, who stood with hands clasped behind her back, every inch prepared. Both inclined their heads as Kira continued, "We offer what aid we can."

"The journey to the Syralen Cove will not be easy," Kira continued. "Especially with humans among your group. On foot, it would take days through dangerous terrain. But our kind can shift into forms large enough to carry riders. We could cut the journey's length significantly."

Calyen stepped forward, his features sharp with determination as he added, "However, the transformation is taxing. While we can carry you, we would need to rest frequently to maintain our strength."

"I can remain with the group for the entirety of the journey," Kira said, her golden gaze sweeping the chamber. "Calyen will stay until we reach the cove and then return to our people to rally further support."

Sidia, who had remained silent until now, crossed her arms and said with firm resolve, "I'll stay here to assist the sanctuary. Our strength is needed in more than one place."

Another swell of murmurs spread through the chamber, but the Shantera's calm confidence seemed to ease some of the tension. Clara's heart swelled with gratitude at their willingness to help. She hadn't thought about how their humanness might be a hindrance to their journey.

One of the Dwarven, his silver-threaded beard framing a face etched with years of endurance, spoke next. The light clink of a satchel at his side accompanied his measured steps as he strode toward the presiding council members. "We, too, have something to offer," he said, his deep voice resonating with steady purpose.

He reached into the satchel and withdrew a small pouch. "I am Torgin," he announced. "This is Kazrakh's Ember, mined from the deepest chambers of our sacred mountain and ground. When the powder is sprinkled on the wielder or their surroundings, it creates a temporary protective barrier, its duration tied to the user's strength. But once the ember's power fades, it leaves the wielder drained."

Malrik, who had been quiet thus far, asked "Why offer something so rare to help us?"

Torgin tightened his grip around the pouch. "Because Veylora's corruption has begun to seep into our mountains. Each year, we retreat further into the depths, but there's only so far we can go. If this ember helps to stop her, then the sacrifice of the three delvers who retrieved it will not have been in vain. Our people cannot remain hidden forever. If Veylora isn't stopped, even the deepest tunnels won't keep us safe."

Torgin passed the pouch to Ashael, who accepted it with a nod of thanks.

Then, from a corner, a lute's soft chord broke the tension. All eyes turned to Rynn, whose mischievous grin was already forming. "The Syralen will be your greatest challenge," he said, leaning lazily against the wall. "And I say this from . . . rather personal experience."

A few eyebrows raised as Rynn strummed another chord. "I once had a, shall we say, passionate dalliance with a Syralen named Merina. Passionate right up until she tried to drown me for composing a ballad she deemed insufficiently flattering."

Scattered chuckles drifted through the room, breaking some of the lingering tension. Even Clara found herself smiling briefly.

Rynn's expression turned serious, his voice taking on a note of caution. "They're not evil, but they are prideful and dangerous. Their songs can entrance even the strongest minds, pulling you into their whims. But they respect those who can match their art, whether in words, melody, or courage. The right response at the right moment might mean the difference between drowning and dialogue."

"Then I'll go as well," Selandor said. He stood tall, resting one hand on the hilt of his sword.

Lythara's brow furrowed, a hint of unspoken concern crossing her face as she faced him. "Selandor . . ." she began, her tone hesitant. But he shook his head.

"My skills will be needed," he said firmly. "And someone has to make sure Ashael doesn't lead them all straight into danger with his usual recklessness."

A soft murmur of subdued laughter passed through the room, briefly breaking the tension. Ashael gave Selandor a wry look, the slightest trace of amusement in his expression.

Elyndra rose, her voice clear and decisive. "I'll join them too. With the uncertainties of the terrain and whatever threats Veylora's forces have in store, they'll need every advantage they can get."

"And I," Vaelin added quietly, his voice smooth but firm.

A hush fell as cautious glances passed between the Aelvor. Nyshara's cryptic warnings about his past settled in Clara's thoughts.

"Are you certain that's wise?" someone asked from the back, their voice careful, almost wary.

Ashael's reply was immediate. "I trust Vaelin with my life, as I have stated time and time again." His words carried a finality that did not invite further debate. A hush fell over fae and human alike.

Ceyndor hit his staff again on the floor, the thud echoing over the room. "Then it is decided," he said. "A small group will journey to the Syralen Cove. Clara and Malrik, guided by Ashael. Elyndra and Vaelin for support. Selandor for his expertise. Kira and Calyen will provide transport, with Kira remaining to assist the group."

He paused, his gaze sweeping over the gathered allies. "Your gifts and knowledge may mean the difference between success and failure. We are grateful for your aid."

"We leave tomorrow," Ashael said. "At first light. We can't risk a delay."

A few murmurs followed the announcement, but no one objected. Ceyndor dismissed the council, and Aelvor and fae flowed out of the chamber. Clara remained rooted as the room emptied.

Tomorrow. The word echoed in her mind, stirring a mix of emotions she couldn't quite untangle. She had known this was coming, wanted to take steps to make the sanctuary and the Aelvor safe, yet hearing it spoken left her breathless.

She glanced at Malrik beside her, his usual steadiness tinged with tension. Her hand brushed the pendant at her neck. Failure wasn't just a possibility; it was a threat that loomed over everyone. If they faltered, the sanctuaries, the people who trusted them, and the hope they carried would all shatter.

Clara exhaled, her resolve hardening. Tomorrow would come, whether she was ready or not. And with it, the first step toward a future that felt impossibly fragile.

CHAPTER 11

As Clara and Malrik stepped out of the council chamber, the cool morning air wrapped around them, a sharp contrast to the heaviness that still lingered in the pit of Clara's stomach. She adjusted the pendant around her neck, its weight a constant reminder of the choices made. She needed to talk to Malrik privately.

Everything had happened so fast. What if he didn't want to go to Syralen's Cove? No one had asked him how he felt about the matter. Now that she thought of it, no one had really asked her either. She supposed speaking about the map and her vision was enough proof of her willingness. But the truth was, none of this had happened because she'd asked for it. She'd been given the necklace and the map because of who she was. Because of her last name. But she was still so confused.

Dad, why did you never tell me more? she wondered.

As she exhaled a shaky breath, footsteps sounded behind her. She turned and froze. Ashael approached, his steps uncharacteristically hesitant. The morning light caught his features, sharp and resolute, leaving Clara momentarily stunned.

"Clara, Malrik," Ashael called, his voice steady and soft, yet somehow carrying enough weight to make them pause. "May I speak with you both for a moment?"

Clara exchanged a quick glance with Malrik, whose brows arched slightly in surprise.

"Of course," she said.

Ashael led them a little way off the path. A veil of vines descended from the treetops, shielding them and giving them privacy. Ashael turned to face them. "I wanted to check in with you," he began softly. "I realize my suggestion to leave tomorrow was sudden. Perhaps too sudden."

His jaw tightened briefly before he added, "If you feel unprepared or overwhelmed, say the word, and I'll do everything I can to delay or adjust the plan. This isn't something you should feel forced into."

Clara blinked, surprised by the unexpected apology. Her chest ached softly. For someone who so often carried himself with unshakable confidence, Ashael's willingness to question his decisions felt deeply human.

Malrik scratched the back of his neck, glancing at Clara. "Tomorrow is . . . soon," he admitted. "But delaying won't make it any easier, will it?"

Clara met his gaze, and something unspoken passed between them. She could see her own uncertainty mirrored in his eyes, but there was also conviction. Her guilt at dragging him into everything eased slightly. "No," Clara said. "We'll be ready. We understand why it has to be tomorrow."

"As much as I want to find a way home, I do want to help. Besides, maybe this is the way?"

Clara nodded and dug her toe into the soft earth. "That's what I've been thinking. We were brought here for a reason, right? The pendant, the map . . . They brought us here. Maybe the way we get home is by finding the Vaelithar. Helping face Veylora's darkness."

Ashael's shoulders eased. "Thank you," he said, his tone earnest. "Your willingness means more than you know. I promise to protect you both with everything I have."

Clara was touched by his words, the sincerity in his tone lingering in her mind. She started to respond, but Ashael spoke again before she could.

Ashael parted the curtain of vines. "Darion wants to see you," he said, gesturing for them to follow. "There's something important he wishes to give you both."

The three walked in silence, Clara's thoughts fixated on tomorrow's departure. Darion awaited them by a table seamlessly shaped from tree roots, Lythara standing nearby, her sharp eyes following their approach.

"They're ready," Ashael said confidently as they stopped in front of the table. "Their bravery and resolve have proven them worthy."

Darion nodded approvingly. "Good." He reached into his robes and pulled out an object Clara immediately recognized, the Zaralis anklet they'd been shown on their first lesson.

Malrik let out a low whistle, his tone caught between awe and nervous uncertainty. "I honestly didn't think I'd see that again."

"Sometimes, crisis reveals truths that years of training cannot," Darion said, holding up the Zaralis. Its surface gleamed subtly, the markings shifting as if stirred by the moment. He extended it toward Clara. "This is yours to bear."

The cool metal felt heavy, strong. She fastened it around her ankle, her breath catching.

At first, nothing. Then, a sudden rush hit Clara, and she gasped, her senses flooding all at once. Every detail sharpened. The rustle of leaves above, the flutter of distant wings in the canopy, the rich, earthy tang of moss and wood smoke swirling around her; everything was heightened. Energy surged through her body, overwhelming at first, making her limbs feel weightless, almost boundless, as though she could run forever.

The chaos pressed in until, suddenly, it stilled. Everything balanced into perfect clarity. Clara exhaled shakily, the power no longer foreign, but hers. It hummed beneath her skin waiting to be unlocked.

"It's incredible," she breathed. She peered down at the anklet, marvelling at the power it had given her. "You feel like this all the time?"

Darion chuckled. "The Zaralis provides a mere taste of what we Aelvor experience." He extended a second anklet to Malrik.

Malrik stepped forward, his grin more uncertain than confident. "Well, let's see what it thinks about me." He froze almost immediately, his brows furrowing. "It's . . . different," he said, his voice laced with confusion. "It's like there's a wall. Like something's holding it back."

Darion closed the lid of the intricate box where the anklets had been stored. "That happens sometimes. The Zaralis isn't rejecting you. It's simply waiting. It's a bond, and like all bonds, it takes time to align."

Malrik's shoulders tensed, and his forced grin faded. "So, I'm supposed to . . . what? Figure it out on my own?"

"It's not unusual," Lythara added. "Many bearers have experienced this. The Zaralis requires trust, growth, or something you may not even realize you're searching for yet. You'll find the answer, Malrik, but it won't come all at once."

Malrik nodded slowly, though Clara could see the frustration simmering beneath his calm exterior.

"It doesn't mean you're not worthy," Ashael added, reading his frustration easily. "It simply means there's more to discover, both for you and the Zaralis. This is part of the process."

"If you're finished deciphering cryptic jewelry, there's still a lot to prepare before tomorrow," said Elyndra as she sauntered up to the table, breaking the tension with dry humor.

Darion nodded. "Go and focus on the path ahead. You've already taken the first step."

Elyndra dragged Clara, Malrik, and Ashael toward the warrior's clearing. She was eager to begin packing. As they walked, the anklet's weight around Clara's ankle felt both present and challenging. She glanced at Malrik whose face was still pinched with frustration. She touched his arm. "Malrik, I—" she began, but the strained smile he gave stopped her.

"I'm fine," he said, cutting off any further attempt, and she let her hand fall, the silence between them heavier than before.

Clara's eyes drifted to Ashael, who was walking ahead. When he glanced back and their eyes met, he flashed her a small, genuine smile. Warmth bloomed in her chest. His promise to protect them echoed in her mind, and for the first time, she felt steadier. He believed in them, believed in *her*, and that was enough to quiet her doubts. For now.

The afternoon passed in a blur of activity. Clara and Malrik returned to the healers' quarters, where Aelina helped them pack essential remedies. Each bundle was carefully labeled, each herb chosen for maximum utility with minimum weight.

While Clara and Malrik worked with Aelina, the sanctuary's transformation carried around them. Musical chimes were replaced by warning bells as warriors converted celebration spaces into fortifications.

Malrik sorted through herbs with unusual concentration, his movements precise but tense. The Zaralis gleamed at his ankle each time he shifted, a constant reminder of its hesitant acceptance.

"These need to be wrapped separately," Aelina instructed, indicating different bundles of leaves. "The night-blooming varieties lose their potency if mixed." She paused, then added more quietly, "I've added extra burn remedies. The Syralen's touch can sear like fire."

Rynn's earlier words about his encounter with the Syralen took on new weight. They finished packing their medicine kit, and Clara tried not to think about what would happen if she were left to face a Syralen alone.

As the light faded, Clara became acutely aware of the Zaralis band around her ankle. Her sharpened senses picked up distant conversations and subtle movements she'd once missed, but they also heightened her awareness of the sanctuary's anxious undercurrent beneath its busy activity.

Malrik worked silently beside her. When their hands brushed while reaching for the same bundle, he tensed. Their once-easy rapport was now strained. Clara's heart twisted in her chest. Was he mad at her or just upset about the anklet's lack of acceptance? She didn't know what to do or how to approach him. He'd been her best friend forever; she couldn't accept his anger. How was this her fault? She would have to talk with him when they were alone.

"The evening bonfire will be your last chance to rest," Aelina said, closing a cabinet of rare herbs. "It's a tradition older than the festival itself. More meaningful now, perhaps." She scooped the remaining cuttings into jars and cleaned her worktable. When everything was returned to its proper place, she shooed Clara and Malrik out the door.

As darkness fell, the sanctuary gathered around a single, massive bonfire, its light casting long shadows on faces marked by both determination and unease. The cool night air carried the earthy scent of the forest.

The laughter of festival nights had been replaced with solemn resolve. Warriors lingered near exits, their weapons close at hand. Survivors from the eastern camp huddled near the fire, seeking its warmth against the chill of what they'd endured.

"A tradition older than memory," Ceyndor said, his voice steady over the crackle of flames. "Each offering represents what we carry forward, leave behind, or hope to return to."

Lythara stepped forward first, dropping a sprig of an herb into the flames. Clara did not miss how her gaze briefly met Selandor's as she returned to stand beside him.

Rynn followed, casting a strand of Syralen pearls into the fire. "A reminder," he said, his fingers brushing the scar at his throat, "that some risks are worth taking." The flames consumed the pearls, releasing an iridescent glow that reminded Clara of the sea from her vision.

When Clara's turn came, she added a dried flower from her first healing lesson with Aelina. The petals shriveled into ash in the heat of the flames. Beside her, Malrik dropped the shaft of an arrow. "To remember where we started," he said quietly.

The ritual continued, each offering adding a spark to the flames. Malrik went to speak with Selandor and a few other warriors. Clara stood at the fire's edge, lost in thought as the Zaralis's subtle hum sharpened her senses. She knew Malrik just needed some time. But even so, she hated this strange dissonance. He'd always been there for her, supported her. She'd done the same for him, especially after his grandfather died. But now, Clara didn't know how to help him. The thought made her sick with worry.

Even with her newly heightened senses, Ashael's silent approach startled her. "You should rest," he said softly.

"I don't think I can," Clara admitted, her voice barely audible over the fire's crackle.

He studied the flames for a moment. "The cove won't be easy. What you saw in your vision is only part of what's ahead."

"Do you think we'll fail?" she asked, giving voice to her fears.

His answer came quickly. "No. I'm more worried about the cost of success."

Before she could respond, Malrik's voice interrupted, cutting through the moment. "Clara! There you are." His tone was casual, but the tension in his stance betrayed him. "Aelina wants to check the healing supplies again. Unless you're busy . . . ?"

"No," Clara said, stepping away quickly. She felt Ashael's gaze linger as she followed Malrik back to the supplies, unspoken words hanging between them. Aelina was nowhere to be found, and Clara got the distinct impression that Malrik had manufactured the excuse to speak with her.

Malrik worked in silence, his movements tense as he double-checked the herbs. "Is the anklet still giving you trouble?" Clara asked gently.

"It's fine," he replied too quickly, forcing a smile. "Who needs magical jewelry when you've got raw talent?"

"Malrik . . ."

"Don't." His tone softened, but his frustration remained. "I just . . . I need to prove something to myself."

"You don't have to prove anything," Clara said, touching his arm lightly. "We came through the portal together. You're here because you belong here."

He stilled at her touch, eyes flicking to her hand, then to her. For a moment, it looked like he might say something, but he only nodded and turned back to his work, focusing on his hands.

"Are you mad at me?" she said, trying to break the tension between them. She could be honest with Malrik, even if it was uncomfortable.

"No, of course not. I'm just upset with the situation." He looked uneasy, tension and tenderness filling his eyes, and she wasn't sure what to believe.

"Okay," she sighed. There was nothing more to say.

As the night wore on, the group prepared in quiet pockets of activity. Lythara whispered a brief farewell to Selandor, their foreheads touching in a gesture that made Clara's chest ache with its intimacy. Elyndra and Vaelin leaned over the map together, their movements smooth and instinctive, like this wasn't their first time doing it. At the clearing's edge, Kira and Calyen practiced their transformations, the shift between human and avian forms mesmerizing to watch.

When Clara finally retreated to her quarters, sleep eluded her. She stood at her window, watching stars wheel across the sky. The pendant hung cool against her chest, but the Zaralis hummed gently at her ankle.

When she finally laid down to rest, her sleep was dreamless.

Dawn arrived in gentle stages, painting the sky in muted colors as the group assembled at the sanctuary's edge. The Shantera stood half-transformed, their features caught between human and avian. Kira's golden hair took on the texture of feathers, while Calyen's storm-gray skin bristled with the promise of wings. Clara adjusted the pack against her back one final time, checking that the map lay secure in her inner pocket. Around her, the others made similar preparations without a word, focused on the tasks at hand.

Torgin had come to give some final words of advice about Kazrakh's Ember. "Use it wisely," he said to Ashael. Its protection is powerful, but brief. Choose your moment with care."

Nearby, Rynn strummed a gentle melody on his lute. "Remember what I said about the Syralen," he called to them. "They appreciate a bit of creative defiance. Though perhaps avoid any songs about their eyes being like stagnant pools. That particular comparison didn't end well for me." His grin carried a hint of remembered pain beneath the humor.

The Shantera's transformation accelerated as dawn brightened. Wings emerged from their backs as their forms grew larger, more powerful. Feathers fluttered across their skin in waves of gold and storm gray. Clara couldn't help but stare.

"It's quite something, isn't it?" Malrik muttered beside her, his attempt at lightness not quite masking his nervousness. He pushed his glasses up his nose with a knuckle.

Clara's heart softened at his attempt to bridge the gap between them.

Lythara stepped forward to bid them farewell, her warrior's composure cracking slightly as she reached Selandor. Their foreheads touched briefly as words passed between them, too quiet for others to hear.

"Keep him safe," she said to Clara afterward, her voice rough with emotion.

"We'll watch out for each other," Clara promised.

Elyndra and Vaelin ran through their final checks in silence, each one always a step ahead of the other. Ceyndor emerged from the sanctuary, carrying a small parcel wrapped in leaves. "A final gift," he said, presenting it to Clara. Inside lay vials of luminescent liquid. "From the heart of our oldest trees. For when darkness presses too close."

Clara secured the vials carefully in her pack, touched by this last offering of trust and protection. The pendant felt warm against her skin for the first time in days, as if it knew they were finally on their way.

"It's time," Ashael announced.

Kira crouched low, allowing Clara to position herself. Darion had fashioned harnesses for her and Malrik, so they might be more comfortable and feel secure while riding on the Shantera's backs. The harness felt sturdy beneath Clara's hands, though her heart raced at the thought of what was to come. Beside her, Malrik gripped his own harness on Calyen's back, his knuckles white but his jaw set with determination.

"Ready?" Kira asked, her voice short and clipped, changed by the transformation.

Clara looked back one final time at the sanctuary. She caught Ashael's eye as he prepared to run beside them and caught a brief change in his expression that made her breath hitch. "Ready," she said.

Before she could finish, wind rushed into her ears as she shot skyward. Kira's powerful wings surged upward, leaving Clara's stomach behind. Each downbeat rolled through the Shantera's transformed body, muscles bunching beneath Clara's legs. She gripped the leather harness tightly, thankful for the secure straps keeping her anchored.

The wind roared past her ears, tears streaming as she squinted against it. The cold pricked her skin until her Aelvor-crafted clothing adjusted, warming her against the biting air. She hunched forward, pressing close to Kira's back, searching for refuge from the wind's relentless assault.

Beneath them, the sanctuary shrank into the forest canopy. This was nothing like flying in a plane. No walls, no engine noise, only the rush of wind and the rhythm of Kira's muscles as they soared through the open sky. Through tear-blurred eyes, Clara saw the landscape below and her stomach sank. Dark, lifeless stretches of corrupted forest spread like ink stains, interrupted by occasional patches of pure forest still glowing with natural light. She hadn't realized how close the darkness was to the sanctuary, and how much of the land it covered.

"The corruption spreads in patterns," Kira's voice carried back to her, somehow cutting through the wind. "See how it follows the valleys?"

Clara nodded, then realized Kira couldn't see her. "Yes!" she shouted against the wind. To their right, she caught glimpses of Malrik and Calyen flying parallel to their course. Malrik's face was pale, his body rigid with tension, but his eyes were wide with wonder as he took in the view.

Far below, she could see Ashael and the others running, their forms barely visible through the canopy but moving with impossible speed. They flowed through the forest like wind given shape, crossing in seconds what would take humans minutes to traverse.

A sudden updraft sent them soaring, Clara's stomach twisting as they rose. Her fingers clenched the harness, knuckles white, heart pounding. She trusted the Aelvor-crafted straps, reinforced for durability, but every instinct screamed against being so high with only leather keeping her secure.

As her terror eased, Clara looked toward the horizon.

Somewhere in that direction lay the Syralen Cove, though she could see no sign of water yet. The landscape ahead showed more patches of untainted forest, giving her hope that not all of Avenora had succumbed to Veylora's influence.

The first descent was almost as challenging as the takeoff. Clara's stomach lurched as Kira banked toward a small clearing, circling once to lose altitude. The ground rushed up at them with alarming speed until Kira's wings spread wide, catching the air to slow their approach. They landed with surprising gentleness, though Clara's legs trembled as she dismounted. It took every effort not to let her wobbly knees collapse completely.

"That was . . ." Malrik's voice shook as he slid from Calyen's back. He steadied himself against a tree, his usual confident grin replaced by a look of stunned awe.

"Incredible?" Clara offered, understanding exactly how he felt. Her own heart was still racing, caught between exhilaration and lingering terror.

The Shantera's transformation back to their fae forms was mesmerizing to watch. Wings folded inward as if being absorbed into their bodies, feathers melting away like golden and storm-gray rain. Both Kira and Calyen breathed heavily once returned to normal, their faces showing the strain of maintaining such powerful forms.

"We'll need an hour," Kira said, settling against a tree. Sweat beaded on her forehead despite the cool air. "The first transformation of the day draws the most energy."

Ashael and the others arrived moments later. Clara marveled at how none of them showed signs of fatigue. The band at her ankle thrummed with energy, making her wonder if she might one day achieve similar endurance.

"We'll continue on foot," Ashael decided, studying the terrain ahead. "The forest grows denser here, and we'll want to stay beneath the canopy. The corrupted areas we saw from above might have patrols."

Selandor and Elyndra moved out in opposite directions, each slipping into motion without needing direction. Clara noticed how Vaelin positioned himself where he could watch both the path ahead and behind. His movements were so quiet she barely heard him pass.

As they prepared to move out, Clara caught Malrik adjusting his anklet again, frustration evident in his quick, sharp movements. The bond that came so naturally to her still eluded him, though she admired his determination to master it.

"Try not to force it," she suggested softly. "The more you fight with it, the more it resists."

Malrik's lips quirked in a half-smile that didn't reach his eyes. "Says the one it instantly accepted." But there was no real bitterness in his tone, just weary determination.

Even with the Zaralis' enhancement, matching the Aelvor's slowed pace tested Clara's limits. Malrik's anklet had not yet unlocked his full potential. It made him faster, but it did not afford him the same speed as the other Aelvor. They adjusted their pace to accommodate both him and Clara.

Ashael led them along paths that seemed to appear and vanish, his knowledge of the terrain proving invaluable. The forest changed subtly as they traveled. The natural luminescence of the trees dimmed, their crystalline veins grew dull. Clara felt the difference in the air itself, which became heavier, almost resistant to their passage.

"Stop." Ashael's command came sharp and sudden. The group halted instantly, and Clara nearly collided with Malrik.

Ahead, the path looked solid enough, covered in the same moss they'd been traveling over. Clara's pendant grew hot against her skin. She reached for it, knowing that it was trying to warn her about some danger she couldn't see.

"Watch," Ashael said softly. He picked up a small branch and tossed it forward. Instead of landing on the moss-covered ground, it fell through what looked like solid earth, disappearing into nothing.

"False paths," Selandor explained, his voice grim. "The corruption doesn't just affect the forest's appearance. It twists the very fabric of Avenora. What looks solid might be void; what appears safe could be deadly."

They detoured around the false path, adding nearly an hour to their journey. The corrupted section of forest pressed around them, its darkness almost tangible. Trees that should have glowed with inner light stood dull and lifeless. Even the moss beneath their feet had lost its natural luminescence.

During their next rest stop, Clara found Malrik sitting apart from the others, staring intently at his Zaralis. His earlier frustration had given way to a quieter, more determined focus.

"The corruption makes it harder," he said as she approached. "I can feel it . . . resisting more here."

Clara nodded, understanding exactly what he meant. Her own anklet's power felt muted, as if the corruption in the air interfered with its connection.

"Here." Ashael appeared beside them, offering each a water skin. His fingers brushed Clara's as she accepted it, sending a shock of warmth through her. She noticed Malrik tense slightly at the interaction, though he said nothing.

They pressed on, alternating between flight and walking, and by afternoon they reached a stark boundary between corrupted and pure forest. The transition was jarring. On one side, trees stood lifeless and gray, while on the other, they hummed with their natural power. Clara felt the change like stepping from shadow into sunlight.

"This is how all of Avenora once looked," Ashael said quietly, his hand resting on a tree trunk that pulsed with untainted light. His expression held reverence and sorrow.

As evening approached, exhaustion began to take its toll. Even the Aelvor showed signs of fatigue, their movements no longer as effortless.

The Shantera's transformations had particularly drained them. Calyen's wings had trembled during their last flight, and Kira's golden feathers had seemed duller than before.

They were about to look for a suitable camping spot when Selandor called out softly from ahead. The group gathered around what appeared to be the largest tree they'd seen since leaving the sanctuary. Its trunk stretched impossibly wide, and at its base was a hollow that hummed with an ancient energy.

"This wasn't shaped by any craftsmith," Ashael murmured, studying the entrance. His hand hovered over the bark, not quite touching. "This is old power. It's tied to Avenora itself. Far older than the sanctuary's barriers."

"Is it safe?" asked Malrik.

Clara felt a pulse of anxiety as she beheld the hollow, too. The last time they'd sought shelter like this, they'd just escaped the Dravok, and Lythara had crept up on them without them even realizing.

"I couldn't pick a more perfect location," Ashael said.

Malrik shrugged. "Good enough for me."

When they entered, the hollow expanded well beyond what its exterior suggested. The walls exuded a gentle warmth, their surface smooth and naturally formed by the tree. Around them, ledges emerged seamlessly to create seating, while the floor softened underfoot, offering a surprising sense of comfort.

"The tree is responding to us, just like the trees in our sanctuary," Elyndra observed, touching one of the walls. "It's protecting us."

Clara watched as everyone settled into the spaces the tree created for them. The Shantera found a corner where the ceiling arched higher, giving them room to stretch their wings if needed. Selandor and Vaelin positioned themselves near the entrance.

As night deepened outside, Clara found herself drawn to the entrance. The Zaralis kept her senses sharp despite her exhaustion, making her acutely aware of every sound in the forest. She could hear the others preparing for sleep and the low conversations about watch rotations.

Ashael sat nearby, methodically inspecting his weapons. She couldn't help but study his profile in the dim light, remembering his words about "the cost of success." Was he simply being cautious, or was there something deeper he wasn't sharing with them?

Further inside the hollow, she heard Malrik shift restlessly. The sound of him adjusting his anklet had become familiar throughout the day. His determination to master it stirred both admiration and concern in her. Their relationship felt different now. It was deeper, but also more complicated, especially with Ashael's constant presence.

"You should rest," Ashael said quietly, not looking up from his work. "Tomorrow will be harder."

"I keep thinking about what we saw from above," Clara replied. "All that corruption spreading across Avenora. It looked like . . ." She paused, searching for words.

"Like a disease," he finished, finally meeting her eyes. "One we have to stop."

A sound from inside drew their attention. Malrik had moved closer to the entrance, his expression carefully neutral. "I can take the first watch," he offered.

"We should all rest," Ashael decided. "The tree will warn us of danger." He stood smoothly, his hand brushing Clara's shoulder lightly as he passed. The touch, though brief, sent warmth spreading through her chest.

Clara watched him disappear into the hollow's depths before turning back to Malrik. "How are you holding up?"

He shrugged, but his usual smile held a hint of genuine warmth. "Better than this morning. At least now I know what being airsick feels like."

She laughed, grateful for his ability to find humor even in difficulty. They sat in comfortable silence for a moment, watching the night deepen outside.

"We're actually doing this," Malrik said finally, his voice quiet. "Following a vision to a cove full of dangerous water spirits, led by a magical piece of jewelry that may or may not think I'm worthy." He shook his head. "If someone had told me this a month ago . . ."

"Would you change it?" Clara asked, genuinely curious.

He looked at her for a long moment, his eyes holding a depth she couldn't quite decipher. "No," he said finally. "Whatever happens, I'm where I need to be."

Clara touched her pendant absently, its familiar weight comforting against her chest. Her Zaralis hummed with energy, and she marveled at how natural it already felt. They'd covered an impressive distance today, but the Syralen Cove still lay ahead, its mysteries and dangers waiting.

"We're almost there," she whispered, the words carrying both hope and apprehension into the gathering night. The pendant hummed, pleased.

Clara settled into the tree's hollow, its warmth easing her aches. Yet sleep eluded her as her mind replayed the soaring view, the stark divide of the forest, Ashael's brief touch and the weight in Malrik's words. Through half-closed eyes, she observed the others preparing for sleep. Elyndra and Vaelin positioned themselves across the hollow, subtly keeping each other in sight. The Shantera, curled together, breathed deeply, their avian grace lingering even in fae-form as they nestled for warmth.

Selandor sat near the entrance, taking first watch despite Ashael's assurance of the tree's protection. His steadfast dedication reminded her of Lythara, and Clara wondered how the sanctuary's defenses were progressing under her leadership.

A soft sound drew her attention to where Malrik lay nearby. In the dim light, she saw him running his fingers over the Zaralis one last time. The gesture seemed different now, less frustrated, more contemplative. When he caught her watching, he offered a small smile.

"Thank you," he whispered, his voice barely audible.

"For what?"

"For believing in me. Even when the jewelry doesn't."

Clara wanted to respond, but her exhaustion finally began to win out. As her eyes drifted closed, she glimpsed Ashael watching them both, his expression thoughtful in the fading light.

CHAPTER 12

Dawn approached on their fourth day of travel, casting a pale glow over the twisted treetops. In the hollow of their latest refuge, Clara stirred, the cool earth a poor cushion for weary limbs. Damp bark and moss thickened the air, clashing with the acrid tang of corruption drifting on the wind. Her Zaralis hummed softly, attuning her to the others as they prepared for the day.

Ashael adjusted his gear, his brow furrowed in thought. Malrik sat cross-legged, fingers drumming against the bow he had brought, his restless energy barely contained. Near the entrance, Vaelin and Selandor spoke in hushed tones, their sharp focus scanning the dark forest beyond.

"Time for the Morsela," Elyndra said, stepping into their quiet circle. She passed each of them a small silver sphere, no larger than a dewdrop.

The traveler's sustenance of the Aelvor, its rarity made it something reserved for warriors on long journeys. Though they had eaten it since the start of their quest, Clara still marveled at how it worked. She rolled the pearl-like morsel between her fingers before placing it on her tongue. The moment it dissolved, warmth spread through her body. Familiar flavors unfolded one by one: fresh-baked bread, golden honey, a whisper of cinnamon.

Malrik bit into his, then paused. He chewed slowly, brows furrowing. "Huh. Last time, it tasted like roasted meat. Now it's spice cakes. The ones my grandmother used to make." He glanced at Elyndra. "How does it keep changing?"

Elyndra smirked. "By now, you should know. Morsela adapts. It becomes what you need most."

Ashael, who had already finished his, frowned slightly. "I don't recognize the flavor."

Clara glanced at him, something tightening in her chest. It was the first time she'd seen him uncertain about something as simple as taste.

The moment passed. They shouldered their packs and stepped beyond their most recent refuge. Mist coiled through towering trees, weaving between branches. The forest thickened, warped by encroaching corruption.

Clara took a steadying breath as she mounted Kira, her hands tightening around the harness. Ashael moved beside her, checking her straps with an almost unconscious familiarity.

"Ready?" he asked. Something in the way he looked at her made her pause. They would reach the cove today. Whatever waited there, it felt a little less overwhelming with him beside her.

She held his gaze, and for a moment, the rest of the world seemed far away.

"As I'll ever be."

The Shantera launched into the air, their powerful wings slicing through the sky. They flew lower today, staying close to the canopy, wary of the darkness spreading below. Hours passed. They flew in careful intervals, alternating between flight and hidden stops to conserve strength. Each league traveled deeper into the heart of subversion.

And then, at last, they saw it.

A sheer veil of mist stretched across the land like a curtain drawn from pale light. At first glance, it looked like a fog rolling lazily from distant cliffs, but Clara felt it. It was power. Old power. The kind that didn't belong to this world alone. Perhaps it was the power of the Vaelithar, resisting manipulation. The tang of it hit the back of her throat.

She dismounted, landing on unsteady legs as Kira crouched to let her slide off. Nearby, Calyen folded his wings, his sharp eyes scanning their surroundings. A low rustle signaled the arrival of Vaelin and the others. They emerged from the trees at a jog, barely winded despite the terrain.

"Three patrols," Vaelin murmured. "Dravok."

Clara tensed, and Malrik swore under his breath.

Vaelin continued. "They're searching for something, but they never go near the cliffs. They keep circling, trying to find a way through."

Selandor's sharp eyes fixed on the mist. "They're being kept out."

The mist had to be a barrier, formed by something beyond the physical. As they drew closer, the air seemed to hum, static crackling between heartbeats.

Clara pulled out the map. It was warm, almost hot. As she unfolded it, the ink shifted, forming new markings that pulsed in response to the magic before them. The pendant at her neck warmed in sync.

The ink swirled, taking on new lines and shapes. After a moment it stilled, revealing a point just a few hundred yards away. "This must be the way in," she said, showing the map to her companions.

Vaelin's eyes narrowed. "That's where they keep circling. If it draws them in, it could be an opening or a trap."

"Which means we tread carefully," Ashael said, his expression darkening. "No unnecessary risks. If they don't see us, we take the chance."

They moved swiftly, steps silent as they made their way toward the location the map had revealed. The air was thick with tension. They stopped a short distance away from their destination. Clara's blood turned cold as she saw a Dravok lumber past the misty veil, though it did not seem to notice them. They watched silently, observing. The patrols moved in the same pattern as before, passing by the hidden path without a glance.

Clara exhaled, relieved. They just needed to time their approach right, so that they could pass by the Dravok undetected. Then, the barrier shifted, yawning open wider.

The Dravok stilled and turned its red eyes, locking onto them. The moment stretched thin, then snapped.

The creature snarled, its form shifting between shadow and substance. For a moment, its body turned translucent, its darkened features blending into the mist. Then, as if locking onto its prey, it stepped forward, drifting through a tree like fog before solidifying again. Claws gleamed like obsidian blades, but beneath the corruption, Clara could still make out the outline of the Aelvor it had once been.

Beside her, the Aelvor unsheathed their swords, awakening their blades. Previously compact daggers expanded in a flash of searing energy. Blades ignited in metal and light, humming with an otherworldly resonance, pulsing in rhythm with their wielders' intent. When Ashael's blade met the first strike, a deep, resonant chime echoed through the trees, as though the metal itself was answering the call to battle.

More shadows emerged from the trees.

Malrik grabbed his bow and nocked an arrow in one smooth motion. Clara had no time to gape at the smoothness of his movement, honed as if he'd been training for much longer. Malrik held tension on the bowstring and the arrow flared to life.

It was not a dull wooden shaft but an Aelvor arrow. Its crystal-forged core pulsed with soft blue light. As Malrik drew it back, the glow intensified, responding to his focus. He released it. The arrow streaked through the air in silver light, splitting into multiple energy points before converging on its target. The Dravok recoiled, its shadow form splintering as the searing light burned through its corruption.

Clara crouched, seeking cover by the roots of trees as Malrik readied another arrow.

Selandor's sword sliced through dark mist, its edge shimmering with ember-like heat as it adapted to the shifting forms of their enemies. Vaelin moved with lethal elegance, his weapon trailing streaks of silver light as it adjusted to each strike. But the Dravok were fast and vicious. Clara spotted Elyndra holding her ground, focused on the fight ahead. Just behind her, a Dravok lunged. Clara opened her mouth to shout, but Kira was already there, deflecting the blow before it could land.

Clara's heart pounded. The chaos around her made it hard to think. She crouched lower, gripping the hilt of her dagger. She thought about pulling it free, about joining the fight instead of hiding behind it.

She was about to move when something caught her eye. The opening behind them flickered, then began to waver.

Ashael saw it too. "Inside!" he shouted. "Now!"

"We can fight—" Malrik started.

"Go! Before the opening seals!" Ashael's blade intercepted a Dravok mid-strike, its glow intensifying as it adjusted to the threat before him. His stance remained unyielding, even as more shadows gathered around him.

"But Ashael!" Clara was torn between instinct and reason.

Her feet refused to move. If she stepped through that barrier, was this the last time she'd ever see him? The thought rooted her in place.

Ashael turned to her, his expression firm but calm. "Trust me."

The world narrowed to him, to his steady gaze.

She hesitated, unwilling to let go. Then Selandor and Elyndra pulled her back. The group rushed into the passage, Malrik the last to enter. The moment they crossed, the misty barrier snapped shut, sealing them inside.

Clara's heart beat harder. Ashael was still out there. Her breath came fast and shallow, panic rising like a tide, threatening to drag her under. He was strong, but the Dravok were relentless. Had they overwhelmed him? Had she just left him behind to—

No. She wouldn't think like that.

Her fingers curled into fists, muscles coiled to move, to tear through whatever power had locked them in. She ignored the calls from the others. They sounded so far away. Every second felt unbearable, stretching into eternity. Mist wrapped itself tightly around her, but she did not move.

Clara noticed a glimpse of movement. A shadow in the mist. Clara barely breathed as a figure stumbled forward, breaking through the barrier.

Ashael.

Relief crashed over her, her vision tunneling on him alone. Her legs moved before she could think, instinct overriding reason. "Ashael!" He was alive.

As she neared, the air around him wavered. The barrier shifted just before he stepped through, parting for an instant, as if responding to him alone. The shimmer lingered in the space behind him before solidifying once more. Why?

The thought barely had time to settle before she saw the red streaks running down his arm, except they gleamed with a silvery sheen. For a split second, she hesitated, her mind scrambling to make sense of it. Then, realization struck. It was blood. Just not like hers. The barrier had let him in but not before the Dravok struck.

Ashael swayed slightly on his feet, his jaw tight, one hand pressed against the gash in his arm.

Clara barely let him take another step before she reached him, hands steadying him. "You're hurt. Sit down, now." Her voice was firm, her nurse instincts snapping into place.

"It's nothing," Ashael muttered, but when she pressed a hand firmly over his bleeding arm, he exhaled sharply and lowered himself to the ground.

"Nothing doesn't bleed like this." She was already taking off her pack, reaching for her supplies, hands moving on instinct.

The gash was deep but clean, likely from a Dravok's claw. Though the wound had begun to clot, it still needed tending. She worked quickly, wrapping it with sure, practiced movements. The Aelvor salve sealed the worst of it in seconds, but the trace of the wound would take longer to fade.

"Better." She pressed her palm lightly against the bandage, securing it, before looking up. Then, she noticed the silence. It wasn't just quiet. It was wrong. A thick, pressing stillness had settled over them, suffocating even the wind. The mist had deepened, snaking through the trees in thick, shifting ribbons.

Clara was alone.

A shiver crawled up her spine. Her hands were still braced on Ashael's shoulder as she looked into his eyes. "Ashael?"

He didn't respond. Her stomach dropped. His posture had changed. He held his body unnaturally still. His sharp eyes had gone glassy, distant.

"Ash?" The nickname came out, unbidden, but there were more important things to focus on. Clara shook his shoulder, but he didn't respond.

Then a voice broke the stillness.

"Vaelin! Vaelin! Look at me!" Elyndra's panicked call reverberated through the mist.

"Calyen, what's wrong?" Kira's voice, sharp with fear.

"Selandor!" Elyndra again.

Clara's breath came in short gasps as a slow, melodic hum drifted through the air. It was barely audible, just at the edge of her hearing, but the moment it touched her ears, something pressed against her mind. A weight. A pull.

She couldn't understand the words. The song was beautiful and haunting. The tones and syllables slipped past her comprehension, as if they were not meant for her.

Clara froze as she realized what was happening. If the Syralen were anything like the sirens from human myth, then the song was not meant for her at all. Where was Malrik?

The mist parted slightly, revealing a beach strewn with small rocks and light sand. Clara scanned the area, frantically searching. She spotted him, walking toward the water. His steps were slow but unbroken, his arms slack at his sides. His boots sank into the shallows. "Malrik!" Clara called.

He kept moving, deaf to her call.

Clara felt torn, locked between choices: stay with Ashael or run after Malrik.

Malrik was knee-deep in water now. Clara's choice was made. Her pulse pounded in her ears as she ran. The mist seemed to tighten, distorting distance, warping sound. Her head ached as the song grew louder.

Clara forced herself to breathe, to think. As she ran, she remembered Rynn's words.

They respect those who can match their art, whether in words, melody, or courage.

This wasn't an attack. It was a test. Clara swallowed as her chest rose and fell with rapid breaths. She had to try. Clara opened her mouth and sang.

At first, her voice shook, the melody hardly threading past the rush of blood in her ears. It was a song she had heard long ago, something her parents had sung to her. What on earth? The melody came easily, though she hadn't thought about it in years. Clara sang as she tried to run through the mist, desperate to reach Malrik.

Kira joined in, then Elyndra. Their voices intertwined, their harmonies pushing against the Syralens' song.

From the water, the Syralen responded. The haunting melody rose, swirling like a current.

Clara pushed back. She wasn't just repeating their song; she was making it her own. Her voice was a tether. A promise. She wasn't just singing to match them, but for her friends. For Malrik and Ashael and all of them. The song came raw and undeniable, shaped by fear and determination.

The Syralens' song weakened. The melody was still beautiful, still haunting, but it was no longer consuming.

Clara's breath hitched as the mist finally loosened its grip. Malrik stopped his slow march into the water. His lower legs were already submerged, but his body stilled. His head tilted slightly. His unfocused gaze shifted to Clara.

"Clara . . ." His voice was barely above a whisper, eyes still distant. "I am . . . always."

Clara's chest tightened. She held out her hand, silently begging for him to take it. Her voice wavered, but she kept singing.

Then, behind her, Ashael's voice rang through the mist. "It's you . . . Clara." His breath was uneven, head still tilted upward, as if seeing something distant.

Her heart stilled. For a moment, she forgot the mist, the song, the danger. Her thoughts tumbled, colliding in ways she couldn't control. What did they mean? What was the Syralen drawing out of them? The Syralens' voices faded, slipping into the mist like a retreating tide.

And then the spell was broken.

Ashael blinked, his breath catching as his eyes finally lifted to meet hers.

"Clara?"

Her lips parted as a flood of relief rushed through her. The mist had stopped its games of stretching time and space. They stood on the beach, Ashael just behind her, Malrik a few paces ahead. Malrik stared at her, truly seeing her, now that the trance had broken.

"Can someone explain why I decided to go for a swim?" Malrik joked, but she noticed he was shivering.

Clara let out a shaky laugh and pressed a hand to her racing heart. For now, they were safe. But the Syralen were waiting.

"Please get out of there," Clara said. "Before I have to drag you out myself."

Malrik sloshed toward shore. "No need. It's freezing."

As the mist thinned, the world sharpened into clarity around them. They regrouped on the beach, checking for supplies and injuries, and took stock of their surroundings.

The cove stretched before them, no longer distorted by shadow and illusion. A vast expanse of water glistened under an eerie, unnatural glow, the surface shifting between stillness and ripples that moved without wind. At its center, a waterfall cascaded over an opening in the cliffs, the water catching light in iridescent colors.

Clara turned back to the group, steadying herself. "So, what now?"

Vaelin scanned the cove. "We need to be cautious. The Syralen don't take kindly to trespassers."

"Then we're wasting time," Malrik said, his stance rigid. "If we're going in, we should all go in together."

Ashael exhaled, considering. "No," he said. "Clara and I should go in first."

Malrik stiffened. "What?"

Ashael turned to him. "Too many of us might make them feel threatened," he explained. "We need to show we're not a danger to them."

Clara nodded, catching on. "We need them to listen, not see us as intruders."

Malrik's jaw tightened. "And if they *don't* listen? If they attack?"

"Then we have backup," Ashael countered. His voice was even but firm. "They expect negotiation, not an invasion."

A brief silence followed. Clara looked between them, waiting for someone to challenge the idea.

No one did. Instead, Ashael turned to her, searching for confirmation. "You and me?"

Clara met his stare and nodded. "Sure. If you think it's best."

Malrik exhaled sharply, shaking his head. "I don't like it."

Clara reached out, brushing his wrist in silent reassurance. "We'll be careful."

His muscles tensed under her touch, but after a moment, he relented. "Fine. But if you're not back soon, I *am* coming in."

Clara gave a small nod before looking back at the others.

"Kira, Selandor, and Malrik will stay close, just outside the cove," Vaelin instructed. "Elyndra, Calyen, and I will watch the perimeter. If anything goes wrong, we'll be ready."

They all nodded.

"One last thing," Elyndra added. "The Kazrakh's Ember."

There was a tense pause. How could they know if now was the time to use it?

"It could give us an advantage," Kira admitted.

"But if we use it now," Ashael said, "we'll be showing them we expect a fight."

Clara chewed on her lip, considering. "The Syralen are clever," she said. "If they can detect it, they might see it as a challenge. Or worse, an insult."

"Then we don't use it," Ashael decided.

No one argued. Clara took a breath, glancing at Ashael before turning toward the waterfall.

Together, they stepped forward.

The sound of cascading water grew louder with every step, and the sharp scent of seawater filled Clara's lungs, briny and heavy in the air. The light tang of salt touched her tongue as spray hit her cheeks.

The entrance loomed before them. Clara hesitated for just a moment before stepping forward, Ashael close beside her. The mist clung to them as they moved beneath the falls. Clara blinked against the spray of water. When she emerged on the other side, her mouth dropped.

The cavern stretched wide, the ceiling lost in a haze of refracting blue light. Water flowed in impossible patterns. Rivers ran up walls, across the air, and along the ceilings before cascading down in suspended streams. Coral-like formations jutted from the ground, glowing with bioluminescent hues. Pools of water mirrored shifting colors, stirred by an unseen energy.

She swallowed, taking in the surreal scene. Her heart stuttered as shadows moved beneath the surface of the largest pool. She fought to remain calm as three Syralen broke the surface of the water and slithered ashore.

Their forms were unearthly—breathtaking, yet terrifying. From the waist up, they had the silhouette of humans. Their skin shimmered like liquid pearl, opalescent and ever shifting. Their hair, weightless and drifting, moved as if stirred by an invisible tide, mirroring the deep green, silver, and blue of their tails, which blended seamlessly with the glistening scales that covered them and crept up their abdomens. The tails rippled across the cavern floor. Their fins fanned out with every movement. Translucent fins were attuned to the water and air alike.

The three fixed their deep black eyes on Clara and Ashael with a strange intensity. They did not speak.

Then, a whisper passed between them.

"Nerissa."

The name echoed through the chamber, carried not by one voice but by many. Clara's body went rigid. Should they run?

The Syralen at the front began to shift. A shiver passed through her. In an instant, she was no longer a creature of the depths but a being standing on two legs. Traces of her aquatic nature remained. Her blue-green hair tumbled around a face that was almost human. Her black eyes lightened into a deep blue, and the delicate fins behind her ears receded, softening into a more human shape.

When she spoke, her voice was music itself, melodic, layered, and almost hypnotic.

"You should not have come."

Clara's pulse quickened. The words were a challenge, a warning. She glanced at Ashael. He said nothing.

A slow smile curled at the corners of Nerissa's lips. "Are you here to take?" she asked.

Clara hesitated, unsure how to proceed.

Ashael shifted slightly beside her, and she sensed the same unease radiating from him. The question was layered with something deeper.

Taking too long to answer felt just as dangerous as answering too quickly.

Clara finally shook her head. "No." There was truth to her words. She wasn't here to claim anything. She only wanted answers.

Nerissa studied her for a long moment. Then her attention settled on Clara's chest.

The pendant pulsed, as if in greeting.

"The Vaelithar bears many scars," Nerissa said softly, her voice weaving through the chamber like a ripple over still water.

Clara's breath caught. What did she mean by scars?

Nerissa tilted her head. "You seek answers."

A statement. Not a question. Clara swallowed. "Yes."

Nerissa's now-blue eyes glittered. "Then let us see if you are worthy of them."

A current moved across the surface of the pool, disturbed, though there was no wind. Nerissa's voice wove through the stillness. The sound vibrated off the cavern walls, the resonance stretching and shifting, as if multiple voices whispered with her. "One among you must descend with true intent."

A second later, the voices of the other Syralen mirrored her words in a ghostly chorus. *"Must descend with true intent . . ."*

The cavern thrummed with sound, reverberating through water and stone. Beneath the surface, the Syralen's tails moved in rhythmic motion, sending waves of color through the depths. Clara couldn't look away. Their movements stirred the water; glowing patterns shifted across the cavern walls.

Nerissa gestured toward the water. "Clarity lies beneath. To the chosen, the answer reveals."

Again, the other Syralen whispered the words in unison, their voices blending into the cavern's song. *"The answer reveals . . ."*

Clara clenched her fists. She knew, deep in her bones, what she had to do. Her vision had led them here. Whatever was hidden beneath the surface, it would show itself only to her.

"I'll go," she said, her voice steady despite the tightness in her chest.

She felt Ashael's eyes on her, sharp and searching. He didn't speak at first, but something in his stance shifted.

"Be careful," was all he said.

Clara exhaled slowly. Too late to second-guess now.

She removed her boots and her coat, laying them on the sand. She stepped forward as the glow of the cove cast golden reflections over the rippling surface. From within her pouch, she pulled out the vial of light Ceyndor had given her, the liquid inside gave off a comforting glow. Tightening her grip around it, she waded in. The water wrapped around her ankles, cool and thick, then climbed to her waist, her chest, her shoulders, pulling her in, pulling her down.

She took a final breath; then, she submerged.

The cavern above became distant, distorted by the refracting water. Below, the darkness stretched endlessly, but it was not empty.

She opened her palm, letting the light from the vial shine. A golden glow unfurled like ink through the water, illuminating an entire world beneath the surface. Her eyes widened. Coral structures sprawled beneath her like the ruins of an ancient city. Towers of red and gold, spires of violet, fields of delicate blue tendrils swayed with the current-like forests.

Tiny, glowing creatures darted between them, their bodies glowed before vanishing into the depths.

The Syralen swam, gliding effortlessly through the water, their forms silhouetted against the glow of the corals. Their tails flicked through the currents, cutting through shafts of dappled light. Their black eyes followed her every movement.

Then she heard it. A song. It wasn't sound the way she understood it. It didn't pass through her ears but resonated inside her. Her chest ached. It was a language she didn't know, yet she understood its message.

Long ago, the Syralen had been entrusted to guard something of great importance. And in return, the power of the Vaelithar protected their home, shielding them, sustaining them. They had waited. Waited for the one who was meant to claim it. Only the chosen would find it.

Clara's lungs began to strain. She thought about returning to the surface, but a flash of light caught her attention.

Below, nestled within the coral, something glowed.

Clara pushed forward, kicking against the heavy water. Her clothes had shifted, pressing tight against her skin, keeping the water out, adapting to her needs. It did little against the pressure of the water that clung to her limbs, dragging at her, but she forced herself closer.

The light came from a clam shell, nestled between twisting coral branches. It was slightly open, golden light seeping from within.

As she reached for it, the shell parted, and Clara was struck with blinding light. She squinted, her eyes adjusting as the glow dimmed just enough for her to see. Inside the clam lay a pearl. It was translucent, perfect, and round as a moon. But inside, it shifted. Sand and water swirled together in an eternal motion, trapped within its luminous depths.

As her fingertips brushed the pearl, a soft hum of energy passed through her. It felt like recognition.

Then the light dimmed, and the shell snapped shut.

A sharp, crushing tightness seized Clara's chest. She had waited too long. Her lungs burned, and the surface was too far.

Clara twisted, pushing herself upward, her arms heavy, legs slower than before. No matter how hard she fought, the water was an immovable force, determined to pull her down and keep her here forever. She kicked harder and looked toward the surface. The glow of the cove above was too distant, a trembling mirage in the dark waters. She needed air. Her vision blurred. A shadow passed in front of her, just as the last ounce of air vanished from her, and black, dark water swallowed her whole.

CHAPTER 13

Malrik

Malrik ran his thumb over the smooth wood of his bow as he paced in front of the misty barrier. Selandor and Kira had gone a few paces up the coast to scout while Elyndra, Vaelin, and Caylen were studying the rocky cliffs around the cavern. The mist undulated softly, shimmering on a light breeze. It was quiet, but he knew the Dravok lingered just beyond the barrier.

He fought the instinct to march into the cave where Clara and Ashael had gone to speak with the Syralen. He didn't like the way Ashael looked at Clara. Or how she always searched for him in crowds or across training grounds. Guilt twisted his insides, and he kicked at the sand. He shouldn't be so worried about that. They were just friends—best friends.

What was his deal with Clara lately? He actually felt . . . *jealous*. Why did he care so much if Clara liked Ashael? He shouldn't begrudge her happiness. And besides, there were more pressing issues to worry about. Like shadow creatures lurking just beyond sight. He shivered, remembering their glowing red eyes.

Malrik paced in front of the veil of mist, boots crunching over damp gravel. The barrier shimmered like moonlight on water, and an unnatural fog hissed when touched by stray shadows. Beyond it, the cave's maw gaped wide and black, swallowing the echo of Clara's voice as she parlayed with the sirens.

He couldn't see her, but he felt her. He was always attuned to her needs, her wants, her hopes. Every breath she took pressed against the sliver of his self-control. But she was inside the cavern with the pretty fae, who, no doubt, had control over vast amounts of power. He had never been able to admit the truth, but he understood it now—he felt a pull to her. And she was powerful in this land, almost noteworthy.

Unlike him. He frowned, feeling jealousy and pride. Malrik tried to ignore the press of his Zaralis against his skin. It wasn't cool or warm. It pulsed weakly, as if its power were buried under all this sand, completely unreachable. Clara had mastered her Aelvor band immediately. Why wasn't it accepting him? At least his Aelvor arrows had worked.

Malrik felt a strange, distant tug coming from inside the cave where Clara wagered with the Syralen. It was more than his desire to be with her. Something must be happening. He ran a hand through his hair for the third time in as many minutes but kept his gaze on the mist.

That's when he saw it. A shift in the fog. Malrik froze, gripping his bow with white knuckles.

Selandor approached, eyes trained on the misty veil.

"Did you see that?" Malrik asked, slowly.

Selandor stepped closer. "Something has alerted Veylora to our presence. They're breaking through."

A hiss rose like a drawn blade from beyond the barrier. Then another, until dozens of terrible sounds reverberated through the ever-thinning fog. The mist writhed violently.

"No," Malrik whispered.

The barrier shuddered. It pulsed once like a dying heartbeat, violent and arrhythmic, then burst.

A sudden wind tore through as the Dravok poured in, their shapes long-limbed and glistening, eyes like voids of black tinged with ruby red. Twisted remnants of what were once Aelvor warriors, their bodies now a patchwork of shadow and bone.

"Positions!" Selandor roared, drawing his sword just in time to deflect a strike from the nearest Dravok, his blade extending in a flash of light, responding to his intent. Black ichor hissed as it splattered onto the rocky beach.

The mist was gone, and Clara was still inside the cave.

One of the creatures lunged. Malrik ducked, dropped to one knee, and threaded an arrow onto his bow. The creature snarled, but Malrik released the arrow. It glowed brilliantly against the shadow and tore sinew and shade. Another came at his side, and he barely escaped its obsidian claws. Kira was there, whirling in a cloud of feathers, caught mid-transformation. She deflected the Dravok, driving a blade through its center.

Malrik dared a glance at the cliffs. Elyndra, Vaelin, and Caylen were rushing toward them, weapons drawn and ready for battle. In a moment, they were there, aided in speed by their fae abilities. The Dravok poured through the rift in the mist, relentless and vicious.

"We can't hold them off like this forever," Elyndra shouted. "Where are they? We need to leave!"

Clara. The name thudded through Malrik's skull like a war drum.

He snarled and loosed another arrow, shouting above the din, "We have to hold them off, no matter what! Clara's not coming out to a slaughter."

Malrik caught a shift of movement in the corner of his eye. The Dravok were angling past them, heading for the cavern's entrance. He nocked another arrow and shot. It scattered into multiple beams of light, hitting four Dravok, but two escaped unharmed.

Malrik felt something tighten in his chest, sharper than fear. He gritted his teeth and aimed for the Dravok. Clara had trusted him to keep her safe. He would die before he let anything happen to her.

The air stank of rot and ozone, and his arms trembled with exhaustion. The Dravok kept coming in wave after wave, each one more frenzied than the last. Then the ground shuddered beneath them.

A low hum vibrated in the air, like the sound of a storm rolling over the bones of the earth.

"What—" Vaelin started, but the words died on his tongue.

From the cave's mouth, light bloomed. A golden pulse surged out in a perfect sphere, smooth and blinding, tearing across the ground in a flash of heat and force. Malrik had just enough time to throw up his arm before it hit him. The shockwave slammed into the sand like a thunderclap, driving the Dravok backward with an inhuman screech. Their shadows writhed in agony before disintegrating into smoke and ash, shriveling like burned leaves in the wind.

The light flared, speeding toward the rift in the fog. As it vanished, the gap in the mist sealed shut, whole once more.

Whatever power had come from the cave changed the veil of protection. The mist glowed, every tendril shot through with veins of gold. Where the Dravok had been, nothing remained but scorched earth and silence.

Malrik blinked through the settling haze, heart pounding. Sweat dripped into his eyes. He had only one thought as he raced toward the mouth of the cavern, desperation making him pump his legs incredibly fast.

Clara.

Ashael

The water was too still.

Ashael stood at the edge of the pool. His chest was tight, breath shallow. Clara had been down there too long.

He had counted every second. Each one stretching unbearably. She should be back by now.

The Syralen watched in silence. Their luminous tails flicked idly beneath the surface, their faces impassive. They did not stir, nor did they move to help.

His ears pricked. It was impossible to hear anything outside the cavern. He hoped that the others remained outside. The Syralen, Nerissa, regarded him with an icy stare. Who knew what she would do if provoked? He kept his focus on the water and the Syralen who observed Clara's descent into their dark water.

Ashael's fists curled. The Syralen were waiting. For her to fail? For her to drown? A muscle tensed in his jaw. No. He would not let that happen. He swore to protect her. A sudden lurch of movement sent a ripple across the surface, breaking his thoughts. That had to be Clara.

But Ashael felt no rush of relief. She was a shadow against the glow of a strange light that pulsed beneath the water. It rose, golden and blinding, sending the surface into a frantic boil. Then it burst from the water, nearly blinding him. A wave of power accompanied it, booming out of the mouth of the cavern. Ashael fought to keep his footing as the immense power surged.

His heart leapt into his throat. Clara must have done something right. Once the light had passed and his eyes had readjusted to the dim cavern light, he peered back into the water. His hope vanished in an instant. Something was wrong. She wasn't kicking upward; she was sinking.

A sharp pang shot through him. The fragment of memory, one he knew he could never forget, threatened to swallow him. He knew exhaustion when he saw it. He knew the exact moment someone crossed the line between fighting and fading. With dreadful certainty, he knew she wasn't going to make it. She wasn't going to make it.

Ashael didn't think, didn't stop to wonder if interfering was wise. Instead, he plunged into the water.

The cold struck like a blade. Pressure clamped around him, the force of the water crushing and all-consuming. Only the deep silence of the depths remained.

He kicked hard, muscles burning as he propelled himself deeper. The weight of the ocean pulled at him, dragging against his limbs. He saw her, drifting in the current.

She was suspended in the glow, her hair fanned around her like a halo, weightless in the water. Her lips were slightly parted, her features eerily still. Too still.

Even now, there was something about her that pulled at him, something that struck deep. But fear swallowed everything. Ashael pushed harder. He pulled his arms through the water, kicked as hard as he could. He reached out for her lifeless limbs, and his hand finally brushed hers.

His fingers brushed something small and solid, clenched in her hand. A sharp current snapped through him at the contact. It was a luminous pearl. The instant his skin touched it, a force rippled outward, like a silent bolt of lightning striking from within. A rush of energy crackled through his veins. His vision sharpened; his heartbeat thundered in his ears. The water no longer felt as heavy.

Something had changed or awakened, but there was no time to question it. Clara wasn't breathing.

Ashael wrapped an arm around her waist and pushed off the coral bed, surging toward the surface. The light above wavered, warped through the refracting depths. Clara was limp against him.

The cove loomed nearer, its radiance stretching toward them. Then they broke the surface. Ashael inhaled sharply, gasping in air as he dragged

Clara toward the rocky shore. Water streamed from them, pooling beneath the cavern's eerie glow. His heart pounded, hands shaking with the residual energy surging through him.

But Clara still wasn't moving.

He lowered her gently, trying to keep his hands from shaking. His fingers pressed against her neck, searching for a pulse. A faint flutter met his touch. It was weak, but it was there. He leaned in, listening for breath. There was nothing. Panic crept up his chest. "Clara," he said, voice barely above a whisper. Her eyes didn't open.

Tilting her head back, he cleared her airway, forcing himself to remain calm. The cavern was too quiet. The air was too still. Ashael sealed his lips over hers, giving a slow, steady breath.

Her chest rose, filling with air.

Still, she didn't wake up. His hand trembled as he touched her cheek. It was cold, and a wave of doubt curdled inside him.

He leaned in and gave her another breath. More forceful this time. His fingers locked against her shoulders, gripping her as if sheer will alone could keep her here. He refused to fail her.

A sound floated through the cavern. Soft, resonant, weaving through the air like the pull of the tide. Ashael stiffened as he realized the Syralen were singing. Their song rose, weightless and haunting, slipping through the cavern. Their voices wove together, layered like echoes in an endless sea. He didn't understand the words, but some part of him understood the Syralens' intent.

Ashael's breath hitched, but he did not leave Clara's side. The song wasn't for him this time. It was for her.

The music wove around them, carrying something unspoken. A farewell. A blessing. Then, without warning, the Syralen vanished. No sound, no ripple, no trace of their presence left behind. One moment, they were there. Next, they were gone. The silence rang too loudly, echoing in his ears. Ashael tore his gaze back to Clara as her chest jerked. She gasped as her body convulsed, fighting against the water in her lungs. Ashael gripped her shoulder and turned her on her side. Water spilled from her lips, her frame shuddering as she sucked in breath after breath.

Relief slammed into Ashael. His hands shook. He hadn't realized he was still holding onto her until he forced himself to let go. "Clara," he breathed.

Her lashes fluttered. Slowly, unfocused, her eyes met his.

Ashael's fists clenched, tension coiling in his chest. She was awake. That warmth stirred again inside him, fighting for recognition. He brushed his fingers against her cheek, trying to put into words how grateful he was. He let his hand fall as the slap of footsteps echoed throughout the cavern.

Malrik and Selandor charged into the cavern, their weapons drawn. Ashael exhaled sharply. The Syralen were gone. Clara was alive, and that was all that mattered.

CHAPTER 14

Clara gasped, her lungs burning as she sucked in a desperate breath. The world spun and her body shuddered, forcing air into her lungs. Each inhale was rough, ragged. But she didn't care. She was alive.

A comforting warmth surrounded her. She became aware of strong arms that held her steady, keeping her close against the lingering chill of the water clinging to her skin. Every fiber of her body felt attuned to him. Ashael.

She blinked, her vision still hazy, but there he was. His mouth pulled into a frown, and his brow creased. The cavern's dim glow reflected in his damp hair, casting shadows across his sharp features. Water clung to his lashes, and his breath was uneven. His grip was strong and caring.

Clara's pulse skipped as something new unfurled low in her stomach. She could feel the strength in his hold, the steady rise and fall of his chest. The space between them was almost nonexistent, and for a moment, she wasn't sure if the shiver running through her was from the cold or something else entirely.

Footsteps sounded, echoing off the damp cavern walls.

"Clara!"

She turned her head just in time to see Malrik stride toward them, his boots splashing against the wet stone. His gaze locked onto hers, his expression shifting the moment he took in the sight of her in Ashael's arms, soaked and breathless. But his features morphed into concern, and the look was gone before she could name it.

Selandor entered the cave right behind Malrik. He exchanged a nod with Ashael, a wordless confirmation that all was well.

Malrik dropped to his knees beside her, his voice lower, steadier. "You all right?"

Clara exhaled, still catching her breath. "I'm okay." Her throat was raw and burned with salt water.

Ashael's hold loosened as Malrik moved in, steadying her as she sat upright. There was a shift in the air, unspoken but undeniable. Together, they helped her to her feet.

"What the hell happened?" asked Malrik. "There was an explosion or something. It chased the Dravok away."

"Dravok?" Ashael's hand drifted to his dagger, and his eyes flicked to the mouth of the cavern.

It wasn't until then that Clara noticed Malrik was covered in sweat and dark, sticky blood. Her heart fell into her stomach. "Mal, are you okay?" She reached out her fingers, ready to check for any sign of injury.

Malrik looked down at himself, noting the state of his clothes. He wiped his cheek, trying to clean some of the blood off. "It's not mine," he said quickly.

"It's Dravok goo. They're gone now," Malrik continued. "The light chased them away, destroyed some, too. They were trying to get to this cave."

Clara's heart plummeted. "How did they get past the barrier?"

"I'm not sure," said Malrik. "It sort of flickered, then went out. They were waiting for an opportunity to breach it."

It was only then that Clara remembered the object she'd dived into the water to retrieve. She uncurled her fingers, revealing the pearl. Its soft glow pulsed gently, swirling light shifting within its depths like an ocean trapped in glass. "Maybe this had something to do with it." Perhaps when she'd retrieved the pearl, the magic around this place had weakened, allowing her to access the orb.

The swirling light reflected in Ashael's gaze. "The Syralen are gone," he murmured, glancing around the cavern. "They left as soon as you woke up."

"A burst of light nearly blinded me when I grabbed it," said Clara as she examined the pearl she held in her cupped hand. Selandor turned, calling the others over, who remained standing guard outside the mouth of the cave. Within moments, their group gathered, forming a cautious circle around Clara.

"What is that?" Elyndra asked, her sharp gaze fixed on the pearl.

Malrik frowned, rubbing a hand over the back of his neck. "It's not the shard, is it?"

Silence stretched between them.

"If it's not," Selandor said slowly, "then what *is* it?"

Clara tightened her fingers around it, the memory of the song still lingering in her mind. "I don't know. But I heard something when I touched it, like a song. It told a story. Maybe I can activate it again."

A hush fell over them.

Then Ashael's eyes snapped to her pendant.

"Clara, your necklace."

She looked down. The Valenwood pendant was glowing softly, a golden glow radiating from its crystalline surface. At the same time, heat spread against her side. Clara brushed the sand from her hand as best she could and reached for her pouch, fingers brushing over the map inside.

It was warm and stayed dry.

She pulled it free, and realization clicked into place. Slowly, she raised the pearl above the map.

The moment they aligned, flames erupted.

Clara inhaled sharply, watching as fire consumed her hand. But there was no pain, no searing heat, only warmth and light. The fire curled around her fingers, shifting in hues of gold and deep red as they danced along her skin.

Then, as suddenly as they had appeared, they vanished.

A single glowing line now burned into the map's surface, stretching toward a distant location. One that had not been there before. The lines of light converged, forming the rough shape of a fiery creature with wings, its form etched in molten gold against the parchment.

Kira was the first to speak. "That . . . that's the Phylarix. The creature of fiery rebirth."

Malrik pushed his glasses up the bridge of his nose, eyes widened. "Wait, so like a Phoenix from our world?" He exhaled, eyes still fixed on the map. "Incredible. Should I be amazed or worried?"

Kira's gaze lingered on the map with reverence. "They are among the oldest creatures ever born of fire itself. My kind has always respected them. Not as kin but as something . . . greater. Stories of the Phylarix were told to us as younglings, but no one has ever seen them. They are elusive, shrouded in myth. No one knows if they still exist or if they ever did."

She reached out her fingers, as if to brush the glowing symbol on the map but then withdrew them. "But if the pearl led us there, then we may be standing at the edge of legend itself."

Selandor crossed his arms. "I've heard tales of this place. It appears the map is showing a Phylarix lair deep inside a volcanic region. If that's truly our next destination . . ." Selandor met Clara's gaze. "Then this journey is about to become even more dangerous."

Clara's pulse thrummed in her ears, her thoughts still focused on the sight of the fire in her palm, of a song she somehow understood. The path ahead was set, should they dare to follow it. Clara clutched the pearl in her fist. Her gaze flicked between Malrik, tired and bloody, and Ashael, soaked and determined. They had already given so much to protect her. But her insides coiled tight with the knowledge that the Dravok would come back. They had followed them here, been waiting for them, patrolling the rift in the mist. What would happen if they got to the next clue in this puzzle before them?

"We should stay here tonight before we set out."

Selandor nodded. "A wise decision. I'll collect the others."

Clara could not meet anyone's eyes as she wrung out her hair and thought about what lay ahead.

Night fell, and the cavern remained quiet, its natural light casting elongated shadows along the walls. No Syralens had returned, but no one felt truly at ease.

Clara sat near the glowing rock formations, exhaustion pressing against her limbs, though her mind remained restless. The near drowning had taken more out of her than she cared to admit, but her thoughts lingered on the Syralens' song. The melody echoed hauntingly in her mind.

Vaelin and Selandor remained crouched near the map, their expressions tight with focus. The others sat around a small fire, warding off the chill that had come with sundown.

A small movement caught Clara's eye. Calyen stepped forward, his presence quiet but firm. "I won't be coming with you," he announced.

No one looked surprised. They had known this was coming, yet now that the moment had arrived, a strange heaviness settled over the group.

Clara's brows drew together. "But Calyen, the Dravok might still be out there."

"I'll be fine. I know how to evade them." He glanced toward the entrance. "Flying makes it easier."

Clara hesitated, glancing at the others, but no one spoke. They knew he was right. He had always planned to leave once they reached the Syralen Cove. His duty was to his people, just as theirs was to continue the journey.

Still, she felt a pang of loss. He had been a steady presence in their group, and now they would be one less.

"Thank you," she said finally. "For everything."

The others murmured their agreement.

Calyen inclined his head. "We will meet again," he promised. "I'll depart in the morning." A few beats of silence passed before Vaelin exhaled, shifting back to the map. "For those of us remaining, we need to decide our next move."

Clara hopped down from her perch and moved to join the others. She sat down next to Malrik. He stopped fiddling with his Zaralis and flashed her a wide grin.

Vaelin traced the parchment with his finger. "We have three possible paths to the Phylarix lair. The first is the fastest but heavily corrupted. Dravok activity will be at its worst here." His hand moved. "The second is longer but avoids the thickest parts of the corruption."

His finger hesitated over an unmarked region on the fringes of the parchment. "Then there's this. Some maps don't even mark it clearly, and no one knows what's out there. It could be corrupted or something else entirely. If we take it, it might be shorter than the second option, but we can't guarantee its safety."

Clara crossed her arms and waited for the others to decide. She didn't know anything about these lands. She would leave the decision to those who knew the terrain.

Selandor finally spoke. "We take the second route. It's safer, even if it's longer. The unknown path isn't an option, and the heavily corrupted route is too dangerous."

Kira crossed her arms. "And how long will that take?"

"Five to six days, depending on travel speed."

The group exchanged glances.

Kira shifted slightly. "With Calyen gone, I will be the only one left to carry someone."

No one needed to say who that someone was.

Malrik stiffened. His lips pressed into a tight line before he spoke softly. "So that means I ride Kira."

Kira nodded slowly. "You're the slowest among us."

The words weren't meant to sting, but they did.

Malrik inhaled sharply, rubbing a hand over his neck. His jaw tightened, fingers flexing before curling into a fist. He didn't argue, but he didn't look happy about it either.

He looked at Clara. "Which means you have to keep up on foot."

"Her Zaralis is working well," Elyndra pointed out. "It'll help."

"That's not the point," Malrik muttered before he could stop himself. "She's still human. That Zaralis helps, but it won't change the fact that she'll have to push herself harder than anyone else here just to keep up."

Clara opened her mouth to argue, but Ashael spoke before she could. "Then I'll carry her if needed."

The words were simple. Matter-of-fact. But Malrik's entire frame went rigid. His head snapped toward Ashael, his expression darkening. "What?"

Ashael didn't even look at him. His gaze remained on the map, voice even. "If it becomes an issue, I'll carry Clara."

It wasn't an offer. It was a statement.

Clara saw a muscle twitching in Malrik's jaw. He was already struggling with the fact that his Zaralis wasn't fully working. He already felt behind. Clara sighed, shifting slightly toward him. "Malrik—"

"I get it," he muttered, running a hand through his hair. "It makes sense."

But he wasn't looking at her.

He pushed himself to his feet and walked toward the mouth of the cave. Tension crackled in the air around him.

Ashael remained still, his face impassive, his eyes giving nothing away.

Clara glanced between them. There was something here, something unspoken, that none of them were acknowledging. But she was too exhausted to pull at the thread.

"We'll leave at first light," said Vaelin. "I suggest we all get some sleep."

The group fell into hushed preparation for rest. Weapons were kept close. Shifts were assigned for keeping watch. No one trusted the silence outside the cavern, but for now they were safe.

Malrik stayed at the mouth of the cave for a long while. From where she lay, Clara could still see him, staring out at the ocean and the starry sky.

Her eyes grew heavy, but her mind wouldn't stop replaying the tension from earlier. The crashing of waves sounded, echoing in the cave, and pulled her quickly into sleep.

The morning light seeped through the cavern's entrance in soft, muted beams. Clara stirred, feeling the stiffness in her muscles as the memory of yesterday's near-drowning clung to her. She rolled her shoulders, testing her strength. Aching, but manageable. The group made quiet, efficient preparations to continue the next leg of their journey as Selandor and Vaelin scouted for a way out of the barrier of mist. When they returned, their features were taut with tension.

"We found a way out," Selandor said. "A clear path past the barrier."

The words set her on edge. A clear path? That wasn't right. She frowned "And the Dravok?"

Vaelin shook his head. "Not a single one in sight."

An unspoken question passed between them. The Dravok had been relentless before. Why had they suddenly withdrawn?

"That's not good," Elyndra muttered.

Kira exhaled sharply, gripping her weapons tighter. "They don't just disappear."

"Feels like we're walking into something," Vaelin murmured, eyes narrowing toward the exit.

No one disagreed.

As they gathered their things, Malrik stood slightly apart from the group, adjusting the straps of Kira's harness. His expression was tight, his movements tense.

Clara noticed the way he kept flexing his fingers, like he was trying to push down his frustration.

"Malrik." She stepped closer.

He exhaled sharply but didn't look at her. "You shouldn't have to run while I just sit there."

She sighed. "It's not like that. My Zaralis is working well. I can keep up. My back isn't even protesting much anymore."

He shook his head. "That's not the point." His voice was gruff, but there was something deeper beneath it. "I should be strong enough to keep up too. I should be able to stand on my own feet."

Clara's expression softened. She understood the feeling of not quite fitting in, of being pushed to the outskirts. "Malrik, you're not weak," she said. "And you're not useless. You're part of this group, just like the rest of us. We all have things we need to overcome. You'll figure it out."

His jaw tightened. He didn't answer for a moment, then finally exhaled. "Yeah. Maybe."

She knew he wasn't convinced, but there was no more time to argue. "We're ready," called Elyndra.

Malrik picked up the harness and headed outside.

The glow of the cavern faded behind them as they stepped outside. The morning air was crisp, carrying the scent of damp earth and fresh leaves.

The Syralen had never returned. Or if they had, there was no sign of them.

Clara blinked in the bright morning light. She touched the pouch at her side where the pearl rested. She didn't know what lay ahead, but for the first time, she felt ready.

The salty air blew against her cheeks, tangling her hair. Ashael turned to Clara, his face solemn. "Tell me if you begin to tire."

Clara nodded and let the tingling surge of power that radiated from her Zaralis flow through her limbs. They walked up the sand toward the barrier. It undulated like the sea, but they knew, instinctively, that they could pass through again. She braced herself. For an ambush. For movement in the shadows.

But nothing came.

They emerged from the mist into the thicket of trees. The forest beyond was empty and silent.

Clara's unease deepened. The Dravok knew they had been here. So, why wasn't anyone watching? Had they assumed the group was still inside? Or had they changed tactics? She exhaled, gripping her bag tighter as they pressed forward. When they reached the safety of the trees, Ashael gave her some last advice. "Trust your instincts. Stay close."

"I won't fall behind."

Kira shifted into her bird form, letting her wings burst forth. Malrik climbed onto her back, and the pair took off into the skies.

Elyndra, Vaelin, Selandor, and Ashael left for the forest. Clara began to jog and found the landscape blurring by with more speed than she'd anticipated. The Zaralis caused her strides to lengthen, her movements to be sharp and precise, her breath to remain slow despite the exertion. She smiled to herself, pleased by how the power coursed through her.

It was easy to stay close to Ashael. Her desire to remain beside him spurred her onward. He never looked back; he knew she was going to make it.

The day stretched on in strained silence. No pursuit. No threats. Just miles of endless trees. By nightfall, they coaxed the hollow of an ancient tree to accommodate the entire group, exhaustion settling heavily over them.

Still, the silence lingered. And somehow, that felt more unsettling than anything else.

CHAPTER 15

Malrik

Malrik lay on his back, staring up at the cool biolumines-cent glow embedded in the earthen ceiling. His body was exhausted, but his mind refused to rest. Sleep had come in short, restless intervals for the past few nights, never deep enough to pull him into true rest, never long enough to silence the frustration gnawing at his chest.

The steady rise and fall of the others' breaths filled the hollow they had made their camp for the evening. They were safe here, the trees providing shelter for them. At least, that's what they all wanted to believe.

But he didn't feel safe. Not from the Dravok. Not from himself.

His fingers curled into a fist, tightening over the edge of his blanket. The band at his ankle, his supposed advantage, his way of keeping up, was still failing him. Sometimes it worked, a surge of power granting him brief bursts of speed. But then, without warning, it would fail, leaving him struggling to keep up.

Useless.

The word clawed at him.

He could fight. He had shown that he could wield a bow and the Aelvor arrows. He had kept the Dravok at bay at Syralen Cove. But what good was any of it if he couldn't even match the others? If Clara was outpacing him?

His jaw flexed. He exhaled sharply and sat up, moving carefully to avoid making noise. The hollow's natural glow cast soft shadows along the walls, shifting with the slow rise and fall of breath around him.

He glanced toward Clara, bundled in her blanket, her face half-buried in the fabric.

Ashael lay nearby, his posture rigid even in sleep. He was irritated, but he pushed the irrational feeling aside.

He grabbed his bow and quiver, then slipped outside the hollow. The cool night air met him, crisp and laced with the damp scent of earth and moss. The towering trees stretched toward the sky, their leaves reflecting the first hints of dawn's approach.

Malrik leaned against the outer curve of the tree, removing his glasses and rubbing a hand down his face. He had to be better.

". . . Help . . . please . . ."

Malrik stiffened. He hastily put his glasses back on and scanned the darkness beyond the treeline.

The voice came again. Soft, barely above a whisper, yet carrying an unmistakable note of desperation.

". . . Please . . . the Dravok . . ."

His breath slowed, his heartbeat picking up in contrast. He turned his head slightly, listening. The Dravok could still be hunting them. This could be a trap.

Malrik hesitated. He should wake the others. But what if this was real? What if someone was out there injured or hunted? He didn't want to risk unnecessary panic. And if it was a Dravok trick, he could handle it.

Hand resting on the curve of his bow, Malrik stepped away from the hollow, moving carefully into the trees.

He followed the cries, stepping lightly among tree roots and the earthen floor. It didn't take long for him to find the source of the pleas.

She was curled near the base of a fallen tree, her form barely visible in the shadows. An Aelvor.

She had olive skin and long black hair that spilled around her shoulders. It was tangled and wild. And her eyes. They were dark, piercing, and locked onto him with something raw. Something pleading.

Malrik swallowed, his mind racing.

She cradled her arm to her chest. Her posture was tense. She was clearly injured and vulnerable.

Dravok didn't look like this. They were twisted, corrupted. Their eyes burned red with darkness. But this woman looked untouched. Beautiful, even.

". . . Please . . ." she whispered, breathless. "The Dravok are hunting me."

Something about her voice hit deep. Malrik hesitated, scanning the darkness beyond her. If the Dravok were close, why hadn't he heard them?

He moved cautiously, each step careful as he approached. "Where did you come from?"

She flinched, as if afraid. "I—I was hiding in the cliffs. They found me." A hitched breath. "I barely got away. I think they're still looking."

Malrik's grip on his bow tightened. Beautiful or not, something wasn't right. He was drawn to her, but he didn't know why.

Then, his instincts screamed.

He scrutinized the Aelvor. The wound on her arm was deep and jagged. But it wasn't bleeding.

Her tangled hair was clean and free of leaves or twigs. Her breath was calm. There was no sign she'd been running at all.

The shadows around her didn't settle right.

Malrik stepped back slowly, keeping his movements calm.

Her gaze wavered for a moment, revealing something dark beneath her stricken face.

And then she lunged.

Her hand shot out, catching his wrist.

The cold was immediate, biting and unnatural.

Malrik gasped as his muscles locked. The air thinned around him as his pulse hammered in his ears. She was no Aelvor, nor was she Dravok. She was unlike anything he knew.

The cold was overwhelming, freezing his limbs, his thoughts, his heart. He heard something behind him, prickling the edge of his awareness, but he couldn't stop staring into the ink-black eyes of the thing that held him captive.

"Malrik, get back!"

A sharp, commanding voice cut through the night.

With a surge of will, Malrik tore his gaze away from the woman and her too-perfect features.

Vaelin burst from the shadows, poised for battle. His blade was already drawn and luminous.

Malrik had fought beside Vaelin at Syralen Cove. He had seen him kill without hesitation. But this time, he wasn't striking.

The woman's gaze slid past Malrik and landed on Vaelin. She gave him a cold, knowing smile.

"Took you long enough."

The words sent another chill down Malrik's spine. Before he could process the meaning, her grip loosened. He yanked his arm free, stumbling back.

"Run. Now." Vaelin's voice was steel.

Malrik didn't argue.

He turned and sprinted toward the hollow. Then he saw her. Clara.

She was running, too, her breath sharp. Her eyes locked onto his, and he felt his heart beat against his ribs.

CHAPTER 16

Clara had watched Malrik leave the hollow of the tree. She'd rolled over, woken up just enough to register him leaving their hollow, then jerked fully awake. For a moment she wondered whether to roll back over and go to sleep, but something in his movements, in the tension between his shoulder blades, made her follow him.

Worry lodged in her stomach as she crept after him, keeping her distance. Her anklet pulsed, sharpening her senses, letting her track him. He walked with care, head tilted, listening hard. Where was he going?

A voice, soft and fragile, drifted through the trees.

". . . Please . . . the Dravok . . ."

Her limbs tingled with adrenaline. Before she could call out, warn him, he stopped in front of a large tree. A figure on the ground pleaded with him.

But something wasn't right. Before she could bridge the gap between them, the figure grabbed Malrik by the arm. A cry lodged in her throat, but Vaelin, fast and silent as the wind, leapt into the clearing before she could call out.

The creature released Malrik. Her pulse pounded in her ears as she ran toward him.

Malrik was fast, but the moment she saw the sheer panic on his face, her pulse spiked. Yes, something was very wrong.

Movement flashed in the corner of her eyes. Selandor, Elyndra, Kira, and Ashael all ran through the trees toward them. They must have heard Vaelin's shout. Or maybe they had felt it too, that unnatural, suffocating shift in the air. Their weapons were already drawn, eyes sharp, closing the distance fast.

For a split second, relief crashed over Clara. Vaelin's voice cut through the dark. "Seraphis."

A single name. A single moment. Then the illusion shattered.

It started slowly. Smoke began to rise. Dark tendrils seeped from the figure, Seraphis's skin, shifting like living shadows. The corruption didn't consume her as it did the other Dravok. It clung to her. Moved with her.

She wasn't twisted or monstrous. She was still Aelvor, but not completely.

Her feet never touched the ground. The darkness lifted her just slightly, letting her drift, weightless, every motion smooth, effortless.

The unnatural stillness stretched for half a breath.

No one moved. No one spoke. Then Ashael stepped forward, his voice sharp. "Vaelin. Explain."

Vaelin hadn't lowered his blade. But his hands shook.

Clara's gaze darted between him and the Aelvor woman. Vaelin knew her.

"Oh, Vaelin." Her tone was light, almost amused. "Haven't told them about me, have you?"

A trace of guilt flashed across Vaelin's face.

"What is she talking about?" asked Selandor.

Vaelin's jaw ticked, but he didn't answer.

Clara barely had time to process the tension before Seraphis turned her gaze to the others.

She smiled, flashing too-white teeth. "They don't know, do they?" She let the words hang, teasing. "Poor Vaelin. Always so secretive." Her eyes grew steely. "Did you really think you could escape us? That we wouldn't find you? You have something we need."

She flicked her wrist in silent command.

The shadows stirred and shifted. A chorus of guttural growls ripped through the air as the Dravok materialized. Dozens of red eyes lit up the dark.

Clara's breath hitched. They'd walked straight into her trap.

Seraphis snapped her fingers and the battlefield erupted.

The Dravok leapt forward at the command, extending their formidable claws. Clara barely had time to react before one lunged at her. Her Zaralis sent a jolt of energy through her with near-lightning force. She hadn't grasped her warrior's training as quickly as Malrik had, but she'd learned enough to know she needed a weapon. She twisted and reached for her side, fumbling for the hilt of a dagger. One she'd hoped she wouldn't need.

As her fingers grasped the hilt and she unsheathed it, her sword ignited into flame so bright it cut through the shadow.

The Dravok shrieked as she drove her weapon deep, its body disintegrating into ash.

Clara exhaled sharply as she staggered and lost her balance. The blade shrank back into a dagger. She barely had time to recover before another Dravok was upon her. Around her, everyone else was locked in battle. Malrik shot arrows with speed and precision. Ashael, Selandor, and Elyndra whirled with their warrior's grace, their movements a blur. Kira slashed at the Dravok, her fingers transformed into talons. Each of them fought for their lives. No one was coming to save her.

The Dravok lunged, taking advantage of Clara's unsteady footing. She tried to throw her body out of the way. The Dravok's deadly claws were an inch away from her throat. Clara squeezed her eyes shut, bracing for impact.

Instead of cold, sharp claws, Clara felt a surge of warmth seconds before a burst of golden light lit up the clearing. A sharp, searing blast erupted from her chest, slamming into the Dravok and obliterating it instantly.

Clara gasped, half from pain and half from shock.

The glow faltered, then diminished. A wave of exhaustion rolled over her, like something had drained her.

She pressed a hand against her pendant, willing it to react. Nothing happened. Her chest rose and fell sharply. She was exposed.

Seraphis, who had been battling Vaelin, evading his strikes with effortless speed, snapped her attention to Clara in the wake of the light. Her eyes, first full of cold hate, shifted as a cruel intent settled there.

Clara was filled with unrelenting dread. Seraphis, floating above the ground, swept forward toward her new target. She dodged Vaelin's next attack without looking, making straight for Clara.

Clara scrambled to get out of the way, to lift her blade and reignite its power, but she was still drained. She took a step back, too slowly, as Seraphis charged.

Around her, blades flashed, Dravok fell, and before she could blink, Ashael was there.

His blade clashed against Seraphis' dark solid tendrils, stopping her inches from Clara.

He stood his ground as Seraphis's eyes flicked to him. She hesitated only for a second, but it was enough time for Ashael to strike.

The force of the blow sent her skidding back, shadows twisting violently around her.

Clara inhaled sharply, gaze snapping to Ashael. Something was different. The air around her felt charged. He had moved faster, struck harder.

She wasn't sure if anyone else noticed.

Clara barely had a second to process before more Dravok swarmed.

Kira's voice cut through the chaos. "Kazrakh's Ember, now!"

Ashael thrust his hand into his shirt pocket. "Fall back!" Selandor and Vaelin were behind him in a moment. Elyndra wrapped an arm around Malrik, sweeping him away from the approaching onslaught of Dravok. Kira whirled in a tornado of golden feathers, coming around the right flank.

As soon as everyone was behind him, Ashael loosened his grip on the Dwarven ember dust, releasing it into the air. The fine particles spread and floated like dust caught in morning sun, forming an almost invisible barrier. Only the faintest glimmer of ember dust remained, suspended like ruby dust.

The Dravok continued with the attack, only to collide with their invisible shield. Their bodies slammed into an unseen force, repelled by something they couldn't fight.

Ashael pressed his hand to the ground. The terrain answered. The earth split open, a jagged rift tearing through the battlefield.

Vaelin, Selandor, and Elyndra moved instinctively, each calling forth the power of Avenora. Vines thickened, twisting into walls of thorns. The roots of nearby trees groaned as they shifted and expanded, forming barriers between them and the creatures snarling on the other side. Stone cracked and rose, reshaping itself to further reinforce the divide. The Kazrakh's Ember was powerful but fleeting. It would only last as long as their energy held.

They couldn't waste time.

"Go!" Ashael commanded.

Kira transformed midair, her form shifting fluidly, her wings spreading wide. Malrik hopped onto her back, gripping her harness as she launched into the sky.

Ashael moved before Clara could react, sweeping her off her feet in one swift motion.

His breath tickled the shell of her ear as he said in a low voice, "Hold on."

Then they ran. The world blurred. Wind tore past Clara's face, her pulse hammering as Ashael surged forward at an inhuman pace.

She barely heard the others behind them, their movements silent shadows in the rush of the escape. The ember dust shimmered in the air behind them, the rift holding for now.

But Clara knew it wouldn't last. Something pricked at the back of her neck. She turned her head.

There, on the other side of the divide, Seraphis floated, still smiling. She didn't move or chase after them. She just watched them go. Still, her voice carried through the distance, drifting past the ember dust.

"You cannot outrun fate."

Clara's lungs seized for a moment. The words reverberated through her skull. Then, Seraphis vanished in a thick billow of smoke.

If Ashael had heard Seraphis's whispered farewell, he didn't show it. He carried Clara without hesitation, his grip secure as he moved with the others. Kira soared above, Malrik clinging to her back, while Vaelin, Selandor, and Elyndra pushed forward on foot.

But as they ran, something shifted.

Selandor's strides grew slower. Vaelin's chest heaved for breath. Ashael's grip around Clara tightened as if he were anchoring himself.

The ember had done its job, but now it was taking its toll.

"We need to stop," Selandor finally muttered, his breath uneven. "The ember, it's pulling too much from us."

Ashael didn't argue. He lowered Clara gently to the ground.

She slid from his grasp. Her legs wobbled beneath her, but she steadied herself.

The rest of the group slumped against trees and fought to catch their breath. Sweat dripped from their foreheads.

After a minute, Selandor straightened. He frowned as he took in the landscape. "I am not familiar with these trees."

Indeed, the trees did not bear the crystalline characteristics of the forest that they had traversed so far. Nor was it corrupted by shadow. Something in the air, in their branches, in the way they leaned close together, was different.

A flap of wings announced Kira's arrival. Malrik slid from her back as the Shantera shifted back into her wingless form. "We're not on the right path," she announced, breathless and exhausted.

"Then where are we?" asked Elyndra as she wiped the perspiration from her brow.

Clara fumbled for the map, hoping it would help. Selandor stepped to her side, gazing at the parchment.

"This isn't the safer route," he said slowly. "And it's not the heavily corrupted one, either."

His finger hovered over the map, tracing a blank space between the two known routes.

Realization hit Clara. They had taken the unknown path.

"We need to turn back," Elyndra said, sounding panicked.

"Turn back to what?" Malrik countered. "The Dravok are still behind us."

Ashael took command with his usual calm. "We're too exposed here. We need to press on, find somewhere we can rest and get our bearings."

The group nodded, too tired to argue. It would take hours before the effects of the ember faded. They needed food and sleep. Dawn was not far off.

Silently, they walked for a few miles, keeping up a steady human pace. Clara focused on putting one foot in front of the other. Though she had not wielded magic after exposure to the ember, she was still tired. She'd gotten little sleep, and the adrenaline of battle had long worn, leaving her tired and shaky.

The sound reached them first, and without a word, the group hurried toward it. A stream.

Clara dropped to her knees, cupping icy water in her hands and drinking. Around her, the others splashed their faces, exhaustion heavy on them all.

For a brief moment, it felt like they could breathe. Then Elyndra went rigid.

Clara noticed it instantly, the way her hand hovered just above the ground, fingers trembling slightly, as if afraid to touch it.

A chill ran through her. Slowly, she followed Elyndra's gaze.

The dirt here wasn't soft like before. No moss cushioned the earth. It was packed down and flattened. Something had moved through here. A lot of somethings. But there were no footprints or claw marks that Clara could see.

Elyndra swallowed hard, her voice barely above a whisper. "Centurions."

"What are they?" asked Clara.

Malrik exhaled sharply. "I read about them during training," he muttered. "They're brutal."

"They don't spare," Elyndra added firmly. "Once they see you as a threat, it's already over. No reasoning, no mercy. If they find us, we won't have time to run."

Clara swallowed hard. It felt like the dangers just kept piling up, one after another. The Dravok, the lingering exhaustion from the Kazrakh's Ember, and now this.

Then she heard it.

Galloping.

Ashael reacted instantly, stepping in front of Clara, his blade half-drawn. The trees shivered. Shadows shifted. The first figure emerged from the pale light of dawn.

For a split second, Clara's mind registered only a horse. Then she saw the rest.

A towering figure, half-man, half-horse, stepped toward them. His broad shoulders were rippled with muscle; his bare torso was laced with scars. He was draped in intricate leather armor carved with unfamiliar symbols. His lower half was that of a massive, battle-scarred warhorse.

And he wasn't alone. More figures stepped forward, forming a silent, watching wall. Their spears were long and sharp. They held them at the ready, scanning them to see if they were a threat. Dread coiled in Clara's stomach, and she feared they had stumbled into something worse than the Dravok.

There were more than a dozen of them now. Clara barely dared to breathe. The Centurions moved as one, a formation of warriors, disciplined and unyielding. Their sheer size, their presence alone, made the forest seem smaller, suffocating.

A single word broke the silence. "Aelvors."

They took a unified step forward, tightened their grips on their spears, and dropped their stances into attack positions.

Clara's breath stalled. This wasn't a warning. This was an execution. Before she could move, before she could even process the inevitability of her body being pierced with spears, a Centurion stepped forward.

He was a towering figure, broad and battle-worn. The silver streaks in his dark mane framing a face carved by war. The others let him pass, deferring to him. Clara knew this must be their leader. His voice, when it came, was like steel over stone. "You trespass."

Ashael, ever composed, started to speak, but the leader cut him off with a sharp, venom-laced growl. "Aelvor words are worthless."

And then he struck. The spear came down, fast and lethal, aimed straight for Ashael.

But the impact never landed. Ashael's blade was already there, intercepting the blow in a flash of steel. The clash rang through the air like a war drum.

Vaelin, Selandor, and Elyndra moved in an instant, weapons unsheathed. Kira let out a low, warning growl as her fingertips morphed into talons.

The Centurions did not back down. The moment teetered on the edge of an all-out battle.

Clara barely had time to register it when Malrik's voice cut through the tension like a blade.

"STOP!"

Everything froze.

The Centurion leader's spear remained locked against Ashael's blade. The others held their attack positions.

The Aelvor and the others did not lower their weapons, but they did not strike.

For the first time, every single gaze turned to Malrik.

A murmur rose from within the Centurion ranks, spoken with a note of surprise.

"Humans."

The leader's head snapped toward the voice that spoke, his brow furrowing slightly before his dark eyes settled fully on Malrik and Clara.

A streak of movement passed through the Centurions. A second Centurion, younger but no less commanding, stepped alongside the leader. His voice was measured, though his tone was edged with caution. "Khazar . . . the prophecy."

The words hung heavily in the air.

Khazar's grip on his spear tightened. After another moment, he lowered his weapon. One by one, the other Centurions followed.

The Aelvor and the others remained tense, blades still drawn.

Khazar's attention swung back to Malrik. "Speak, human."

"We didn't come here to fight," he said, his voice surprisingly steady. "We were running from the Dravok. We didn't know we were trespassing."

Khazar's expression remained cold as he contemplated this.

"You will come with us." His words left no space for debate.

The Centurions shifted, ready to move.

Just as the tension began to ease, Khazar's sharp gaze whipped back to Ashael and the others. In a single, effortless motion, he raised his spear again. "The rest do not belong here."

The Centurions moved in unison, stances dropping back into attack formation. It was only the humans they had reconsidered. The other fae were still trespassers.

Clara opened her mouth to defend them, but Malrik beat her to it.

"They are with us!" Malrik's voice rang out, unwavering.

Khazar's spear hovered in place. Then, he gave a sharp nod and lowered his spear once more.

Malrik had spoken, and for whatever reason, Khazar had chosen to listen.

CHAPTER 17

Malrik

M alrik still wasn't sure how any of this had happened. The Centurions had listened to him. *Him.*

The realization settled upon him as they passed through the heart of the Centurion settlement. It was unlike anything he had ever seen.

The Aelvors had crafted dwellings, seamlessly woven into nature, but here, Malrik found no individual shelters. Here, the trunks and branches of massive trees twisted together, standing so closely aligned that their canopies formed an unbroken shield overhead. The dense foliage swallowed most of the light, casting the camp into a realm of muted shadows. There were no walls and no clear boundaries, just a fortress of nature, where the Centurions made their way without effort, adjusting to the path as it changed beneath them.

But as they moved silently through the settlement, Malrik leading his group, it wasn't the architecture that caught his attention. It was the structure of their society.

The warriors who had surrounded them in the forest were almost all male. Malrik saw a male Centurion step instinctively in front of a female as their group passed. His posture adjusted slightly, shoulders squaring, eyes tracking their movement without a word. The gesture was subtle, but Malrik understood that the Centurions followed a patriarchal hierarchy. Malrik saw female Centurions working in small groups, tending to the young, preparing supplies, and sharpening weapons. But he did not see any females dressed for battle, wearing leather armor, or bearing any spears themselves.

He realized why the leader had listened to him. It wasn't just because he was human.

It was because he was male. A notion that felt ancient back home. He doubted Clara liked the idea, but the Centurions left them no room to argue.

A glance at Clara confirmed it. She walked beside him, steady but silent. The Centurions barely acknowledged her, but he could feel the eyes of many of them trained on him.

A thought settled deep inside him, a realization that felt both instinctive and foreign. They saw him as the one responsible for her.

Malrik squared his shoulders slightly, becoming what they wanted to see. He wasn't just a bookstore owner anymore. Never in his life had he imagined standing in a place like this, playing a role he had only read about in stories. Like . . . a *hero*. No chance. But still, he couldn't let her down. He knew he would be the one expected to negotiate on their behalf.

He and Clara had spent the last several weeks relying on the Aelvor. Not because they were inferior, but because they had needed to. The Aelvor understood this world. He and Clara had not.

But now? The Centurions weren't even looking at Ashael or any of the other Aelvor.

Malrik cast a glance toward him. Ashael remained silent, walking behind him and Clara.

The Centurions were ready to kill the Aelvor on the spot. But why?

A voice pulled him from his thoughts. "You are uneasy, human."

Malrik turned. One of the Centurions had fallen in step beside him. He looked young, his face unlined, but he walked with the same calm focus as the rest.

Malrik forced a breath. "I didn't expect to be the one worth listening to."

The Centurion regarded him for a moment before responding. "It is rare for outsiders to be given an audience." His eyes darted toward the Aelvor walking behind them. "Some are less welcome than others."

Malrik frowned. He chose his words carefully. "I'll make sure we don't waste the opportunity."

The Centurion gave a small, approving nod before stepping ahead to rejoin his kind.

Malrik exhaled slowly. He had saved them from immediate execution. That much was clear. But if he couldn't do this, reason with them, make them understand that they weren't trespassing intentionally, then they were all doomed. And being male had never made him all that confident in the human world, but he needed to do this for her. For them. Everyone was depending on him for once. The world felt weighty with the expectation.

They were ushered deeper into the Centurion stronghold, past branches that weaved together to make four-inch thick barricades. Their escorts surrounded them, beckoning them to continue with an unspoken command to follow.

They entered a clearing where large stones formed a rough circle, a space clearly meant for gathering. Even without a word, the setup told him this was where choices were made.

The Centurions took their places around them, forming a loose perimeter. They were no longer aiming weapons at their throats, but their guarded stances made their feelings clear. Khazar stood at the front, his sharp gaze swept between them, his expression impossible to read.

"Our kind has heard stories," he said at last, his deep voice steady. "Stories of a prophecy. One that speaks of humans."

Malrik felt Clara stiffen beside him. He fought the urge to reach for her hand as a murmur passed through the Centurions. Some seemed intrigued, others skeptical. But none of them dismissed it outright.

"It is only one interpretation," Khazar continued. "No one can know for sure. But it is not something I can disregard."

His attention settled on Malrik. "What brought you here, human? And why," Khazar's scrutiny turned toward the Aelvors and Kira, "do you travel with them?"

Malrik concentrated on the feeling of the earth beneath him, grounding his thoughts and emotions. He would only have one chance. "Before I tell you our story," he said carefully, "I need to know that the Aelvors and Shantera will not be harmed."

Silence followed.

A few of the Centurions exchanged glances, but Khazar's expression did not shift. "Our distrust is not without cause," he said, his voice edged with something old and worn by time. "The Aelvor were entrusted to protect Avenora. To protect all within it. Including Centurions."

His dark eyes moved to Ashael, Selandor, and the others. Though he did not speak their names, the next words were aimed at them. "They failed."

The weight of the accusation hung heavy in the air.

"When Veylora's reign began," Khazar continued, "when the corruption spread, my people were left with no choice but to disappear. We fled. We hid away to survive." He gestured to the warriors around him. "We found refuge here, deep in these lands, and have defended it ever since. We fight anything, and anyone that dares threaten what little we have left."

His words weren't angry. He sounded almost sad. A kernel of distrust lodged itself in his heart. Why would the Aelvor, who seemed so keen to protect him and Clara, turn their back on other fae?

"The Aelvor failed us," Khazar continued. "So, we learned to rely only on ourselves. Our kind shares a bond with the earth itself. Its rawness, its unyielding strength, we draw from it." He gestured to the ground beneath them. "We shield our lands with protective wards, carve runes to keep the worst evils at bay." His jaw hardened. "But it is never enough."

The Centurions around him murmured their agreement. Some stamped their hooves.

"We lost many," he finally said. "Some died in the war. Others were taken. Our numbers are fewer now. That is why we protect our females and younglings fiercely. For our survival."

Malrik pushed his glasses up his nose. He let Khazar's words sink in.

"I hear you," he said. "I won't pretend to understand the pain your people carry, but I recognize it."

Khazar studied him, his gaze unwavering.

Malrik took a slow breath. "But the Aelvor," he glanced at Ashael, then to the others, "have been nothing but allies to us. They protected us when we knew nothing of this world. They stand with us now not because they must, but because they choose to."

Khazar's dark eyes moved from one of them to the next. His fingers tapped once against his spear, steady and slow. The air around him tensed, like a bow drawn but not yet released. Malrik's hands curled into fists at his sides, bracing for the answer he didn't want to hear.

"For tonight, you will have shelter," he said, but the lines around his mouth stayed tight. "You will not be harmed."

His gaze lingered on the Aelvors a moment longer, as if silently warning them.

Malrik heard Clara exhale in relief.

"Now, human," Khazar said, his tone sharp but measured. "It is time for you to answer my question. Why travel with the Aelvor?"

Malrik nodded. This was going better than he had hoped. "Clara and I were chased by the Dravok into this world when the Aelvor found us."

241

Khazar's expression remained impassive. "And why is that?"

Malrik met his gaze. "We believe it's connected to restoring the Vaelithar. That is what brought us here. We are making for the volcanic lands. We were ambushed by the Dravok and its commander on our way there."

A murmur spread among the Centurions, subtle but unmistakable. More than a few warriors tightened the grip on their spears.

"Then there may be truth in the stories foretold," one of them said.

Khazar held up his hand in silence. "We have fought the Dravok since the beginning. We do not tolerate their presence near our lands. When we patrol, we make sure none come close to our borders." He hit his spear on the ground. "You will leave at first light. I will not risk harm to my people by sheltering you for longer. We will show you the way to the volcanic lands, and you will not return."

"We thank you for sheltering us," said Malrik.

He glanced at Clara, whose shoulders had visibly relaxed. She looked tired, as they all did, still feeling the effects of a sleepless night and the ember, but she was much more at ease. For now, it was enough.

CHAPTER 18

After Malrik had successfully negotiated with the Centurions, they'd led them to a small sleeping area between two large trees. In the dim light of the canopy, it was easy to fall asleep.

When she woke, the light had changed and grown darker. It was well into the evening. She sat up and rubbed her eyes. She must have slept the whole day. Her companions had long since awakened. They stay in uneasy silence, watching the camp.

Malrik, however, was in a good mood. He spoke with some of the Centurions near the border of the sleeping area. She remembered the confidence with which he had led them and smiled to herself. She was proud of him. He had saved them and spared further bloodshed.

A few of the Centurions who stood watch over them brought them all wooden bowls filled with steaming broth, along with plates of roasted vegetables, nuts, and dried herbs. Clara accepted it gratefully. She hadn't realized how much she had missed the comfort of a hot meal until now. The vegetable broth, the roasted roots, and the fresh nuts were simple but satisfying. For the first time in days, Clara felt full. The warmth of it still lingered in her stomach, a small but precious relief after the day they had endured.

After she ate, Clara looked around, taking in the camp. The trees here were colossal and tightly packed, their massive trunks aligning so closely that they formed a near-perfect circle, enclosing a space vast enough to hold all the Centurions along with their group. Their canopies intertwined above, creating an impenetrable shield that let no rain seep through. Only a single narrow opening disrupted the enclosure, just wide enough for one to pass. The air within was cool and dry, a stark contrast to the dampness of the forest beyond.

Scattered across the soft, moss-covered ground, Centurions lay in deep rest. Some stretched out with their arms crossed over their chests. Others leaned against the bark, seemingly asleep, even while standing. A few rested against each other, their massive forms pressed together in peaceful repose, breathing steady and untroubled.

Clara's eyes drifted toward Ashael. He sat apart from the others, lost in thought, his expression shadowed beneath the dim firelight. He studied the flames with his usual calm. The sight brought her comfort.

Clara exhaled softly. They had survived the Centurions. They had shelter. They had food. She watched the rest of her group. Elyndra and Selandor sat close to one another, their heads bent and voices lowered. Kira, who had been lying down, started to sit up. She had used the ember's power and carried Malrik. No wonder she looked tired.

Vaelin, however, sat apart from the group. There hadn't been time to confront him about Seraphis. Why had she known him? Clara rested her chin on her knuckles, her gaze narrowed slightly as she watched him in silence.

He sat rigidly, fingers flexing at his sides, jaw tightening. As if he wanted to say something but didn't know how.

Clara frowned and pushed herself to her feet. She walked toward him with purpose, ready to ask him what he knew about Seraphis and her trap. From across the clearing, Malrik moved toward them. Ashael, too, roused himself from his contemplation and moved toward the others.

She opened her mouth, about to demand Vaelin spit it out, but Selandor beat her to it.

"Vaelin," Selandor's voice cut through the quiet, firm but steady. "We've been scouting together for ages, but I never knew about Seraphis."

Elyndra crossed her arms. "Neither did I. You clearly had a history with her." She looked away for a moment, then back at him. Her voice wavered slightly before she caught it. "All we ever knew was that you were once part of Veylora's army. But maybe you have something more to tell us."

The words hung thick in the air.

Vaelin exhaled slowly, running a hand over his face. He looked tired. "I don't know if I will ever truly earn your trust," he admitted. "I don't know if I ever had it to begin with." His eyes darted toward Selandor, then Elyndra. "But I did know that telling you about my sister would have made earning it even harder."

Clara's mouth dropped. His *sister*?

Vaelin sighed. "I should have told you before. I know that now. I just—" He hesitated, then shook his head. "No excuses. I should have told you."

Selandor's expression hardened. "Yes. You should have."

Elyndra's lips pressed into a thin line. "So that's it," she murmured. "That's why you've been pushing me away."

Vaelin's gaze snapped to her.

She let out a sharp breath. "I thought you didn't trust me. That you wanted to keep your distance. But it was never about that, was it? You were hiding this from me."

Vaelin opened his mouth, but before he could defend himself, Ashael spoke.

"He's fought with us." His tone was calm and measured. His sharp blue eyes locked onto Vaelin. "Even when Seraphis was there, you still chose to fight against her." A small pause. "That means something."

Vaelin's jaw tensed. For a moment, he looked at Ashael, searching for something in his expression, then nodded.

"I used to be one of Veylora's commanders," he said. "At the time, I thought I was doing what was best for Avenora." His fingers twitched against his knee. "But I was wrong."

Clara exchanged a glance with Malrik, whose mouth was set in a grim line.

Vaelin's gaze darkened. "My sister, Seraphis, was always ambitious. Always ruthless. When I started to see the truth, when I realized I was on the wrong side of this war . . . I left." His fingers curled into a fist. "I tried to take her with me. She refused. She knew that when I left, she could take my place. She wanted that power."

Malrik's frown deepened. "If you were a commander before and now Seraphis is, how come she looks like that, but you look like this?"

"I left before the corruption could take hold. Veylora chooses who receives her power. Not all of her followers are given it." His jaw set. "The Dravok are nothing but weapons. They follow orders. Nothing more. But commanders like Seraphis? They're different. More powerful."

He exhaled, his voice lowering. "The Dravok are the blades. Commanders like Seraphis wield them."

Clara's throat felt tight. "So, not everyone under Veylora is like them?"

Vaelin shook his head. "No. Most of them are just people. They aren't corrupted, but they live under her rule, terrified of what will happen if they disobey. Not everyone who follows her does so by choice."

Clara's mind raced, piecing everything together. The whispers, the tension she had noticed before, the way the other Aelvors had looked at Vaelin. They had known something about him was different but not everything. And now the truth had finally surfaced.

She studied him carefully. The way his shoulders held that subdued guilt, the way his voice didn't waver even under scrutiny. But could he really be trusted?

Beside her, Kira stayed silent, her sharp eyes sweeping over the group, listening to every word. Selandor's expression remained wary, his jaw tight. Elyndra's wasn't much different. Malrik, for his part, remained neutral, but Clara could sense his skepticism.

Then there was Ashael. He kept his gaze locked onto Vaelin. "I believe in second chances," he said simply. "And you've proven yourself time and time again."

Vaelin held his stare for a moment, then gave a small nod.

The conversation drifted into quieter voices, tension lingering but no longer suffocating.

Clara caught Vaelin and Elyndra moving slightly farther away, their hushed voices just out of reach.

Vaelin's tone was low and careful, and Elyndra's was still sharp, but something had changed. She wasn't walking away.

The longer Clara watched them, the more she could see it. Vaelin wasn't just trying to explain himself. He was trying to pull her back in. And Elyndra, after a moment, let him.

Clara let out a slow breath, forcing herself to look away. She should have felt relieved that the tension in the group had settled. That the night wouldn't end in a rift.

But something else burned at the edge of her mind. Something important. Something she had almost forgotten in all the chaos.

The Syralen Cove. The words Ashael and Malrik had spoken in their trance. Clara's stomach tightened. She longed for answers. And she wasn't letting it go this time. The words Ashael and Malrik had spoken under the lure of the Syralens' song refused to fade. They looped through her mind like an unsolved puzzle, pressing against her with underlying urgency.

Maybe it was nothing. But how could she even begin to ask them?

"Clara."

Her thoughts snapped into focus at the sound of Ashael's voice.

He was watching her. His piercing blue eyes fixated on her face. His head tilted just slightly, the way he did when he was picking up on something others might miss. It was something she had seen him do when training, or during council meetings.

"What's on your mind?" he asked.

Clara's shoulders tensed, and she looked away. "It's nothing," she said quickly.

When she glanced back, his eyes were still on her. Clara felt her cheeks grow hot under his scrutiny.

Then, Malrik, ever perceptive, leaned forward, his brow arching. "Yeah, Clara," he said, voice laced with amusement. "You're acting fidgety all of a sudden. I know something's up."

Clara hesitated for half a second longer, then sighed, pressing her hands together in her lap. "All right," she muttered. "Fine. I just . . . I wanted to ask you both something."

Ashael and Malrik exchanged a brief glance.

She took a slow breath. "Do you remember anything from the Syralen Cove? When you both went into that trance?"

Malrik stared at the ground, like the answer might be buried beneath it. "I . . . I'm trying," he admitted, rubbing the back of his neck. "But it's cloudy. I remember the feeling of being pulled into something, like I was on the verge of understanding." He exhaled in frustration. "But the details are gone."

Clara tried not to let her disappointment show, but Ashael must have noticed.

"I remember bits and pieces," he said.

Clara's breath hitched as she turned to him. "You do?"

Ashael's expression was thoughtful. "Not everything," he admitted. "But there was something. A strong feeling, like I was realizing something. Like something important had come to the surface."

Clara stiffened. Her mind raced back to the words Ashael had spoken in the trance—the way his voice had sounded when he said them.

"It's you, Clara."

The memory sent a rush of heat through her. Was that what he had realized about her? The way he had looked at her made her stomach feel like it was filled with fireflies, warm and bright and buzzing. She curled her hands into fists, trying to will the feeling away.

Ashael's focus settled on her, his gaze searching, as if sensing her sudden shift in demeanor. "Clara?"

She swallowed hard, forcing a quick nod. "I'm fine."

That came out way too fast.

Ashael raised an eyebrow, not convinced. His lips parted slightly, as if on the verge of saying something. The moment stretched, then he blushed.

It was barely there, almost hidden beneath the firelight, but Clara saw it.

And Clara, already flustered beyond reason, felt her own face burn hotter in response. She immediately dropped her gaze, mortified.

Ashael cleared his throat and stood. "We should get some rest," he announced briskly. "We have an early start tomorrow."

Malrik raised a brow at him but didn't argue, stretching out with an easy yawn. "Not a bad idea."

Clara barely nodded, her mind still spinning. So many questions. So many tangled feelings. But right now, there was nothing she could do about any of them.

"Wait, Malrik."

He paused and looked at her expectantly. His gaze was soft and warm. It felt like home.

"I never said thank you. For speaking with the Centurions. You saved us all."

Malrik squirmed and pushed his glasses up his nose. "Well, they were only going to listen to a human male, and seeing as I was the only one available—"

Clara cut him off. "But you stepped in before you knew that. I should have said it earlier. Thank you."

Malrik shrugged and gave her a wry smile. "You're welcome."

A moment of comfortable silence wrapped around them. Clara felt her eyes grow heavy. Her insides still stirred with emotion, but exhaustion was pulling her under. She murmured goodnight and lay down, forcing her mind to quiet. Tomorrow, she would find her focus. Tomorrow, there would be no distractions.

CHAPTER 19

Morning arrived in silence. The air was crisp, the settlement still wrapped in the hush of dawn. But beneath that stillness, anticipation hummed. To Clara, it felt like a low, restless energy that coiled in her chest.

Clara adjusted the strap of her pack, fingers brushing against the pendant at her neck. It wasn't warm, not yet, but there was a sensation there, a subtle awareness. As if it, too, knew they were drawing near to something important.

Khazar and a small group of Centurions waited at the edge of the settlement. The Centurion leader was as imposing as ever, his eyes cool, assessing, as the group approached.

"Your path is set," Khazar said, his voice like stone over steel. "With Aelvor speed, you will reach the volcanic lands before noon. But tread carefully. Fire has a way of revealing truth."

Malrik hesitated, then stepped forward. "Thank you for sparing us, though I still don't see how I made a difference."

Khazar's gaze was unyielding. "Human, you showed three things that deserve respect."

Everyone stilled.

"Courage. Selflessness. Hope." His voice was firm. "Perhaps sparing you will not be for nothing." His tone hardened. "Do not make me regret it."

Malrik held his gaze. Then, finally, he gave a small nod.

Khazar shifted his attention to a young Centurion. "Baragh, show them the way out."

The Centurion inclined his head and stepped forward, motioning for them to follow. He led them through the narrow passage to where the trees thinned, revealing the first stretch of their journey. Baragh pointed toward the distant horizon, where a wispy plume of steam drifted into the sky.

"Follow this route." There was something softer in Baragh's expression as he looked at them. Unlike Khazar, his words lacked the same hardened steel. "May the path be kind to you."

Clara inclined her head in return. "And may yours be safe."

Baragh gave a brief nod before stepping back, watching as they prepared to leave.

An uneasiness still clung to the group. Clara's gaze flicked to Elyndra. Her silence cut sharper than any words. And though no one said it, Malrik's glance toward Vaelin held an unspoken edge of suspicion.

Without a word, Kira shifted and lowered herself, allowing Malrik to mount. As he adjusted his grip, her talons flexed briefly against the earth, wings rustling as though barely restraining themselves.

"To the Phylarix . . ." she murmured, almost to herself.

Malrik glanced down at her, then forward. They shot into the skies in a gust of wind.

Ashael led the group from the ground. He waited as they secured their packs and weapons. Clara rolled her shoulders, preparing for the journey ahead.

"Let's go," commanded Ashael.

They ran into the trees, heading for the craggy landscape.

Their journey to the volcanic lands was smooth. The Centurions had directed them well. The path was clear, and no Dravok haunted their steps. They ran most of the day, stopping only occasionally to let Kira rest. As they neared the edge of the volcanic lands, the change in the environment was undeniable.

Instead of a barren wasteland, life flourished. The flora here was lusher, more vibrant, untouched by corruption. Clara had expected an ashen wasteland, but the volcanic rocks were covered in a jungle-like ecosystem. Trees bearing thick, broad leaves glowed softly, while flowers bloomed in breathtaking hues of deep blues, fiery oranges, radiant purples. The air itself felt different, charged, humming with unseen energy.

Up ahead, the closest volcano loomed, just minutes away. Clara slowed, a strange sensation prickling against her skin.

"A barrier," Ashael murmured, his pace faltering. "Not like the others we've encountered. This one is . . . magnetic. It's drawing at something we don't understand."

Clara resisted the urge to shudder.

Kira and Malrik descended from the sky to join them on the ground. Malrik stretched his arms above his head. Kira shifted, then conferred with Ashael as the group continued on foot, reporting on what she had seen.

A strange smell tickled Clara's nose as they walked, sulfurous yet sweet. Was it the barrier? They continued onward, pushing softly against the magical barrier, stepping over black stone. They rounded a bend and Clara gasped.

Dozens of hot springs, their surfaces shimmering with soft steam, reflected the sky in deep sapphire hues.

Splash!

Water sprayed into the air as Malrik launched himself into the nearest spring, emerging with a wide grin. He'd removed his Aelvor coat and shirt, and his glasses faster than she could blink. "Well? Don't just stand there."

Elyndra and Selandor followed, removing their outer garments and wading into the water, sighing as the warmth enveloped them.

Clara hesitated for only a moment before kicking off her own shoes, removing her overcoat, and sliding in. If it was dangerous, Elyndra and Selandor wouldn't have gone in. The heat wrapped around her like a forgotten embrace, melting the exhaustion from her bones. She let the water hold her and floated idly for a moment, taking in the wide expanse of sky above her.

"Didn't take you for the type to enjoy this," Malrik teased, floating beside her.

She smirked, lazily swiping a hand through the water, sending a small wave toward him.

Malrik raised a brow. "Oh, that's how it is?"

Before she could blink, he lunged.

Clara let out a startled laugh as he splashed water straight at her face. "Malrik!" She coughed, pushing her soaked hair back.

His grin widened. "You started it."

Then, before she could retaliate, Malrik sank beneath the surface.

Clara waited, expecting him to pop up behind her to pull another prank, but he was gone long enough that her attention wavered. Steam floated around her. Then the wind gusted, blowing away the clouds of warm fog. A splash behind her caught her attention. Clara whirled, prepared for Malrik, but her heart stuttered as Ashael emerged from the water.

His head tilted back, as he brushed strands of damp golden hair away from his face. Sunlight caught the droplets clinging to his skin, tracing the sharp angles of his cheekbones, the smooth line of his jaw. He exhaled slowly, blinking the water from his lashes, and met her stare.

Clara's breath stalled. For a moment, everything else faded—the laughter, the heat, even the sensation of water against her skin.

Ashael didn't move, didn't speak. He just . . . watched her.

Clara tore her gaze away from him, heart thudding, willing the moment to pass.

A sudden surge of water crashed over her, followed by Malrik's laughter.

"Thought you'd be safe while I was gone?" he teased, grinning as he surfaced.

Clara turned too quickly, ready to scold him, but her foot slipped against the smooth stone beneath the water. She yelped and tipped sideways. The water rushed up to swallow her. Before she crashed in, Malrik's hands gripped her arms, steadying her. His grip was firm, heat radiating from where he held her. His laugh softened, eyes glinting with amusement.

"Careful, Valenwood," he murmured, voice lower than before. His smile pulled at his lips, which were unnervingly close. His laugh, low and rich, sent a strange twist through her stomach.

What is wrong with me?

She tried to brush it off, the strange swell of emotion, shaking her head as she pulled away, but the moment had already lodged deep in her chest.

Clara shut her eyes and dipped beneath the water, hoping the heat would drown out her conflicting thoughts. She needed to get a grip. Enough distractions. She'd vowed to put her emotions aside, to remain focused. She surfaced, gasping for air.

"The water will not slow your journey, but time will." Kira stood at the edge of the pool with her arms crossed. "I tried to shift, to scout above, but something is holding me back."

Just like that, the moment was gone.

Clara exchanged a glance with Malrik, then Ashael. One by one, they pulled themselves from the water, the warmth fading into the air as quickly as it had settled. The fun was over. It was time to move.

Clara exhaled in relief as the last of the moisture evaporated from her skin, her Aelvor underclothing drying as swiftly as always. At least that was one thing she could be grateful for in this unpredictable world. She fastened the rest of her outerwear into place and pulled on her boots before glancing at the others.

Ashael turned to Kira. "Try shifting again."

Kira's expression darkened, but she obeyed, closing her eyes, attempting to transform. She let out a sharp breath. "Still nothing."

Ashael frowned.

Selandor tensed. "It's not just her. Something is wrong."

Clara watched as the other Aelvor subtly shifted their weight, expressions tightening with realization.

"My senses . . ." Elyndra murmured. "They're weaker."

Vaelin flexed his fingers. "There is something dampening our power."

Clara glanced at her Zaralis, expecting the faint hum of energy she had begun to grow used to. But there was nothing. The anklet felt muted, like it had never awakened at all. "Was it the water?" she asked. They'd all jumped in, too eager for relief to really weigh the consequences.

Ashael shook his head. "Kira did not join us in the springs."

"It has to be the volcanic lands themselves," Malrik said as he ran his thumb along his jaw. "A protective measure. A ward. Something keeping outsiders from using their strengths."

Clara's throat felt dry. Whatever this place was hiding, it didn't want them at full strength.

Selandor exhaled, nodding ahead. "Good thing we're almost at the foot of the volcano."

They set off again, their pace slower as an invisible weight pressed against them.

As they walked, Clara sidled up beside Elyndra. "You've been quiet," Clara murmured. "Something's bothering you."

Elyndra hesitated before saying, "Sel and I were talking earlier. We've been thinking about . . . Vaelin."

Clara's stomach tensed. "What about him?" Vaelin walked at the front with Ashael. Given how their powers were dampened, it seemed unlikely that he would hear them.

Elyndra exhaled. "What if he led Seraphis to us?"

Clara's mind faltered, but before she could respond, Malrik's voice cut in. "You're not the only ones wondering."

He stepped up to walk alongside them, his expression grim. "I've been thinking about it too," Malrik admitted. "He left Veylora's army, but who's to say he won't switch sides again?"

A sharp inhale came from ahead. Vaelin had stopped walking.

So much for him not hearing them.

Slowly, he turned to face them, his features guarded, but his fists were clenched at his sides. "If I were going to betray you, I would have done it a long time ago."

No one spoke.

Vaelin's features hardened. "I would give my life for this cause. For all of you."

Clara swallowed hard, her thoughts tangling. Elyndra's concern, Malrik's suspicion, Vaelin's conviction all weaved together to create a web of uncertainty.

"Enough," Ashael said, stepping forward, his voice commanding. "We don't have time for this. I've made my stance clear, as has Vaelin. To continue to question is to harm our progress."

The conversation effectively ended. Clara felt a pang of guilt as Vaelin walked ahead, distancing himself from the rest of the group. They walked at a steady, slight incline in silence.

Clara let out a slow breath, her fingers instinctively brushing against the pendant at her chest. A sudden warmth pulsed against her chest and her side. It wasn't just the pendant that radiated warmth. She halted. "The map," she whispered and fumbled for her pocket.

Ashael was already beside her, glancing at it. Clara unfolded the parchment, watching as new markings glowed against its smooth surface.

"It's guiding us," she said, her voice tight with certainty.

Their eyes lifted toward the towering volcano ahead.

"The path is clear," Ashael murmured.

They moved forward, following a trail previously hidden from view that wound up the volcanic rock. They would never have found it without the map's help. It was tucked between two pillars of black, pocked rock, only visible if you knew where to look. The rocks created a mirage, obscuring the path unless you knew right where it was. It was wide enough to walk two across, but as they climbed, the path narrowed, and the heat thickened.

Slowed by their lack of magic, Clara felt entirely human. She could tell that Malrik, who groaned now and then, did too. Sweat dripped down her brow and back as they climbed for what felt like hours. Her back ached, and her breath came in gasps. Then, the map pulsed hotly again, and Clara saw it. A dark opening, set into the side of the volcano.

She looked up at the volcano. They weren't quite at the peak, but they were far above the foot of the mountain.

Her pendant pulsed again as she squinted at the mouth of the cave. Her stomach twisted, but not with fear. It was drawing her in. "This is it," she murmured.

Without another word, the group stepped forward into the darkness.

CHAPTER 20

The air was thicker inside the cave. It wasn't just the silence, though it stretched, vast and hollow, as if the cavern itself were watching. It was the shift, the way the space around them seemed to hold its breath.

Clara's boots scuffed against the uneven stone as she stepped forward. The cave was massive, its walls towering so high they disappeared into darkness. The only light came from the entrance, barely stretching past the threshold before the shadows swallowed it whole. She reached for the light vial Ceyndor had given them, its glow spilling into the cavern, pushing back the darkness as they ventured deeper.

With bated breath, they walked as silently as possible through the cavern. Suddenly, the ground vanished. A jagged cliff cut through their path, plunging into a seemingly endless abyss. Clara's stomach plummeted as she stepped closer, peering down into the void. The blackness stretched infinitely, swallowing all light and all sound, pulling her in. She felt the darkness reach up for her; her chest swayed forward ever so slightly, carrying her closer to the void.

"Clara, step back!" Malrik's voice rang out.

She blinked, suddenly aware of how close to the edge she was, how far she leaned over. She took a quick step back to prevent herself from falling.

Before Clara could catch her breath, the earth trembled.

A deep, low groan echoed beneath them, as the cavern floor vibrated. A sharp crack split through the stone, fissures splintering below.

A dull red glow pulsed from the depths, faint at first, then deepening, shifting from ember-red to molten gold.

Ashael yanked her back, and the party scurried away from the lava that slithered through the cracks. Glowing veins pooled into a slow-moving river below. Heat licked Clara's skin.

And from the inferno something moved.

A shape, engulfed in flames. Dripping lava, trailing fire, wings unfurling like banners of molten light. It ascended, regal and commanding, before descending in a slow, deliberate arc.

With a burst of heat and flame, it landed on a small, narrow stone jutting from the cavern wall. It was just near the edge of the ledge where they stood, slightly above, no higher than the tallest among them.

Roughly the size of an eagle, its body glowed, streaked with hues of crimson and deep orange. Its feathers shifted in color like dying embers, while its long, flowing tail trailed behind it.

Even as the flames around it faded, the creature itself remained luminous, its radiance painting the cavern walls in shifting shadows.

It stared at them but did not speak. It did not need to. Its presence alone demanded reverence.

Beside her, Kira lowered herself onto a knee without a word, her entire body sinking in silent awe.

To Kira, this was sacred.

The Phylarix remained still, its piercing amber-gold eyes observing them. Then, as if the earth moved with it, it lifted its wings in a steady arc. Heat rolled through the air, and embers drifted from its feathers like fading sparks.

Another deep rumble echoed through the cavern.

From the lava below, a single stone pole shot up. It was cylindrical, rough-edged, and wide enough for only one person to stand on.

Then another emerged, bursting from the lava, heading the Phylarix's call. And another. One by one, seven stone poles broke through from the molten river, forming a precarious path toward the other side of the abyss.

Beyond them, another ledge stretched from the cavern wall, its base disappearing into shadow. At the far end, atop an elevated rock platform, something lay shrouded in darkness.

Clara's pendant pulsed against her chest. In her pocket, the map grew warm. This was it. Clara knew what to do.

The Phylarix gave its wing a slow sweep, like a silent push forward.

Vaelin exhaled sharply. "A trial." He stepped forward first. "I'll go."

He stepped forward before anyone could stop him. Clara bit her lip and knew that their conversation earlier drove his determination to prove himself. But the moment his boot touched the first stone, it gave way.

The pole trembled, dropping fast, sinking toward the lava below.

Malrik swore.

Elyndra gasped and yanked Vaelin back just as the stone plunged lower. The instant his foot left the pedestal, the rock halted. Then, it slowly rose again, reforming and resetting.

Clara's pulse pounded in her ears. The Phylarix's gaze lingered, unyielding, piercing, as if seeing through her. Weighing her. Waiting.

A silent certainty settled over her. She felt it in her bones, and in the pendant's pulse, the map's silent pull. Clara turned to the others, steadying herself. "I think . . . I think it's me."

A hand shot out to stop her. Before doubt could creep in, she stepped forward.

One foot onto the stone. Clara held her breath, waiting for the pillar to begin sinking into the boiling lava below. But it held.

She looked forward. Her ears were ringing; she couldn't hear what the others were saying. A dangerously wide gap yawned between the next set of poles. Clara tensed. Moments like this really made her wish for longer legs.

She inhaled sharply, bent her knees, and leapt.

"Clara!" Malrik's voice slashed through the silence.

A rush of gasps echoed, magnified tenfold by the cavern's echo.

Her boots hit the stone, then slipped. She lurched forward, panic spiking, but her arms flung out, catching her balance just in time.

She exhaled shakily, heart hammering. Whatever this was, it was meant for her. She leapt forward, gritting her teeth as she sailed through the hot air. Again and again, until the final step was within reach.

Clara exhaled as the heat of the lava below lapped against her skin. She brushed a bead of sweat from her eyes, blinking away the sting. One more step. Just one.

She lifted her foot, ready to launch herself onto the last pillar, then slammed into something unseen.

A force, invisible yet solid, pushed against her like a wall that wouldn't budge. She tried again, harder this time, frustration rising in her chest. Nothing.

"I can't move forward," she called over the sounds of burbling lava below.

The group went still. A few shifted where they stood.

"What is it?" Malrik called.

Clara pressed her palm against the air in front of her. It rested against a barrier. "There's something here." She turned, pulse quickening. "Something's stopping me."

Malrik adjusted his glasses, then scanned the standing stone poles before them. "We're missing something."

They all studied the seven stone poles rising from the lava, rough and solid, forming a treacherous path ahead.

Clara pressed her lips together, her eyes narrowing as she tried to piece it together. Something about this felt intentional.

The Phylarix remained motionless on its perch, its glowing eyes fixed on them. Watching. Waiting. When no one moved, the Phylarix let out a sharp, resonant cry. Then another, and another, until seven distinct cries echoed through the cavern, each one falling like the next tick of the second hand of a clock.

Clara's stomach twisted. Her gaze traced between the Phylarix and the stones. Seven cries. Seven steps. Realization settled over her. "There are seven of us," she called back.

"And seven stones. That can't be a coincidence," Selandor said.

Malrik frowned. "But what happened to Vaelin earlier? The step rejected him."

"Maybe it's Clara who has to go first," Elyndra said, glancing at the Phylarix, whose glowing eyes still bore into them, unmoving. "Maybe that's the order."

"But who follows?" Selandor challenged. "If we're wrong, the step could sink again."

Ashael's voice was quiet but certain. "We all have to be on the steps."

A long silence. How were they to know who should follow behind Clara?

"Only one way to find out." Ashael stepped forward.

Clara barely breathed as his boot met the next stone. It held. Tension knotted in her chest.

Ashael exhaled, testing his footing. "It's good."

The ache in Clara's chest eased slightly as Ashael leapt to the next step, then another. He made it look effortless. Every motion was controlled, like he was back in the warrior's training ring.

He reached the step beside Clara and stopped. They both looked behind to the others who waited on the ledge.

Malrik rolled his shoulders, inhaled sharply, then smirked. "My turn."

He stepped forward, and the stone pillar held his weight.

One by one, the others followed suit. Vaelin, Elyndra, Kira, then Selandor.

No sinking. No rejection. They had all been meant to stand here.

Clara smiled in relief as Selandor leapt onto the last pillar. They had passed the Phylarix's first puzzle. Then the stones shuddered beneath them.

The stone poles beneath their feet began to sink, slow at first, then faster. The lava below churned, bubbling violently as the heat rose. Sweat formed at Clara's brow.

"No, no, no," she breathed.

"We need to get off—" Elyndra's voice sharpened with alarm.

"There's nowhere to go!" Selandor shouted.

The sinking quickened. The molten river rose, and flecks of molten rock and burning embers reached for them. Clara's knees shook as unbearable heat rose, threatening to choke her. She couldn't think, couldn't move as the pillars sank lower and lower.

A keening wail split the air. The Phylarix dove, blazing. It plunged past them, skimming the molten river, then surged upward.

It circled once, then shot toward the far ledge, fire trailing in its wake.

With a final burst of flame, it landed directly before Clara. Light erupted. Fire flared across the cavern, shadows recoiling.

It had descended, only to rise again. Its very movement was a message.

Ashael's eyes snapped to the Phylarix. "A phoenix doesn't just burn," he said. "It must rise from the ashes."

Kira whispered, soft and reverent. "Rebirth." The word left her lips like a prayer.

But Clara still didn't move. The Phylarix didn't just rise. It burned first. Her mind raced, the heat pressing down on her like a living thing. "What if . . ." She hesitated, then forced the words out. "What if it's not just about standing here?"

The Phylarix's golden eyes glowed, unblinking. Its gaze bore into her, expectant.

"It's not enough," she whispered. "It's not enough to just be here. We have to acknowledge something. Burn something away."

Vaelin's fists clenched. "I carry the sins of my past." His voice was hoarse, unsteady. "But I want to be more than my mistakes."

The moment the words left his lips, his step began to rise.

Clara's pendant pressed against her chest, insistent and heavy. Uncertainty threatened to pull her under. She closed her eyes. "I am torn," she whispered, steady despite the war inside her. "But I will find clarity."

Her step rose, pulling away from the fiery lava.

"It's working!" Malrik's voice rang out, full of disbelief and hope. With a steady breath, he squared his shoulders. "I have doubted myself, but I choose to believe I can be more."

His step rose.

Ashael's gaze wavered, then steadied. "I have feared what I'm becoming." A breath. "But I will not fight it."

His step rose.

One by one, the rest followed, voicing their truths, admitting their burdens, their hopes for renewal. The stone pillars continued to rise, higher than before, reaching for the ceiling of the cavern.

The roar of the molten river below softened, fading as they rose. Heat still swirled through the air, but the threat of the fire receded.

The pillars shuddered to a stop. Clara's step abutted the lip of the ledge they had been trying to reach. Clara stepped forward, leaving space for the rest of the group to follow. The last of them reached the other side, stepping onto solid footing at last.

For a moment, no one spoke. Clara exhaled, letting her shoulders drop. Her frantic pulse began to slow. They'd made it. They were alive. Ahead, the Phylarix rested atop a nest of coals, perched on a low stone platform that rose to about Clara's hip. They glowed fiery orange and red, their heat rippling through the air. But something about the creature itself had changed. It no longer held itself tall and poised.

Its wings drooped, the fire along its feathers dimming to a weak glow. Its piercing eyes, once so watchful and intense, seemed dim and clouded.

She stiffened, every sense suddenly on edge. Something wasn't right. Before she could react, the Phylarix's body ignited, its entire form swallowed by fire.

Clara gaped, too stunned to speak.

The flames blazed impossibly bright, so intense that Clara had to shield her eyes, squinting against the glare. The cavern around them flashed gold, orange, and red before plunging into darkness.

Clara blinked, adjusting to the sudden dimness. The nest was still there, but the Phylarix was gone. Her heart clenched. She took a hesitant step forward. Then another.

At the center of the smoldering coals, a pile of soft, gray ash rested where the Phylarix had been. Smoke rose in thin curls from it, spiraling into the air. It was gone.

A lump formed in Clara's throat. Even though she had barely known the creature, even though it had felt almost unreal, its absence hit her like a loss.

The ashes shifted.

The movement was subtle, small but unmistakable.

Slowly, Clara stepped closer and leaned in to examine the remains. Something round peeked from beneath the ash. Her pulse quickened. She reached out, brushing away the soot with careful fingers, and revealed an egg.

A thin, radiant crack split its shell as soon as her fingers grazed it.

Hope swelled inside her.

Another crack formed. Then another. A soft glow pulsed from within the shell.

Then, the egg shattered. A newborn Phylarix emerged, small yet brilliant, its form bathed in molten radiance. It gave a small, uncertain shake, wings twitching, then flapped once. Then twice.

Before their eyes, the tiny creature expanded, its form shifting, stretching, flames rippling along its feathers. Its wings broadened, its glow intensified, and within moments, the majestic Phylarix stood before them once more, fully grown.

Clara stared, entranced.

The Phylarix opened its beak, and a soft, melodic sound filled the cavern. It reminded Clara of a harp, each note smooth and light. Her chest loosened. Her shoulders dropped. It felt like hearing a favorite song after a long day. Warmth spread through her limbs, steady and quiet, easing a tension she hadn't noticed until it was gone.

A golden tear slipped from the Phylarix's eye. It fell, landing on the broken eggshell. The Phylarix stretched its wings, fire gliding along its feathers. Then it vanished. A tender warmth lingered in the air.

Clara exhaled. Where the Phylarix had gone, she did not know. Her gaze dropped. The broken eggshell still lay there. Nestled inside, something gently aglow caught her eye. Curious, she reached down and carefully lifted it from the fragments of shell. It was smooth and warm in her palm. A semi-translucent sphere, swirling with molten gold and ash. The two elements danced within it but never merged, just like the pearl from the Syralen Cove.

Her pendant gave a muted throb where it lay against her chest. Clara frowned. It was the same size and had a similar appearance to the pearl, but inside, this item was different.

Her fingers tightened around it. What did it mean? Another artifact. Another clue.

Were they really getting closer to the Vaelithar shard? Or just gathering more unanswered questions?

As she held the artifact, the air cooled down. The heat that had pressed against them since the beginning of this trial faded. The molten river was gone. The cracks in the ground sealed themselves, the cavern falling into deep, reverent silence.

Behind her, Kira gasped.

Her form shimmered, then shifted into wings, talons, feathers. She looked down at herself, stunned. "I can shift again."

Selandor flexed his fingers, testing his grip. "I can feel it too."

The weight was gone. Their senses were clear and unburdened.

Clara curled her fingers around the artifact. Her Zaralis hummed pleasantly, waiting for her to use its power.

Behind the nest of coals, now gone dark and quiet, a crack of light filtered through the gloom. Wordlessly, the group made for it, walking along the sturdy ledge. They emerged back onto the side of the mountain.

As they stepped outside, Clara turned to the others and held up the lava sphere.

Elyndra's eyes narrowed. "It looks like the first clue."

Malrik crossed his arms. "First water, now fire." He exhaled. "What's next?"

Clara dove her fingers into her pocket. "The map will show us the way. Just like before."

The group gathered close, ready to see what the Phylarix's treasure would reveal to them. Clara hovered the lava sphere over the map. Heat surged through the parchment. She flinched, fingers tightening around the sphere.

A gust of wind erupted from the map, bursting outward as if the map itself had exhaled. The force ripped the parchment from her grasp.

"No!"

The wind howled, and the map spiraled forward, carried as if by unseen hands.

They all ran after it.

It danced around them, borne on gusts of wind that jerked it out of reach from their fingers, as if it were playing with them. Clara's knees barked as she jumped from a ledge of lava rock, her fingertips brushed the edges, but it pulled away from her.

They ran, down then up, cresting over ledges and plunging back down in a mad dash. As they circled around to the north side of the volcano, the map faltered on a dying gust.

Clara lunged and caught it just in time.

But as she lifted her head, ready to shout to her companions that she'd caught it, she froze. There, before them, suspended in the sky just beyond reach, was a floating island.

Clara stared, disbelieving. Her mind reeled. This wasn't possible. Not in her world. Islands didn't float. Land didn't hover over nothingness.

Malrik, out of breath from their chase, placed his hands on his knees. "Unbelievable."

The island hovered close enough so that they could see the outline of its forests and waterfalls that cascaded over its edge, spilling into nothingness.

On the map, a new symbol had appeared, the outline of a floating island. An exact match to what was before them.

Selandor exhaled sharply. "The Floating Island of the Nyths." His voice was barely a breath. "It never stays in one place. It's not meant to be found. And yet . . . here we are."

The map had led them to their next location. An island in the sky, just out of reach.

CHAPTER 21

The fire crackled low, its embers casting long shadows across the stone outcrop where they'd made camp. Above them, stars scattered across the sky. The scent of ember and ash still clung to their clothes, reminding them of the hell they'd just survived. Clara sat a short distance from the others, the warmth of the fire at her back, the chill of the altitude brushing her cheeks. She held the pearl and the lava sphere in cupped hands, watching the swirling elements beneath the surface.

The trial had left its mark, not just in the soot that clung to her hair and clothes, but to her heart. Malrik and Ashael had nearly burned alive. She'd almost lost them, all of them. If they hadn't figured out the Phylarix's puzzle, they'd be dead.

Malrik's low laugh reached her ears from where he sat with Selandor and Elyndra. Clara squeezed her eyes shut. They were fine. They had survived and had work ahead of them.

Clara exhaled slowly and pulled the map out of her pocket once more. The parchment unfolded like it had a will of its own, glowing lines blooming to life across the surface. She studied the golden thread that was their path, the symbol of the floating island above them. Suspended in the sky, cradled in mist and silver light.

Their next trial.

Clara held the map tighter, half afraid it would blow out of her hands again. So far, it had never led them astray. Through forests to the Syralens and into the heart of a volcano. Each step had drawn something new from them. From her.

She barely recognized herself anymore. Someone who charged head-first across boiling pits of lava, who would face danger head on instead of observing it from the sidelines. She thought back to New York and how small and insignificant the towering buildings had made her feel. How lost she felt in a crowded subway, or how invisible she was on a street corner.

But here in Avenora, she had purpose. She bore magical artifacts and was being pulled deeper and deeper into a myth of people who battled against the darkness. She traced the lines of the map with her eyes, reflecting on the places she had been and where she still needed to go. At home, she was a nurse, tending to wounds. Here, she was powerful.

Malrik plopped down next to her, his voice low. "You're staring at it like it might disappear."

Clara glanced at him, the corner of her mouth curving. "Wouldn't be the strangest thing we've seen."

He chuckled softly. "It sure wouldn't."

They looked up at the floating island in companionable silence.

"I keep wondering," said Clara, giving voice to what was weighing on her heart. "What happens when the map runs out of places to lead us? What if it doesn't help the Aelvor in their fight against Veylora? What if it's all for nothing?" Her lips quivered.

Malrik threaded his fingers through hers. His palm was warm and soft. "Wherever you go, I'll go with you. Your dreams, the map, your pendant led you here for a reason. We just have to trust that something is waiting on the other end of all of this."

Clara nodded slowly, her eyes never leaving the island in the sky. "I guess you're right."

Malrik grinned. "I always am."

She laughed and shook her head. They stayed for a little while longer, her heart easing a little.

When she turned to find sleep, Ashael's gaze was fixed steadily on her. Her cheeks flushed, her heart squeezed, and she quickly shut her eyes. She didn't dare wonder why he was staring at her with such intensity. With what looked suspiciously like longing.

The next morning, the party clustered around an overlook where they could clearly see the floating island. Mist wound around its edges, mixing with low clouds that had descended on them in the night. After a good night's sleep, the island looked even farther away. Clara bit the inside of her cheek and reached her fingers toward her pendant. Malrik ran a hand through his hair. "Well. We need a way across. Or up, rather."

Kira crossed her arms. "That much is obvious." She studied the island, her sharp gaze narrowing. "I'll have to shift," she said finally. "I can take one of you across, maybe another after, but I can't promise more. I don't know how this place will react to me."

Clara turned to her. "You're not sure?" Kira was the only hope they had at reaching the island. If she couldn't bring them . . .

Kira's expression darkened. "This place . . . I don't know what it is." She exhaled. "Flying through normal air is one thing. Flying into that?" She nodded toward the island, where mist curled at its edges. "It could be like the Phylarix cave. I won't know until I try."

Ashael's gaze remained locked on the floating landmass, clearly thinking. Elyndra exhaled softly, her sharp eyes lingering on the shimmering treetops.

Clara frowned. "What even are the Nyths?"

Selandor glanced at her. "Tiny winged fae." His tone was quiet and serious. "Quick. Elusive. Almost impossible to catch."

Elyndra inclined her head. "And difficult to understand."

Clara blinked. "You mean they don't talk?"

"They do," Elyndra said, wrinkling her nose. "But not in ways that make sense."

Selandor's gaze was thoughtful, distant. "There are stories, but who can say how many of them are true? It is said that the Floating Island is their home, but some claim they were once seen beyond it, appearing and disappearing as they pleased."

Vaelin gave a slow nod. "I've heard the same. But since the corruption? No sightings. No whispers. It's as if they vanished." He glanced toward the island. "I wonder if they're even still there."

Elyndra exhaled. "There or not, we need to be careful. The Nyths are known for their tricks, and this island is no ordinary place."

Malrik exhaled sharply. "So, we could be walking into their game."

Selandor regarded him evenly. "Illusions. Challenges. Perhaps worse."

Malrik scoffed, crossing his arms. "Yeah, that sounds about right."

Clara looked at him. "What?"

His expression hardened. "If they're anything like the fae stories from where we come from, then we'd best be careful." His voice dipped lower. "What you see may not be real. What you hear may not be meant for your ears. And what seems safe—" he exhaled sharply. "Might be the trap itself."

Clara's stomach tightened. "So, how do we deal with them?"

Selandor answered before Malrik could. "Do what they least expect."

"I was hoping they'd be more like Tinkerbell," she muttered.

Malrik let out a sharp laugh. "Yeah? And which of us is Peter Pan?"

She cast him a look. "Obviously me."

Ashael blinked, clearly trying to make sense of the conversation. "You are . . . Peter?"

Elyndra arched a brow. "And what manner of bell does one tinker?"

Malrik huffed a laugh. "Forget it. They're just human folk tales."

Selandor, ever pragmatic, ignored them entirely. "This is wasting time. We need to decide who goes first."

Clara already knew the answer before anyone could argue. "I'm going."

Malrik muttered something unintelligible under his breath.

Ashael straightened, accepting her answer without question. "Then when it is possible, I will follow."

Malrik's chest rose sharply as he spoke. "You think I'd let you go before me?"

"We don't have time for this," Clara snapped. She was stressed and impatient. "We don't even know if Kira can come back."

Ashael's eyes darkened, but he said nothing. Malrik said something to himself.

Kira took a step back. Her form blurred. Shifted. Grew. She shook out her wings. "Are you coming or not?"

Clara swung herself onto Kira's back. With a lurch, they leapt into the sky. The wind churned against Clara's face, hot and restless. She tightened her grip. Kira's wings snapped downward, sending gusts of air swirling around them.

Clara squinted against the wind, trying to make out their surroundings. The volcanic lands stretched on for miles. Clara could see nothing but rock. She twisted in the harness, and behind her she could make out the edge of the forest. There was no sign of the Dravok, Seraphis, or the corruption. But that didn't mean it wasn't there.

Clara tightened her hold onto Kira's harness as they descended, the island emerging through a thin veil of mist. The smell of damp earth and wild flora permeated the air. Below, the land shimmered in emerald, sapphire, silver, and gold, as if it had been crafted from precious stones. Clara wondered if Veylora's corruption had ever touched here. It was so perfect. Maybe *too* perfect.

Kira landed with a soft thud onto grass that sparkled with dew, wings folding tightly. Her breath was unsteady, shoulders tense. "That flight drained me more than it should have."

Clara slid off, boots sinking into the cool, impossibly soft earth. "You okay?"

Kira shook herself out. "The longer I stay, the worse it gets," she rasped. "I need to go now before I lose too much strength. Stay here. Don't move until I return."

Without waiting, she pushed off into the sky, leaving Clara alone.

She remained where Kira had left her. She studied her surroundings, admiring the beautiful scenery. From the skies and below, the island hadn't looked too big. But now that she was here, surrounded by trees and a lazily curling mist, it was hard to tell how big the island actually was.

Clara fought the urge to plop down onto the grass. Time stretched, though the sunlight did not shift. Kira should've been back by now.

Her eyes searched the sky. Nothing. The others would follow soon, wouldn't they?

"Clara?"

She spun, heart lurching.

Malrik stood a little way off, dark hair tousled by the wind. Clara let out a sigh of relief. She hadn't even heard Kira return, but Malrik must have been dropped off farther away.

She hurried toward him. "Malrik!"

His grin widened, and he matched her pace. The tension in her muscles uncoiled. "I thought Ashael was coming next," she said.

Malrik smirked. "I won that argument. That's why I'm here first."

She rolled her eyes. Of course he did. Then, the island froze. The birdsong vanished. The wind died in an instant.

Dread coiled in Clara's stomach, settling like a weight. Malrik's stride faltered. The teasing spark in his expression dulled. The mischief in his eyes drained away. Something about it didn't seem right.

Clara took a step back, then another. "Malrik?" Her voice barely carried.

His hand lifted, reaching for her. "Clara, it's okay. I'm here."

She hesitated. "You're . . . here?"

"Yes." His voice dipped a fraction lower than usual, warping mid-sentence before snapping back to normal. "You were waiting for me, weren't you?"

Something inside her twisted. His lips moved, but they weren't in sync with his words. Like a delayed echo.

Her pulse pounded in her ears, nearly drowning out all sound. "I was," she admitted slowly. "But why did Kira drop you off so far from me?"

His steps remained too measured. Unnaturally precise. "She must have miscalculated."

Miscalculated? No. It wasn't like Kira to make a mistake like that. A nervous chuckle left Clara's lips, forced. "Well, as long as we're both here now."

Malrik tilted his head. "You don't seem happy to see me."

The words should have been teasing, but he sounded almost accusatory.

"Of course, I am." She wanted to believe it. Wanted to step forward. But something was wrong.

The Malrik she knew would have cracked a joke by now. Thrown an arm around her. Told her she looked ridiculous for how worried she was.

This wasn't him. The realization settled like ice in her veins.

Not-Malrik took another step. Too smooth, too controlled. Like a marionette suspended on invisible strings. He was usually so casual.

Clara's instincts screamed at her to run. But she couldn't. Something pressed against her limbs, dragging her forward, urging her to believe.

Her nails bit into her palms. Her breath came in shallow bursts.

Everything inside her told her to trust, to step forward, to let go of doubt. "It's a trick," Clara whispered, shutting her eyes tight. "It's a trick."

Silence.

Then his voice, softer now. "Clara, what's wrong?"

She forced herself to think of the real Malrik. The sharp edge of his laughter. The smirk that always meant trouble. Stubborn, reckless, too bold for his own good.

She opened her eyes.

The imposter was still there, his hand nearly touching hers.

Panic surged. The unseen force tightened, pressing her forward. She screwed her eyes shut again.

She clung to what mattered: Malrik showing up unannounced when he thought she was in trouble, pretending he just happened to pass by. Him always being there for her, even when it meant stepping through a portal into another world.

Where are you, Malrik?

A ragged breath escaped her as she opened her eyes. This time the illusion cracked.

The false Malrik wavered, then shattered into nothing. He dissipated into the air like a fading projection.

Clara staggered and gasped. The weight pressing on her lifted, but a prickling sensation remained on her skin.

Leaves rustled. Birds stirred in the trees. The island breathed once more.

Relief washed over her, nearly buckling her knees, but it was fleeting. She was alone again. And now, more than ever, she longed for the real Malrik. For Ashael. For someone.

What if Kira was too drained? What if she didn't come back? What if no one did?

Clara's fingers curled into fists as she scanned the empty expanse of the island. The island didn't feel like a perfect paradise anymore. She scanned the trees, hunting for any sign of movement. Her throat tightened. She couldn't trust her own senses. So, what was she to do?

Clara waited.

And waited.

CHAPTER 22

Clara hugged her arms to her chest, shifting her weight from foot to foot. The island remained deceptively peaceful.

Kira still wasn't back yet.

Clara continued to scan her surroundings, searching for anything useful: a landmark, a clue, a sign of what the Nyths were protecting. Was this truly leading them closer to the Vaelithar shard? Was this island their test?

The map had led her here for a reason. Her pendant was warm against her chest. She'd been the one to volunteer to go first. Clara clung to these facts and swallowed her fear. Then, she stepped further into the island. A twin-trunked tree stood just ahead, its silver-veined leaves dancing in the sunlight. Its gnarled roots twisted over moss-covered stones. The trunk split in two before curving back together, as if reaching for itself.

Clara noted the unique tree, then kept walking. She passed more trees, little pools of water that flowed into streams. She strained her ears for any sound, but all was quiet. She walked a few more minutes; then her stomach sank.

Another tree with a split trunk rose before her. Was this a unique species to the island, that the trees grew this way? Clara squinted at it. Then she had an idea.

She bent down, picked up a smooth stone, and carefully placed it atop one of the lowest branches.

Then she turned and walked in the opposite direction, heading back to the spot where Kira had dropped her off.

Minutes passed.

She breathed in the crisp air, watching the way light moved through the branches, trying to shake off the unease winding inside her.

Her stomach plummeted as her suspicions were confirmed. The tree stood before her again. The stone was still there.

A chill prickled down her spine. Clara spun on her heel and strode in a different direction, quickening her pace.

But the tree was waiting for her, the stone unmoved.

She tried again.

And again. Every direction, every angle, every possible route. Each time, she ended up in the same place. Desperation and loneliness crashed inside her. She tried not to think about what would happen if she was stuck here forever.

A soft, breathy giggle wove through the air. Clara stiffened, her skin crawling. She spun toward the sound, scanning the trees.

She swallowed, fighting to calm her rapid breaths and keep the panic at bay. *The Nyths. They're toying with me.*

Her fingers balled into fists. *Think. There has to be a way out.*

She dug through her memory, through everything they had pieced together about the Nyths.

And Selandor's voice echoed in her mind: *Do what they least expect.*

But what did that mean?

Her jaw clenched. Then it clicked. Do the opposite. If walking forward kept her stuck—

She took a slow step backward. Then another. The air rippled, wavering like heat waves rising off pavement.

Clara's pulse leapt, but the tree remained. She was close to breaking out of this illusion; she could feel it. But the Nyths would not be shaken so easily.

Another memory from childhood flashed. Her family had once visited her mom's hometown, a place steeped in superstition, with stories of beings they called *engkatos* that lured kids into forests and left them wandering in circles. She remembered the local kids wearing their clothes inside out to keep from getting trapped, and she had laughed at it back then. A shiver ran through her. This felt too much like those stories.

She yanked off her jacket, flipped it, and shoved her arms back through the sleeves.

The forest around her hushed. The skin on the back of her neck prickled, like she was being watched.

Her breath came shallow as she took a slow, deliberate step backward, then another, and another.

The tree blurred at the edges. The ground beneath her shifted. The air felt different.

"Are you there? Clara?"

Her heart stammered. Ashael was here.

She inhaled sharply. His voice was close. She should be able to see him. Or was it another part of the trick?

"Ashael?" she called.

"I hear you," he answered. "Clara, I'm walking in circles."

"If you are," she called back, "walk backward! Invert your clothes!"

A pause.

"You want me to . . . invert my clothes?"

Clara fought the urge to laugh. There couldn't be any doubt this was Ashael. His serious voice and skepticism rang true. "Yes!" she called.

"All right," Ashael's voice came again, resigned to his indignity.

Clara swallowed hard, her pulse pounding as she kept moving backwards out of the illusion.

She collided into something firm and solid. A sharp gasp tore from her lips. She pressed her weight into the person behind her. When it didn't vanish, she turned. Ashael was there, his blue eyes trained on her face. Her breath left her in a rush.

Relief crashed over Clara. Ashael stood before her, solid and real. Yet the moment stretched too long, and doubt crept in. She tilted her chin up and studied his face. She needed to be sure that this was him. The illusion of Malrik had been so convincing at first.

Her mind scrambled. Before she could stop herself, she blurted out, "Have we ever danced together?"

Ashael blinked, caught off guard by the suddenness of the question. A slight furrow formed between his brows, his lips parting as if trying to make sense of it. "No," he answered.

Clara's stomach plummeted. It wasn't real. She felt foolish. She took a step back, her heart thudding against her ribs.

Ashael frowned, his confusion clear in his eyes. "Why?"

But she didn't answer. She turned away. A lump formed in her throat. She couldn't do this again. Couldn't let herself fall for another trick.

"It was a game," his voice called out, steadier this time. "We were trying to hold an orb between our chests."

Clara froze mid-step. She spun back around, her eyes wide. It *was* him.

The relief was so sudden, so overwhelming, that she didn't think. She flung herself at him.

Ashael barely had time to react before she collided with him, her arms wrapping tightly around his middle. His body stiffened beneath her touch, his arms awkwardly hanging at his sides as if unsure of what to do.

For a second, he simply stood there, unmoving.

Tentatively he placed one hand on her back. "I'm here," he murmured.

Clara squeezed her eyes shut, pressing her forehead against his shoulder. *He's real. He's real. He's real.*

The illusions, the isolation, the fear crashed into her all at once. A tear slid down her cheek.

Ashael's other arm wrapped around her, and this time, it wasn't hesitant. It was warm, reassuring. She felt his breath against her hair, felt the way he held her just a little tighter, as if *he* needed this too.

Clara didn't want to move. Didn't want to let go. When she finally pulled back, her gaze met his. The world shifted. Clara wasn't sure what changed, only that something did.

His arms were still around her. Hers around him. His eyes, intent and searching, held something unspoken, something that sent a slow heat flowing through her chest. She felt a connection, a pull, drawing her to him.

Her heart fluttered, her fingers still resting lightly against his back. Their gazes remained locked.

Clara blinked as music floated through the air. A melody both fleeting and lingering, peaceful yet stirring. It hummed, like the island itself was singing just for them.

Clara startled as a tiny glowing light drifted into her peripheral vision. She glanced around and saw what looked like fireflies swirling through the air. The lights floated around them, casting a soft warm glow.

Ashael's hand shifted, his fingers brushing against hers. She inhaled sharply at the contact.

His lips quirked in a small, almost teasing smile. "This . . ." he murmured, his voice low, a hint of warmth beneath it. His fingers clasped around hers. "This is a real dance."

Clara barely had time to react before he twirled her. A surprised laugh escaped her as she spun beneath his hand, the air wrapping around her like silk.

Then he pulled her back in, one hand settling lightly at her waist.

Clara smiled.

They moved, swaying to the distant melody, the lights drifting around them like tiny constellations. She felt light and free. She was able to forget for the moment that there was any threat of danger, that they were supposed to be looking for an artifact to banish the darkness. She let herself sink into the moment, her steps and heart light as a feather.

And then she realized they were floating. She gasped, eyes widening as she glanced down.

The ground was a foot beneath them. They rose effortlessly, as though carried by the rhythm itself.

Ashael chuckled softly. "Seems we've been chosen for the Nyths' dance."

Clara's heart pounded. She met his gaze again, and this time she *felt* it. The pull. Like a thread between them, tightening, drawing her closer.

The world outside ceased to exist. There was just Ashael and her. Clara could have stayed like this forever.

Ashael's fingers tightened at her waist, his intense gaze fixed on hers. "You are beautiful."

A warmth spread through her, sinking deep, different from anything she'd felt before. It blossomed in her chest, pulsed through her veins, made the world beyond this moment blur into nothing.

Ashael traced the line of her cheek, his fingers featherlight, lingering. His touch burned in the best way, his warmth pulling her in like gravity itself.

The space between them narrowed. His breath ghosted against her skin, warm and steady. Clara's fingers dug into his tunic, clutching the fabric without thinking, anchoring herself.

Ashael hesitated, hovering, his lips just a breath away. A silent question in his eyes.

She bit her lower lip, tilting her head up in answer, anticipation thrumming through her—

"Clara!"

The voice, sharp and urgent, shattered the moment.

Clara jolted, pulling away from Ashael.

Malrik.

He stood a short distance away firmly on the ground, staring at them. But he wasn't looking at her. His gaze was locked on Ashael. On the way Clara was still in his arms.

The spell wavered. The soft, glowing lights scattered like startled embers. The ground below seemed impossibly far. Clara didn't realize how high the dance had carried them. Gravity seized them. Ashael pulled her closer. The wind rushed past them as they fell. He hit the ground first, his arms still locked around her, breaking her fall.

For a moment, Clara lay frozen, her heart hammering. Her hands were braced against his chest, fingers gripping instinctively into the fabric of his tunic. He was warm beneath her touch, his heartbeat a steady rhythm against her palm. His breath fanned against her cheek, close. Too close. Heat flushed through her.

Clara scrambled back, pushing herself upright in a flurry of movement. "A-Are you okay?"

Ashael exhaled, his chest rising and falling as he blinked up at the sky before looking at her. "I'm fine." His voice was softer then. "Are you?"

She nodded quickly, trying to ignore the way her skin still tingled where he'd held her.

"Glad to see you two had a graceful landing." Malrik's voice was light, but something in it felt off. A brief surge of emotion surfaced in his eyes before it vanished. Then, as if nothing had happened, a smirk slid into place.

Clara groaned, shoving herself to her feet. "Shut up."

Ashael sat up as well, but before anyone could speak, the ground beneath them shifted.

Ashael's expression darkened as he glanced down. Malrik took a cautious step forward, his smirk fading.

Clara followed Ashael's gaze and felt the blood drain from her face.

They stood on massive piles of bones. They were pale, brittle, and half-buried in the earth.

Some lay intact, others were fragmented.

Clara's breath came shallow.

Ashael rose slowly to his feet. Malrik adjusted his stance, arms crossing over his chest.

No one spoke.

Clara studied the bones, then Malrik. The reality of the situation, of the Nyths' tricks, settled over her once more. "How do I know you're really Malrik?" she asked, her voice barely above a whisper.

Malrik gave her a look and, without missing a beat, sighed dramatically. "Clara, I know you ate all those chocolates from my backpack in third grade."

Clara choked. "You *knew* about that?"

His grin returned. "I found the wrappers in your desk the next day, you little thief."

Her face burned hotter, if that was even possible.

Ashael blinked between them, clearly not understanding but sensing this wasn't the time to ask.

"Okay, I'm glad it's really you." She straightened her own tunic and tried to ignore the lingering tension in the air. Clara tore her gaze back to the skeletons, forcing herself to breathe. "What is this?"

Ashael crouched, running his fingers over the brittle remains. His brows drew together, his shoulders stiffening. "Some are in pairs."

Malrik frowned. "And some aren't."

Clara went cold. A closer look confirmed it. Many skeletons lay side by side, their fingers barely inches apart, as if reaching for each other even in death. Others lay scattered, alone, untouched by another.

"Couples?" she whispered.

Ashael's gaze darkened. "Or people who got lost in the illusions."

Malrik exhaled, scanning their surroundings. "If they were trapped in a trance, they probably never found their way out." His tone turned grim. "And if they fell for it. . ."

Clara swallowed. "They were lost forever."

A sick feeling settled in her gut.

Ashael's voice was quiet, thoughtful. "The Nyths don't just create illusions. They weave them." He stood. "If someone believes in their trick, it becomes real. And they never wake up."

His gaze lingered on Clara as something deeper stirred in his eyes.

Her stomach knotted. They'd almost kissed. A single moment more, and she and Ashael might have joined these bones.

Had any of it been real?

She clenched her fists. Forced herself to shake the thought away even as she fought the urge to be sick.

Malrik, too, seemed unusually quiet. He glanced at Ashael before looking away, jaw tight. If seeing them together had affected him, he wasn't letting it show. It was hard to tell how Malrik felt.

"So," Clara cleared her throat. "Where are the others?"

Malrik exhaled. "Kira's drained. She needs rest before she can bring the next person."

Clara nodded slowly, unease still prickling under her skin.

A glint of light caught her attention. The same tiny glowing orbs, no longer drifting aimlessly, but now aligned, stretched forward like a path into the trees.

Ashael noticed it too. "What do you think?" he murmured.

Malrik stepped closer. "Either it's another trick . . ." His voice was dry. "Or the Nyths want us to go somewhere."

Clara swallowed. "There's only one way to know." She took the first step forward.

The lights thickened as they walked, blinking in and out like fleeting sparks, shifting into patterns that urged them forward.

Then they heard whispers.

Clara tensed. The voices were soft and distant, just out of sight. There was another hush of giggles, then a sharp *shhh* like someone had been scolded.

Malrik tensed beside her. "All right. That's eerie."

Ashael remained quiet.

Clara strained to listen. The voices . . . they were no longer just whispers. They were words.

"They have shown strength . . . and willpower . . . But only one may retrieve what they seek."

She went still. The lights hummed around them, spiraling in slow, deliberate motions.

"Did you hear that?" she asked, her voice barely above a whisper.

Ashael glanced at her. "I did."

Malrik frowned. "I heard *something* but not clearly. What did it say?"

Clara hesitated. "It said . . . we've shown strength and willpower, but only one of us can retrieve what we seek."

Malrik exhaled sharply, running a hand through his hair. "By now, we all know who they want." His gaze landed on Clara.

Ashael's expression darkened. "Because of your pendant."

Before anyone could say more, a sudden gust of wind spiraled before them. The tiny lights surged, forming a twisting vortex. A whirlwind of golden embers, laced with soft blues, silvers, and violets.

The wind wrapped around itself, spinning tighter and tighter until it wasn't just wind anymore.

A shape took form. An orb. It hovered before them, glowing, pulsing. Large enough for someone to step inside.

Clara's heart pounded.

Ashael and Malrik both turned to her.

Clara exhaled, then took a step forward.

The second her foot crossed the threshold, the wind brushed against her skin, welcoming her. She stepped inside the orb. Once inside, she saw that the little lights were not fireflies. These must be the Nyths.

Tiny beings hovered all around her, no taller than her thumb. Their wings gleamed like glass, bodies lit from within. Their skin—mahogany, ivory, amber, and warm brown—was dusted in thick glitter. It caught the light, reflecting silver, gold, sapphire, or violet. Their hair flowed in colored strands, their features sharp, almost Aelvor-like, but impossibly small.

Their wings fluttered so fast, they blurred, just like a hummingbird's.

They flitted around her, some hovering close, observing her intently.

Clara barely dared to breathe.

One of them, a Nyth with deep indigo glitter and silver-dusted wings, drifted close, its tiny glowing eyes studying her. It darted away just as swiftly.

Another followed, brushing past her cheek before vanishing into the swirling lights.

Her heartbeat pounded in her ears.

The Nyths parted, making space at the heart of the glowing sphere.

Clara held her breath. In the center, floating weightlessly, was a small orb. It pulsed softly, wind and soil swirling inside, circling yet never merging. The Nyths shifted, their tiny glowing faces expectant.

Clara stepped forward, drawn by something deep in her chest. She reached out.

The second her fingers wrapped around the sphere, the entire glowing vortex collapsed in a whisper. *"The elements must remember."*

Clara staggered back, the weight of the sphere solid in her hands. The air around them settled. The island stilled once more.

Malrik and Ashael rushed toward her, their eyes locked onto the sphere she now held.

Clara turned it in her palm, watching as the forces inside danced, bound together yet never one.

She swallowed, glancing up at the Nyths, but they were already drifting away, their glowing forms vanishing into the mist.

Had they just given her a clue?

Her grip tightened on the sphere. *The elements must remember.* But remember what?

The sky deepened into hues of navy and violet, the last remnants of daylight fading beyond the treetops. Clara exhaled, wrapping her arms around herself. The air had cooled, laced with moss and the hushed sound of waterfalls in the distance.

Still no sign of Kira.

"Kira's been gone too long," Clara murmured, glancing at the sky.

Malrik stretched his arms behind his head, leaning against a twisted root. "She looked drained when she dropped me off. She probably needs a full night's rest before making another trip."

Clara pressed her lips together. "I hope she's okay."

"She will be," Ashael said, his tone calm but firm. He stood a few steps away, scanning the surrounding trees. "And so will the others. They know how to handle themselves. Right now, we should focus on getting through the night."

Malrik exhaled, glancing around. "Looks like we're safe, at least for now."

Clara nodded, her gaze drifting toward the tiny glowing lights still hovering around them, their movements slow and unthreatening. "And it seems like the Nyths have accepted us."

Malrik scoffed lightly. "Or they're just waiting to mess with us when we least expect it."

Ashael turned toward them. "Either way, we should get some rest. I can find a tree and coax it into a shelter for the night."

"We can help," Clara offered, pushing off from where she sat.

But Ashael shook his head. "No need. I'll be back soon." His gaze darted toward Malrik. "Just . . . try not to get into trouble while I'm gone."

Malrik smirked. "No promises."

Ashael disappeared into the trees, his silhouette melting into the twilight.

Clara watched him go, her gaze trailing after him a beat too long. She didn't know why she was so drawn to him. After the dance they'd shared, the Nyth's dance, it felt like her heart had never come back down to earth. She found herself glancing at Ashael even more than usual. The Nyths were tricksters. How could she be sure that the moment they'd shared, their almost-kiss, wasn't a part of their games? Clara shuddered, remembering the piles of bones they'd stood on. Malrik noticed her staring.

His smirk lingered, but something in his posture shifted. He leaned back against the tree root, stretching his legs out. "Well, looks like we're stuck with Ashael."

Clara gave a low chuckle, but Malrik's words lingered. *Stuck with Ashael.* The words were half teasing and half laced with something else. Clara didn't know what to say. Because the truth was, Ashael being here changed things. He wasn't just another person in their group. He was *Ashael*. And Malrik knew it, too.

She exhaled, brushing the thought aside. "Yeah. Until Kira finally shows up."

For a moment, they sat in comfortable silence, the distant sounds of the island filling the spaces between their thoughts.

Then Clara turned to him. "Did the Nyths play games with you too?"

Malrik's smirk faded slightly. He tilted his head back against the bark. "Yeah. Had their fun."

Clara studied him. "How'd you escape?"

He shrugged. "Wasn't that hard, really." He smiled. "I'm a master of escape rooms. This was basically the same thing."

Clara almost believed him.

Suddenly, the humor faded, and he tapped his fingers idly against his knee. "At least, that's what I tell myself."

"Of course."

Malrik didn't continue. Instead, he stared off into the darkening sky, the easy confidence from before slipping away.

Clara waited, half-expecting him to throw out another joke, but he didn't.

Then, so softly she almost didn't hear it, he murmured, "But sometimes . . . illusions are better than reality."

Clara frowned slightly, studying his profile. The smirk was still there, but it didn't quite reach his eyes. She dug her fingers into the grass. She wanted to ask what he meant. But she didn't.

CHAPTER 23

Malrik

The night pressed in, the island settling into an eerie stillness as the minutes crawled on. The only sounds were the occasional rustle of leaves and the whisper of water in the distance. Malrik sat still, arms resting against his bent knees, watching the tiny glowing orbs drift lazily through the air.

But his mind was nowhere near the present. They lingered on Clara and on Ashael. His jaw clenched. The image refused to leave him. Clara in Ashael's arms, his hands on her waist, her face tilted up toward his. Too damn close.

He hoped it was just the Nyth's and their illusions. Perhaps that's all it was. But something else nagged at him.

It wasn't just the possibility that they had kissed. It was the way she looked at him, even before they'd come to this floating island in the sky. But ever since he'd found them, she couldn't stop staring at him. Like nothing else existed. Like Ashael was the only thing in her world.

Something twisted deep in his chest. He shouldn't care so much. He should be *happy* for her. He and Clara had been friends forever. That was all.

Malrik rubbed the back of his neck, exhaling sharply. He didn't know what to think anymore.

Clara wasn't just his closest friend. She was his person, the one constant in his life that never changed. But lately, things were changing, and he didn't know if it was just this place, this journey, or something deeper than that. Could it be that he wanted to be more than friends? Or maybe he just didn't want to share her.

Malrik followed one of the little floating orbs, watching it as it drifted lazily over the grass and through the trees. He stifled the urge to sigh. It wasn't just that Ashael was in the picture now. Malrik could see the way Ashael held himself around her—always calm, always controlled, but never indifferent.

And worse, there were moments, small and fleeting, that Malrik felt something between him and Clara, too.

And that scared him.

He wanted to talk to her. Needed to. Before whatever this was, whatever was happening, slipped beyond his reach. His fingers curled into a fist, then loosened again. Screw it.

"Clara."

She glanced at him, brow lifting slightly.

"There's something I wanted to talk to you about."

Clara sat up, her body tense. He could see the way her shoulders stiffened, the way her fingers stilled in the grass. "What is it?"

His stomach twisted. That wasn't the reaction he wanted. He wondered if she already knew what he was about to say. She looked like she was bracing herself for it, like it was bad news. His heart plummeted into his stomach.

Still, he forced himself forward. Now or never. "It's about Ashael."

The words stuck in his throat. One wrong move, and whatever they had, whatever they were, might never be the same. His fingers tightened against his knee, a brief squeeze before he dragged a hand down his face, exhaling sharply. He could press. He *should* press.

Instead—

He forced himself to smile and sighed. "I wonder if he already found our shelter. You must be tired."

Clara exhaled, relief flashing across her face. "Oh. Yeah, I hope so."

That should have settled something. Should have made things easier.

But instead, it only left a deeper knot in his chest.

Clara shivered, rubbing at her arms.

Malrik chuckled, shifting closer. "All right, come here." He slung an arm around her shoulders, his smirk teasing but his touch warm. "I'm your heater now. And your pillow. Until golden boy comes back, anyway."

Clara hesitated for only a second before leaning into him, resting her head lightly against his shoulder.

He should say something. Crack a joke. Make it feel normal. But for some reason, he didn't. Instead, he just let her stay there, the warmth of her pressed against his side. He felt her relax, the tension slowly easing from her.

He let himself settle into the moment, cherishing their closeness. It was over too soon.

Malrik glanced up just as Ashael emerged from the trees, his sharp gaze locking onto them.

Clara straightened slightly but didn't pull away completely.

Ashael's expression remained steady, but something in him had changed. His whole body stiffened subtly.

"I found a place," he said. "We should move before it gets colder."

Malrik smirked, his grip on Clara tightening briefly. "Right. Wouldn't want our fearless leader to freeze."

Ashael didn't rise to the bait.

Clara cast him a sharp glance, then stood and brushed off her clothes. "All right. Let's go."

Malrik followed suit, stuffing his hands into his pockets.

As they walked, he threw one last glance toward Ashael. Something had changed. And for the first time, Malrik wasn't sure where he belonged.

CHAPTER 24

Ashael

shael walked slowly, his movements purposeful. Every tree he passed was unsuitable for their needs, or so he tried to convince himself. Truthfully, he was stalling.

Finding shelter wouldn't take long. The trees here were ancient, their hollows large enough to provide cover. He could easily coax one to widen, to shape itself into something safe for the night. But as he walked, he savored the solitude, the chance to sort through his tangled mess of thoughts.

His mind churned with everything that had happened since leaving the camp. He thought of the lands they had crossed and of his own abilities, sharpening in ways he barely understood. Whatever the reason for these changes, he would turn them toward their cause. His people needed him to succeed, and he intended to give everything he had. They had passed each trial placed before them, and the more they endured, the stronger his conviction grew that they truly had a fighting chance against Veylora's corruption. And then there were the dreams. Fragmented, slipping away the moment he woke, yet leaving behind an unease he could not shake.

And Clara. Always Clara.

He exhaled, pressing a hand against the rough bark of a tree. He had never wanted anything before. Not like this.

His mind flitted back to the dance they'd shared. The way her body felt pressed against his, warm and soft. The look in her eyes, dark brown and full of yearning. The way her mouth would have felt against his own. He had wanted it to happen. He still did. It unsettled him. Not because he regretted it, but because the depth of his want felt completely foreign.

He had lived a long life, much longer than any human. But never once had he felt this kind of pull. Not toward another Aelvor. Not toward anyone. And Clara was human.

It wasn't unheard of. But it was rare. Very rare. He really should not be with a human woman.

Did she feel it too, the pull toward him? What would it feel like for a human? The Nyths loved their games. The whole moment could have been one of manipulated thoughts and feelings. If it had gone too far, if the illusion had ensnared them completely, it could have ended badly for both of them. And yet he couldn't shake the feeling that the tension between them hadn't been the result of the Nyths' spell.

An Aelvor and a human.

Clara would want to return to her world when this was over. That was her home. He knew that. But the thought of her leaving, of this pull between them ending before he even understood it—

He exhaled sharply, shaking his head. He'd tarried long enough. He needed to find shelter. Spotting a large tree with a hollow trunk, Ashael placed a palm against the bark. He reached inward, coaxing it open, shaping it into something they could use for the night. The wood obeyed, shifting with ease beneath his touch. Within moments, the space inside had softened, the floor padded with moss, and the air warm and insulated.

It would do.

He turned back toward the others, weaving through the trees, only to stop cold.

Clara and Malrik sat close together. Too close.

Ashael's steps faltered. His grip tightened at his side, fingers balling into fists before he forced them to loosen. His chest felt tight, something sharp twisting deep inside him, unexpected, unwanted.

Malrik's arm rested around Clara's shoulders, holding her against him. She didn't seem to mind. Her head rested lightly against his shoulder, her body relaxed.

Ashael swallowed hard as something cold settled beneath his ribs. It shouldn't matter. They were just friends. Weren't they?

Even if they weren't, what right did he have to feel so jealous?

He exhaled, schooling his expression before stepping forward.

The moment Malrik noticed him, his smirk returned, lazy and knowing.

Clara shifted but didn't pull away completely.

Ashael forced himself to keep his voice steady. "I found a place," he said. "We should move before it gets colder."

Malrik's grip on Clara tightened briefly. "Right. Wouldn't want our fearless leader to freeze."

Ashael ignored the comment, but it was clear Malrik was irritated with him. Or jealous. Or something. Still, his focus was attuned to Clara. She yawned as she stood. She was exhausted. He silently chastised himself for taking so long to find shelter. She needed rest.

"All right. Let's go," she said.

As they walked, Ashael felt her glance at him more than once. As if she could sense something was off. Her attentiveness gave him hope, but it also made him uncertain.

Once inside the hollow, the warmth of the tree settled around them. It was a quiet space, safe, enclosed. Malrik barely hesitated before flopping onto the moss.

Ashael's gaze lingered on him.

Malrik and Clara had always been inseparable. It had never mattered before. Now, it was impossible to ignore the way he looked at her or the way she laughed with him. Clara trusted him in a way that only came from years of knowing someone.

He couldn't possibly be what Malrik was to her. That kind of closeness, that kind of history, it wasn't something he could just step into. Nor did he want to. He knew the value of such loyalty. Of his friends.

Ashael clenched his jaw and forced the thought away. He sat at the entrance, back straight, gaze fixed outward. "Get some rest. I'll take first watch."

Clara hesitated. He could feel her looking at him. But then, she lay down, curling slightly into herself.

The minutes stretched. Silence filled the hollow.

He exhaled slowly, willing his mind to settle. It was useless. The thoughts, the questions, the ache, it was all still there, gnawing at him in the quiet.

And then he heard a whisper, soft and tentative.

"Ashael?"

He turned. Clara was awake.

CHAPTER 25

The hollow was warm, the moss soft beneath her, but sleep didn't come easily. Clara shifted, adjusting her position, trying to will her thoughts to settle. They didn't.

Malrik. Ashael. Their quest.

Her mind spun in circles, each thought bleeding into the next. She turned slightly, stealing a glance at Ashael where he sat near the entrance, his back straight, shoulders rigid. He looked on edge. Why?

She had noticed it earlier. The way his expression was a little too controlled, the way something shadowed his eyes before he hid it away.

Beside her, Malrik was sound asleep. He had been restless earlier, but now he was at ease, his breaths even and deep. She was grateful for that. He needed rest. They all did.

She tried to fight it, but sleep pulled at her eyelids. Eventually, exhaustion won, and she drifted off.

Warmth. Stillness. And something else, something that pulled her from sleep.

Clara blinked, disoriented for a moment, her thoughts sluggish. But then her gaze instinctively landed on Ashael.

He hadn't moved. He sat, guarding the entrance with his back to them, his eyes fixed on the sky and the stars, as if the weight of the night was his alone to carry.

He should sleep too.

Carefully, she sat up. Malrik's breathing remained steady beside her, undisturbed. She didn't want to wake him, so she moved as quietly as she could.

"Ashael," she whispered.

Ashael tensed and turned toward her, blinking once as if clearing his mind before meeting her gaze.

"Clara," he murmured. "You're awake."

She nodded, then hesitated before saying, "I can take the second watch. You need to rest too."

Ashael shook his head slightly. "The tree is protecting us. I would have sensed if something was wrong by now." His gaze drifted briefly toward the hollow's entrance, the tension in his shoulders easing just a fraction. "It's safe here." He exhaled, quieter this time. "You should go back to sleep. I will follow in a few minutes. I just . . . need some air. I'll return shortly." He pushed himself to his feet and stepped into the quiet of the night.

Clara studied him for a moment. Something about the way he said it made her hesitate.

As she watched him rise and step just outside the shelter, a nagging feeling stirred inside her. He was troubled. It was obvious.

And it nagged at her more than it should.

She glanced at Malrik, still fast asleep, before stepping outside to follow Ashael.

The air outside was crisp and cool, carrying the scent of damp earth laced with a subtle hint of flowers. The sky stretched above, a vast expanse of black and silver, with the full moon casting its soft glow over the island.

Clara inhaled softly. It was beautiful, but it was not what stole her breath away.

Ashael stood just beyond the shelter, bathed in moonlight. His hair gleamed, his sharp features softened by the silvery glow, his presence striking against the quiet backdrop of the trees.

Their eyes met. There was something raw and unspoken in his gaze.

She swallowed, forcing herself to take a step forward. He didn't look away. Her pulse quickened.

"Ashael," she said softly, stopping just inches from him. "Are you all right?"

He didn't answer right away. Instead, his gaze lingered on her, as if weighing his response. Then, quietly, he said, "I have been plagued by thoughts I can't shake."

Clara hesitated, then asked gently, "Do you want to talk about it?"

Ashael let out a soft exhale, glancing up at the sky. Then, shaking his head, he murmured, "It is nothing to bother you with."

Something about his tone made her chest tighten. She searched his face, as if hoping to find answers in the way his jaw tensed, in the way his shoulders carried invisible weight.

Still, she gave him a small nod. "All right, but I hope you know I'm here for you."

He inhaled sharply, as if weighing the risk of speaking at all. His fingers curled at his sides. And then, finally he spoke. "It was real."

Clara went still, every nerve focused on him. "What?"

Ashael met her gaze, hesitation tightening his features. "The dance. It was real."

Her heart pounded. He had been thinking about it too? The way they had moved together, the way she had felt in his arms. She had tried to convince herself all night that it was nothing, a fleeting moment, a trick of the Nyths. But hearing him say it now . . . Her face grew hot. "I—" Her voice faltered. She tried again. "A-Ash . . . I'm . . ."

Before she could form the words, he spoke again.

"You are beautiful, brave, and kindhearted." Ashael's gaze softened, something almost pained surfacing in his expression. "You don't have to say anything," he murmured. "I just need you to know . . . you deserve more than this. More than danger at every turn."

His voice was quiet, steady, but there was something in it that made her chest ache.

"I will stand by you," he continued. "I will do everything in my power to see this through, to help you, to help our people. And when it's over, I'll make sure you get home safely."

Home. The word should have comforted her. But instead, it sent a pang of something close to loss through her chest.

Going home meant leaving this place. Leaving him. She swallowed past the sudden knot in her throat. "I know," she said slowly. "You've saved me more times than I can count. I . . . I haven't even thanked you for it."

Her heart felt heavy as it pounded against her ribcage. "Thank you, Ashael." She forced a small, grateful smile, even as a dull ache settled in her chest. "I hope I won't be a burden much longer."

Ashael's brows drew together. For a split second, it looked like he wanted to say something more. His fingers flexed at his sides, as if aching to reach for her. He merely nodded.

Clara turned back toward the shelter, her thoughts more tangled than before.

She had wanted answers. Instead, she walked away feeling even more lost.

She slipped back inside the hollow, laying down on the moss. Moments later, she heard the soft tread of Ashael's footsteps.

He settled onto the other side, his presence a quiet weight in the darkness. Clara closed her eyes, unsure if sleep would come again.

Clara stirred awake at the sound of soft movement, her body heavy with fatigue. Malrik was already up, stretching out his limbs as the dim morning light seeped into the hollow. His movements were careful, but something about the way he held himself felt tense.

She blinked, rubbing the sleep from her eyes before scanning the hollow. Ashael was gone.

Malrik caught her searching gaze and spoke before she could ask.

"He's out." Malrik's voice was even, but his gaze dipped briefly, as if hiding something behind lowered eyes. A beat passed before he looked up again, his expression carefully neutral. "Checking the area. Making sure it's safe before we head out."

Clara hesitated, but instead of pressing, she gave a small nod.

They settled into a simple routine. She and Malrik each took a Morsela, the small sustenance more than enough to satisfy their hunger. She took a sip from her flask, the cool water easing her throat.

By the time Ashael returned, the tension in her shoulders had lessened, but the moment he stepped inside, something shifted.

"The coast is clear."

For some reason, she couldn't meet his eyes. Her fingers curled slightly against the fabric of her sleeve, then smoothed it out as if that would steady her. She took another sip from her flask, fidgeting to keep from looking at him.

"We should make use of our time while waiting for Kira," he said. "We need to figure out where to go next."

Clara nodded quickly, latching onto the distraction. "Yes, of course."

She knelt and reached into her pack, retrieving the wind sphere. Then she withdrew the map from the pocket of her tunic. She hovered the sphere over the map, just like every time before.

Clara braced herself for a rush of wind, for the map to light up with their next path. Nothing happened.

Her brows furrowed. She adjusted, moving the sphere over the surface more slowly this time.

Still nothing. Confusion pressed into her chest. It had worked before with the other spheres.

She frowned and tried again, this time waving the sphere over the ground, the gnarled roots weaving through the hollow, over the small pool of water collected in the tree's natural crevices.

Still nothing.

"This doesn't make sense," she muttered, pacing slightly as frustration crept in.

Malrik leaned against the hollow's entrance, watching her with raised brows. "Maybe it's just being difficult," he said. "Or maybe the Nyths tricked us, and it was never supposed to work in the first place."

Clara exhaled sharply. "No, it should work like the others. Why can't this one?"

Malrik hummed in his throat, thinking. "All right, well—Nyths! A little help over here?"

Only silence met his outburst.

Clara scowled. Malrik shrugged. Then, something clicked. A whisper of a memory.

The elements must remember.

"Wait," she said suddenly, turning to them. "The Nyths said something to me when they gave me the sphere. I forgot until now."

Ashael and Malrik both turned to her, alert.

"They said, 'The elements must remember.'"

Ashael frowned. "The elements . . . must remember?"

Clara dug into her pack, pulling the other spheres out. She knelt and laid them gently on the moss. Three in total.

Malrik and Ashael moved to crouch by her side and examined them closely.

The first, retrieved from an ocean pool, contained swirls of blue and gold. Water and sand. The second was filled with embers shifting alongside dark ash. Fire and rock. The last sphere from the Nyths held a translucent substance that danced inside, kicking up small tornadoes of dirt. Wind and soil. They were all elements.

"The elements must remember." Malrik muttered, brushing the center sphere with his finger. "What does that even mean? Are they supposed to think? Are they . . . sentient?"

He tapped a knuckle against one of the spheres. "Hello? Give us a sign if you understand us."

Silence.

Ashael sighed, rubbing the bridge of his nose. "It may not be that literal."

Clara sat back on her heels and tried not to feel so disappointed in her own inability to figure out what the Nyths meant. "What do you mean?"

Ashael studied the spheres, his fingers brushing absently over them one by one. "What if they're meant to work together?"

Malrik scoffed, then froze. His expression shifted, brows drawing together. "Wait, you mean they should remember each other?"

A realization rushed through Clara like a spark catching flame.

"And how will they remember each other?" Malrik asked, his voice thoughtful but impatient. "By placing them . . ."

And at the same time, the three of them breathed, "Together."

Clara immediately handed them each a sphere. To Ashael she gave the one from the Syralen's Cove, to Malrik the sphere that swirled with fire and rock. She clutched the one from the Nyths in her hand as she spread out the map.

They hovered them together over the map and waited. Clara didn't dare breathe. The silence stretched, thick with anticipation.

Something in the hollow stirred, light as a breath. It wasn't something she could see, at least not at first, but she could feel the air around them change.

The distant roar of rushing water grew loud. A fresh scent rolled through the hollow, crisp and clean like mist and river stones. The moss beneath them was cool, the dampness seeping through the fabric of her clothes, as if fresh rain had passed nearby.

A strange, weightless touch traced over Clara's fingers, almost curious. Her fingers twitched instinctively, a prickle running up her arm. She glanced down. The map rested motionless on the ground, yet she still felt the presence, like water slipping through her grasp.

Her eyes darted up, searching for the others.

Malrik's eyes were wide. "What the hell was that?"

Ashael flexed his fingers subtly, as if testing the unfamiliar force. His gaze met Clara's. "Do you feel it too?"

She exhaled, relieved to know she wasn't imagining it, yet uncertainty still coiled inside her. She gave a small nod, unable to find her voice.

Finally, the map reacted.

A pulse spread across the surface, the lines stretching and bending like ink swirling in water. The lines glowed softly, then grew bright.

The light rose from the map, unfurling into something Clara couldn't yet make out. Ashael inhaled sharply. Malrik leaned in, his eyes widening. Above the map, a three-dimensional projection wavered, rippling like heat over stone.

Clara's heart pounded as the image cleared. She saw a towering cascade of water, jutting out from a flat, stone plateau. Mist swirled around the waterfall. Malrik let out a breath, shaking his head with a crooked grin. "Finally."

Ashael's gaze swept over the scene, calculating. He bent forward and examined the map, which had shifted to reveal a more detailed sketch of the floating island. He traced a path along the map with his finger, before stilling on a point in the center of the island, slightly northeast of dead-center. "That's where we need to go."

Clara inhaled deeply, tension loosening in her chest. "It worked."

Malrik's grin faded slightly as he studied the display. "Yeah, but what exactly is waiting for us there?"

The group watched the wavering golden waterfall. Clara couldn't help but feel wary. It was beautiful but hinted at danger. Like all the previous places they'd been to before. It seemed this next stop would be no different.

CHAPTER 26

Clara panted as they followed the winding path upward, the damp ground uneven beneath her boots. The rush of water echoed from above, growing louder with every step.

She exhaled sharply, glancing back. Malrik and Ashael were close behind, moving steadily up the trail. The incline wasn't impossibly steep, but the moss-covered stone made footing tricky. More than once, she had to slow her pace to keep from slipping.

It seemed almost too good to be true that their next destination, the towering waterfall, was on the floating island. Then again, the map had led them to the spheres in a particular order. Clara felt a surge of uncharacteristic confidence. If they'd made it this far, surely, they were nearing the end of their journey.

At last, they reached the top of the craggy path. Clara braced her hands on her knees, catching her breath before straightening. Triumph swelled in her chest. They made it.

The view stretched vast and untouched, more breathtaking than she had imagined. The waterfall thundered beside them, its force vibrating through the ground. The air was thick with moisture, cool droplets clinging to her skin and seeping into her sleeves.

They moved carefully, edging forward, their boots pressing into the damp ground. The stone plateau leveled out, its smooth surface slick with running water. Clara stepped cautiously, testing her footing. Slippery, but manageable. *As long as I go slow, keep my weight balanced, and—*

Her foot slipped.

Well, so much for that.

She tipped backward, the world tilting with her, until strong hands seized her. Ashael's grip held firm, halting the fall before it could take her. Her heartbeat hammered.

She looked up into his eyes.

Time slowed. His fingers tightened just slightly, his touch warm despite the cool air. There was no space between them, nothing but the pull of something neither of them spoke aloud.

"I swear, you're trying to give me a heart attack." Malrik's voice cut through the moment like a blade, rougher than usual. He was already stepping closer, his arm extended before she could even think.

Ashael released her slowly. She could still feel the warmth of his hold as she regained her balance.

"Come on," Malrik muttered, his tone edged with something between exasperation and insistence. "Hold onto me this time."

Clara hesitated for a fraction of a second before taking his outstretched arm.

Taking a steadying breath, Clara forced herself to look down, her knees wobbling at the sheer height. Below, a dense shroud of mist swallowed the base of the falls, concealing whatever lay beneath.

Malrik let out a low whistle. "Glad the map didn't send us up from below. Climbing this beast? No thanks."

He paused, brow furrowing as he eyed the drop. Then, with a slight tilt of his head, he muttered, "All right, seriously, where does all this water go?"

Clara frowned, the question sinking in. She had assumed there had to be a river or a pool to catch the thundering water, but she couldn't see anything from this vantage point. "A river, probably . . ." she said, sounding uncertain.

Ashael glanced at her, as if voicing the thought forming in her mind. "If there is one."

The moment dragged, too heavy to be comfortable.

A waterfall this massive should have a clear destination, but no streams branched away. No gaps in the fog revealed the path below. And it wasn't like they were standing at the edge of the floating island. They were somewhere in the middle.

Yet somehow the water just disappeared.

Malrik leaned forward, scanning the depths below. "That doesn't add up."

Clara squinted, trying to make sense of the drop. She could hear the water below, or at least she thought she could. The sound was there, but something about it felt off. It didn't trail away like a river flowing downstream. Instead, it hovered, looping back on itself, like it had nowhere to go.

Ashael studied the mist. "Something's not right . . ."

The map had led them here. But why?

Malrik broke the silence. "So, what now? We jump?"

It was a joke, but Ashael took it seriously. "You may be right."

Malrik turned to him. "Seriously?"

Ashael's expression remained thoughtful. "In every clue we've gathered, there's always been some kind of test. This could be another."

Malrik let out a dry laugh. "A test? Or suicide?"

Ashael ignored the remark. "If this place is guarding something, it makes sense there would be a way to prove our worth."

Clara barely listened as they argued. Something about this place called to her. She'd felt it grow stronger as they climbed. A pull in her chest. Her pendant had warmed against her skin too, as if pleased.

Malrik gestured sharply toward the mist. "Right, so we just leap into a void and hope it doesn't kill us?"

Ashael exhaled, shifting his weight as he glanced at Malrik. "We've passed every trial that's come our way, Malrik. There's no reason to think this will be any different."

Malrik's voice dropped, edged with something heavier. "And what if this is the one time we're not supposed to make it through?"

Ashael held his gaze, unshaken. "Standing here won't change that."

The tension between them thickened. Clara sighed to herself. *Seriously, what is up with these two? Is Malrik jealous?*

She opened her mouth to stop them, but a whisper made her freeze.

"Clara . . ."

She let go of Malrik's arm and whipped around. He didn't notice. He was too busy arguing with Ashael.

Clara turned once more to the waterfall. It thundered, drowning everything else.

"Here."

The voice was clear. Her pendant pulsed strongly as she gazed into the void. Her fingers brushed over it instinctively, the heat pressing into her skin.

She inhaled deeply. This wasn't the Nyths. This was something else.

Ashael and Malrik were still arguing when she cut in. "Did you hear that?"

Both turned to her. "Hear what?" Ashael asked.

She hesitated, her voice quieter than before. "A voice."

Malrik tensed. "The Nyths again?"

"No." She shook her head, a tremor running through her. "It's . . . different."

She knew this voice. It was familiar. Distant, yet impossibly close. She had heard it before. In her dreams.

She hadn't had them since their journey began. The whispers. The guiding presence. The pull toward something unknown.

Now, it was back. Urging her forward.

Malrik's gaze darkened. "Clara?"

She turned to them, heart racing. "It's the voice from my dreams."

Ashael's expression sharpened. "You're sure?"

She nodded. "It led us to the first clue that brought us here. And now I hear it again. But this time I'm awake."

Malrik exhaled, dragging a hand through his hair. "What did it say?"

Clara hesitated, pulse hammering. Speaking it aloud made it feel more real.

"My name," she said slowly. "And . . . 'here.'"

Malrik's brows knit together. "Here?"

Clara nodded and pointed into the thick fog. "And it sounded like it came from below."

Ashael studied her closely. "If the voice has guided us before . . ."

Malrik cursed under his breath. "You can't seriously be considering—"

Clara interrupted, stepping closer to the edge. "The map led us here, exactly here. It didn't tell us to go below another way. This is the spot."

Ashael hesitated. Even *he* looked uncertain now.

Malrik shook his head in disbelief. "You're both insane."

Clara had heard enough.

This was it. The voice, the map, the journey . . . everything led here. She thought of the dreams that had guided her, the whispers that had pulled her forward, and the weight of the pendant against her chest. She had come too far to turn back now.

She took a breath and steeled herself. She walked a few paces away from the edge, back toward the center of the plateau. She paused. Ashael had told her to trust her instincts. And every instinct inside her was screaming at her now. She faced the falls. Before she could reconsider, she

317

ran forward. One, two, three paces before she reached the edge. Then she hurtled herself forward until there was nothing beneath her feet but the thundering of water.

Malrik shouted, his voice raw and frantic, cutting even through the roar of the water.

Heavy footsteps pounded the stone behind her. A rush of movement. Ashael, lunging. She felt him reaching, heard the scrape of boots on wet rock, the sharp inhale of breath.

For a single, breathless second, the world held still and Clara hovered, weightless, before gravity caught up to her. She fell.

The wind rushed up to meet her, tearing at her clothes, yanking her hair back. Her stomach lurched. A jolt of fear shot through her, sharp and sudden. *What have I done?*

The air howled past, cold against her skin, needling her cheeks. Water droplets lashed at her face, sharp as pinpricks. She squinted against the sting, the world blurring, the waterfall's roar consuming everything.

But as she fell, the terror did not consume her. The fear faded. The wind wasn't just biting, it was exhilarating. The cool mist wove around her, seeping through her sleeves, sending a shiver down her spine. And for a split second, she *liked* it.

She kept her gaze forward, refusing to look down, letting herself surrender to the weightlessness. It felt *freeing*. The longer she fell, the more it didn't feel like falling at all.

Then she made the mistake of looking down.

The thick fog stretched beneath her like a bed of translucent cotton, soft and endless. If only it would feel that way when she landed. But she had no idea what was waiting below.

Her body went rigid. The fog was close enough to touch, yet it revealed nothing beneath. She squeezed her eyes shut and braced for impact, for her body to crash against stone or plunge into freezing water, but nothing came.

Something should have happened by now. Clara opened her eyes and saw only white. She had stopped falling. She was floating.

Suspended in the thick fog, warmth wrapped around her, gentle and steady. Clara felt like she was being held. The fog was safe and welcoming. She sucked in a breath and tried to get her bearings. She felt a subtle pull, guiding her lower.

Her feet met something solid. The light dimmed. She blinked, and the world solidified before her eyes.

Smooth white stone curved around her in a perfect circle.

She was in a chamber that had no doors or windows, just an unbroken expanse of pristine walls that felt untouched by time. Overhead, a dense layer of fog blocked any view of the ceiling, concealing whatever lay beyond. *Was it still the waterfall above? Or something else entirely?*

Something glinted in the dim light.

Clara slipped a hand into her satchel, fingers wrapping around the cool glass of her light vial. Holding it up, she let the soft glow spill over the walls.

Embedded in the stone were tiny fragments of an unfamiliar material, neither metal nor crystal. The pieces reflected the dim light, forming delicate patterns and symbols in a mix of colors. She studied them, brow furrowing. *What could they mean?*

A soft *whoosh* caught her attention.

Clara turned just as Ashael landed, his descent graceful, controlled. His sharp gaze swept the chamber, alert for any sign of danger.

Finally, his gaze found her.

He closed the space between them swiftly, voice edged with concern. "Clara, are you hurt?"

Before she could answer, there was a *thud* and a muttered curse.

Malrik stumbled forward with a grunt. "Damn it—" He straightened, shaking off the landing before his head snapped up, scanning the chamber. "Clara!"

Ashael was already at her side, checking for injuries, but Malrik was right behind him, his urgency palpable. He reached them a moment later, still trying to catch his breath.

"Don't—" He let out a sharp exhale, his frustration spilling over. "Don't you *ever* do that again."

Clara spread her hands wide, hoping to calm him. "I'm fine."

Malrik took off his glasses and dragged a hand down his face. "Yeah, well, my heart isn't."

Ashael watched her for another moment before letting out a slow breath, his shoulders finally relaxing. "That was reckless," he said, his tone softer, "but I'm proud of you."

His words hit deeper than she expected, sending her a rush of warmth she hadn't realized she needed. Malrik, blunt and clearly on edge, didn't bother hiding his concern, and somehow, that got to her too. Different, yet both affected her more than she cared to admit.

She offered a shaky smile before turning back to the stone walls. "There's something here," she murmured. "And above . . . we can't be sure what's beyond that fog."

Malrik and Ashael shifted their focus to the walls, and Clara hoped they could help her figure out this next puzzle.

"What do you think it is?" Malrik asked quietly.

Ashael ran his fingers lightly across the surface, his expression thoughtful. "It might be another clue. Or a way forward."

They began moving slowly around the chamber's perimeter, examining each shimmering pattern. No matter how long they stared, they still couldn't decipher its meaning.

Malrik frowned. "And what if this is a trap?" His voice was edged with unease. "We don't even know how to get out of here."

Clara forced herself to remain calm, even though it suddenly felt like the walls were pressing in on all sides. He was right. If this was a test, how would they know if they were meant to pass it, or if they were simply walking into something they couldn't escape? There was no way out of this chamber.

Then, light stirred within her pendant, a pull in the dark.

Clara stiffened, her gaze dropping to it.

A slow, steady heat spread against her skin as the pendant warmed. The glow intensified, shining brilliantly.

Malrik went still. "Clara . . ." His voice was wary as the light reflected in his widened eyes.

Ashael's gaze sharpened, assessing her.

Her feet moved before she could think, following a strange tug to the center of the room. Drawn forward, she stepped toward the center of the chamber, the pendant's light strengthened with each step, shadows stretching long across the stone.

A small, round table rose from the chamber floor. It was made of the same stone as the room. Four concave circles were carved into it. Three formed a perfect triangle that glowed with a different color. Cobalt blue, ember red, and pearly silver.

At the very center lay a fourth concave, smaller than the others. Its surface gleamed like flawless crystal, the depths sparkling as though a thousand tiny stars were trapped within.

Clara reached out, her fingers tingling as they grazed the edge.

The colors were vibrant, the texture smoother than anything she'd ever felt. It was like nothing she had ever encountered, overwhelming in its strangeness. Avenora was always different, always more, and it left her breathless.

Malrik let out a slow breath. "Well, I don't know about you, but this seems fairly obvious to me."

He was right. There were three waiting slots for the three spheres they had collected so far.

Clara's heart pounded as she reached into her satchel, fingers brushing the smooth orbs she had kept safe. Drawing them out, she felt a surge of certainty. They were meant for this place.

Malrik drew in a low breath. "They're a perfect match."

Clara cradled the spheres in her hands. Water, Fire, Wind. It felt right. This had to be the key.

Ashael inclined his head toward the table. "You do the honors, Clara."

She fit the water orb into the blue concave, her breath quickening as it slid in with ease. She did the same with the fire sphere and the red awaiting slot.

The final sphere rested in her palm. The seconds felt heavier, each one stretching as the weight of the moment settled on her. Slowly, she set it into the silver-white hollow, watching as it settled, as if it had always belonged.

She stepped back and waited for the truth to be revealed.

Once again, Clara felt disappointment roil in her gut. Nothing was happening. It made perfect sense. The spheres matched the pedestal perfectly. So, why was nothing happening?

Malrik exhaled sharply. "You've got to be kidding me." He waved a hand through the air, as if brushing away the frustration. "That should have done something."

Clara's stomach twisted into tighter knots. It had to be right. But the table remained unchanged, the spheres sitting there as if mocking her.

Ashael frowned. "Unless we're missing something."

A bright light carved through Clara's vision, emanating from her chest. She looked down and saw her pendant blink slowly, pulsing like a heartbeat. Each flash came quicker now, stronger, more insistent. She clapped a hand over her chest, as if trying to soothe it. She squinted at the pedestal, and as her fingers curved around her necklace, she realized what the missing piece was.

Her fingers fumbled with the clasp before freeing the pendant, its warmth pressing into her palm.

She lowered it into the final hollow. Light erupted. Three brilliant rays, white-hot and precise, shot from the pendant in perfect lines, striking each of the spheres. The orbs responded instantly, releasing their own radiant beams of ruby, cerulean, and silver, twisting toward one another in an unbreakable cycle of energy.

Clara's jaw dropped as the spheres rose into the air.

They lifted from the concaves, weightless, spinning slowly at first. Then they picked up speed, spinning until they blurred into streaks of color, impossible to track.

The hair on Clara's neck and arms rose as the room became charged with energy. A terrible *crack* made her gasp. The spheres shattered. But they were not broken. They dissolved into swirling wisps of energy, twisting and coiling above the table like a living storm.

The walls shifted. Malrik cursed as symbols began to emerge, rising from the stone as if waking from a long slumber. The carvings unraveled into streams of light, joining the churning energy above them.

Clara's body locked in place, eyes wide, as the air around them vibrated, heavy with something ancient.

A voice, delicate as a breeze, resounded through the room.

"Bearer of light."

Before she could react, the light began to take shape.

Ashael tensed. Malrik's fingers twitched toward the bow slung across his back.

Then Clara saw herself. Her own face, suspended in the air, rendered in light. It wasn't just a projection. It held warmth, a silent gratitude, as though welcoming her at last.

Clara's lips parted. It knew her.

The face quivered before morphing into a flood of images. Flashes of Avenora's past spun around them, unraveling history as they knew it. The disruption of balance and the shattering of the Vaelithar, the artifact that was the key to the Veil Gate that separated the land of Avenora from the human realm. War followed, and darkness spread like a plague. But then the vision lingered on the moment the Vaelithar broke. It splintered into three pieces.

Clara felt Ashael stiffen beside her as the vision began to fade.

The swirling lights and symbols collapsed inward, condensing, folding into themselves, shrinking until the air itself seemed to constrict around them.

A burst of white light made Clara shield her eyes. The light dimmed, and Clara dropped her arm.

Suspended in the air above the pedestal was a single, solid object. Clara stepped forward, her breath unsteady. One side was smooth and curved. The other was jagged, fractured. A shard, roughly the size of her palm. Its crystalline surface shimmered, shifting between translucence and a swirl of interwoven colors like smoke trapped inside glass. Then clear again. Then colored once more.

She knew what it was. "The Vaelithar . . ." she whispered, caught between awe and disbelief.

Above the shard, words took shape. Floating, as if written by fire.

Ashael read the words that blazed above them. "When the veil quakes and shadows rise, two shall stand to mend the broken."

Ashael read the words evenly, but Clara caught the tension laced in his tone.

The letters quivered in the air. Another line formed.

One shall bear—

It wavered like it was struggling to hold itself together. Then the words faltered and broke apart like smoke on the wind.

Clara held her breath, waiting. But no more words came.

The air around her stilled. The message had been cut short.

The three of them stared at the floating shard. Clara inhaled deeply, trying to calm the rush of emotions inside her. They had found it. After everything they had endured, the searching, the close calls, the trials, they'd found the Vaelithar shard. It was real. Malrik let out a sharp breath, dragging a hand through his hair. "Did that just happen?" he said, voice rough with disbelief. He turned to them, his brows drawn tight. "After all this time, after everything we've faced, we actually found it?"

He let out a slow breath. "I mean, I still can't believe I actually jumped." His lips curved into something between a grin and a grimace. "But I did it for you."

His gaze held hers, not quite letting go. There was something raw in it, something honest and exposed.

Something tugged at her chest.

Before she could respond, Ashael stepped closer. "I knew you'd make the right call." His bright blue eyes sparkled with pride. "I'm glad you remembered to trust your instincts."

Clara's cheeks warmed as she held his gaze. He was right. She had remembered. It had given her the courage to jump.

"We found it," she said. She cleared her throat, trying to sound composed. "Together."

The realization hit Clara hard. Before going through the portal, she'd felt so isolated. Stuck, too, as if she was only going through the motions of her life, not truly living it. Even though the arrival of the pendant and the terror that followed had thrust her into a strange new world, she didn't feel so alone. She'd had a purpose back in New York, and she was happy to take care of others at Brookhaven. But here, in Avenora, when she was stacked against impossible odds, she didn't have to face them alone.

Clara's eyes pricked with tears. She turned and blinked them away before Ashael could see. Her chest warmed, strengthened by his and Malrik's presence. But another look at the pedestal, at the shard floating above it, made her come back to the present moment. "I think we just saw the truth," she said.

Malrik adjusted his glasses. "What do you mean?"

"A confirmation," she said slowly, "of the scholars' records, of what people believed about the Vaelithar, but also something else. Something no one knew before."

Ashael nodded, a hint of relief in his voice. "It revealed knowledge that's been lost for centuries. Now we know there are three shards, and we have one of them. We're not totally in the dark about what we're looking for anymore."

Malrik shook his head. "True, but it didn't give us everything."

Clara frowned. "You're right. The words . . ."

Ashael rubbed his chin. "I know what it was."

Malrik didn't wait for him to finish. "Yeah, it's just like the prophecy. The way it showed up, how it burned into the air. Exactly like Ceyndor said." He let out a frustrated sigh. "So, what if we just saw a piece of the prophecy that everyone else saw back then? Only this time, it's just the three of us who got to see it."

Ashael wasn't so discouraged. "Then that means we may only see the full prophecy when the Vaelithar is whole again."

A heavy silence stretched between them. The implications settled like a weight over their shoulders.

Malrik crossed his arms. "All right. Let's break down what we know."

He glanced at Clara. "'One shall bear . . .' That has to mean 'bear the light,' right? We heard that whisper. 'Bearer of Light.' It has to be you."

Ashael gave a small nod. "It confirms your role in this, Clara."

Clara crossed her left arm over her stomach, resting her chin on her right hand as she thought. The whisper that had unsettled her before now felt real, like a truth she couldn't deny. She was the Bearer of Light. It wasn't just a title anymore. It was becoming part of her. Her fingers found the pendant and fastened it back on her neck, taking a slow breath.

"I guess I am," she murmured.

The thought wasn't as shocking as it might have been a few weeks ago. After everything that had happened, the trials she'd endured, and the way her pendant and the light had kept her on the right path, it only made sense. It didn't feel as though fate had forced her here. It felt more like every choice she had made had slowly uncovered the strength already within her, a strength capable of more than she had ever believed. And somewhere deep inside, she knew she could be worthy of this responsibility.

Malrik exhaled, rubbing his jaw. "But if you're the one bearing the light, then who's the second person in the prophecy?"

No one had an answer.

Malrik forged ahead. "You know what I don't get? The prophecy that was shown all those years ago appeared in both realms, right? How did everyone understand it?"

Ashael's eyes shifted toward him, thoughtful. "A good question." He ran his fingers over the ancient carvings, his expression pensive. "I believe the prophecy adapts."

Malrik raised an eyebrow. "Adapts?"

Clara's eyebrows also shot up. It didn't make sense for a prophecy to change. Then, it wouldn't be much of a prophecy, would it? More like a prediction.

Ashael nodded. "The Eternals would have ensured that their words could be understood by anyone who witnessed them. The prophecy was meant for both fae and humans. So it wouldn't be bound by a single language. It would manifest in a way that the person receiving it could comprehend, whether through words, symbols, or even visions."

Clara considered this. It made more sense than the actual prophecy changing meaning. "People might have interpreted it in different ways, then."

Ashael stared hard at the floating shard. "Exactly. And maybe that's why no one today knows the full prophecy, because it wasn't recorded the same way by everyone who saw it. Just stories, theories, fragments passed down over time."

Malrik let out a sarcastic chuckle. "Great. So, not only do we have to find the shards, but we have to piece together an ancient puzzle that no one has ever fully understood."

Clara followed Ashael's gaze and turned back to the shard, watching it hover in silence. "Where do we even begin with the other two pieces?"

Ashael shook his head, voice low. "I don't know. But we do know that Veylora is searching for them too."

"And what if she finds them first?" asked Malrik.

Clara's stomach dropped. She, too, was wondering what would happen if Veylora got her hands on a piece of the Vaelithar.

Ashael's gaze remained locked on the shard. "She won't. At least not easily."

Malrik narrowed his eyes. "What makes you so sure?"

"Because of what we just witnessed." Ashael gestured toward the carvings around them that were embedded into the walls of the chamber. "The Eternals' essence still lingers within the Vaelithar, even in its broken form. The shards weren't just scattered. They were cleverly hidden. This first shard wove itself into the elements, creating those orbs of power that needed to be reunited in this specific place in order to be revealed. All while the shard's memories remained bound to this place, waiting for the right connection. Clara's pendant."

Clara shifted back on her heels. "You're saying the Vaelithar chose where to hide?"

"Yes. And the remnants of its power shield the places where it rests."

Malrik let out a slow exhale, shaking his head. "That would explain why certain places, like the Syralen Cove, remain untouched by corruption. They're protected."

"And it explains why Veylora had her Dravok surrounding it," she said.

Ashael's expression darkened. "She must have sensed something. Or maybe she just believed the whispers were true. The fact remains that now that we have uncovered this shard, she will be even more dangerous."

Clara's hands tingled as fear sent a spike of adrenaline through her. Ashael was right. Veylora would do anything for the shard, and if she could sense the magic surrounding it, they might already be surrounded by Dravok. "Then we don't have much time."

Ashael let his hand drift to the hilt of his dagger. "No. We need to find the other shards as soon as possible."

"No pressure, right?" Malrik said.

Clara bit her lip as Ashael turned toward her.

"We should take it now."

Clara nodded, though something itched at the back of her mind. What would happen when she touched it? Would the places it had been protecting remain untouched, or would they fall once it was removed from its resting place?

Whatever happened, it wouldn't be worse than Veylora getting to the shard first. Clara shuddered as the memory of the Dravok leapt to the front of her mind.

She reached out, hesitating for just a heartbeat, then closed the distance.

CHAPTER 27

Clara's fingers were tense as they closed around the Vaelithar shard, being careful not to cut herself on its jagged edge. Its surface was cool against her skin, unexpectedly solid for something that had hovered so weightlessly before her. She drew it away from the table, cradling it in her palm as if it might shatter at the slightest pressure.

"It's beautiful," she whispered, unable to tear her eyes from the crystalline fragment and the colors that swirled inside it. The shard seemed to welcome her touch, almost purring beneath her fingertips.

Her gaze flitted to Malrik and Ashael's faces. They were both equally transfixed by the shard. Malrik let out a long breath, the tension easing from his shoulders. Ashael stared at it, then shifted his eyes to her.

Clara stood stock still, waiting for a sudden shift in the chamber, anything to indicate that the shard had been removed from its resting place. The room remained unchanged. The patterns on the wall still glimmered, but there was no sudden rush of darkness or impending danger.

"Thank goodness, I was expecting—"

A tremor stirred beneath her boots.

"Do you feel that?" Malrik asked, throwing out his hand.

A crack split through the air like brittle ice snapping. Hairline fractures stretched across the walls, creeping like veins of lightning. The ground lurched. A droplet of water landed on Clara's cheek. She looked up, only to see that more water followed, seeping through the fog overhead, turning into a downpour. Oh my God. What was happening? "It's collapsing!" Malrik shouted.

Water jetted through the walls in bursts, biting and icy. The floor groaned beneath their feet, splintering with each passing second. Streams surged from below, the water rising to flood the room.

The water rushed in, and they were helpless to stop it.

It was already at Clara's knees, then her waist. The cold bit through her clothes, stealing the breath from her lungs. She gasped and clutched the shard tightly to her chest.

Ashael strode through the water and gripped her shoulder with startling force.

Malrik splashed toward her from the opposite side and grabbed her hand.

"Hold on!" they shouted together, their voices echoing above the din.

Clara looked between them. Their faces were taut with urgency, and for a brief second, their eyes locked over her head. Clara saw the tension in that glance, sharp and wordless.

Before she could register more, the floor crumbled beneath them. Water exploded upward, swallowing them. Clara was pulled under the icy waves. She didn't even have time to scream. Roaring filled her ears, and the water pounded against her body.

Ashael's grip vanished. Malrik's hand was ripped away.

Clara clung to the shard with both hands, holding on like it was the only solid thing left in the world. She would not let go of it. Not after all they had endured to get it.

Water was everywhere, pushing her down. She kicked but had lost her sense of direction. Her lungs burned, screaming for air. Fear threatened to drown everything out. Her mind began to spiral. This was how she was going to die.

A pulse of warmth from the shard stilled her thoughts. It pulsed again, stronger, and wrapped around her. Suddenly, her body shot upwards.

Her head broke the surface. She gasped, air flooding her lungs. She coughed hard, sputtering, and blinked against the blur of water and light.

She treaded water, still clinging to the shard, and took in her surroundings. Clara was in a river. There were trees on both sides, and muddy banks that sloped into the water. Her heart stilled. There was no sign of Malrik or Ashael.

She screamed their names but was met with only the sound of the rushing river.

Clutching the shard in one hand, she fought her way through the water, her strokes lopsided and frantic. Her breath tore in and out, sharp and uneven.

No. Please. No.

Movement on the bank caught her attention. Her name echoed over the water, frantic and pleading.

Ashael.

Without hesitation, he splashed into the river and reached her fast. His hands gripped her arms, eyes scanning her face like he couldn't quite believe she was real. He helped her swim to the bank and continued to cling to her as they stumbled to shore.

He placed his hands on both sides of her face, and their eyes locked.

The way he looked at her made the rest of the world blur. His gaze rooted her to the spot, like he was trying to say everything at once but couldn't find the words. Then, he exhaled, blinked, and pulled her into a fierce embrace.

Clara let herself sink into his arms. His chest rose and fell against her temple. She clutched the shard to her chest and closed her eyes.

"I thought I lost you," he murmured close to her ear.

The words hit her somewhere deep, stealing the air from her lungs. She wrapped her arms around him, bringing their bodies closer together. For a brief moment, there was nothing but the rhythm of their breath, the pounding of their hearts.

Then Clara jerked back to reality.

"Malrik," she whispered, a new wave of panic rising.

She pulled away and turned, scanning the river. "Where is he?" Her voice cracked as she searched the water's surface.

Still nothing. Her nerves screamed for action. "I have to go back!"

Ashael caught her wrist. "Clara, wait! I'll find him—"

A splash sounded just upstream. Clara spun toward the sound, rushing a few steps along the muddy bank.

Her heart jumped. "Malrik!" she shouted, as relief made her knees wobble.

He paused mid-stroke as he turned his head toward her voice. Clara waved frantically and splashed into the water up to her knees.

Malrik drove forward with uncanny speed, each stroke stronger than the last.

His face broke into a grin as he neared the bank. He stood and waded through the water.

Clara ran forward as he reached the edge and stood, soaked to the bone. Without thinking, she threw her arms around him, nearly knocking him off balance.

"I was so worried." Her voice cracked as she spoke.

He didn't move at first, like his mind hadn't caught up to the moment. But then he slowly wrapped his arms around her, holding him to her.

"I thought you—"

Malrik's fingers slipped from her hair to her back, settling in a way that felt like a promise.

"Shh . . . I'm here. I'm all right."

Clara leaned into him, swallowing a sob, letting herself feel his body beneath her own. Something pulled at the edge of her awareness. A prickle rose along her back, impossible to ignore.

Clara disentangled herself from Malrik's arms and turned slowly.

Ashael stood a short distance away, water dripping from him, his eyes locked on hers. He broke his stare before Clara could decipher the look on his face.

Clara felt a pang ripple through her. To ease the tension, she gave a crooked smile. "Malrik, I never knew you were such a good swimmer."

He gave a breathless laugh. "Neither did I."

His eyes dropped to his leg, where the Zaralis shimmered faintly. "I was sinking. The current kept pulling me under. But then something changed. "I felt sharper. Stronger. Like the Zaralis actually listened this time."

Clara's smile widened, her voice light with relief. "I'm glad it worked when you needed it most." She glanced at him, teasing gently. "Or maybe it was you who finally believed you could."

Malrik looked at her, a surprised smile pulling at the edge of his mouth. "Maybe."

Ashael nodded approvingly. "The Zaralis recognized your strength because you stopped holding back."

Malrik's eyes narrowed. "I didn't think I was holding back to begin with."

"I meant that you connected with a purpose that the Zaralis found worthy. It reacted to the shift in you, aligning with you," explained Ashael.

Malrik thought about Ashael's words for a moment, then nodded. "I understand."

Clara wondered what had changed. He seemed the same. "So, what, you're like a whole new person now?"

He laughed and bumped into her shoulder. "No chance. Still me. Just that, while I was in there, I wanted to *live*. When I jumped from the cliff,

335

it was to come after you. But when I was in there," he jerked his head back toward the roaring river, "I wanted to live for *me*. If that makes sense."

Clara understood. She was forever thankful that Malrik would always be there for her and would do the unthinkable, like jump off a cliff, to protect her. But their time in Avenora had shown them that they needed to trust in themselves, in their strength and in their courage. When they did, the path before them was clear. Clara knew she could take care of herself. She was so glad Malrik had wanted to live for himself too.

She smiled at Malrik and returned the bump to his shoulder. "Makes sense to me."

Clara clutched the shard to her chest and looked between her friends. "Now what?"

"First, we need to dry off. Then we'll decide what our next course of action should be," said Ashael.

They waded back up the bank and into the forest. As they walked, Clara felt the bands around her chest loosen a little. They were alive, and they had the shard. But she knew, deep down, that everything had changed.

Clara perched on a sun-baked boulder at the river's edge, emptying water from her boots before setting them nearby. The humid air clung to her skin, but thankfully her clothes had started to dry. Aelvor fabric truly was a gift.

She felt the weight of the satchel against her hip but couldn't shake the unease crawling up her spine.

"I was afraid this would happen," she murmured, fingers brushing the hard outline of the Vaelithar shard through the satchel's fabric. "I think the protection's gone."

Malrik rubbed the back of his neck as he settled down onto a patch of grass nearby. He waved his glasses through the air, trying to dry them. "You mean that's why we almost drowned? So, that place existed outside time or something? A pocket dimension that collapsed when we took what it was guarding? And then the real world snapped back into place, river and all?"

Clara tilted her head, considering. "It would seem so."

Malrik said, "The Eternals just had to hide that magical room under a freaking waterfall. What's wrong with a nice, dry cave? Or a temple? Or literally anywhere that doesn't involve plummeting to your death?"

Clara crossed her arms at her chest lightly. "Since when has anything been simple here?"

"Fair point." Malrik let out a sigh and flopped back onto the grass with a soft *thump*, arms sprawled out.

Ashael had taken a seat on another boulder nearby, one leg bent, his right elbow resting on his knee as he rubbed his jaw in thought. "I believe you're right, Clara. The Eternals' essence may no longer shield this place or the others. Or, at least, the protection is beginning to fade."

Clara glanced around, her voice quieter now. "So, we need to be careful."

Ashael nodded slightly, looking at the satchel. "The Eternals' essence must be condensed inside the shard now. Maybe we can still access it somehow and use it to fight Veylora's forces. Or maybe it's dormant. Waiting to be whole again."

Clara brushed her fingers against the familiar weight of the pendant. "It's hard to say. It helped me, I think. In the water."

"It's fickle, then. Like your pendant," Malrik said, picking up a small pebble and tossing it into the river. It hit the surface with a soft *plunk*.

337

"Half the time you don't even know when it's working. No control. And when it does help, it leaves you drained."

Clara exhaled, her shoulders slumping. "Yeah." It would be better if she could control it. The pendant or the shard. As it was, they were at their mercy.

Ashael sat still, posture tight, his striking blue eyes scanning the treeline like he expected it to rearrange itself at any moment.

Clara could see it on Ashael's face: Something was wrong.

A breeze rippled through the trees, carrying with it a sharp chill that raised goosebumps across her arms.

Malrik, still sprawled on the grass, squinted up at the sky. "Wait, what is that?" He jerked upright. "Is it getting darker?"

At the same moment, a shadow slipped across the ground.

Clara's gaze snapped upward, scanning the sky. "Kira?" But even as the name left her lips, her heart sank.

The shadow split, then split again, multiplying like dark smoke across the sky, bleeding into the blue.

Ashael shot to his feet, hand flying to his weapon. "Dravok," he growled.

Malrik surged forward, seizing Clara's wrist. "Move!"

"Wait, my boots!" She dropped, fumbling to pull them on, fingers slipping against the leather.

"There's no time!" Malrik shouted, panic rising in his voice. He reached for his bow and unsheathed an arrow from the quiver strung to his back.

A triumphant shriek tore through the sky. A Dravok had spotted them.

"I'm almost—" Clara managed breathlessly, shoving her heel into the last boot. But before the buckle snapped into place, Malrik yanked her up.

Clara sucked in a sharp breath. The treeless bank left them fully exposed. There were no shadows to hide beneath, no chance to vanish.

"Find cover!" Ashael shouted, already sprinting. "Somewhere dense where they can't spot us from above!"

They bolted for the forest. Branches slapped at Clara's arms and snagged at her sleeves as they plunged into the trees. Dark shapes streaked overhead, silent, swift, and all too aware.

Terror clawed at her, urged her to move faster.

"Then what?" Malrik rasped behind her, close enough that she could hear the strain in every word. "We're stuck on this floating chunk of rock!"

"The Nyths—" Clara gasped, breath tearing from her lungs. "They might—"

"Oh, the invisible faeries who like to play tricks on us?" Malrik shook his head. "Not much help right now."

They ducked beneath low branches as shadows passed through gaps in the canopy. The Dravok circled above, patient, inevitable.

Clara's foot caught on an exposed root. She stumbled forward. Not even her own Zaralis could fix her human reflexes completely. "How do we get off this island without Kira?"

Ashael leapt over a massive boulder, then spun back. Clara pulled herself up. "We don't."

"Fantastic." Malrik scrambled over with unexpected agility. "Trapped here with Veylora's pets. When will Kira be back?"

"Soon, I hope," Clara said, her voice cracking with desperation. "She has to."

She glanced back, expecting to see a shadow creature hot on their trail, but there was nothing. The Dravok was gone, and there was no sign of movement in the trees. Maybe they'd outrun it.

She turned forward again, and a gust slammed into them from behind, sending leaves spiraling into the air. Clara whirled, heart in her throat.

But it wasn't a Dravok.

The Shantera landed hard on the path, golden wings folding as she shifted into her more humanoid form.

"Kira!" Clara nearly collapsed with relief.

"I'm sorry," Kira said quickly, breathless. "It took longer than I'd hoped to recover after our last flight."

Ashael appeared beside them without a sound, his blade still in hand. "The protection around this island is weakening," he said. "Not completely, there's no corruption here yet, but the barrier's thinner than it was. The Dravok got through."

Kira's expression tightened. "I saw. Even from the volcanic lands, I felt a change. And the air here is not as dense as before. Easier to fly through. They must have felt it too."

Malrik's gaze sharpened. "They were waiting for this," he said quietly. "Just beyond reach, until the moment they sensed an opening." He turned to Kira. "Below, is it still safe?"

"For now." Her eyes lifted to the sky. "But not for long."

A chill skittered down Clara's spine. "How do they know exactly where we are?"

"They shouldn't," Ashael said, eyes narrowing. "Not unless something's guiding them."

Malrik cursed under his breath.

"We need to get Clara out. Now." Ashael's tone left no room for debate.

Clara shook her head. "I'm not leaving you two—"

"You must." The fear in Malrik's eyes contradicted his firm voice. "You have the shard. If Veylora gets her hands on you—"

"You matter more than either of us now," Ashael interrupted, his usual stoicism fracturing.

The protest died in Clara's throat. She didn't want to admit it, but she couldn't argue either. The shard at her hip felt like the weight of the world.

Malrik tightened his grip on his bow. "We'll hold them off."

"Kira can return for us," Ashael added.

Clara looked between them. Malrik, her childhood friend, the one who had crossed worlds just to keep her safe. And Ashael. She felt like she'd known him longer than she had any right to. She drew the satchel closer to her side. The thought of leaving them behind tugged at something tender inside her. It felt like betrayal.

Kira seized her arm, grip like iron. "Now, Clara." She shifted forms, wings unfurling in a gust of wind and feathers. "Get on."

Clara turned to them one last time, words tangling with fear, affection, and a hundred things she hadn't yet sorted through. "Don't you dare die," she managed, voice tight.

Their eyes met hers—Ashael's striking blue, Malrik's storm gray—and both nodded, determination etched in the lines of their faces.

Heart aching, Clara climbed onto Kira's back, fingers gripping the makeshift harness. The Shantera gathered herself, then launched skyward with a powerful thrust that left Clara's stomach behind.

Wind tore at her hair as they climbed. The forest below shrank, and with it, the two figures who had somehow become essential to her world.

Stay alive, Clara willed, throat too tight for prayer. *Please stay alive.*

As Kira carried her away from the island, from danger, Clara pressed a hand to her satchel. She could feel the shard inside. It was no longer just an artifact but a responsibility. A promise. She would keep it safe. For all of them.

Kira descended toward a narrow ledge jutting from the volcano's side, cutting through the thermal currents with steady control. Clara clung to the harness, the wind whipping tears from her eyes as they spiraled down. Below, an opening cut into the rock face. A dark mouth leading back to the cavern where the Phylarix had appeared to them before vanishing.

The landing was swift and sure. Kira touched down on the stone ledge, her wings folding with a graceful snap as Clara slid from her back, legs unsteady after the frantic flight.

"We made it," Clara said, her voice barely audible over the wind that howled across the ledge.

Kira wasted no time. "Hurry. Inside."

They ducked through the opening, leaving the screaming wind behind. The air inside was warm and still, carrying the scent of ash and fire. Clara had barely taken three steps when a figure broke away from the others and rushed toward her.

"Clara!" Elyndra's voice echoed off the walls as she flung her arms around Clara, pulling her into a fierce embrace. "Thank the stars. We were so worried."

Clara returned the hug, surprised by how much she needed it. "I'm all right."

Elyndra pulled back, scanning Clara's face. "When Kira returned yesterday, she was barely able to stand. We wanted to go after you immediately, but . . ." She trailed off, glancing at Kira.

"I couldn't carry anyone," Kira said, her voice low as she stood beside Clara, gaze dropping for a moment. She gave a slow shake of her head. "Not after the journey there."

Elyndra nodded. "We decided that the moment she recovered enough, she would go back for you."

"Flying alone is faster, less taxing," Kira added. "I can take a smaller form and move quicker. The plan was to assess what you needed, whether you required me to return with the others, or to bring one of you back." She looked at Clara. "Good thing I arrived when I did."

Clara reached out, resting a hand on Kira's shoulder. "You were just in time. The Dravok started swarming right before you arrived."

The reaction was immediate. Heads snapped up; bodies tensed.

"Dravok?" Selandor pushed forward, his usually composed features tight with alarm. "On the island? That shouldn't be possible."

"What about Ashael and Malrik?" Vaelin demanded, stepping closer.

"They stayed behind," Clara said, her voice catching. "To hold them off while Kira got me away."

Selandor's face paled. "Ashael is reckless enough on his own, and now he's facing them without me." His hand moved instinctively to his blade.

"And Malrik was no less reckless," Vaelin countered, frustration evident in the set of his jaw. "I told him it should be me who went after Ashael, but he refused to listen. Shoved past me and took Kira's harness before I could stop him." He shook his head, eyes narrowing. "Always charging ahead, never thinking beyond the moment."

The two men exchanged a glance, their worry for their respective friends momentarily bridging the tension between them.

"And the Nyths?" Selandor asked, voice regaining control. "Did you reach them before the Dravok came?"

Clara clutched her satchel. "We met with them. They put us through their trials, and we passed."

A trace of relief softened Selandor's face. "Then something was gained, at least."

"But why were the Dravok there at all?" Elyndra's brow furrowed. "How did they find you? How could they have passed through the protection?"

Slowly, Clara reached inside and withdrew the Vaelithar fragment, holding it in her palm where they all could see it.

Gasps rippled through the group. The shard caught the ambient light of the cavern, colors dancing within it like liquid fire.

"You found it," Elyndra whispered.

"The Vaelithar shard," Selandor breathed.

Clara nodded, then carefully returned it to her satchel. She told them everything about the chamber beneath the falls, the three elemental spheres that had combined to form the shard, how it had hovered in the air as if waiting for her. She described how it seemed to recognize her somehow, then the collapse, the water rushing in, the river that had appeared where before there had been only mist and the unknown.

"I wish I could have been there for you sooner," Kira said when Clara finished, her fingers brushing across her brow as she looked away. "If I had recovered faster—"

"Don't be so hard on yourself," Clara said firmly. "Without you, we wouldn't have reached the island in the first place."

A smile touched Kira's lips, small but genuine. "I believe I'm ready now." She straightened, rolling her shoulders. "I should go back, bring one of them here."

A knot formed in Clara's stomach. "Be careful."

"I'll return soon," Kira said, then moved toward the cavern entrance.

The others stepped back, giving her space. In one smooth motion, she shifted, her form narrowing, wings snapping open in a sleeker, lighter shape. She took to the sky without another word, a shadow streaking into the distance.

Clara watched until she disappeared, then turned back to the group. Her gaze drifted to the cavern entrance, heart heavy with worry for the two who had come to mean so much to her.

Ashael's warning from earlier about something guiding the Dravok returned to her thoughts.

"Do you think . . ." she began, then faltered. "Do you think Seraphis is with the Dravok?"

Vaelin's expression darkened. "She cannot manage sustained flight like the Dravok. If she's involved, she won't be far. Likely giving orders from cover." His eyes narrowed. "We must remain alert. Even here."

Clara nodded slowly, unable to shake the feeling that something was wrong. If Seraphis was controlling the Dravok, she had to wonder how the woman had known exactly where they were. The island wasn't easily found, so how had they been discovered?

She glanced at Vaelin, studying his face. His eyes met hers for a moment before looking away.

A shiver crawled up her spine, one that had nothing to do with the air.

Was it the power of the Vaelithar that led the Dravok to them, or something else?

CHAPTER 28

Malrik

Malrik watched as Kira and Clara disappeared into the sky. She was safe. That was what mattered. The shard was safe.

"They're coming," Ashael warned, his voice low and tense.

Malrik turned. Dark shapes circled above the treeline, dipping and weaving like vultures searching for carrion. He counted six of them. He prayed they would not see Kira and Clara as they soared through the air.

"This way," he said, plunging deeper into the forest. "Let's lead them away from Clara's direction."

Ashael followed without question, his steps nearly silent behind Malrik. They moved swiftly through the undergrowth, leaving just enough of a trail for the Dravok to follow.

It worked. The shadows swooped down, cutting through gaps in the canopy. Malrik caught glimpses of their movements. They were being herded deeper into the forest, away from any escape route.

"Where are the Nyths when you need them?" Malrik muttered, scanning the trees for any sign of the elusive little lights. But the forest was empty, save for them and the shadow creatures.

Malrik paused, catching his breath as he took in their surroundings. The trees here were still vibrant, untouched by the decay that usually followed the Dravok. No blackened bark, no withered leaves.

"The corruption hasn't spread," he said quietly. "Maybe there's still some protection from the shard lingering here. Or maybe it takes more than six Dravok to corrupt an area like this."

Ashael didn't answer. His eyes tracked something above them, body tense as a drawn bowstring.

Malrik didn't have time to wonder further. A shadow dropped from above, unfolding as it fell. Its tendrils spread outward like roots reaching through dark soil.

Ashael drew his dagger, and the blade responded instantly, elongating into a sword that glowed with fiery red light. It illuminated the shadows around them, dispelling the gloom.

The Dravok lunged, its arm solidifying into a long black tendril sharp as a blade.

Malrik pivoted, his body responding with new control as the anklet hummed against his skin. The Dravok's strike missed him by inches. Malrik reached for his bow, but the Dravok was too close.

"Here!" shouted Ashael. He threw a silver-handled dagger to Malrik.

Malrik lunged and swiped the weapon out of the air as it spun. His anklet hummed with power, sending a rush of energy through him. As he wrapped his fingers around the pommel, the blade extended and ignited.

The Dravok lurched forward, swinging its deadly claws.

Malrik countered, swinging his sword in an arc that forced the creature back. He felt different. Lighter, faster, and more connected to his own movements. The Dravok struck again, and Malrik parried, the impact jarring but not overwhelming.

They danced in deadly rhythm. Malrik kept the creature at bay, looking for an opening. When it came, he didn't hesitate. He thrust forward, driving his blade into the center of the Dravok's chest.

The creature froze, its form shuddering. Then, like dust scattered by wind, it simply evaporated into nothing.

Not bad. I can handle this, he thought, a grin tugging at his mouth. Malrik spun, searching for Ashael. What he saw made him stop short.

Ashael was a blur of movement, so fast Malrik could barely track him. He fought two Dravok simultaneously, his blade flashing as he wove between them. He'd strike one, spin away before it could counter, then appear on the other side of the second.

Malrik had never seen anyone move like that.

A sudden brush of wind against his ear jolted him back to his own fight. He turned just in time to meet the attack of another Dravok.

Malrik brought up his sword, blocking the blow, but one of the tendrils slipped past the blade and grazed the back of his hand. Pain seared his skin, hot and sudden.

Focus, you idiot.

He gritted his teeth, readjusted his grip despite the burn, and kept moving.

Each Dravok that fell evaporated into nothing, leaving no trace. Malrik felt a surge of confidence as he dispatched another.

More shapes descended through the trees. Not six Dravok anymore. At least a dozen.

Malrik and Ashael fought back-to-back, their blades carving through the air. Malrik's arms burned with exertion, but the Zaralis anklet kept him moving, keeping him one step ahead of death. They thinned the Dravok's numbers, fighting with desperate intensity.

A flash of gold caught Malrik's eye. He risked a glance upward.

Kira was back, weaving through the canopy, careful to stay out of the Dravok's sight as she descended toward them.

"Malrik!" Ashael shouted, his voice cutting through the chaos. "Go! This is your chance!"

Malrik hesitated, slicing through another strike. "What about you?"

"I'll hold them off!"

"But you'll be alone," Malrik argued, even as he backed toward Kira.

Ashael shook his head, dispatching another Dravok with terrifying efficiency. "Just go!"

Still, Malrik hesitated, unsure why he couldn't just leave. This was Ashael—the man who'd been little more than a frustrating mystery since they'd met. The man who seemed to know Clara better than he did, who moved with an otherworldly grace even among the Aelvor.

And yet . . .

"Come on!" Kira hissed. "Before they see us!"

Decision made, Malrik vaulted onto Kira's back, grabbing the make-shift harness. As they rose, he looked back at Ashael, surrounded by shadows but holding his own.

A screech tore through the air above them. Malrik's head snapped up. A Dravok had spotted them. It ripped through the air toward them.

"Hold on!" Kira warned, then banked sharply, swerving between trees.

The Dravok followed, undeterred by Kira's evasive maneuvers. Malrik grabbed his bow and reached for his quiver, fingers closing around his arrows. They expanded in his hand, the Aelvor material responding to his touch. He nocked one, trying to steady himself as Kira ducked and wove through the forest.

He drew back and fired but missed.

The Dravok shrieked, closing the distance.

Malrik knocked another arrow, forcing himself to breathe. Kira dove beneath a massive branch, then shot upward. The sudden change in direction gave Malrik his moment.

He aimed, exhaled, and loosed the arrow.

The arrow struck true, burying itself in the center of the Dravok's chest. With a sound like a sigh, the creature evaporated into wisps of darkness.

Kira didn't slow, climbing higher until they broke free of the canopy. The sky opened above them, vast and clear. Malrik looked back at the island growing smaller beneath them, searching for any sign of Ashael.

"He'll be all right," Kira said, as if reading his thoughts.

Malrik wasn't sure when he'd started caring whether Ashael lived or died. But he found himself hoping Kira was right.

The rocky, volcanic land grew larger ahead of them, its rugged silhouette a promise of safety. Malrik clung to the harness, his body aching from the fight, his mind racing with everything that had happened.

As they descended toward the narrow ledge jutting from the volcano's side, one thought rose above the rest.

Clara.

CHAPTER 29

Ashael

Ashael turned to face the remaining Dravok as Kira and Malrik vanished into a bank of cloud cover. He scanned his surroundings, noting the terrain, the light, how his enemy moved through the trees. He was alone and could not risk any mistakes. The weight of his blade was familiar in his hand. There were at least eight of them left, circling like predators around wounded prey.

But he was far from wounded.

His awareness heightened, intensified by adrenaline and his wordless promise to Clara to stay alive. His senses sharpened until he could hear every rustle of leaves, feel every shift in the air. Time seemed to slow around him as the first Dravok lunged.

Each movement of the shadow-beast appeared almost languid to his amplified senses. His blade sliced through the creature with perfect precision, and before its form had even begun to dissolve, he was already engaging the next. He flowed between them, each strike deliberate and exact.

He had always been quick, even by Aelvor standards. But this was something else entirely. It was as if his body had remembered something his mind had forgotten. Something long buried had sparked to life.

A Dravok's tendril lashed toward his face. He twisted, feeling it pass through the space he had occupied an instant before. He countered, his blade piercing the center of the creature's form. It disintegrated into a whoosh of smoke.

Two more converged on him from opposite directions. Ashael leapt, impossibly high, letting them collide beneath him. His sword swept down in a single, fluid motion, dispatching both before his feet touched the ground again.

He didn't know how long he could maintain this pace, but it didn't matter. He had to survive. For Clara. The thought of her strengthened his resolve as he faced the next wave. He knew she could fend for herself, deep in his heart. She had a special connection to the world, stronger than other humans.

Still, he hoped she cared for him. And that was a reason to stay alive. Would she miss him if he was gone? He wanted to be someone she would miss.

A sharp, high-pitched sound cut through his concentration. Tiny cries, unlike anything he'd heard before, echoed across the battlefield. Ashael turned instinctively toward the sound, his focus broken for a split second.

It was enough.

Pain lanced through his thigh as a Dravok's claw sliced into him. Ashael staggered, his rhythm breaking, the clarity of his senses wavering. He twisted away, just in time to dodge a second strike aimed for his head.

Warm blood trickled down his leg. The wound wasn't deep, but it burned like fire. Three Dravoks converged on him, sensing weakness, their forms rippling with anticipation. The smell of blood was thick in the air.

Ashael gritted his teeth, forcing his mind to clear. He parried a tendril, sidestepped another, but the third lashed across his forearm. He stumbled back, the pain sharp and immediate, but he didn't let go of his blade.

The cries came again, more urgent and desperate than before. Ashael whipped around, searching for the source despite the danger.

There, just a few paces away, a cluster of floating lights darted frantically between the trees. Dravok swarmed around them, tendrils reaching for the tiny glowing forms of the Nyths.

Despite his wounds, despite the Dravok still focused on him, Ashael surged forward. Pain flared through his thigh with each step, but he pushed through it, his blade carving a path toward the lights.

He managed to force the Dravok back as a tiny, glowing creature hovered right in front of his nose. No bigger than a berry, its wings moved so fast they blurred at the edges, scattering a tiny cloud of glitter behind it. Its face looked oddly like a miniature version of his own.

A sound like wind chimes mixed with distant echoes filled his ears, but somehow, he felt it inside his mind as well, clear as a thought.

Help us. Our home. Our Mother.

Ashael flinched, startled by the strange dual sensation of the voice in his head and the sharp chime.

"Your voice . . ." he murmured, disoriented.

The Nyths squealed in warning as another Dravok lunged. Ashael whirled and slashed it down without hesitation. Four Dravok down.

The musical voice came again, both echoing around and within him.

Follow. Hurry!

The Nyth darted upward, and Ashael traced its path to the crown of a massive tree that towered above the others. His heart sank in horror. More shadows swarmed there, engulfing the highest branches in darkness.

Ashael started toward the tree, intending to climb, but the Nyth zipped in front of him, stopping him short.

No time.

Before he could react, a breeze brushed past and light circled him, lifting him off the ground.

Think. Where you wish to go. Think it.

Understanding flashed through him. He focused his thoughts upward, visualizing the crown of the massive tree. His body responded instantly, rising through the air as if he weighed nothing at all.

Higher and higher he flew, the Nyths forming a shimmering escort around him. As they neared the treetop, Ashael saw the full extent of the attack. A group of Dravok surrounded an enormous, enclosed nest woven from living branches and leaves, their shadows creeping into its walls.

Ashael tightened his grip on his sword and thought himself forward. He shot through the air, closing the distance with startling speed. The first of the Dravok never saw him coming. The second barely had time to turn before his blade found its mark.

He moved among them as if he'd been born into the air, twisting and turning with the same fluidity he'd found on the ground. The pain in his thigh and forearm stayed at the edge of his focus, distant and pushed aside by the task at hand.

The Nyths joined the battle, their tiny forms glowing brighter as they unleashed streams of sparkling light that burned through their enemy like fire through dry leaves. Around them, vines curled down from the massive tree, snapping at the shadows and hurling their attackers away with startling force.

Together, they drove the shadows back. For each one Ashael struck down, the Nyths felled another with bursts of searing light.

The battle raged around the heart of the Nyths' territory, the place they fought to protect. He could feel the urgency in the Nyths' every move.

Sweat dripped into his eyes and blood spattered the leaves of the giant tree as he worked in tandem with the tiny fae to defend their home.

The last Dravok dissolved into nothing, leaving only clear air and the soft glow of the Nyths around him.

Ashael hovered just at the tree's nest, his breaths deep and uneven. Whatever magic kept him airborne hadn't faded yet, but the sharp clarity he'd felt during the fight was slipping. Pain returned, each throb a reminder of what the battle had taken.

The woven walls of the Nyths' home began to part. Light spilled out from the heart of the nest, a gentle, steady glow. A figure emerged, taller than the others, soft gold light trailing behind her. She held herself with a serene grace, though she was no taller than his thumb.

Her long blonde hair was streaked with hints of different colors just below the tips. Her wings, larger than the rest, were adorned with intricate patterns too small for him to make out, but they glittered in various hues, changing with each movement. She appeared ageless, yet her eyes radiated an undeniable aura of wisdom.

The Nyths whispered as she moved closer, their voices filled with reverence. "Mother, Mother." The sound of their words filled his ears, but almost immediately, the message also rang in his mind, clear and direct.

The Nyths' mother regarded him with solemn intensity. Then she spoke into his mind. *You fought for us when you had no obligation. You risked your life for strangers. You bled for our people.*

Ashael inclined his head slightly, wincing as the motion sent a flood of pain through him. "It was the right thing to do."

The light around her pulsed gently. Then she bowed.

We will remember you, Ashael of the Aelvor. And repay this debt.

Ashael inclined his head, returning the gesture.

The Nyths' mother was pleased. The light shimmered around her. *I know the task laid before you,* she continued. *The Vaelithar has thought you worthy. We will offer what aid we can. But be warned, Ashael of the Aelvor, your time grows short.*

Surrounded by the Nyths' light, Ashael's thoughts turned to Clara. The thought of her was enough to help him master the pain. This boon from the Nyths would not be wasted. If they could help him and Clara save Avenora, the pain would be worth it.

"Thank you," he said. Blood continued to seep from his wounds. "I don't suppose you could help me now, could you?"

The Nyths' mother smiled and extended her hand.

CHAPTER 30

Wings beat against the sky as the sun began to set, casting long shadows over the rocky ledge where Clara stood, scanning the horizon. Her heart kicked up as Kira approached, her feathers glinting in the setting sun. The moment she touched down, her wings folded inward, and her form shrank until her humanoid shape stood on the stone beside them.

Malrik slid from her back, landing with a slight wobble that he tried to pass off with a confident step.

"Malrik!" Clara rushed toward him, her breath catching. "You have no idea what I was imagining."

He ran a hand through his windswept hair, a crooked smile forming on his lips. "I hope it involved me fighting like a champion."

"You know what I mean," Clara said, feeling heat rise to her cheeks.

"You doubt me after everything we've been through?" He spun in a slow circle with his arms wide. "See? Not even a scratch."

A pale gleam caught on a dark line across the back of his hand. Clara stepped closer and grabbed his wrist.

"Then what do you call this?"

A thin gash stretched across his skin, the blood dried to a dark crust.

"That?" Malrik blinked, as if just noticing it. "Barely a graze."

Clara shook her head and guided him toward the back of the cavern. "Sit. Let me treat it before it gets worse."

Malrik dropped to the ground with a groan and stretched out his legs. Clara knelt beside him, pulling her satchel forward. She opened a small tin of Aelvor salve and gently dabbed it onto the wound.

Malrik winced.

"Does it hurt?" she asked, looking up. His face was scrunched in discomfort.

He nodded, leaning back against the cavern wall with a sigh. "Clara, everything hurts."

"Where exactly?" she said, her voice low with worry. She checked his arm, pressed gently along his sides, and felt around his abdomen for any hidden injuries.

He didn't answer.

Clara glanced up again and caught the slight curve of his lips, as if he were trying not to laugh.

She narrowed her eyes. "You're impossible."

She gave his arm a light smack. He caught her hand before she could pull it back, his fingers warm around hers.

"And yet here you are," he said, grinning. "Still fixing me."

A shadow approached from behind. Vaelin stepped into view and stopped just beside them. He didn't speak right away, his gaze drifting between Clara and Malrik.

Without a word, he gave Malrik a quick jab to the shoulder. "As I recall, I was meant to fly with Kira after Ashael. But then I was pushed aside by a certain stubborn human."

Malrik blinked, then grinned. "Were you worried about me, Vaelin?"

"I was simply thinking of the mission," Vaelin said. His voice was calm, but something in his eyes made Clara pause. Maybe he cared more than he let on.

Selandor crouched beside them, his sharp features curious and alert. "A human returning from battle against multiple Dravok," he said. "Not something we often witness."

Malrik rubbed the back of his neck. "I had some help."

"Oh?" Selandor raised an eyebrow.

Malrik tapped the anklet on his leg. "The Zaralis. It finally responded. For once, it didn't feel like I was wearing it. It felt like we moved together."

Selandor's eyes gleamed. "Then the bond has awakened. These things happen only when both sides are ready."

Elyndra stepped into the edge of the circle, her movements as graceful as ever. "Fortunate timing, Malrik. Any longer and Clara might have worn a trench into the stone."

Clara gave her a look, but Elyndra just shrugged, a small smile tugging at her lips.

Malrik laughed under his breath, though his attention drifted back to Clara. He took her hand in both of his, holding it gently. "I told you I'd come back," he said softly.

Clara looked up at him, her hand resting between his palms. His gray eyes drew her in. She blinked back tears, smiling softly. "I'm really glad you're here," she managed.

Kira lowered herself next to them, resting against the wall. She unscrewed a water flask and took a long drink, her movements slower than usual.

"Kira," Clara said, her nurse's instincts taking over. "Are you all right?"

"I'm fine," Kira replied. Her voice was rough, and she moved slowly, as if wading through mud. "Just need a moment before I go back for Ashael. The trip wasn't as hard. I'll be ready."

His name hit Clara like a wave, pushing everything else aside.

"Ashael," she whispered, her body tensing. How had she let herself forget, even for a second?

Malrik gave her hand a gentle squeeze. "He's fine. You should've seen him. The Dravok couldn't lay a finger on him. He was fighting two at once when I left," Malrik added. "Faster than anything I've ever seen."

Selandor's expression didn't ease. "His skill is considerable. But even the strongest can't stand when the odds grow too heavy."

Malrik nodded. "There were more coming. A lot of them."

Clara stood and walked to the cavern's entrance. The wind brushed past her and carried with it the scent of ash and stone. The sky had grown darker, its colors deepening as the last of the light faded.

She began to pace, but she kept her eyes trained on the sky and the island that floated in the distance.

Inside the cavern, Kira rested with her eyes closed, her breathing steady. Malrik leaned against the wall, one knee propped up, his head bent as if lost in thought. Elyndra sat cross-legged, her hands folded calmly in her lap.

Outside, just beyond the entrance, Vaelin and Selandor stood watch at the ledge.

Time stretched. Clara didn't want to rush Kira, but what if Ashael needed them? She twisted her hands as worry turned her stomach leaden.

"I see something," called Selandor.

Everyone rushed toward the opening.

A figure approached from the floating island, but it didn't move like a Dravok. There was no shadow swirling in its wake, no hint of darkness. Instead, a trail of gold streamed behind it like a comet tail.

"What is that?" Vaelin asked quietly.

Clara leaned forward. "Ashael?"

"Is he . . . flying?" Malrik asked, almost too stunned to believe it.

Ashael soared across the sky, golden dust swirling around him. He didn't fall or falter. He glided, calm and sure, like the air itself carried him.

He descended toward the ledge and landed without a sound.

There was blood on his sleeve and down one leg, but he held himself upright. His eyes went straight to Clara.

She couldn't move. The intensity of his blue eyes kept her rooted to the spot.

Clara couldn't tear her gaze away from him as the golden dust trailed off into the twilight, back toward the island.

Without warning, he staggered forward.

Selandor caught him before he could fall. Vaelin moved to his other side, and together they supported his weight.

"Get him inside," Selandor ordered, his voice tense.

They guided Ashael into the cavern and carefully lowered him to the ground. Clara rushed to his side, heart racing as she knelt beside him. He was paler now, his breathing uneven.

She quickly assessed his condition, noting his pallor. "He's lost a lot of blood," she said, forcing her voice to remain calm, her nurse instincts taking over. She would not allow herself to panic. Clara fumbled with her satchel, hands shaky as she dug through it.

"Help me with his clothes," she said.

Selandor and Vaelin eased his coat from Ashael's shoulders, then his tunic. Clara inspected the wound that slashed across his forearm. A sick feeling pooled inside her. It was deeper than she'd first thought, still bleeding continuously.

"I need a clean cloth and water," she said, trying to sound calm.

The others scurried to help, bringing her supplies.

She cleaned the wound carefully, wiping away dirt and dried blood. Her fingers worked quickly, applying pressure to stem the bleeding before reaching for the Aelvor salve. The thick, green paste felt cool against her fingertips as she spread it over the cut.

"The salve will take time," she murmured, wrapping the wound with a strip of cloth. "It's deep."

On his other side, Elyndra was already tending to the gash on his thigh. "This one isn't as serious," she said, inspecting the wound with a light touch. "But it's good we're treating it now."

Between them, they managed to stop the bleeding. Ashael's breathing grew steadier, though his eyes remained closed and his face too pale.

"He needs water," Clara said, reaching for her flask. "And this."

From a small pouch, she shook a fine, silvery powder into the water. It dissolved instantly, turning the liquid an icy blue.

"Aelina gave it to me," she explained, noticing Selandor's questioning look. "It helps with hydration after blood loss."

Clara slipped her arm beneath Ashael's shoulders, lifting him slightly. "Ashael," she said softly. "I need you to drink this."

His eyes fluttered open, unfocused at first before finding her face.

"Clara," he breathed.

"Here," she said, bringing the flask to his lips. "Small sips."

He complied, drinking slowly. When he'd had enough, Clara eased him back down, his head resting on her lap. His eyes drifted shut again, the tension in his face softening as exhaustion pulled him under.

But just before sleep took him, his lips parted. "You're safe," he murmured.

Clara stilled. The words landed harder than she expected. Even now, when he could hardly stay conscious, he was thinking of her. Not the pain. Not the blood. Just her.

Clara brushed a strand of hair from his forehead, her fingers light and careful.

Her lip quivered as she whispered, "Yes. I'm safe."

She paused, then added softly, "Now rest. Let me take care of you. You've done more than enough, Ashael."

She waited a moment, then gently shifted, reaching for a rolled blanket to use as a pillow. She eased her hand beneath his head, ready to slide out from under him.

But as she moved, Ashael turned onto his side, his face now angled away from hers. In his half-sleep, his fingers closed around her arm and pulled it beneath him, anchoring her in place.

Clara froze, caught somewhere between surprise and warmth. His grip wasn't tight, but it was firm enough to hold her there. She didn't want to wake him. So she stayed.

The cavern grew quiet around them. Elyndra moved in silence, packing away the remaining supplies.

At the entrance, Selandor stood watch, scanning the horizon. "We should all get some sleep," he said. "I'll take the first watch."

Vaelin nodded but didn't move far. Instead, he joined Selandor at the entrance, his gaze sweeping across the darkened sky. For a moment, neither of them spoke.

"You should rest soon too," Selandor said quietly after a beat.

Vaelin gave a slight nod, though he remained where he was.

Clara wondered if either of them would sleep at all.

She turned, catching sight of Malrik standing across the cavern. He was watching her and Ashael. His eyebrows were slightly drawn, his lips pressed together. He took a step, hesitated, then turned too sharply and bumped his head against a low stone ledge. He hissed and clutched his head.

"Malrik?" Clara asked, keeping her voice low so she wouldn't wake Ashael. "Are you all right?"

"I was just examining the structural integrity of this extremely low ceiling," he said, rubbing the spot and straightening with as much dignity as he could manage.

Clara raised an eyebrow. "Really."

He sighed. "Okay. I was just . . ."

"What is it?"

He didn't answer at first. Then, with a slow breath, he walked over and sat beside her. He saw Ashael's resting form, his jaw clenching briefly before he tipped his head back and exhaled.

"I'm glad he made it back," he said quietly.

Clara looked up, surprised by the genuine concern in his voice.

"He saved my life by staying behind," Malrik added. "Bought us time to escape."

Her eyes settled on Ashael's face. "He deserves to get better." Her voice dropped. "He will, won't he?"

Malrik's mouth lifted at the corners. "There's no better nurse than you." His voice held a trace of pride as he met her eyes for a moment. Then he glanced at Ashael. "He should be fine. He's too stubborn not to be."

He gave her shoulder a gentle touch. "Get some rest. You did good."

Across the cavern, Kira had already drifted into much-needed sleep. Elyndra soon joined her, wrapping herself in a light blanket and curling up on the cave floor. Malrik stayed by her side and tilted his head back to rest on the wall.

Clara mirrored him and let her eyes close. The sound of Ashael's breathing, the low murmur of Selandor and Vaelin near the entrance, and the reassuring presence of her friends wrapped around her like a soft blanket. They were alive and safe for the moment. Sleep claimed her quickly as her body sagged with relief.

Clara woke up with a groan. Her neck was stiff, and her back hurt from sleeping against the hard cavern wall all night. Golden light spilled through the narrow entrance, catching dust particles that floated lazily in the air. She blinked a few times, adjusting to the brightness, and glanced down.

Ashael was still asleep, his head resting gently against her leg.

She stayed completely still, not wanting to wake him. Color had returned to his cheeks overnight. The lines between his eyes had faded, leaving his face smooth. Gone was the fierce warrior.

Clara couldn't help but study him. His features were almost perfectly balanced. His brows were thick but neatly shaped. His jaw had a sharp, clean angle, softened only by the light stubble along his chin. A slight bump along the bridge of his otherwise well-formed nose should have disrupted the symmetry, but somehow, it only added to his charm.

Her eyes drifted lower. His lips, slightly parted. Heat crept up her neck and flushed her cheeks. She tore her gaze away and did not let herself think about how it would feel to place her lips against his. Slowly, she pulled herself back to the moment and looked around the cavern.

Elyndra was still wrapped in her blanket nearby, one arm flung over her face. Malrik had somehow managed to sprawl across his own blanket, one leg propped up awkwardly against the wall. Both were sound asleep. From outside, she could hear low voices talking quietly.

Vaelin and Selandor.

She squinted toward the cavern entrance, sunlight temporarily blinding her. They must have stayed up all night.

Clara finally gave in, adjusting her position to ease the growing ache in her back. The subtle movement was enough to wake Ashael. His eyes snapped open and locked onto hers.

Her body stilled. His gaze pulled her in like the sea, deep blue with flecks of gold catching the morning light. Despite the brightness spilling through the cavern entrance, his pupils widened as he stared at her.

She watched as the fog of sleep slowly cleared from his face. His gaze darted around for a second, like he was trying to remember where he was. Then it clicked. His face turned pink, the color spreading all the way to his ears.

He sat up abruptly, rubbing his eyes with the back of his hand. He cleared his throat and ran fingers through his hair, all while avoiding her gaze.

"I—I'm sorry," he said quickly, his voice hushed and oddly unsure. "I didn't mean to—I fell asleep on you. That couldn't have been comfortable. I didn't intend—"

Clara just stared at him, surprised. He was stumbling over his words. She had seen Ashael wounded, calm under pressure, even quietly amused, but never flustered.

She smiled at him and shook her head. "It's all right. You had us worried. I'm just glad you're awake." She tilted her head slightly. "How are you feeling?"

His fingers gently touched the bandages wrapped around his arm and leg. He looked back up, eyebrows slightly raised. "You . . . did this?"

Clara tucked a loose strand of hair behind her ear. "It was the least I could do."

His ocean-blue eyes stayed on her face. Slowly, he reached toward her hand, like he couldn't find the right words and hoped his touch might say what he couldn't.

But before his fingers could touch hers, a loud voice came from the cavern entrance.

"Ashael!"

They both jumped.

Selandor walked in, shaking his head with that familiar look of annoyance and brotherly concern. "I can't leave you alone for one second without you coming back half-dead?"

Ashael laughed softly and stood up, dusting off his trousers. "Selandor. Good to see you too."

They clasped hands and pulled each other into a quick hug. Selandor muttered something that sounded suspiciously like "reckless idiot" before letting go.

Vaelin followed behind him, his black hair neatly tied back. He nodded at them both, quickly assessing Ashael's condition.

Clara stretched her arms over her head, letting out a small groan. Her legs felt numb and tingly.

The others were waking now. Everyone was glad to see Ashael. They fell into their usual morning routine, sharing Morsela and water.

Kira appeared in the cavern's entrance, her hair slightly damp with morning dew. She joined their circle, taking her share silently.

"So," she said after a moment, looking at Ashael. "How exactly did you manage to fly back on your own?"

Everyone stopped eating and turned to look at him.

Ashael sat down, one knee pulled up to his chest, his expression turning serious. "After you flew off with Malrik, the Dravoks kept coming. I held them off as long as I could." He ran a hand through his hair, then glanced around at the others. "Then I heard the Nyths. They needed my aid, so I followed them to a large tree. The Dravok were attacking it."

Clara leaned forward, intrigued.

"The Nyths covered me with this dust," he continued, gesturing with his hands. "It let me fly. Just long enough to help protect what I assume was their home at the top of the tree. We pushed back the last of the shadows. And afterward . . ." He paused. "I met their leader."

"And?" Selandor prompted, curiosity brightening his expression.

"They call her Mother," Ashael said.

"Mother?" Elyndra repeated, her lips parting in surprise.

Ashael nodded. "She thanked me. Said they would remember what happened. That they owe us a debt." His voice grew quieter. "She also knew about the shards. She knows what we're trying to do."

Clara sat up straighter. "Did she tell you anything that could help us find the others?"

Ashael shook his head. "Not directly. But she warned that our time is limited. The shard we found is connected to the others. And Veylora can sense that connection."

"How?" Elyndra asked. "How can she possibly know?"

"She's one of the Eternals," Malrik said, brushing crumbs from his shirt.

"Was," Vaelin corrected quietly but firmly, crossing his arms. "She *was* one of them. Now she's something else. Something darker."

"There has to be something connecting her to them," Kira said thoughtfully, tracing a finger along the sharp line of her jaw. Her delicate features remained composed, but her eyes narrowed slightly as she considered the possibilities.

Clara swallowed. "I sensed a kind of force pushing into my dreams before. Ceyndor believes it could be her."

Vaelin's face darkened. "Veylora keeps secrets, even from those closest to her. There's a section of her palace no one is allowed to enter. Only her." He drummed his fingers against his arm. "If there's a reason, that's where it's hidden."

They fell quiet, each lost in thought.

Finally, Elyndra broke the silence. "So, does this mean we don't have any clues about the next shard?"

Ashael shook his head, his expression troubled. "Nothing specific."

"We shouldn't stay here much longer," Kira said, rising to her feet. "If the protections are failing, Seraphis won't be far behind."

Suddenly, Kira went still. Her head tilted slightly, and her nostrils flared.

Clara set down her water flask. "What is it?"

Kira didn't answer right away. Her shoulders had tensed like she'd caught something no one else could. "Something's not right," she said quietly.

Without another word, Kira ran out of the cavern. Seconds later, they heard the rushing sound of wings as she took flight.

When Kira returned moments later, her face was tight with worry. "It's starting," she said. "I saw steam and smoke rising from the north side."

She glanced around at their confused faces.

"The volcano—"

A low rumble rolled through the ground, a vibration that sent small stones skittering across the cavern floor.

Clara flinched as the sound crawled up her spine. A sharp, sulfurous scent hit her nose, burning the back of her throat. A gust of warm wind shot through the cavern.

She staggered back just as a thin crack split the rock beside her, hissing. A ribbon of steam rose from it like breath from a beast.

"Oh no," Clara whispered. Realization struck hard. "The protection— it wasn't just shielding us. It made the volcano dormant."

The rumble intensified. Larger rocks clattered down from above, crashing against the stone floor.

"We need to get out of here," Ashael said, already reaching for his pack.

They scrambled to their feet, snatching up their things. Another tremor shook the ground, stronger than the first. Clara nearly lost her balance, but Malrik grabbed her arm, steadying her.

"Move!" Selandor shouted, waving them toward the exit.

They ran, dodging falling debris. The ground lurched, then settled, then bucked again beneath them. The cavern entrance was just ahead.

They were only a few steps away. Clara could see the craggy landscape and the trees in the distance.

A deafening crack split the air. Massive boulders broke free from the ceiling, slamming to the ground with thunderous force, inches in front of them. She crouched and threw her hands over her head as dust swirled through the air, making her cough. Darkness fell, swallowing them. The cavern entrance collapsed in a storm of stone and dust.

The floor continued to rumble and shake, the volcano roaring to life after centuries of silence. Clara's stomach twisted as she lowered her arms and saw the mountain of rock that now blocked the way out.

They were trapped.

CHAPTER 31

Dust settled around the wall of fallen rock as Clara stared at what had been their only exit. She pressed her palm against the stone, feeling for any weakness, any gap that might offer hope.

"We need to move these rocks," Malrik said, already grabbing at a loose stone and yanking it free.

"Stop!" Selandor pulled him back as more debris showered down from above. "You'll bring the whole ceiling down on us."

The cavern had become a furnace. Sweat ran in rivulets down Clara's neck as she dabbed her face with her sleeve, her tunic clinging to her skin. Her lungs burned with each breath, the sulfur stench making her dizzy. Eyes stinging, chest constricting, she found herself taking quick, shallow gasps that did little to satisfy her need for clean air.

She glanced at her companions. Elyndra brushed sweat from her brow, eyes fixed on the cracking ceiling. Selandor's jaw worked silently as he scanned for any escape. Kira paced, shoulders tense. Even Vaelin's calm had cracked, his fingers tapping against his leg betraying his worry.

"We need to find another solution," Ashael said, his voice calm despite the situation. "And quickly."

"Your pendant," Elyndra said suddenly, her voice cutting through Clara's spiral of fear. "It responded to danger before. It might help us now."

Clara's shaking fingers found the pendant resting against her chest. She closed her eyes, willing it to activate, to show them a way out.

Nothing happened. The stone remained cool and dormant beneath her touch.

She squeezed the gem as hard as she could, pleading as sweat ran down her face. But the pendant did not answer her.

"It's not working," she gasped, desperation edging into her voice.

Another violent tremor shook the cavern. A shower of rocks crashed down mere feet away from them.

"The shard," Ashael said, his composure beginning to slip. "Try the shard, Clara."

Malrik nodded urgently. "It responded to you before. It helped you in the water when we were separated."

Clara fumbled with her satchel, her fingers clumsy with urgency and slippery with sweat. She pulled out the crystalline fragment, clutching it tightly in both hands, terrified it might slip from her grip.

"Please," she whispered. "Help us."

The shard remained cold, its surface dull and unresponsive. The colorful light that had danced within it had gone dark.

Clara closed her eyes tighter, focusing every ounce of her will into the fragment. "Please!"

Nothing.

Her shoulders slumped. "I can't make it work," she admitted, her voice breaking.

Vaelin turned away, searching the walls for any weakness. Selandor placed a hand on Ashael's shoulder, their eyes meeting in silent understanding. Kira stood motionless, her face set in resigned determination.

They were out of options.

Then, warmth bloomed against Clara's palm. She looked down, startled. The shard was changing, colors suddenly swirling within its clear depths. Red, orange, and yellow with trails of ash drifting through them like smoke.

"It's working!" she gasped, choking back a sob of relief.

The ground lurched beneath them, more violent than before. The shard slipped from her grasp.

"No!"

Clara lunged forward, her hand outstretched, fingers splayed. The shard tumbled through the air, spinning, its colors blurring together. Her fingers closed around it just before it hit the ground.

Another tremor rocked the cavern. Rock cracked and split. The ledge they stood on began to fracture, large chunks breaking away and plummeting into the darkness below.

"Move back!" Ashael shouted, grabbing Clara's arm and pulling her toward the wall.

They pressed themselves against the rock face, watching in horror as their standing room crumbled away piece by piece.

The shard had woken, but the volcano continued to erupt. A high pitched, familiar sound echoed through the cavern.

Clara's head jerked up. "Did you hear that?"

Malrik frowned, straining to listen above the volcano's rumble. "Hear what?"

The cry came again, closer now, piercing through the chaos. A rush of air brushed her cheek, carrying with it a warmth unlike the volcano's suffocating heat.

"There!" Elyndra pointed toward the open space beyond the crumbling ledge.

Clara stared, wide-eyed. The Phylarix had returned.

Its magnificent form swept toward them, wings spread wide, each feather edged in living flame. It circled once, twice, its eyes finding Clara's before it dove closer.

"It's come back," she whispered, the shard warm in her palm.

The ledge gave another lurch, dropping several inches. They crowded closer together, backs pressed to the wall, the edge now mere steps away from their feet.

The Phylarix flew around them in faster, tighter circles, drawing nearer with each pass. The flames along its wings grew brighter, stretching outward like reaching hands.

"What's it doing?" Malrik shouted, his voice barely audible over the volcano's roar.

The heat intensified; the Phylarix's fire was so close now that Clara could feel its caress against her skin. Fear surged through her as the creature drew even closer, its flames now dancing across her clothes, her hair.

"It's burning us!" she screamed, instinctively trying to bat away the fire that crawled up her arm. But there was no pain.

The fire spread across her body, wrapping her in a cocoon of vibrant red and gold, yet her skin remained untouched. The flames didn't burn; they embraced, shrouding them in protection.

She looked around in disbelief. The others were covered in the same beautiful, painless fire. Ashael stood behind her, his arm circling her shoulders protectively, his own form aglow with living flame. Malrik's gray eyes were wide with wonder.

"It doesn't hurt," Elyndra gasped, staring at her hands engulfed in fire.

The Phylarix's wings beat faster, its form blurring until it was nothing but a streak of fire circling them. The flames rose higher, swirling into a vortex that consumed them entirely.

Light flashed. Clara covered her eyes with her forearm as the roar of the volcano dulled to a distant echo.

The ground's violent shaking slowed, as if moving through honey. Heat receded from her skin, replaced by a strange, suspended coolness.

The ledge finally gave way, cracking with a sound like thunder, falling into the abyss below. Clara's feet lost contact with solid ground.

Instead of falling, a sensation like lightning coursed through her veins, a rush of energy so intense it felt like running a marathon in the space of a single breath. Her body hung suspended, neither falling nor flying, caught in a moment between seconds.

Then, like a rubber band snapping back into place, the world came back into focus. Fresh, cool air filled her lungs. Birdsong rang in her ears.

Clara lowered her arm slowly, blinking against the sudden daylight. Gone was the dim, smoky cavern. They weren't in the volcano anymore. They stood in a grassy field, surrounded by trees. The sky was blue and cloudless above them.

The Phylarix swooped down and hovered before her, its wings sending small embers drifting to the ground where they faded into nothing. Its fiery eyes met hers, holding her in place with an intensity that made her forget to breathe.

In that moment, the world around her disappeared. There was only Clara and the creature of fire, locked in a silent connection that went beyond words.

A presence touched her consciousness. There were no sounds, no actual words spoken. Just meaning, flowing directly into her mind like water finding its path through stone. The Phylarix didn't need language to communicate, and somehow, Clara understood.

The path you seek lies where you began. The last burns darker than you think.

The Phylarix's message still echoed in Clara's mind when a sharp intake of breath from behind her broke the spell. Her companions stood scattered across the grass, looking dazed but unharmed. Relief flooded through her at the sight of them all. They were safe.

Elyndra brushed her fingers against the soft grass. Selandor stood perfectly still, his gaze fixed upward. Vaelin had already drawn his blade, scanning their surroundings with wariness. Kira stood apart from the others, her head tilted as if listening to something only she could hear.

Malrik and Ashael were closest to Clara, both staring at the Phylarix with expressions of stunned wonder.

"What was that all about?" Malrik asked, nodding toward the Phylarix. "That was some intense eye contact."

"It communicated with me," Clara said, her voice barely above a whisper.

Ashael stepped closer. "What did it say?"

Before Clara could answer, the Phylarix's wings spread wide. A bright flash of light forced her to shield her eyes once more. When she looked again, the creature was gone.

"What did it tell you?" Ashael pressed, his voice gentle but urgent.

Clara hesitated, the cryptic message turning over in her mind. "*The path you seek lies where you began. The last burns darker than you think.*"

A hush fell over the group as they absorbed the words.

"Where you began," Elyndra repeated thoughtfully. "That could mean many things."

"And what burns darker?" Selandor wondered aloud.

Malrik rubbed the back of his neck. "Whatever it means, I'm more interested in what just happened. Did that thing just teleport us?"

"The Phylarix," Ashael corrected. "And yes, I believe it did."

"Teleportation." Malrik spread his hands. "I shouldn't expect anything less."

Clara pulled out the map from her satchel. "Maybe the map will show us where we are now."

She unfolded it carefully, the others gathering around to look. The parchment lay flat in her hands, the familiar markings visible, but nothing new appeared. No glowing point indicated their location; no path illuminated to guide them forward.

"Nothing," she said.

Ashael frowned slightly. "Perhaps the map only responds to the spheres or to specific locations."

Clara glanced down at her satchel, feeling the weight of the shard inside. "Remember the sphere we found at the volcano? The one the Phylarix was guarding? That became part of the shard."

"A connection," Ashael nodded. "The shard responded to the Phylarix, or perhaps the Phylarix to the shard."

"Either way," Vaelin said, "the question remains. Where are we?"

They all looked around at the unfamiliar landscape. Rolling hills stretched before them, covered in tall grass that rippled in the breeze. Sparse trees dotted the terrain, their branches reaching toward a clear blue sky. In the distance, mountains rose like jagged teeth against the horizon.

"I'll scout," Kira offered. Before anyone could respond, she shifted forms, wings unfurling as she launched herself into the air.

While they waited, the others spread out, examining their surroundings. Clara wandered a short distance away, taking deep breaths of the clean air. After the suffocating heat and sulfur of the volcano, each breath felt like a gift.

When Kira returned, she seemed puzzled. "I don't recognize this region. We're definitely still in Avenora—the light has that same quality. But I've never flown over this area before."

"Could we be near Veylora's territory?" Malrik asked, sounding tense.

Kira shook her head. "No signs of corruption. The land is healthy here."

"She's right," Vaelin added, his jaw tightening slightly. "This place is unfamiliar, even to me."

"That's something, at least. If we don't know where we are, then neither does Veylora." Malrik said. "We should find shelter before we make any further plans."

"Malrik is right. Shelter and water are our primary concerns," Ashael agreed.

Clara stifled a smile at the smug look of satisfaction on Malrik's face.

They trekked across the rolling grassland, keeping the mountains to their left. For hours, they walked, with Kira shifting to circle ahead every so often, scouting for any clues to where they were, making sure they weren't being pursued by Dravok. Normally, Clara would have been exhausted. Her uncomfortable night of sleep didn't do much to ease her already aching muscles. They'd had little rest since she was first deposited onto the Nyths' floating island. She'd jumped into a waterfall, nearly drowned, and now had walked for hours. Thankfully, her Zaralis gave her the strength and stamina to keep going.

As the light began to fade, Selandor spotted a cluster of trees with wide trunks. "These will do," he said, approaching the largest one. He placed his palm against the rough bark.

Within moments, the tree had formed a spacious hollow, complete with moss bedding and woven branch-shelves.

Vaelin cocked an eyebrow as he glanced around their shelter. "Really, Selandor? Interior decorating?"

Selandor held up his hands. "I wanted it to feel homey, all right?"

The shelter was comfortable enough to fit their entire group, protected from wind and weather. Clara helped arrange their supplies onto the ornately crafted shelving as they settled in for the night.

"There's water nearby," she called to the others, already moving toward it.

A narrow stream wound its way between the hills, the water clear and cool. Clara knelt beside it, dipping her hands into the refreshing current. She splashed her face, washing away the grime and sweat of the volcano.

One by one, the others joined her, taking turns to clean themselves and fill their water skins. As twilight deepened around them, they returned to the shelter, settling in for the night.

Elyndra and Vaelin took the first watch. Malrik had already stretched out on his makeshift bed, one arm flung over his eyes. Kira sat near the entrance, gazing out at the darkening sky. Selandor was busy organizing their remaining supplies, counting what they had left.

Ashael sat apart from the others, examining the bandage on his arm. Clara approached him, settling down beside him.

"Let me see," she said softly.

Ashael looked up, a hint of surprise crossing his features before he offered his arm. Clara gently unwrapped the bandage, revealing the wound beneath. The gash had already begun to close, the angry red fading to pink at the edges.

"It's healing well," she said, reaching for her satchel. "The Aelvor salve is remarkable."

"Aelvor healing at its finest," Ashael agreed, watching as she applied a fresh layer of the green paste.

Clara worked in silence for a moment, her fingers gentle against his skin. "I wish we had something like this in my world. It would make healing so much easier."

"Your experience as a healer serves you well here," Ashael observed, watching her work.

Clara looked up, a little surprised. "You remember."

"That you were a nurse? Of course." A ghost of a smile touched his lips. "I pay attention, Clara."

She continued tending to his wound. "It was different, though. In the nursing home, I mostly cared for the elderly. People in their final years."

"That takes a different kind of strength," Ashael said. "There's a warmth to your care that I've rarely encountered. I've come to depend on it more than I should admit."

The rare moment of vulnerability caught her attention. The intensity in his blue eyes sent a flutter through her chest. Ashael was usually so reserved, keeping his thoughts and feelings hidden away.

She wondered what had changed. Was it their brush with death at the volcano? The strange journey through fire? Or perhaps the quiet of this moment, away from immediate danger?

"How do you feel about it?" he asked. "This journey, I mean. It's asked much of you."

Clara covered the salve and tucked it safely into her satchel, considering the question. "Mixed feelings, honestly. Sometimes I'm terrified. Sometimes exhilarated." She paused. "But mostly, I feel it's changed me. It's turned me into someone I didn't know I could be. Someone who would jump off a cliff on nothing but gut instinct."

"The trainings helped, I hope?" There was a hint of lightness in his voice.

Clara laughed softly. "They did, though you weren't exactly gentle." She remembered how he had made her go through the forms again and again, perfecting her balance.

"Not bad for a human girl," he said, the corner of his mouth lifting in what might have been a smile.

"Have you met many humans before?" she asked, curious.

Ashael shook his head. "Never, actually. Just you and Malrik."

"Really? But you must be . . . How old are you?" She didn't stop to think if it was really polite to ask or if she actually wanted the answer, but she was so surprised that she was the first human he'd met that she didn't stop to consider.

"Many human lifetimes," he answered vaguely.

Ashael's face bore no lines, no signs of age. Yet his eyes held a depth that spoke of years beyond her imagination.

"Did you have family here? Before all this?" The question slipped out before she could stop it. He hadn't seemed to mind her asking about his age, anyway.

Something shadowed Ashael's expression. For a moment, she thought he wouldn't answer, and she felt a sudden surge of guilt for prying.

"My parents were killed during an attack from Veylora's forces," he said finally, his voice low. "I was young. Ceyndor took me in, raised me in the Aelvor Sanctuary."

"I'm sorry," Clara said softly. "Do you remember them?"

Ashael's gaze drifted to the shelter's entrance, where stars had begun to appear in the darkening sky. "Fragments. My mother's voice. My father's hand on my shoulder." He shook his head. "Not enough."

"And Ceyndor? Did he know them?"

"He claims that he didn't know them well. Said they lived in another, smaller Aelvor camp. They had met only a few times before . . ." He trailed off, then added, "I know little of my family line."

Clara could hear the grief in his voice. He mourned not just the loss of his parents, but of his history, his roots.

"After they died," Ashael continued, "I swore to become stronger. To be a better fighter." His eyes found hers again, their blue depths holding something fierce. "I couldn't protect them then. But I swear to you, Clara, I won't fail you."

The intensity of his promise caught her off guard. In the dim light of their shelter, with the others around them, she felt something change between them. Like a wall had just settled between them. She remembered what he'd said about getting her home, and her chest squeezed.

Clara didn't know what to say. Her gaze dropped involuntarily to his hand resting on his knee, just inches from hers. She stared, noticing the long, tapered fingers and the fine blue veins visible beneath his pale Aelvor skin. Her own hand twitched, as if contemplating reaching out to him.

Ashael caught her staring. Heat rose to her cheeks, and she began to draw her hand closer to herself, suddenly self-conscious.

Then, with a gentleness that surprised her, Ashael's hand moved to bridge the gap. His fingers found hers, a light touch that felt significant in its restraint.

The next morning, Kira announced her decision over breakfast.

"I need to fly farther out," she said, taking a small piece of Morsela from her pack. "We're not getting anywhere with these short trips."

"How far are you thinking?" Vaelin asked.

Kira shrugged. "As far as needed to find something I recognize. A mountain range, a river, anything that might help us pinpoint our location."

Selandor nodded. "It makes sense. And this place seems safe enough for now."

The night had passed peacefully. There was no sign of the Dravok, Seraphis, or corruption. Clara glanced around their makeshift camp. Selandor's homey touches made their hollow feel like a luxury. "We could all use a few days' rest," she said.

So, Kira left, promising to return within a week. And for once, they had time to breathe.

The days that followed held a strange peace that Clara hadn't experienced since their quest started. Without immediate danger driving them forward, they settled into a simple routine. They conserved their Morsela and made do with fresh berries, roots, and small woodland creatures that

Elyndra, Malrik, and Vaelin brought back from hunting. For the first time since their stay with the Centurions, they enjoyed hot meals cooked over a small fire, a luxury that boosted everyone's spirits.

Clara noticed other changes too. Elyndra and Vaelin had started speaking again; really speaking, not just exchanging necessary information. One evening, as they gathered firewood together, Elyndra confided in her.

"The time here has been good for us," she said quietly, gathering fallen branches. "Vaelin and I are finding our way back to each other."

"What about his sister?" Clara asked, scooping up her own armful of kindling. "Seraphis, I mean."

Elyndra's hands stilled for a moment. "It's complicated. But we've both realized that holding onto anger doesn't help anyone." She smiled a little. "Sometimes, you need quiet moments to remember what matters."

Not everyone seemed to find peace, though. Clara often caught Selandor sitting alone, his gaze distant as he stared in the direction they'd come from.

"He's thinking of Lythara," Ashael told her when she asked. "The longer we're away, the harder it gets."

One evening, as they sat around their small fire, Ashael looked up suddenly. "We should send word to the Sanctuary. To Lythara and Ceyndor. Let them know we're alive."

Selandor's head snapped up, hope flaring in his eyes.

"Is that even possible?" Clara asked.

"It's risky," Vaelin said, "but we're far from Veylora's stronghold here."

"Why haven't we done this before?" Malrik asked, poking at the fire with a stick.

Vaelin gave him a flat look. "In case you hadn't noticed, we've been busy running for our lives."

"How would it work?" Clara asked, leaning forward with interest.

Selandor set down his water flask. "We can call a bird and attach a message to its leg. I'll guide it through intention. It's how we've sent messages for centuries. The bird won't know the path on its own, but if I focus, it'll feel the pull. Avenora's energy connects everything."

They weighed the risks, debating what information would be safe to share if the message were intercepted.

"Keep it simple," Ashael advised. "Just that we're alive and safe."

"And that we've found the first shard," Elyndra added. "But maybe be vague about that part. Put it in a way that Ceyndor would know, but no one else would."

In the end, they agreed on a brief message. Selandor fashioned writing implements from items around camp, mixing ash from their fire and carving a slender twig into a pen. He coaxed a leaf to grow as big as his hand before writing a few lines. Clara caught glimpses of the elegant Aelvor script as he worked, flowing like water across the leaf's surface.

Once finished, he rolled the tiny note tightly and secured it with a thin thread from his supplies.

Clara watched, fascinated, as Selandor stepped away from camp and closed his eyes. His lips moved in what looked like a silent song, his hands held gently before him.

Within minutes, a small bird with iridescent blue-green feathers appeared, landing lightly on his outstretched finger. Selandor spoke softly to it, stroking its head with one finger as he carefully attached the rolled note to its leg.

Then he touched his forehead to the small creature's head, his eyes closed in concentration.

"Is he . . .?" Clara whispered to Ashael.

"He's imprinting the path," he said quietly. "And how to avoid harm."

After a moment, Selandor raised his hand and the bird took flight, quickly disappearing into the brilliant blue sky.

"Do you think it will reach them?" Clara asked.

Selandor nodded, his expression lighter than she'd seen in days. "It will. And Lythara will know we're safe."

What Clara noticed most was the change in Ashael. When they were alone, collecting water at the stream or taking the dawn watch together, he spoke to her differently. He shared small stories of his training years, asked about her life in her world, even smiled. But whenever Malrik approached, Ashael would withdraw behind his usual reserve, his words becoming measured and practical again.

She caught him watching her sometimes when he thought she wouldn't notice. Something in his gaze made her chest tighten in a way she wasn't ready to examine.

Malrik remained himself—intellectual, strong, observant—but something had deepened there too. He sat closer to her at night, his shoulder pressing against hers. His hand lingered when passing her a water flask. Small changes that spoke volumes.

Clara felt the pull toward both of them and hated herself a little for it. They were trying to save a world. There wasn't time for whatever this was, these feelings tangling inside her. But they were stuck here, waiting for Kira to return. Instead of fighting them or trying to figure out what she wanted, she simply let everything be. It felt good not to worry for once.

On the seventh day, Kira returned just before sunset, landing with a heavy thud that suggested exhaustion. They gathered around her immediately.

"Did you find anything?" Elyndra asked, offering her water.

Kira drank deeply before answering. "Yes. I know where we are."

That night, they crowded inside the hollow, sitting in a circle on the moss floor. The tree's luminescent veins cast blue-green light across their faces as Clara spread the map between them.

"Show us," Ashael said.

Kira leaned forward, her finger hovering over the map. "I flew north first, following this range." She traced a path along a line of mountains. "Nothing familiar. Then west, where I found this river." Her finger moved again. "And finally, southeast."

She tapped a spot decisively. "This forest matches what I saw. And beyond it, I recognized the cliffs of Sarien." She drew an invisible circle. "Which means we're here."

Clara studied the spot, unsure of its significance until she heard Elyndra's sharp intake of breath.

"But that's . . ." Elyndra started, her eyes widening.

"The Veil Gate," Vaelin finished, voice tight. "Or at least, the area where it's supposed to be."

Silence fell as they absorbed this.

"What do you mean 'supposed to be'?" Malrik asked, leaning forward to study the map more closely. "It's either there or it isn't."

Selandor shook his head. "The Veil Gate isn't like a normal doorway. It's not a physical structure you can simply walk up to and touch."

"Most of the time, it's invisible," Elyndra added. "It appears only under specific circumstances, but it is usually contained to this region. At least, it last appeared here."

"Like what?" Clara asked.

Selandor's fingers traced a circle on the map. "Historically, it would appear for the Eternals themselves, of course. And for the royal family of the Aelvor and the chosen human guardian family." He paused. "Or for those who carried the Vaelithar."

"The Vaelithar acts as both key and keeper," Ashael explained, his gaze drifting to the shard in Clara's hands. "It maintained the balance between worlds, stabilized the gate, and helped it judge who should pass through."

"Judge?" Malrik repeated.

Elyndra nodded. "The gate can sense intention. In rare cases, if someone's purpose had aligned with the greater balance between worlds, the gate would appear and allow passage, even for those without royal blood or the Vaelithar."

Clara turned the shard over in her hands, watching the colors shift within it. "What does this mean now? With the Vaelithar broken?"

No one spoke for a moment. Then Clara remembered what Mrs. Alcott had whispered to her before she died. The elderly woman had gripped her wrist with surprising strength and said, *"The veil is thinner than you think."*

At the time, Clara had dismissed it as confusion. But now, it made sense. But how on earth did Mrs. Alcott know about Avenora and the veil to begin with? Clara's mouth twisted in thought. She may never know the answer to those questions.

"The gate is weaker now," Ashael said, voicing her thoughts. "Probably erratic, appearing and disappearing without purpose or pattern."

"But not completely broken," Selandor added quickly. "As long as the shards exist, even separated, they still exert some control. The worlds haven't merged. Not yet."

"What about the Dravok shadows?" Clara asked, shivering as she remembered the terror of being stalked by the creatures. "The ones that came through to my world?"

Ashael's expression darkened. "They must have watched, waited. Perhaps they found moments when the gate briefly manifested."

"Staying in shadow form probably made it easier," Vaelin said. "Without ever solidifying, they could slip through even the smallest crack in the veil."

"The gate momentarily loses control over judging intention," Elyndra concluded. "That's how they passed through."

Malrik sat back, his face grim. "So, the Dravoks have been here before. Which means they can come back."

"And next time," Clara said softly, "they might bring Seraphis with them."

The hollow seemed to grow colder at the thought.

"The message," Clara said, reaching for her satchel. She pulled out the shard, its surface gleaming in the dim light. "'The path you seek lies where you began. The last burns darker than you think.'"

"We've been trying to decipher the second part," Ashael said, "but maybe the first part is the key."

"'Where you began,'" Malrik repeated, brows furrowed. "The Veil Gate isn't where we started, though. We came from the Aelvor Sanctuary, then the Syralen Cove, then the volcanic lands . . ."

They went back and forth, offering theories and discarding them just as quickly. Could it refer to where the Vaelithar originally broke? Where the corruption first appeared? The beginning of Veylora's rise to power?

Clara listened, turning the shard over in her hands, feeling its weight and warmth. The conversation blurred around her as her mind worked through a different possibility.

The Phylarix had spoken only to her.

Malrik must have noticed her expression change. He stopped mid-sentence and turned to her.

"Clara," he said, his voice cutting through the others, "what are you thinking?"

The hollow fell silent. All eyes turned to her.

Clara looked up, meeting their gazes one by one, the realization settling over her with absolute certainty. "The Phylarix only spoke to me. So, I was thinking of where all this began for *me*."

Her friends stared at her, waiting for her to finish.

As she turned the shard over again in her hands, admiring the jagged edges, it struck her how much the swirling colors inside reminded her of home. Of brilliant, flashing lights that never went out, that rippled across tall buildings in a kaleidoscope of color.

"New York City," she whispered.

Malrik swore under his breath.

Clara's eye flicked up, finding Ashael's. His face was set in a stoic mask. Clara felt her heart harden, too, shielding her from what she knew was coming. To see this through, she would have to return home. The only problem was she wasn't sure she wanted to.

CHAPTER 32

Clara had barely slept. After her revelation about New York City, the group had debated for hours, voices rising and falling as they worked through the risks, the what-ifs, and everything in between.

In the end, the plan was set: She and Malrik would cross through the Veil Gate back to their world. Alone.

Her fingers brushed the shard through the side of her satchel. The pendant pressed against the hollow of her throat. Both artifacts were never far, serving as constant threads that tied her to all that had changed.

"You're still thinking about it," Malrik said, matching his stride to hers as they left the hollow to search for the Veil Gate.

Clara nodded. "I asked Elyndra again why none of them are coming with us." She kept her voice low, though the others had spread out ahead of them. "I understand Kira staying behind, but . . ."

"But you wondered why Ashael isn't coming," Malrik finished for her, his expression carefully neutral.

"All of them," Clara corrected quickly. "I just don't understand why we're splitting up."

Malrik shrugged. "They explained it already. The Aelvors will protect the Gate from any threat that might try to follow us back. And to be honest, we know our world better than they do."

"I know," Clara said. "It makes sense. It's just . . ."

"Hard to leave them," Malrik said softly.

She nodded, swallowing the lump in her throat.

"We'll come back," he reminded her. "They'll be waiting for us right here."

"If we can find the Gate at all," Clara said, kicking at a stone. "And if it lets us through."

Clara's thoughts turned to her family. It had been more than a month. By now, her parents must have realized she was missing. She pictured her mother pacing the floor, calling hospitals and police stations. Her father driving to New York, checking her apartment, and questioning her neighbors.

"Do you think we should try to contact your dad right away?" Malrik asked, as if reading her thoughts. "About the Valenwoods, I mean."

Clara nodded. "I'll probably need to go back to Ohio. As far as I know, Dad's an only child. My grandparents died when I was young, so I don't have much family history to go on."

"Valenwood," Malrik said thoughtfully. "It definitely sounds like a guardian name."

"That's what Mrs. Alcott said," Clara said softly. "I didn't really take it seriously because I thought it was a product of her dementia, but thinking back . . . she knew more than she let on. She gave me the map. I wonder if there were others like her who knew more."

"That's another mystery to solve when we get home." Malrik shook his head and sighed.

Up ahead, the group had spread out. Vaelin and Elyndra walked close together, heads bent in conversation as they examined the eastern perimeter. Selandor moved methodically through a small grove of trees, touching each trunk as if the bark might reveal secrets. And Ashael . . .

Ashael stood apart from the others, glancing straight at her. When their eyes met, he quickly looked away, turning to walk in the opposite direction.

Clara frowned. Just when she thought they'd been growing closer . . . her heart constricted.

"Hey, don't worry about my bookstore," Malrik said suddenly, breaking into her thoughts. "I'm sure someone's watering the plants."

Clara blinked at the abrupt change of subject. "You have plants?"

"No, but if I did," he said with a grin, "I'm sure someone would be watering them."

Despite herself, Clara laughed. "You're ridiculous."

"I'm serious! I keep wondering if I remembered to lock up. And what my customers think happened to me." His smile faded slightly. "We're probably on some missing persons list by now."

"I just hope our families are okay," Clara murmured. "I don't even know how we're going to explain where we've been all this time."

They continued walking, scanning the area for any sign of the Veil Gate. Clara was about to suggest they try another direction when the air around them changed.

It became heavier, thicker, like walking through invisible syrup. A sensation similar to static electricity raised the hair on her arms.

Malrik stopped suddenly and waved his hand in front of him, trying to touch the source of the strange feeling. "Do you feel that?"

"Yes," Clara whispered, hardly daring to breathe.

They moved forward, and the hair on the back of her neck rose. Her scalp prickled, and her lungs even burned a little. She smiled. This had to be it. They must be close to the Veil Gate.

They waved to the others, gesturing for them to come quickly. Clara reached forward, fingers stretching, searching for anything that felt like a gate.

Then it was gone. The air returned to normal. The electric sensation vanished, as if it had never been there.

Clara's hand dropped to her side. "No," she murmured. "No, it was right here."

Malrik kicked at the ground in frustration. "We were so close!"

By evening, their frustration had grown. It was almost worse that they had gotten a taste of the Veil Gate's power. They gathered around a small fire outside the hollow, the rich scent of roasting meat filling the air.

"The disturbance Clara and Malrik felt is a good sign," Selandor said, crouching by the fire. He turned the skewer slowly between his fingers, juices hissing as their dinner cooked over the glowing coals. "It suggests the Gate is trying to manifest."

"But it's unstable," Ashael added. "Without the Vaelithar to anchor it, the Gate appears briefly then fades."

"If we keep searching, we'll catch it eventually," Elyndra said. "We just need patience."

Clara nodded, agreeing quietly. The fire crackled between them. For a while, no one spoke. They just sat there, letting the quiet settle around them.

A strange warmth prickled along her side. She turned her head slightly and caught Ashael staring at her, his blue eyes intense in the firelight. The moment their gazes connected, he looked away, suddenly engrossed in conversation with Selandor.

Clara started to rise, determined to finally talk to him about his strange behavior, when Malrik returned from the fire pit carrying two portions from their earlier hunt, now well-cooked and steaming.

"Here, eat!" he insisted, pulling her back down beside him. "You've barely touched food all day."

She sat reluctantly, accepting the plate, but her attention kept drifting across the fire. Ashael never looked her way again, but Clara couldn't help wondering what thoughts lay behind his guarded expression.

Clara pushed aside the leafy curtain of the hollow, squinting as morning sunlight hit her face. She hadn't slept well. Ashael's continued avoidance had bothered her more than she wanted to admit, leaving her restless.

She'd never anticipated feeling this way about his distance or about him at all. The realization unsettled her.

The others had already left to search for the Veil Gate, and she'd stayed behind longer than she meant to. She hurried outside, turning right without looking, and slammed directly into a solid figure.

"I'm sorry," she and Ashael both said at once.

They stood awkwardly, too close, both leaning back slightly. His hair was damp. She could smell the light herbal scent that clung to him.

"I was just—" Clara started.

"I should have—" Ashael said simultaneously.

They both stopped. Ashael looked somewhere over her shoulder, his jaw tight.

"I was just heading this way," he said formally. "I think Malrik might be down the eastern path."

Before she could respond, he stepped around her and walked away, his stride quick and purposeful.

Clara started in the direction he'd indicated, but something inside her snapped. The frustration she'd been suppressing bubbled up, hot and demanding. He couldn't just push her away like this. Not after everything they'd shared.

She spun around and marched after him.

"Ashael!"

He stopped, his shoulders going rigid. When he turned, his eyes darted everywhere but her face. He opened his mouth, probably to make another excuse.

"Why can't you look me in the eye?" she demanded. Even as anger simmered through her, it could only conceal so much of her hurt. Her chest was hollow, her heart caved in from sadness.

His gaze finally met hers, and Clara's anger faltered. The vibrant blue of his eyes seemed dulled, like a light had gone out behind them.

Clara swallowed hard, pressing on when he remained silent. "I can't take this anymore. Did I do something wrong?"

He looked away for a second, then back at her. "No, Clara, please don't say that." His voice dropped. "It's not what you think."

"Then tell me what it is," she said, hating the way her voice wavered. "Because I know you feel it too."

Ashael ran a hand through his hair, the gesture uncharacteristically agitated. "I promised to protect you. This is how."

"How is this protecting me?" Clara stepped closer, forcing him to really see her. Tears welled, but she refused to let them fall. "And when the hell did you decide I needed protection? I have the map. I have the pendant. I am capable of protecting myself."

He moved toward her, closing the distance between them. "I know, I know. I'm sorry." He paused, his eyes downcast. "Clara, you have no idea . . ." he trailed off, looking away.

"Is it because I'm going back to my world?" She searched his face. "You changed the moment we decided. But I am coming back—"

"Even so," he said quietly, "your path leads elsewhere. Your life, your people . . ." His hand opened and closed at his side. "Our worlds are not meant to . . ."

Clara stared at him, the truth finally sinking in. How deeply he'd been thinking about this, not just where they stood now, but what it all meant.

"We don't have to think so far ahead," she said softly. "The future isn't guaranteed. The present is all we know for certain, and I choose to live in it."

Ashael's expression changed, and something like hope passed across his face.

Before he could respond, footsteps approached them from behind.

"Clara! Ashael! I have good news!" Malrik jogged toward them, slowing as he approached, his expression shifting as he took in the scene.

"Vaelin's found the Gate," he said, his voice infused with false brightness. He moved closer to Clara, a subtle positioning that spoke volumes. "You okay?"

"Fine," Clara said, not quite meeting his eyes. "That's great news about the Gate."

Malrik glanced between them once more, clearly unconvinced but unwilling to press the issue now. "We should hurry before it moves again."

Clara turned toward Malrik, her conversation with Ashael hanging unfinished in the air between them. She felt pulled in two directions—toward the Gate they'd been searching for days to find and back to Ashael to finish what they'd started. But the mission had to come first.

"Lead the way," she said, following Malrik while remaining acutely aware of Ashael's presence behind her. This wasn't over.

They followed Malrik toward the rising hill. Clara's heart pounded, not just because the Gate might finally be here, but because what she'd left unsaid still burned inside her.

CHAPTER 33

Malrik

Morning dew clung to the grass as Malrik combed through the meadow, scanning the horizon for any hint of the Veil Gate. They'd been searching since dawn, each taking different routes to maximize their coverage. His boots left damp impressions in the soft earth as he walked.

He'd left Clara sleeping in the hollow. They'd been able to breathe a little easier in this area for the past few days, with no immediate threats and the worst of the terrain behind them. It had given everyone a chance to recover, at least physically.

Even so, Clara had looked worn lately. The shadows under her eyes had deepened, and she moved with a kind of heaviness that hadn't been there before. Something was bothering her. He just didn't know what it was. He had his guesses, but she hadn't confided in him.

The sky stretched clear and blue overhead, a stark contrast to the troubles that had plagued their journey. For a realm in the midst of a struggle against darkness, Avenora certainly knew how to present a beautiful morning.

Movement caught his eye. Vaelin approached at a half-jog.

The Aelvor warrior's expression was different today. He looked alert, focused, but there was something else beneath it. A restlessness.

"Malrik," Vaelin called, slowing his pace. "I found it."

Malrik stopped in his tracks. "Found what?"

"The Veil Gate," Vaelin replied, eyes bright with intensity. "Or at least, the place where it should appear."

Malrik's heart skipped. "You're sure?"

Vaelin nodded once.

"Have you told the others?" Malrik asked, mentally calculating the fastest route back to Clara.

"I've informed Selandor and Elyndra. Kira as well," Vaelin said, glancing back over his shoulder. "They'll meet us at the clearing. I came to find you. Can you locate Clara and Ashael? We should move quickly." His fingers flexed at his sides and inched almost imperceptibly toward his weapon.

Something in the gesture unnerved Malrik. The Aelvor's stance was tense. Was it simply from his anxiety to get everyone to the Gate or something else? "Everything all right?" he asked, watching Vaelin closely.

Vaelin blinked. "Of course. We've been searching for this Gate for days. Finding it is significant."

Malrik nodded, deciding not to press further. "I'll get Clara and Ashael."

As Vaelin headed back toward the meeting point, Malrik paused, letting reality sink in.

The Veil Gate. They'd found it. They could go home.

Home. A world where his biggest concerns had once been bookshop inventory and making rent payments. The simplicity of it all seemed almost foreign after everything they had experienced.

But going home also meant leaving Avenora behind. Leaving the Aelvors, who had become more than just allies. In his world, it would be just him and Clara, navigating whatever came next. No Selandor's wisdom. No Elyndra's insights. No Kira's strength.

No Ashael.

His stomach twisted at the thought, a complicated mix of emotions rising inside him. He wasn't blind to what had developed between Clara and Ashael. The glances they shared, the way they always found each other during quiet moments. But for a few days now, something between them felt different. An awkward tension had crept in, and Malrik wasn't sure what it meant.

And what about his own feelings? The fierce protectiveness he felt toward Clara had deepened into something more. Somewhere along this journey, amid danger and discovery, Clara had become more than just his closest friend. He cared for her deeply, in a way that sometimes ached.

But did she feel the same? Sometimes, he thought she might.

Malrik shook his head. This wasn't the time to untangle that particular knot. They had a Veil Gate to find, a journey home to prepare for, and a world to save.

He headed back toward the hollow, picking up his pace with each step. The forest thickened around him, now familiar after days of calling it a temporary home. As he approached the massive tree that housed their shelter, voices floated through the morning air.

He slowed, already reading what he might find.

It was Clara and Ashael. Their voices were low but tense, enough for Malrik to catch the emotion behind them. He couldn't make out every word, but the tone said enough. Clara sounded hurt, frustrated. Ashael's voice was quieter, like someone trying to explain something he didn't really want to admit.

From what Malrik could gather, it was about the distance between them lately. About Ashael pulling back. And more than anything, it confirmed what Malrik had suspected for a while now. There was something real between them. Something neither of them seemed willing to let go of no matter how complicated it had become.

The ache in Clara's voice hit him harder than he expected. Whatever she felt, it mattered. And as much as he wanted things to be different, he couldn't pretend he hadn't seen it coming.

Malrik stood frozen for a moment. But seeing Clara like this, upset and vulnerable, wasn't something he could just walk away from. If she wanted Ashael, he wanted her to have him. He could not begrudge her happiness, even if it meant he lost her. They would always be friends—best friends.

He stepped forward, making sure his footsteps were loud enough to be heard.

"Clara. Ashael!" he called out, putting a bit of forced brightness into his voice. "I have good news!"

They both turned, surprised by his sudden appearance.

He jogged toward them, stopping beside Clara. Whatever came next, he would be by her side.

It was time they went home.

CHAPTER 34

Clara hurried after Malrik, her heart still racing from her confrontation with Ashael. She could hear his light footsteps behind her, barely audible even in the quiet forest, a stark contrast to the chaos inside her chest.

The path widened as they reached a sunlit clearing where Kira, Selandor, and Vaelin waited. Kira's posture was tense, ready to spring into action at any moment. Selandor paced the perimeter, his expression alert and watchful. Vaelin stood still at the center.

"You found it?" Clara asked, trying to steady her voice. The air here felt normal. How could he be sure it would appear here?

Vaelin nodded. "Not quite manifested yet, but I can feel it. It's like a thin spot in the fabric between worlds. The disturbance is stronger than anything we've encountered so far."

Selandor approached, the sunlight catching in his auburn hair. "How close?"

"Very," Vaelin replied. "The Gate is on the verge of manifesting fully."

Clara glanced around the clearing, noticing the absence of their sixth companion. "Where's Elyndra?"

Clara caught the slight twitch in Vaelin's jaw. "She's waiting at the location. I thought it best not to leave it unattended."

"It's finally happening," Malrik said, adjusting his glasses. "We're actually going back."

"Then let's not waste time," Ashael said from behind Clara. His voice was cool and commanding, reminding her of the aloof warrior she'd first met in the Aelvor Sanctuary, not the warm person she'd come to know. She didn't turn to look at him, but she felt his presence like a physical touch.

Vaelin led them through a narrow path between tall, swaying grasses. The vegetation grew thicker as they progressed, eventually giving way to a grove of massive trees whose branches intertwined overhead, creating a natural cathedral of leaves and light.

As they walked, Clara noticed Selandor's tense posture, his eyes constantly scanning the surroundings as if expecting danger from any direction. His hand rested lightly on the hilt of his blade. Kira had noticed it, too, her gaze following his vigilant movements.

Clara leaned toward Malrik. "Is it just me, or does everyone seem unusually on edge?"

Malrik frowned, glancing ahead. "You're telling me."

The path narrowed as they continued, forcing them to walk single file. Clara found herself between Malrik and Ashael, hyper aware of each breath, each footstep. A knot formed in her stomach. Something wasn't right. The forest had grown too quiet. What was happening?

When the path widened again, Selandor dropped back to walk beside Vaelin. His voice was low, but Clara caught fragments of their conversation.

"You've been off since you returned from scouting," Selandor said. "What aren't you telling us?"

Vaelin kept his eyes forward. "We're walking into unknown territory."

"We've been in unknown territory for weeks." Selandor's tone hardened. "This is different. You're different."

Vaelin's jaw tightened. "Focus on the mission."

"I *am* focused," Selandor countered. "Which is why I need to know if there's something you're not saying."

Clara's pulse quickened. The tension between them felt like a physical thing, pressing in from all sides. She glanced at Ashael, whose face revealed nothing, but she noticed how his stride had shortened. He was listening too.

A flutter of wind brushed the leaves overhead, sending dappled shadows dancing across their path. The air grew heavier, thick with an uneasy stillness that made Clara's skin prickle. Her fingers found the pendant at her throat, its familiar warmth offering little comfort.

Ahead, the trees thinned. Vaelin raised his hand, signaling them to stop.

"We're close," he whispered.

Clara peered ahead, her heart hammering against her ribs. The air was still. There was no prickle of electricity, no hum in her bones that hinted at a hidden power.

"Something's wrong," she whispered to Malrik. "I can feel it." She took a step back.

Malrik nodded. He unslung his bow from his back and grabbed an arrow from his quiver. "Stay close."

Before she could respond, Vaelin stopped and gestured to a small clearing ahead. "There."

The air in the clearing seemed to shimmer, though not with heat or light. It was more like looking through water, the space beyond wavering and indistinct. Clara stepped forward cautiously, drawn by the strange distortion. It didn't feel the same as before, but there was no doubt that something powerful lay ahead.

As the group stepped out of the safety of the trees, out into the open, the air continued to shimmer.

"The Gate," she whispered. "It's really here."

Malrik moved up beside her, eyes wide. "Our way home."

A snap of branches cracked through the air like a whip. Clara whirled around as a figure emerged from the shadows of the massive silverbark trees.

Seraphis stood at the opposite edge of the clearing, a cold smile on her face. Her black hair fell in a sleek cascade down her back; her dark eyes glittered with triumph. Beside her, held firmly in the grip of a Dravok, stood Elyndra.

"Looking for someone?" Seraphis asked, her voice smooth and tainted with poison.

"Elyndra!" Selandor lunged forward, only to freeze as the Dravok tightened its shadowy tendrils around Elyndra's throat.

"Well done, brother," Seraphis said, turning her gaze to Vaelin. "Right on time."

Clara turned to Vaelin, the truth hitting her like a physical blow. "You—"

"There was no other way," he said quietly, not meeting anyone's eyes.

A low, animal sound escaped Selandor's throat as he advanced on Vaelin. "I knew it! You traitor!"

"He did what any sensible brother would do," Seraphis said, stepping fully into the clearing. Behind her, dark forms shifted and coalesced. Dravoks, at least a dozen, took shape around her, shadow bodies solidifying, smoky swirls trailing from them.

"Let her go," Selandor demanded, unsheathing his weapon. The blade lengthened and burned with a fatal glow.

Seraphis smiled, the expression never reaching her eyes, wholly unthreatened by Selandor. "When I have what I came for." She turned her gaze to Clara. "The key. Hand it over, willingly, and your friend lives."

Clara's hand went instinctively to her pendant. It pulsed against her skin. "Why would I give this to you?"

"Because when given willingly, it won't fight its new bearer," Seraphis explained, her tone almost conversational. "I think we both know that after our last encounter. It's rather particular that way." She gestured toward Elyndra. "And because I need the Aelvor woman alive for now, but that could change if you refuse."

"You promised you wouldn't harm Elyndra!" Vaelin's voice cracked with desperation, his eyes darting between his sister and the captive Aelvor.

Seraphis's lips curled into a cold smile. "I promised I would spare her life if you cooperated. Your cooperation isn't complete until I get everything I want." To emphasize her point, she nodded to the Dravok, who constricted its hold around Elyndra's throat, making her gasp for air.

"Don't," Elyndra managed to choke out. "Clara, don't give it to her."

Clara looked around desperately. Selandor and Kira stood rigid with tension. Malrik had edged closer to her, his fingers resting lightly on his bowstring. Ashael had moved to her other side, his presence solid and reassuring despite everything left unsaid between them.

"You're surrounded," Ashael said to Seraphis, his voice level. "You won't leave this clearing alive if you harm her."

Seraphis laughed, the sound like breaking glass. "Bold words from a lone warrior. Look around you," she gestured mockingly. "You're the ones surrounded."

As if on cue, more shadows materialized among the trees. Dravoks emerged from their hiding places, forming a ring of darkness around the clearing.

Clara's heart raced as she looked at her trapped friends. Her mind worked frantically, searching for options, for escape routes.

"What will it be, human?" Seraphis asked. "Your friend's life or your stubborn pride?"

Clara reached for the cord around her neck. "If I give you this, you'll let her go?"

"Clara, no!" Elyndra struggled against her captor.

"Your word," Clara insisted, looking directly at Seraphis. "Swear it."

Seraphis placed a hand over her heart, the gesture a mockery of sincerity. "You have my word. The pendant for the Aelvor's life."

Slowly, Clara lifted the pendant over her head. The crystal felt heavy in her palm, almost reluctant to leave her possession. It pulsed feebly. She stepped forward, every instinct screaming at her to run.

Seraphis extended her hand, triumph gleaming in her eyes.

Clara placed the pendant in her palm, then stepped back quickly.

"Now let her go," she demanded.

Seraphis closed her fingers around the pendant, a smile spreading across her face. "Of course." She nodded to the Dravok. It released Elyndra with a shove.

Elyndra stumbled forward, caught by Selandor before she could fall.

Clara's heart raced. At least they didn't know about the shard. Maybe there was still a chance they could escape. "Oh, and I'll take the shard as well," Seraphis added, her gaze sliding to Clara's satchel. "Yes, I know you have it. Did you think Veylora wouldn't sense its awakening?"

Clara felt sick. They knew everything. She shared a quick glance with Malrik, whose face had gone pale.

"And now," Seraphis said, slipping the pendant into a pocket, "the shard."

Clara's hand moved to her satchel. Her pulse thundered in her ears. The clearing around her faded, sounds muffled, as if the world had narrowed to this one moment. She saw Elyndra swaying, held upright only by Selandor's arm. Seraphis tilted her head slightly, already certain of victory. At the edge of the clearing, the Dravoks had shifted into position, waiting for their commander's word.

Then Clara's eyes found Ashael's. A question passed between them without words. He gave the slightest nod. She didn't hesitate.

With a sudden burst, Clara yanked the satchel from her shoulder and hurled it high toward him. "Catch!"

For one stretched second, the world stood still. Then chaos erupted.

The satchel arced high overhead, spinning once, the weight of its contents pulling it slightly off course. For a heartbeat, it felt like it might fall short.

Seraphis moved like a blade through the air, eyes locked on the prize.

She was fast. But Ashael was faster.

His fingers closed around the satchel just as hers missed by inches, her momentum carrying her past him with a hiss of frustration.

The Dravoks surged forward like a dark tide.

Kira didn't fully shift. Her form stayed humanoid, but golden wings burst from her back. She unsheathed her sword which glowed red and gold. She looked like an angel casting her fury on the forces of darkness. She launched into the fray with a blast of wind, her blade slashing through shadow.

Selandor and Elyndra whirled, their blades gleaming as bright as beacons.

Shouts rang through the clearing. Steel clashed with shrieks of inhuman voices. Light met darkness in a storm of movement and chaos.

Clara ducked as a Dravok's tendril whipped past her, its arm stretching farther than anything should. She didn't hesitate. She drew her dagger, which instantly flared into a fiery blade in her grip.

Ashael's training kicked in. Her body moved on instinct, the Zaralis sharpening her reflexes. She slashed upward, cutting clean through the extended limb. The blade hissed as it sliced, and the Dravok recoiled, its shadowy form rippling with pain.

Malrik appeared at her side and let loose an arrow. It struck its target, bursting like a firework. "Nice!"

They moved together without needing to speak. Years of friendship shaped every turn, every step. When Clara stumbled on uneven ground,

Malrik caught her arm without looking. When a Dravok lunged at him from behind, Clara shouted a warning and drove her blade into its side before it could strike.

Across the clearing, Selandor had turned his blade toward Vaelin. His face was a mask of fury, barely contained.

"You lied to us!" he roared, closing the distance in three strides. "You led us into a trap!"

"Selandor, no!" Elyndra cried out, struggling to rise. Her voice broke as she reached toward them. "He was trying to protect me!"

But Selandor didn't hesitate. He struck, his blade aimed not to threaten but to harm.

Vaelin drew his weapon at the last second, parrying the blow. "Let me explain!" he shouted, breathless, his stance defensive. He blocked another strike, then another, refusing to counter.

"I trusted you!" Selandor bellowed, each attack sharper than the last. "We all did!"

"I didn't want this," Vaelin said, his voice raw. "She had Elyndra. I had no choice."

"You always have a choice!" Selandor spat, driving him back step by step, his anger flaring with each clash of steel.

"What would you have done if it were Lythara?" Vaelin pleaded.

Selandor would not hear it. "I would never have betrayed my friends!"

Vaelin held his guard, refusing to retaliate. Clara saw it in the way his shoulders drew tight and his steps grew heavier. The guilt was crushing him.

Ashael had landed atop a large boulder, the satchel secure in his grip. Three Dravoks closed in, their forms coiling and stretching unnaturally as they attacked. His blade cut through the air, metal gleaming and fire trailing in its wake as he fought them back, each strike precise and deadly.

Across the clearing, Seraphis remained still. She stood with eerie calm, watching him with a focused, calculating gaze. Her lips parted slightly, as if tasting the moment. Then, slowly, she raised her hand.

More Dravoks emerged from behind trees and stones, creeping into position around Ashael like predators encircling their prey.

Clara and Malrik moved together, fighting side by side. Their training with the Aelvor warriors had honed them into a formidable pair, their different fighting styles complementing each other. Clara guarded Malrik as he shot arrow after arrow into the fray.

A Dravok lunged at Clara, and she rolled under its attack, coming up behind it to strike at its back.

But there were too many. For every shadow they drove back, two more took its place. Clara's arms ached; her lungs burned with every breath. A quick glance around the clearing showed the others faring no better. Kira darted above, diving to strike then soaring out of reach, but even she couldn't keep pace with the endless shadows.

The air shifted around Clara. A jolt of electricity raised the hair on her arms. The same sensation as before, but stronger now. At the center of the clearing, the light bent and warped.

"The Gate!" she called out, pointing to the distortion. "It's opening!"

Ashael dispatched the last of his attackers and leapt down beside her, his breathing labored but controlled. He pressed the satchel into her hands, his fingers lingering against hers for a heartbeat longer than necessary.

As Clara took the satchel, she felt warmth radiating through the fabric, a soft glow visible at its edges.

"The shard is responding to it," Ashael said.

She opened the satchel to reveal the Vaelithar fragment, now glowing with inner light, its colors swirling rapidly.

The air around them shimmered more intensely, the warping space expanding until it formed an oval that reached above their heads. The edges wavered and thinned in places, the portal fading and solidifying erratically. Through it, when distinct enough, Clara could make out blurry shapes of buildings, people, and lights.

New York. Their way home.

"It doesn't look stable," Ashael said urgently. "The shard seems to be helping, but without the full Vaelithar, I doubt it will hold for long."

"We have to go *now*," Malrik said, grabbing Clara's arm. "Just like we planned. You and me."

But all around them, the battle raged on. Kira had taken a hit, one wing folded awkwardly as she fought on. Elyndra had joined the fight, keeping Dravoks away from Selandor as he continued his confrontation with Vaelin.

"We can't just leave them like this!" Clara protested, looking at their embattled companions.

Ashael's eyes met hers, hardening with resolve. "All of you go through!" he shouted, loud enough for everyone to hear. "I'll stay and hold them off as long as I can!"

"That wasn't the plan," Selandor called back, blocking another strike from Vaelin. "We were supposed to guard the Gate until they returned!"

"Plans change," Ashael shouted. "We're outnumbered. The Gate is our only chance now."

Before she could protest further, a scream rang out. They turned to see Selandor landing a fierce blow that Vaelin barely managed to block, the force driving him to one knee. Blood streamed from a gash across Vaelin's side, his face contorted in pain as he struggled to maintain his defense.

"No!" Elyndra cried, lunging toward them. Kira caught her mid-stride, restraining her with surprising strength for her slender frame.

"He is a traitor," Selandor said, his voice raw with pain.

"He saved my life," Elyndra countered, tears streaming down her face. "Seraphis would have killed me if he hadn't brought you here."

Confusion crossed Selandor's face, his blade wavering for a moment.

"Go!" Ashael shouted. "All of you! The Gate is closing!"

Kira dragged a struggling Elyndra toward the glimmering oval. Selandor hesitated, then moved to follow, throwing one last pained look at Vaelin.

Not far behind, Seraphis rose slowly, shadows curling around her like smoke. Her gaze locked onto the retreating group, cold and unblinking.

She sneered. "Useless," she muttered, watching the Dravoks falter. "Do I have to do everything myself?"

Then, louder, she refocused her command, pointing toward them. "They're not leaving with the shard!"

Darkness surged around her as she lifted from the ground, hovering for a breath before launching forward, fury trailing in her wake.

Ashael charged forward to intercept her, his blade ready to defend his friends' escape.

"Your turn," Ashael called to Clara and Malrik over his shoulder. "Go!"

"Not without you," Clara insisted, reaching for his arm as tears blurred her vision. The thought of leaving him behind tore at her heart.

"I'll be right behind you," Ashael said, though the look in his eyes held something final.

Clara started to speak, but Malrik caught her arm. "Clara, we have to go. Now."

In the next instant, Ashael surged forward, placing himself between Seraphis and the others. Steel clashed with a thunderous sound, their movements a blur of fury and precision.

Ashael pressed the advantage, each strike driving Seraphis back. For a moment, it looked like he might overpower her.

Then Seraphis twisted, feinted left, and spun around. Her blade found its mark, slicing across Ashael's shoulder. He staggered from the impact, but his feet held firm and his grip remained strong.

He stumbled but didn't fall. His counterattack came swift and sharp, catching Seraphis off guard.

His blade struck deep into her abdomen. She gasped and dropped to her knees, her weapon falling beside her as she slumped forward, hands pressing to the wound. Then she crumpled to the ground and went still.

The Dravoks froze, momentarily disoriented without her control.

Clara broke free from Malrik's grip and ran to Ashael. "Come on! The Gate is still open!"

Ashael turned toward her, breathing hard, his expression set. "No, Clara. I need to make sure none of them follow you through. I'll stay behind."

"Ashael." Her voice cracked. The clearing felt distant, the noise of battle fading beneath the rush of her pulse. A hundred things rushed to the surface. Feelings she hadn't named, questions she hadn't asked, moments she hadn't let herself feel fully until now.

Not knowing if this would be the last time she ever saw him, Clara stepped in and gripped the front of his tunic. She leaned in and kissed him.

His hand rose to her cheek, his touch trembling, then steadying, as he kissed her back. Warmth bloomed between them, anchored in a breathless sliver of time, where nothing else mattered.

She pulled back just enough to look up at him, her voice barely a whisper. "Come with me."

Ashael stared at her for a moment longer. There was longing in his gaze, but something resolute, too. Then, he turned. His blue eyes caught hers, and she had a sudden flashback to before she left New York. Blue eyes. Ashael's eyes. She had seen them in the beginning, before they even arrived here. It occurred to her—she was meant to know him. To be with him. He needed to follow her into New York. It was meant to be.

"Go. I'll be right behind you."

In a blur, he rushed toward the Dravoks gathering around Seraphis. His blade moved with perfect aim, cutting a path through them. Clara stood frozen for a breath, watching as he reached Seraphis, as if searching for something.

"Clara! The Gate won't hold long!" Malrik's voice broke through her thoughts.

She turned and watched as Kira and Elyndra vanished through the Gate. Selandor guarded the threshold with his weapon drawn. Malrik waved frantically, pleading with her to hurry.

She turned, glancing back at Ashael one last time as he sliced his way through the Dravok.

Clara's mouth opened in horror as Seraphis's limp form stirred. She wasn't dead. The Dravoks jolted into motion, their focus snapping back as if her presence had pulled them together. Before Clara could yell a warning, Malrik wrapped his arms around her and tugged her toward the Gate.

Clara stumbled through the opening of light. The world spun and tilted around her. She searched desperately for Ashael. The edges of the Gate began to shrink, closing in rapidly. She couldn't move, couldn't breathe. He wasn't going to make it.

As the portal flickered, she saw Vaelin, launching forward and shoving Ashael through.

At the same moment, a quick flash tore through the air, fast and sharp, falling short.

Seraphis's outstretched hand dropped as her body slumped back down.

The Gate closed, and the world spun as color and sound blurred together. For a moment, Clara felt weightless, formless, suspended in a place between places. Then her feet struck solid ground, and she staggered slightly, trying to steady herself as the shock traveled up through her legs.

She blinked, trying to orient herself. The sound of traffic filled the air. The smell of car exhaust, trees, and the elusive scent of city grime rushed in all at once.

They had arrived in Central Park.

It was night. The city lights gleamed in the distance, and streetlamps cast soft golden light across the walkways. But here, where they had landed, the trees offered a canopy of partial cover, shielding them from prying eyes.

Cold air brushed against her cheeks, and only then did Clara realize how much the temperature had dropped. Winter had arrived. Frost dusted the grass nearby, a thin silver sheen clinging to the blades. She hadn't even noticed the shift in seasons while in Avenora. Time had passed, but the land never seemed to change.

Kira and Elyndra stood nearby, their expressions a mixture of wonder and disbelief at the towering skyline visible beyond the trees. Elyndra cringed as a car honked its horn, the sound familiar to Clara but startling to the Aelvor. Selandor turned in slow circles, taking in the unfamiliar world with wide eyes, hand still on his weapon.

Then, she saw Ashael. He stood a few paces away, catching his breath, but unharmed. Her chest heaved in a silent sob. He made it.

At the corner of her eye, she caught a movement beside her. Malrik.

"We're home," Clara whispered, her voice catching on the words as she continued to watch the skyline.

He stared up at the buildings that framed the park. "Home," he said, his voice oddly distant, as if he couldn't quite believe it.

Clara smiled as her eyes filled with tears. Somehow, they had made it back. She wiped her cheeks and turned to face him, ready to share in this moment of triumph.

Malrik's face was deathly pale. He swayed slightly where he stood, one hand clutching at his chest. Blood seeped between his fingers, soaking his shirt in an expanding crimson stain.

Clara inhaled sharply, eyes going wide. Panic surged through her.

"Malrik! You're bleeding!"

His eyes met hers, confusion swimming in their depths. "I don't . . . feel right," he managed as he fell to his knees.

Clara threw herself to her knees and gripped his shoulders to catch him. She gasped as she beheld the jagged, black object that jutted out from his chest.

Malrik's fingers were wrapped around it, as if he'd been about to pull it free.

"Don't!" Clara cried. "You could make it worse."

He blinked at her, swaying again.

"You need to sit," she said quickly, guiding him to the ground with careful hands, doing her best not to jostle the wound.

Malrik winced as he sank to the grass, but he didn't protest.

A few figures appeared at the edge of the trees. Joggers, maybe, or people walking home. One of them stopped, eyes wide at the sight of the group. A phone came out. Another person pointed.

Clara barely noticed. Her focus stayed on Malrik.

Around them, the sounds of the city grew louder. Horns blaring, distant shouts, and now, rising over all of it, the wail of sirens weaving through the night.

Clara stayed by Malrik's side, her grip firm on his hand as she looked around desperately for help. They had the shard and had made it through the Gate, but they had not emerged unscathed. As Clara took stock of the situation, calling for her friends to help, one thought floated to the back of her mind.

This was far from over.

Acknowledgments

To you, dear reader, thank you for opening this book and stepping into this world with me.

I poured so much of my heart into these pages, and writing this story became my joy, my escape, and my quiet miracle.

If it brings you even a fraction of the wonder and comfort it gave me, then it has all been worth it.

To my husband, Charles, whose love, patience, and unwavering support kept me going through every late night and self-doubt. This book would not exist without you.

To my family, who has always been proud of me in everything I do, and who never stopped believing that I could turn my dreams into something real. Thank you for surrounding me with love.

To my dad, Dr. R. Kadile, my first and number one biggest cheerleader. Thank you for your forever support. The light and kindness you shared with the world will always live on in my heart.

To my friends, both near and far, and my online friends who cheered for me through every chapter. Your encouragement meant more than you know.

To the editors and creative professionals who helped me refine this story, thank you for your skill, your insight, and your care in bringing this book to life.

And finally, to you again, the reader. Thank you for being here. You are the reason stories live beyond their pages.

Thank You for Reading

Every story lives through the hearts of its readers, and I'm so grateful you chose to step into this one. I hope *Realm of the Fae*, *Book One* of *The Veil* series, brought you wonder, escape, and a spark of magic to carry with you.

If you enjoyed the journey, I would be truly grateful if you left a review. Your words help other readers discover this world and keep it alive.

I hope to see you again in Book Two.

You can connect with me on my socials, where I share updates, behind-the-scenes moments, and glimpses of what's coming next.

Thank you for reading and for believing in this world.

About the Author

S.J. Kadile is an RN and author whose life across the Philippines, Dubai, Belgium, and the United States shaped her voice and imagination. The challenges and beauty of rebuilding life in different countries inspired her debut novel *Realm of the Fae, Book 1* of *The Veil* series, a story born from her desire for escape, wonder, and self-discovery. Since then, she has kept going, one story after another.

When she isn't writing, she enjoys cozy cafés, nature walks, pickleball, table tennis, escape rooms, board games, and quiet nights watching shows with her husband.

[www] www.tealinkpress.com

[♪] @sjkadileauthor

[◉] @sjkadileauthor